T0127723

SHEARCLIFF
AND FAMILY

ALBERT G. MILLER

authorHOUSE®

AuthorHouse™
1663 Liberty Drive
Bloomington, IN 47403
www.authorhouse.com
Phone: 1 (800) 839-8640

Published by AuthorHouse   05/06/2018

ISBN: 978-1-5462-4017-4 (sc)
ISBN: 978-1-5462-4016-7 (e)

Print information available on the last page.

This book is printed on acid-free paper.

I'll keep this short,
so this one's for the original Matt.

Summer, 1524
years post crisis

PROLOGUE

Everise Longbrook played quietly by the hearth. Her father had fashioned her a small doll from straw and scraps of cloth earlier that day, and she was content with filling her six-year-old head with its adventures as she marched it back and forth across the floor—one moment a mighty hero, the next a damsel in distress.

Everise heard something strange. This late in the day all the adults had already gone to their shops, so she wondered why she heard voices. They seemed excited about something; perhaps there was a festival today she had forgotten about? Curious, she discarded the doll and pushed a chair toward the small window, so she might catch a glimpse of whatever was causing such a stir. Clambering atop the chair, she was about to pull back the curtains when she heard the scream. It was an inhuman noise, impossibly loud and painful to hear. Everise covered her ears and shut her eyes tightly, trying to block out the sound, but it was to no avail.

The scream ended, but Everise remained motionless, too afraid to move. Slowly, she opened her eyes and pulled her hands from her ears. Her ears were ringing, but she could still make out screams coming from outside, this time of human origin. Steeling herself, she pulled back the curtains and stared out into the street. She saw people running as fast as they could toward the center of town. She saw her friends being dragged along by their parents and even caught sight of her uncle running toward her house. He looked frightened. She looked frantically for her parents in the crowd but was unable to spot them.

Without warning, everyone was gone. There was a noise like the world's largest forge igniting, and all Everise could see was fire. The flames gushed down the street like a river, and wherever they touched, people vanished. She fell from the chair as the fire engulfed the window, causing the glass to shatter. She scampered backward as the fire crept slowly through the window. Everise ran to the door hoping to escape, but with a splintering crash, the thatch roof fell in, showering her with sparks. Panicking, she ran back toward the bed and crawled beneath it. She watched slowly as the fire spread and felt the air growing hotter by the second. She began to cry, crying for her mother, for her father. Still, the fire grew closer, the air became hotter. She found it was getting difficult to breath, and her cries were interrupted by ragged coughing. She tried to draw a breath but found the air had grown unbearably hot, scorching her lungs.

The fire reached her and Everise screamed.

CHAPTER ONE

Christian Shearcliff ran his thumb along the edge of the ring he wore. Not one to wear rings, he found himself still growing accustomed to its unfamiliar weight even after several weeks of wearing it each day. That being said, he enjoyed his new adornment, mostly due to what it represented.

"Chris, what are you doing? I told you I wanted you to run three more sets, not stand around daydreaming!" Sarah chastised as she marched out from within their home.

Tall, with bright red hair and striking blue eyes, Sarah Shearcliff was by far the most skilled warrior Chris knew. While Sarah could normally be found clad in large spiked armor hauling a small arsenal of weapons, today she wore only a leather tunic and carried a wooden practice sword. It was plain, practical garb, and her only adornment was a simple golden ring engraved with intertwining vines, identical to Chris's own.

"Sorry, I finished that and was taking a break," Chris told her, hastily picking up his own practice sword.

"If you ran those sets correctly, you would still be working," Sarah said with a frown. "Run them again and show me your form," she commanded.

Chris began moving through the complex series of strikes and movement Sarah had had him doing all morning.

"Your timing was off on that last strike," Al whispered in Chris's head.

"I didn't ask you," Chris thought irritably in reply.

The problem with sharing your thoughts with a master swordsman was that they couldn't help interjecting from time to time, he decided.

"Wrong. Your last strike was too slow," Sarah chided.

"Told you," Al chuckled.

"Here, let me show you," Sarah said and raised her sword.

Chris gave a silent groan. He had come to realize that whenever his wife wanted to *show him* something, it usually ended up with him battered and bruised. Sure enough, Sarah launched into a blinding series of slashes and thrusts. He managed to block right up until the strike she had deemed too slow, at which point he found he was unable to raise his blade fast enough to avoid a wicked strike across his shoulders, courtesy of Sarah.

"Point taken," Chris grumbled as he nursed his shoulder, which was slowly turning purple.

"That looks like it hurts," Sarah said, slightly surprised as if someone else had just smacked him with a large wooden sword.

"Yeah, it does," Chris complained as he lowered his sword.

"I thought your fancy cloak is supposed to protect you from that type of thing. Why didn't it stop the blow?" Sarah asked.

"It's indestructible, so it won't let me get cut in half or anything, but it doesn't do anything when I get bludgeoned like that!" Chris explained. "Besides, it's not meant to be armor; it's meant to hide me. That's what the enchantment was made for."

"That's why I keep telling you to get proper armor!" Sarah told him firmly. "Even Matt wears *some* armor; you need to get with the program."

Chris realized she had baited him into this trap and searched frantically for a way out.

"Armor would only slow me down, and my sword does a fine job of protecting me," Chris argued, dreading the idea of being encased in a heavy steel cage.

"Until your sword decides it doesn't want to cut whoever you're fighting, which brings us back to why I'm training you to use a regular blade in the first place," Sarah told him.

Chris could find no fault in her logic. It was true his sword was enchanted; so long as he wielded it, he was a master swordsman, but the blade also had a fatal flaw—it refused to harm any individual it deemed *good*. This had proven dangerous in the past when in the middle of a battle his sword became unusable due to the nature of his opponent.

"I see your point, Sarah, which is why I agreed to train in the first place, but you have to understand the reason for the enchantment. I'm not supposed to be killing the type of people the sword won't fight," Chris told her.

"Well, while that sounds great when you say it now, how has that ideology helped you in the past? That sword has almost gotten you killed as many times as it's saved you, and one of those times was because it refused to fight me when I was hell-bent on killing you! That sword has proven that it values its morals more than your safety, so stop complaining, and let me help you. I'm in no hurry to become a widow," Sarah told him angrily, ending their discussion.

Chris sighed and readied his sword. One rapid exchange of blows later, Sarah landed another crushing blow to the same shoulder.

"Gods, Sarah!" Chris gasped as he dropped his sword, clutching his shoulder, which was now swelling quickly.

"I actually didn't mean to hit you there that time; you moved," Sarah said, slightly embarrassed.

"I thought the idea of this training was to keep me alive!" Chris said, voice warped in pain.

"Let me look at that," Sarah commanded as she walked toward him.

With gentle fingers, she inspected his wound.

"It looks like it's dislocated; you'll have to go see Matt. I'm sorry, Chris," Sarah said with concern.

"It's fine; I'll be right back," Chris said with a wince.

"You've done enough today," Sarah said, patting him on the shoulder, causing him to grimace. "Sorry!" Sarah gasped before hastily picking up the training swords and disappearing from sight.

"Time to find that cleric...*again*," Chris grumbled as he walked inside the house.

The house itself was a massive log cabin sitting in a secluded valley within the Godspine; the largest mountain range on Targoth. Chris and his companions had earned the property several weeks ago after killing the evil Governor Sorros. The estate was immense, and Chris had yet to learn the secrets of all its rooms.

"Good day, Master. You appear to be hurt. May I assist you?" asked a maid who suddenly appeared in front of him.

"No, Flora; I'm fine. I just need to know where Matt is," Chris told her.

"Master Bleakstar is currently in the library, and my name is Fiona," Fiona told him.

In addition to the lands and estate, Chris had earned the service of a pair of maids, Flora and Fiona. As it turned out, the maids were identical, impossible to distinguish from one another. Chris had attempted to release them from his service at one point, seeing no need for servants, but the maids had refused and continued to live within the estate. Seeing no way to be rid of them, Chris had grown to accept their constant presence and allowed them to continue the house's upkeep.

"Sorry, Fiona; thank you," Chris told her.

"Will you be needing anything else, Master? I need to go do a load of laundry," Fiona told him.

"No, that's fine. Sorry to trouble you." Chris winced as he turned toward the library, his shoulder throbbing.

Sure enough, after a short walk, he found his friend Matthew Bleakstar sitting with his nose buried in a familiar book, a book with sapphires set into the cover.

"That's strange; Ge's showing me a passage on how to heal deep muscle bruising. I wonder why?" Matt asked without looking up.

"Three guesses," Chris groaned as he slumped into a chair beside him.

"I see you were sparring with Sarah again. So, tell me, did you win this time?" Matt laughed.

"Spare me the jokes until after you've healed my shoulder; it hurts like hell," Chris pleaded.

Matt sighed and began praying softly, his hands beginning to glow. Much rougher than Sarah, he set his hands on Chris's injured shoulder, and Chris felt it slip back into the socket with a pop, followed by instant relief as his injuries were magically healed.

"There. Good as new," Matt said proudly as he sat back.

"Thanks, buddy, I really owe you one," Chris told him as he tested out his newly-repaired shoulder.

"I thought the point of all this training was to keep you alive? I swear every other day I end up having to put you back together again," Matt said with a bemused smirk.

"It's not as bad as it originally was; at least she's using practice weapons now," Chris argued.

"Only because I told her I wouldn't put your arms back on for the fifth time," Matt laughed. "I swear I spend more time reattaching your limbs than anything else."

"Yeah, it's remarkably hard to train without your arms," Chris said dryly. "I really hope she decides I'm capable enough soon. I don't know how much more of this I can take."

"Do you want my advice?" Matt asked as he ran his hand through his short bleach-blond hair. "Get her out of the house; hell, get all of them out of the house. We've been sitting around for over a month now. Getting out will do everyone some good."

"What do you mean?" Chris asked with concern. "I thought everyone liked the estate."

"Oh, we do, don't get me wrong. But while I'm happy to relax and read my book, the others are going a little stir-crazy. Ditrina's taken to shooting fireballs at the mountainside whenever she gets bored, and Cassy has been driving me insane," Matt told him.

"Speaking of Cas; where is my sister?" Chris asked. "I haven't seen her in a while, and it's not like her to be quiet for so long."

Matt pointed a finger at the ceiling.

There, suspended in an opaque bubble, was his sister. She was currently screaming down at them, treating Chris to a good view of her fangs. Thankfully, the bubble seemed to block sound as well as imprison her because judging by the gestures she was making, her words were less than flattering.

"Why is my sister on the ceiling?" Chris asked calmly.

It was hardly the strangest thing he had walked in to find, after all.

"She kept bugging me, so I threatened to stick her up there. She called my bluff," Matt explained.

Chris nodded as if this was the most logical thing in the world.

"That's a handy spell. Did Ditrina teach you that?" Chris asked.

"No, this one Ge showed me in the book," Matt explained.

Much like how Chris had Al stuck in his head helping him use his sword, Matt shared his mind with the spirit Ge, who aided Matt in the use of his magical book, though Ge only spoke to Matt in his sleep. Chris also had another spirit named Mi living in his head that shared his dreams along with Al, making his evenings more eventful than most.

"You know once you let her down, she's going to kill you, right?" Chris told him.

"Who said anything about letting her down?" Matt asked with a laugh. "Actually, that brings me back to the whole *getting them out of the house* bit. If I let her out, would you mind taking her down to the Lonely Elf for a while? That may help her cool off."

"How do you recommend I convince her of that? She looks pretty intent on butchering you," Chris remarked.

"Convince Ditrina. If Cassy hears her girlfriend is going, she's likely to tag along," Matt told him.

"Fair enough; you did fix my arm, after all. Let her down, and I'll see about getting her out of the house," Chris told him.

Matt snapped his fingers, and the bubble vanished. Cassy began to plummet toward the ground but twisted in the air like an acrobat and landed lightly on her reptilian legs. While her body appeared normal enough, curvy with caramel-colored skin, she was impossible to mistake for a human. The farther away from her main body you looked, the more reptilian she appeared, with bright emerald green scales covering much of her arms and legs, and fingers capped with talons. She didn't wear much, only a short skirt and a bright cloth wrapped several times around her chest.

Naga like her were uncommon on this side of Targoth, and, as such, she often drew strange stares whenever they went into town. At this moment, her pretty face was contorted with rage as she stared at Matt with her piercing green eyes.

"You, *asshole*! You filthy little midget! How dare you stick me up there?!" she hissed as she marched toward him, claws bared.

"I hardly think five-foot-three classifies me as a midget," Matt said calmly as he looked at Chris expectantly.

As funny as it may be to watch his sister assault Matt, Chris honored his arrangement.

"Hey, Cas! Ditrina and I are heading down to town. Go get her for me, will you?" Chris called.

Cassy spun on the spot and looked at him excitedly, all trace of her wrath forgotten.

"Oh, fun! I'll be right back!" she chirped before disappearing from sight.

Matt shook his head in disbelief.

"How does she just change tracks like that?" he wondered aloud.

"Don't go thinking you're out of the woods yet. I doubt she'll forget about that little trick," Chris cautioned.

"Noted," Matt said as he settled back to read his book.

"Not coming with us?" Chris asked him.

"Seriously? This will be the first peace I've had all day," Matt said with a content smile.

Chris left the library and hurried to his room. If he was to be making a trip to the village, he wanted to have his sword with him—just in case. As he rounded a corner, he crashed into a maid carrying an armful of clothes, causing her to scatter them across the floor.

"Oh, I'm sorry Fiona; let me help you with those," Chris said quickly as he began picking up clothes.

"Thank you Master, and my name is Flora," the maid told him.

Chris paused and looked at her suspiciously.

"Wait a moment. Fiona told me she was doing laundry earlier...who are you?" he asked slowly.

The maid looked shocked for a moment but recovered quickly.

"Very good, Master; you are correct. My name is Fiona. I was just testing you to see how well you could tell us apart," she told him cheerfully.

Chris shook his head in confusion but had managed to accept this when a second maid rounded the corner.

"Flora hurry up, we don't have all day," this new maid chastised.

Chris sprung to his feet.

"Wait a moment, you just told me your name was Fiona! You two do this on purpose!" Chris yelled in outrage.

Flora/Fiona, he had no idea who was who at this point, rushed to gather the rest of the clothes before moving to her sister's side. They both curtsied hastily.

"We have no idea what you're talking about, Master. Have a nice day," the maids said in unison before disappearing around the corner.

Chris shook his head in disgust before continuing to his room.

Upon arriving, Chris found his sword exactly where he left it, as he expected. Being enchanted, the sword prevented others from touching it without his permission. On a whim, he took a moment to admire it. He drew the blade and was greeted by three feet of razor sharp steel engraved with an intricate pattern of overlapping squares. The hilt felt familiar under his hands as it always did, and the pair of rubies set in the cross guard flickered with burning light. Looking in the mirror standing in his room, Chris sighed as he saw his eyes had yet to return to their natural color. Once dark brown, now stained maroon. His eyes were a harsh reminder of his unnatural fusion with Al.

The reflection stared back at him—the same narrow face, the same black hair—holding the same sword, but Chris saw a different person.

He blinked, and the red-eyed stranger did the same.

"I am sorry, you know," Al said in his head.

"So you keep saying," Chris thought in reply.

"I feel the need to say it often," Al told him.

"It's fine, really; I honestly don't mind the eyes," Chris thought.

"The eyes are the least of your concerns," Al told him.

Chris sighed and slid the sword back into its scabbard. The red eyes were more of a side effect of his fusion than anything else. The main problem, as Al constantly reminded him, was he may be unable to cross over into the afterlife at the time of his eventual death.

"We've been over this, Al; neither of us knows how to fix my soul. More importantly, neither of us knows if my soul is actually in any danger to begin with! This is all just your theories, so stop worrying about it," Chris thought irritably.

"I spoke to Ge. He thinks as I do; you're in danger, Chris!" Al exclaimed.

"In danger of what? I'm no more likely to die as I am now than I was before. You're worried about what comes after my death, but my main concern is delaying it as long as possible. If you come up with some solution to this, feel free to let me know, but for the last time, stop apologizing every time I think about you!" Chris thought angrily.

Al said nothing, and Chris made his way back down to the common room where he found Cassy and Ditrina waiting.

"Then he stuck me to the ceiling!" Cassy exclaimed angrily to Ditrina, and Chris saw her black eyes widen in surprise.

Like his sister, Ditrina was far from human. Being an elf, she sported completely black eyes with thin white rings for irises and pointed ears. Her skin had a faint green tint to it, and her veins stood dark on her arms like a leaf.

"Do you know what spell he used?" Ditrina asked her eagerly.

"The spell's not important, Di," Cassy said irritably.

"I beg to differ; the spell is the most interesting part of this story!" Ditrina exclaimed, looking far more animated than usual.

Few things manage to rile up the strange pyromancer; however, new spells ranked highly on that short list.

"Di, you know I don't know what spell he used. Right now, you need to help me think up a way to get even with Matt," Cassy scolded.

"Perhaps we could prime a fireball to go off when Matthew enters his quarters?" Ditrina proposed, brushing back a strand of long blue hair that had drifted across her face.

Chris decided it was time to join the conversation before the situation degraded any further.

"Ditrina, remember the rules. No fire magic in the house," Chris said quickly.

"Yes, leader," Ditrina said sadly.

"Don't call me that," Chris snapped.

"Sorry, leader," Ditrina said, nodding seriously.

Chris sighed and turned his attention to his sister.

"Could you try to limit your revenge to things that don't destroy the house?" Chris pleaded.

"He stuck me to the ceiling! Do you think I should just let it go?" Cassy demanded.

"No, I'm just telling you that your revenge isn't worth blowing up the house," Chris explained, dumbfounded that he was even having this conversation.

"Well, how do you propose that I get even?" Cassy demanded, clawed hands on her hips.

"Maybe try ignoring him for a few days; that would teach him a lesson," Chris told her, praying to the gods she would buy it.

It seemed one of the ten was listening.

"Having Cas ignore you would be horrible," Ditrina declared loudly without any trace of guile, as she often did.

Chris let out a silent sigh of relief.

While he didn't quite understand the root of the relationship between his sister and the strange elf, he knew Cassy put heavy stock in whatever Ditrina had to say. Stranger still, Cassy seemed to be the only one who could put social conventions in a way the elf could understand, making for what could only be called *interesting* conversations between the two.

"You really think that would work?" Cassy asked hesitantly.

Chris couldn't believe she was actually buying it.

"Absolutely," Ditrina said with conviction.

Cassy nodded, and Chris cheered silently in his head.

"You can start by heading down to town with me," Chris told her, seeing she had taken to the idea of ignoring the cleric.

"Why are we going to town?" Ditrina asked.

"I'm going to talk to Sam; maybe he'll have work for us," Chris told them.

"A new contract would be a welcome change of pace," Sarah said as she walked into the room.

Cassy jumped in surprise.

"Don't sneak up on us like that!" she hissed.

Sarah ignored her and looked at Chris.

"Is your shoulder all right?" Sarah asked with concern.

"Yeah, Matt fixed it up. Don't worry about it," Chris said with a wave of his hand.

It was hardly the first time he had been wounded in practice, after all—a fact they knew all too well.

"I'm not trying to hurt you, you know. I'm really trying to help!" Sarah told him, still looking worried.

"It's fine, really," Chris said with a smile. "I've seen what it's like when you're trying to hurt me. Compared to that, this is nothing," he assured her.

"I don't know; you walked away from your first fight with a couple of scars. After your first bout of *training*, you had to have your arms reattached. I'd say this is *waaaaaay* more dangerous," Cassy said with a laugh.

Sarah was not amused.

"Being my sister in law will not stop me from skinning you," Sarah said darkly.

"So you keep reminding me. I'm shaking in my scales," Cassy taunted, but Chris noticed she danced out of immediate skinning range.

"*Anyway*, I was just about to take these two down to the tavern, so we should probably get going," Chris said trying to prevent his wife from making him an only child.

"I'll see you later tonight then," Sarah said, giving him a peck on the cheek.

Thankful that he had managed to yet again prevent an unpleasant incident amongst his party members, Chris began heading toward town, far more tired than he should be that early in the day.

CHAPTER TWO

The town lay a few minutes' ride away from the valley. Nestled at the entrance to a hidden pass within the Godspine, it had no official name and served as a favorite location for smugglers and those wishing to avoid the King's taxes. Arguably, the most noticeable feature of the village was the inn. While the building itself was nothing remarkable, the innkeeper was one to draw special attention from Chris and his friends.

"Welcome to the Lonely… Oh, it's you guys! Come on in!" Sam called as Chris entered the bar.

With short blue hair, green skin, and pointed ears, Sam and Ditrina were two of a kind. Uncommon enough that most considered them extinct, the elves were a rare sight on Targoth, and Chris counted himself lucky enough to know two of them.

"Morning, Sam," Chris called back cheerfully as his companions entered the inn behind him.

As usual, Sam bowed deeply as Ditrina entered.

"Princess," Sam said reverently.

"Hello, Samasal," Ditrina said.

Cassy giggled.

"I still can't believe you're royalty, Di," she said.

"I assure you, she is," Sam said as he returned behind the bar.

"Yeah, she's our Fire Princess," Chris told him cheerfully.

"Please do not call me that," Ditrina said flatly.

"Sure thing, Fire Princess," Chris told her.

"Please do not call me that," Ditrina said again, in exactly the same tone as before.

Chris raised an eyebrow and decided that irony was lost on the girl.

"So, what brings you all down from the valley today? It's a bit early to be drinking, don't you think?" Sam asked.

"Actually, Sam, we were wondering if you had any new leads for us. It's about time we started looking for work again," Chris told him.

He had asked the elf to keep an eye out for any potential jobs they could take, but so far, he had nothing for them.

"Sorry, Chris, I've got nothing for you," Sam said with a shrug. "None of the smugglers heading through the pass has said anything about any contracts needing fulfilling, and, as for rumors, I've got nothing worth chasing down."

"Come on, Sam, you have to have *something* for us," Chris pleaded quietly, leaning forward so he could whisper to the elf. "Some of the others are going crazy being cooped up all day; there's got to be something, anything!"

"I am not going crazy!" Cassy yelled.

Chris found it easy to forget her hearing was far better than average.

"I didn't say you specifically!" Chris said quickly.

"Bullshit! Matt put you up to this, didn't he? He was tired of me hanging around the library and made you try to get rid of me!" Cassy exclaimed in outrage.

"No...I...You have the wrong idea..." Chris began, frantically thinking of a way to pacify his sister.

"All right, all right, I may have heard something, but I didn't want to say anything," Sam admitted, interrupting Chris's excuses before they began.

Chris looked at him strangely, so he elaborated.

"It just didn't seem like a job for you is all," he said with a shrug.

"We can't afford to be picky right now," Chris told him.

"Running that low on funds?" Sam asked.

"Running low on patience," Chris sighed.

Sam shrugged.

"Suit yourself then. Rumor has it a large monster was sighted farther south along the Godspine. Normally that wouldn't be a big deal, but it was seen heading toward a small village. I'm sure the villagers would be grateful if you killed it for them before it starts eating them or their livestock," Sam told them.

"Just saying it's a monster doesn't help us any. What is it?" Chris asked

"It's a…dragon," Sam said and braced himself.

"*Noooooo*!" Ditrina screamed, causing Chris to almost jump out of his skin.

"Gods, Ditrina, what the hell is wrong with you?" he demanded.

"*Nooooooo*," Ditrina moaned quietly in reply, curling into a ball on her seat.

Chris looked at Cassy for some form of explanation.

"Di's terrified of dragons, remember?" Cassy told him like it should have been obvious.

"Well, how the hell was I supposed to know?" Chris asked, looking at the quivering ball of fright that his friend had evolved into.

"She told us the first time we came here. How could you have forgotten?" Cassy demanded while trying to comfort Ditrina.

"Oh, *excuse* me! She also told us she was royalty and cursed that same day, so forgive me for forgetting something trivial like that!" Chris yelled.

"I remembered; that was why I didn't want to say anything about it," Sam admitted.

"Dude, not helping," Chris said, shooting him a look of betrayal.

"It's all right, Di; we're not going anywhere near the dragon," Cassy said softly.

"Like hell, we're not! We need to kill it before it destroys that village. Ditrina will just have to deal with it," Chris said firmly.

"Look at her, Chris!" Cassy said, pointing to Ditrina's pathetic whimpering form. "You can't possibly expect her to do this."

"We'll just leave her behind then," Chris said.

"You cannot go! The dragon will kill you," Ditrina wailed suddenly, springing upright.

"Di, if we don't go, the dragon will kill a lot more people. You don't want that, do you?" Chris asked her.

Ditrina sniffled but shook her head.

"I do not think I will be much help," Ditrina admitted quietly.

"Think about it, Ditrina. You said yourself that your fear of dragons was irrational. Maybe seeing us kill one will help you with your fear." Chris told her, managing to remember her choice of words from weeks before.

"You are a cruel leader," Ditrina said with a sniffle but protested no further.

With that handled, Chris returned his focus to Sam.

"Where did you say the dragon was sighted?" he asked.

"About a three weeks' ride south of here, by Rooksberg. The reports I heard said it was a female, so it's possibly looking for a place to nest which would explain why it's hanging around the mountains. News will spread quickly about the dragon, so if you want the job, you should probably hurry," Sam advised.

"We'll leave the day after tomorrow. That should put us near Rooksberg before the end of the month," Chris said.

"Does Rooksberg have a glyph?" Ditrina asked quietly.

"A what?" Cassy asked.

"A glyph. It is a symbol used for teleportation. Usually, you can only teleport to somewhere you have been before, but if you know a place's glyph, you can go to it," Ditrina explained.

"I don't think so, but I know the Glenord glyph is nearby," Sam told them.

"Why have we never heard about these glyphs before?" Chris asked.

"Well, the glyphs were created before the crisis, when magic was in its prime. Seeing that humans can no longer use magic freely, most simply forgot they existed. Though few know it, most of the villages and cities are still fairly close to where they were before the crisis. The castle in Bleakstar, for example, is actually the original one from before the crisis, making it one of the oldest structures on Targoth. With that in mind, the glyphs that once aided teleportation are still fairly close to their respective destinations, assuming wherever you're going has roots that predate the crisis," Sam explained.

"So, this Glenord place, it's an old village?" Chris asked.

"No, Glenord was a city before the crisis. The city itself has long since crumbled away, but the glyph still works just fine. If you use that one, you should put yourself about a day's ride from Rooksberg," Sam told them.

"I thought you knew all about magic stuff, Di. Why didn't you know about this glyph thing?" Cassy asked.

"I know about glyphs. I was just unaware of where they are," Ditrina told her.

"Don't you have your glyph book?" Sam asked.

When he saw Chris and Cassy looked confused, he elaborated.

"All Rikes are issued a book containing the locations of all known usable glyphs before they leave on their quest. I would have figured that she had hers still," he said with a shrug.

"Where's this book, Ditrina?" Chris asked her, as he had never seen any such thing in her possession.

Ditrina mumbled something unintelligible.

"What was that, Di?" Cassy asked.

"I burned it," Ditrina said quietly.

"You what!?" Sam yelled.

"It was not my fault!" Ditrina wailed. "I was poking around some ruins before I met Shearcliff and Company, and I tried using a fireball to blast open the entrance. The doors had an enchantment on them, and the spell rebounded and hit me. While fire is more of an inconvenience to me than anything else, my clothes and all my things were burned to a crisp." Ditrina pouted.

"You tried using a fireball to open a door?" Chris asked, dumbfounded.

"It was the first thing I had tried to explore since leaving home! The doors were too big for me to open on my own, so I thought exploding them open might work!" Ditrina argued.

"So, what did you do when your spell went off in your face?" Cassy asked.

"I walked to the nearest town," Ditrina said as if it should have been obvious.

"Wait, I thought you said your clothes got burned up as well...you didn't mean the ones you were wearing, right? Those were protected like you are, right?" Chris asked, dreading her answer.

"Of course not, those were just regular clothes. They were incinerated," Ditrina told him.

"So, what did you wear when you went into the town?" Cassy asked.

"Nothing. I told you, all of my clothes were destroyed," Ditrina said, staring at them blankly.

Chris and Cassy looked at each other in disbelief while Sam choked on his drink.

"Princess, you don't mean you wandered into the village *naked*, do you?" Sam asked, almost begging her to deny it.

"Are you three all right? I have already said several times now, I had no clothes and went to the village. What is so hard to understand about that?" Ditrina asked tilting her head to the side.

"Di, people don't go wandering around town naked! That's not ok!" Cassy yelled.

"I know that now. The people in the village told me after a while," Ditrina said.

"After a while?" Sam asked, still not believing what he was hearing.

"Yes, I stayed in that village for three days, on account of the tailor making me new clothes. The morning of the third day, a kind woman gave me a cloak and said I could not go walking around without clothes any more. Stranger still, I saw a lot of the men exchanging gold with one another when I put on the cloak. You humans are a strange bunch," Ditrina declared.

Chris couldn't think of any intelligible reply, and it seemed Cassy was in the same boat. Sam looked horrified.

"Nobody understood why the Fire Princess was locked in the palace for so many years. All of the other royal family members toured the city, but nobody ever saw little Ditrina. Now I know why," Sam said as if in a trance.

"My father told me I needed to study and to stay in the palace most of the time," Ditrina agreed.

"He was worried you'd do something like that!" Sam yelled.

"Like what? Buy new clothes?" Ditrina asked, not understanding.

Sam made small movements with his hands and mouth, but no words were completed. He looked at Chris in desperation.

"Cas, deal with this," Chris said as he buried his face in his hands.

"*Me*!? Why me?!" Cassy demanded.

"She's your girlfriend for one, and on top of that, I refuse to have a conversation with *Ditrina* as to why clothes are needed in public!" Chris yelled, shaking his head angrily.

"I know you need to wear clothes in public; those nice villagers told me," Ditrina reminded them.

"Ditrina, please, no more words. I'm begging you," Chris pleaded.

"Yes, leader," Ditrina said.

They departed for Glenord two days later. Chris counted those two days before departure as some of the best days he could remember, with Cassy refusing to speak to Matt whatsoever, and, as such, staying relatively quiet whenever he was in the room. Chris spent a lot of time with Matt during those days. When it came time to depart, they gathered their horses and loaded their gear, and awaited Ditrina's instruction. What would have been a several-week trip was shortened to seconds by her magic; however, teleportation was not without its own drawbacks.

"Are you all right, Di?" Cassy asked as Ditrina stumbled, having just arrived at their destination.

"I will be ok, Cas, I have just never teleported so much so far before," Ditrina panted. "You four, plus the horses, proved more difficult than I expected. Next time, I will brace myself a bit more."

While Ditrina seemed exhausted after her display of magic, Sarah was obviously unwell. She had stumbled away from the group and began to heave uncontrollably seconds after arriving.

"All good, Sarah?" Chris asked with concern.

Sarah continued to vomit.

"Sarah…" Chris began.

"I'm…fine…I just…need…a minute," Sarah panted as she recovered her breath.

Cassy giggled.

"I hate teleporting! Every time I do it, I feel like I turn inside out!" Sarah complained.

"None of us have that problem. I think you're just looking for attention," Cassy taunted.

"Teleportation affects everyone differently," Ditrina explained. "Some people become quite ill after doing it, while others feel perfectly fine. I, for one, actually enjoy the feeling of teleporting. It tickles."

"Well, that makes me feel *sooooo* much better," Sarah said with a roll of her eyes.

"Glad I could be of assistance," Ditrina said happily.

Sarah looked at her blankly.

"Sarcasm, Ditrina," Matt said with a sigh.

"Oh, sorry! I thought she was serious that time!" Ditrina complained.

"You really need to work on that, Di," Cassy told her.

"I am trying! I am three for forty-three this week! That is two better than last week!" Ditrina argued.

"Wow, you're turning into a real expert on sarcasm, aren't you?" Sarah asked, shaking her head.

"Thank you!" Ditrina exclaimed, beaming.

"Three for forty-four," Matt whispered to Chris.

Ditrina's spell had landed them atop a hill, within the center of the ruins. They weren't much to look at. What had once been the proud city of Glenord now stood around them as a few scattered chunks of rubble discarded around the hill. Nothing that could have been mistaken for a building could be seen, and the group saw no reason to linger.

"So, where's Rooksberg in relation to Glenord again? We should probably start heading toward the village," Chris said.

Matt pulled out his book and began to flip through the pages.

Magic as it was, it could show him a wide range of things, for better or worse.

"No, no, no, gods *damn it*, Ge! I need a recent map! Showing me maps from fifteen-hundred years ago doesn't help me at all!" Matt complained.

"Anyone else?" Chris asked.

"I believe Rooksberg is located directly against the mountains. That puts it slightly to the west of us, but I am unsure of whether or not it lays farther north or south of here," Ditrina told him.

Matt gave a triumphant shout.

"*Finally*, Ge! About time. This map puts Rooksberg due west of here. All we have to do is ride toward the mountains, and we'll be at the village by sundown," Matt told them.

"Wow, Matt actually did something useful for once," Cassy said with surprise.

"What the hell is that supposed to mean? I do helpful things all the time!" Matt yelled indignantly.

"I'm not saying you're not *helpful*; I'm just saying it's not like you to do anything useful when we're out and about. Your skills are better suited for when Chris inevitably does something stupid and ends up hurt," Cassy explained.

Both Matt and Chris looked offended.

"I do more than just heal Chris!" Matt yelled.

"Yeah, and I don't need healing *that* often!" Chris said indignantly.

Everyone laughed at him, including Matt.

"Not to offend you, buddy, but you're pretty fragile," Matt told him. "I can't deny I've spent a lot of time putting you back together again."

"That's hardly fair…" Chris began.

"Let's see, you were knocked out after your fight with Droga and needed me to heal you then," Matt told him.

"Then again, after your fight with Sarah. Had Matt not put you back together again, you would have bled to death," Cassy pointed out while Sarah looked embarrassed.

"Then there was Purevein. You were out for two days after that," Sarah said trying to move the subject away from herself.

"Oh, come on! You can't count Purevein against me! Everyone except for Ditrina was down after that!" Chris yelled.

"I wasn't," Sarah reminded him.

He ignored her.

"She used a sleep spell, then fed me a potion that made me sleep while I couldn't fight back. That one's not my fault," Chris insisted

"So, you admit the others were your fault?" Matt asked innocently.

"Shut up, Matt. You almost died in Purevein after casting a *light spell*. I don't want any shit from you," Chris retorted.

"Still, the first time you used magic you went into a coma for two weeks and lost part of your soul. I believe that is much worse than what happened to Matthew," Ditrina told him.

"Which is why Chris isn't allowed to use magic," Sarah said, giving him a sharp look.

She had forbidden him from trying to use his magic again with the fear of him accidently hurting himself.

"No, no, *you're right*. I'm just a bumbling idiot who almost dies every time he trips!" Chris yelled.

"I detect sarcasm," Ditrina said.

"Hey, nice job! That puts you at four for forty-five!" Matt said proudly.

"I am setting a new record for myself!" Ditrina said happily.

"We're all *soooooo* proud of you," Chris said, rolling his eyes.

"Thank you," Ditrina said with a blissful smile.

"Four for forty-six," Sarah sighed.

They set a leisurely pace toward Rooksberg. Along the way, Chris took the time to admire his surroundings. He had never been this far south before, and he was beginning to notice plants he didn't recognize.

"How far away from Shearcliff are we from here?" he asked as they rode.

"About a month or two's ride, why?" Matt replied.

"Just curious. I've never been this far south before," Chris replied.

"I've been a bit farther south, but we're rapidly approaching the extent of my travels," Matt admitted.

"What about you, Sarah? Have you been this far south before?" Chris asked.

Sarah gave a snort.

"Please, I've been as far south as the southern passes, and as far east as the eastern desert. You won't find many places on Targoth I haven't been," Sarah told them.

"How far north have you gone?" Ditrina asked.

"About as far as you'll find people. I stopped before I reached the tundra," Sarah said.

"That is a shame. Had you pressed on, you may have found yourself near the elven city. Not that you would have been able to get in. The protective barriers would have turned you away, but at least you could have said you got close," Ditrina told her.

"What's the elven city like, Di?" Cassy asked.

"Well, it is a lot like a human city, to be honest. It is surrounded by farmland that grows year-round, so we do not need to worry about food. Inside the walls, we have all sorts of shops and buildings. You can buy a magic sword, a potion to cure the common cold, and a sweet roll all on the same street. The center of the city houses the palace, where the Gel live. Anyone not affected by the curse is referred to as a Gel. The Gel do not leave the palace very much, and they are not allowed to leave the city at all. Their jobs are to raise as many children as they can in the hopes of making more Gels," Ditrina explained.

"You said you grew up in the palace, right, Di?" Cassy asked.

"That is correct. My father is the current king, so my brothers and I all grew up in the palace. Two of my brothers are Rikes like me, but one was lucky enough to be born a Gel. He will be the next king," Ditrina said.

"Being a Gel doesn't sound all that great. You're a prisoner in your own city," Sarah said.

"Oh no, the Gels are the most respected people in the entire city! It is up to them to bring up our future generations. Quite literally, our survival as a species rests on their shoulders," Ditrina told them.

"So, if they're not allowed to leave the city, what do they do all day?

Elves don't have children that often from what I understand, so that must give them a lot of time on their hands," Chris remarked.

"The Gel do whatever they like. Because they are so vital to our existence, they do not follow the same laws as the Rikes. They can go wherever they like, within the city, of course, take whatever they like, and say anything they like. If a Gel gives a Rike an order, it is borderline treason for the Rike to disobey," Ditrina told them.

"But what if a Gel is tormenting a Rike? You make it sound like a Gel could get away with murder!" Matt exclaimed.

"Well, so long as they do not murder another Gel, they could. Regardless of their birth, the Gel are considered royalty and harming a Gel is punishable by death," Ditrina told them.

"So, does that mean that you have the same rights as a Gel because you're a princess?" Chris asked.

"Technically, yes, though I am not bound by the laws that keep the Gel in the city. As a Rike, I am expected to do my duty and explore the world looking for a way to break the curse, but as a princess, I am entitled to special treatment from the other elves. This proves complicated because technically, I am supposed to marry another high-ranking elf as a member of the royal family, but as a Rike, I hold the right to choose my partner—man or woman. All of my brothers have already married for political reasons, but I decided to leave before my father could find me a husband," Ditrina explained.

"So, they just let you leave without any problems?" Sarah asked skeptically.

She doubted Ditrina was telling the whole story.

"Well, I remember that some of the guards were unhappy when I said I was leaving. They kept saying something about bringing me to my father, but I blew up a couple of buildings, and they decided that they had to deal with that instead. After that, I walked to the stables and rode south," Ditrina told them casually.

The others exchanged uneasy looks.

"Ditrina, you realize that they're probably looking for you, right?" Matt asked.

"Why?" Ditrina asked, not understanding.

Matt and Chris looked at each other, unsure of how to put it in a way that the elf could understand. Luckily for them, Sarah spared them the need to speak.

"Because you blew up a building! That makes you a criminal, Ditrina!" Sarah yelled.

Ditrina shook her head.

"Nobody was in the buildings I blew up, so it was not an issue," Ditrina told her as if this made everything better.

"Di, you can't just go blowing up buildings!" Cassy yelled.

"I told you, I have the rights of a Gel. Nobody cares if a Gel blows up a building or two from time to time," Ditrina told them.

They stared at her in mute disbelief. Ditrina seemed to recognize they wanted further explanation.

"All elves can use magic; fixing a building only takes a few minutes," she said with a shrug.

"Be that as it may, the rest of us don't go around blowing up buildings!" Chris told her, hoping this didn't need explaining.

"Oh, I know that now," Ditrina said, nodding her head enthusiastically.

Chris was afraid to ask how she leaned this after hearing about how humans taught her about clothes. Matt seemed to have no such fears.

"How did you figure that out?" he asked with a chuckle.

"Do you know the town of Forhelm? Near the northern tip of the Godspine?" Ditrina asked.

"Yeah, as a matter of fact, I do. I went there once visiting a temple. It's a really nice place," Matt told her.

"Not anymore," Ditrina said, shaking her head sadly.

They decided that was enough questions about Ditrina's past for the time being.

As the day stretched on, they grew closer to Rooksberg. When they were about five miles away by Matt's calculation, Cassy began looking around strangely.

"Do you guys smell that?" she asked as they rode.

"No, what is it?" Chris asked her.

He trusted she had smelled something. As a naga, her senses were far superior to those of a human.

"It smells like smoke," she said as she continued to sniff the air.

"You're probably just smelling the village's cook fires," Matt said dismissively.

"I don't think so. I've never smelled something like that from so far away before," Cassy told him.

"Perhaps we should hurry?" Sarah proposed.

They urged their horses faster and sped toward the village. As they grew closer, Chris began to smell it too—the smell of smoke hanging heavy in the air. He realized that he smelled something else as well, something strangely sweet and sickening.

"Gods...what happened?" Chris asked as they broke through the tree line.

Before them was a scene from a nightmare. Charred husks sagged where buildings once stood, and the streets were blackened and scorched. Slowly, as if afraid to disturb the horrid vision before them, they dismounted and walked into the town.

"What could have done this?" Cassy muttered.

"It must have been the dragon; we are too late," Ditrina said with a tremble in her voice.

"Gods damn it!" Matt yelled. "We should have ridden faster. We took too long getting here!"

"Calm down, Matt..." Sarah began.

"Don't give me that *calm down* shit! We took too long, and these people died because of us!" Matt yelled, infuriated by what he saw.

"Calm down," Sarah repeated coolly. "These buildings have been burned out for a day or two now. It's likely that the dragon destroyed this place before we even knew about the contract," Sarah explained slowly.

"What do we do now?" Ditrina asked, looking around nervously at the husk of what had once been a town, like the dragon was somehow hiding in one of the buildings.

"Start looking around for survivors. It's possible someone escaped the dragon's fire and is still hiding in the village. Right now, we need to be concerned with the lives of the villagers, if there are any of them left," Chris told them.

They broke into groups, with Matt, Cassy, and Ditrina heading one way and Chris and Sarah heading the other. As they looked for survivors, Chris became more and more nauseated, with the stink of the smoke and smell of burnt flesh clogging his nose. Finally, Chris could stand it no longer.

"How do you do it?" he demanded as they walked.

"How do I do what?" Sarah asked.

"How are you so at ease right now? How are you not appalled by all of this?" Chris demanded in disbelief.

So far, as they had searched, Sarah hadn't shown the slightest sign of emotion, not even when Chris saw her pulling charred corpses from within the shells of the buildings.

"I'm used to it, I guess. As horrible as it sounds, this is by no means my first time exploring a burned-out village. When I was still part of the Band of the Boar, we chased several groups of bandits across the countryside. Sometimes they would leave towns looking like this. Hell, when we sacked that coastal city all those years ago, it looked a lot like this when we were done with it," she told him.

Sarah gave a small, sad laugh.

"What is it?" Chris asked.

"Once the city was ours, there wasn't a useable building still standing, yet they still called us liberators. The crown praised us as heroes and saviors, but we did more damage to that city than the raiders ever did," Sarah said shaking her head.

She was quiet for a while.

"Don't try to emulate me, Chris. It's good you're revolted by this. Nobody should have to get used to seeing something like this," she said suddenly before returning to their search.

They reconvened in what used to be the town's square an hour later.

"Did you guys find any traces of survivors?" Chris asked, fearing the answer.

"Nothing. How about you?" Matt replied.

Chris shook his head sadly.

"We should get out of here. I don't wanna spend another minute in this depressing place," Cassy said, looking at the ruins in disgust.

"Agreed. I see no reason for us to remain," Ditrina said hastily.

Chris shook his head.

"We can't leave yet; the dragon is still out there," Chris told them.

"But Chris, the villagers are all dead. There's nobody left to offer us a contract, so who's gonna pay us?" Cassy asked.

"We're not doing this for gold. We're doing this because it's the right thing to do. That dragon slaughtered an entire village. Who's to say it won't do it again? We do this to avenge the fallen and to protect those who have yet to feel its fire," Chris told them.

"You've been talking to Al too much," Cassy grumbled but protested no further.

Suddenly, they heard a scream. It echoed off the mountain and drifted down to them like an eerie melody. It was high-pitched and harsh, almost metallic in its nature, and it chilled them to the bone.

"I think we should leave," Ditrina said softly, shivering despite the warmth of the summer day.

"Ditrina, we need to kill it, or else this will happen again!" Sarah said angrily.

Ditrina looked totally unconvinced.

"If you want to go so bad, fine, go. Teleport on home, and we'll see you in a month, assuming the dragon doesn't kill us. To pass the time while you wait, you can flip coins to decide whether or not we get eaten. Does that sound fun?" Sarah demanded.

Ditrina shook her head.

"If you don't like that plan, you can march up that mountain and help us kill that dragon!" Sarah yelled.

"I hear something," Cassy said suddenly.

"What is it?" Chris asked.

"It sounds like someone's crying," Cassy said, puzzled.

"Where?" Chris demanded.

Cassy listened intently.

"It sounds like it's coming from that building over there," she said,

31

pointing to a husk that appeared slightly more intact than the others. "It's strange, I didn't hear anything until after the dragon roared," she told him.

Chris barely heard her. He was already racing toward the building.

"Hold on, Chris, I'll help," Sarah said as she followed close on his heels.

As he reached the building, he found the doorway blocked by a portion of the roof. He searched frantically for another way inside as he became aware of faint whimpers coming from within.

"Hold on; we're coming!" he yelled as he crawled in through the window beside the door.

Once inside, he found the fire had gutted the house. Tables, chairs, even what had once been the floor of the second story coated the abode in a thick layer of ash. The only thing that even mildly resembled furniture was a lone bed sitting pressed up against the far wall, charred, but still partially recognizable. The whimpers came from beneath it.

"It's ok, you can come out now," Chris said kindly.

The whimpers made no move to stop, nor did the person show themselves.

"Let me try," Sarah said as she approached.

It had taken her longer to enter on account of her armor.

"What's your plan?" Chris asked. "Whoever's under there is terrified."

"We don't have time to deal with that," Sarah declared and picked up the remains of the bed with a heave, tossing it behind them.

Their eyes widened in shock, and they stood in mute horror for a second.

"Matt! Matt, get in here; right now!" Chris screamed and rushed to the girl.

She lay on her right side, and from the way she looked, there should have been no way she was still alive. The left half of her body seemed to have been burned away, along with her clothes and hair, leaving half of her face a charred skull. The rest of her seemed to have fared no better, and her blackened, skeletonized hand reached out to him like a claw, almost nothing but bone. Her bloodshot eyes darted around the room in fear, and her breathing was ragged and irregular. From time to time, she would make a small whimpering noise.

"What seems to be the…oh, gods," Matt said quietly as he saw bone gleaming through charred flesh.

Without further delay, he rushed to the girl's side and began to pray, laying his glowing hands upon her.

"Is she going to be ok?" Sarah asked with concern.

"I have no idea how she's still alive. Those burns should've killed her," Matt said, shaking his head. "I don't know how much help I'm going to be," he admitted.

"But you can keep her alive, right?" Sarah asked nervously, looking at the little girl.

Matt said nothing but continued to work diligently.

"We need to help her," Al said in Chris's head.

"Matt is doing everything he can," Chris thought in reply.

"It's not enough; she's going to die!" Al replied angrily. "I refuse to stand by and watch a child suffer like this!"

"What do you want me to do?" Chris wondered irritably. "The only way I could help her at all at this point is to put her out of her misery, and you and I both know that's not going to happen."

"There is another way," Al told him.

"No, absolutely not! The last time we did that, I went into a coma for two weeks!" Chris thought angrily.

"I'm losing her," Matt said quietly.

"Save her, Chris! Take up the sword and save her!" Al urged.

Chris drew his sword.

"Gods damn it," he cursed and walked toward her.

"Chris, what are you doing?" Sarah asked cautiously.

"I'm going to try to save her," Chris said as he knelt beside her, planting the sword in the ground.

"No offence, buddy, but you're not exactly a healer. Unless you suddenly pledged yourself to a god without me knowing, please get back so I can work—" Matt started, but Chris pushed him aside.

Without waiting for an explanation, Chris gripped the sword by the hilt and saw the rubies flare up as Al channeled his power through him. He prayed he knew what he was doing.

"Chris, no! You promised you wouldn't try to use magic again!" Sarah yelled.

"We don't have a choice here, Sarah; she's dying," Chris said, and as he looked at her, Sarah saw his eyes were glowing red.

He looked at the girl and saw she was shaking with fear and pain.

"It's ok, I'm going to help," he assured her and placed his hand on her burned face.

Immediately he felt the power flowing from his sword into her, using him as a conduit. He watched in amazement as skin began to regrow where once bone had gleamed, and the blood drained from the girl's eyes, revealing they were brown. Stranger still, her hair regrew slightly, and he saw it was black like his. A few seconds later, Chris sat back and saw the girl's burns had been replaced with scarred skin. Despite this, half of her face still appeared as a leering skull with the scarred, discolored skin stretched taut across the bone, and her left arm still looked boney and ended in a claw-like hand.

Chris sat back, exhausted, and the girl instantly fell asleep.

"Are you all right?" Matt asked in amazement.

"Yeah, I just need a minute," Chris panted.

"I only healed her enough to keep her alive. Had I used more power, I could have repaired her completely, but that would have been dangerous for you. Better I sacrifice her looks rather than risk your life," Al told him.

"Will she be all right now?" Chris wondered.

"Yes, her body will function as it normally would, but her voice may be…damaged. Her vocal cords were seared, and seeing as they weren't essential, I only repaired them a little bit," Al explained.

"She will be able to speak, though, right?" Chris wondered.

"Yes, but like I said, it may be difficult for her at first," Al said.

"What the hell did you do?" Sarah demanded.

"Al healed her, enough so that she'll be able to live a normal life. He said he could have fixed her looks, too, but that could have put too much strain on me," Chris explained.

"That's remarkable," Matt said quietly.

"How do you feel?" Sarah asked him.

"To be honest, kinda like my blood's on fire. I'm not doing that again any time soon," Chris told her.

"What's going on in there? Is everyone ok?" Cassy called from outside the building.

"We're ok! Chris used magic and healed the girl!" Matt called.

"What!? I wanted to see him use magic again! Why did you not call me inside?" Ditrina asked indignantly.

"Your curiosity wasn't exactly high on my list of priorities!" Chris called irritably.

"It should be!" Ditrina called back.

"You're right, the next time I'm about to save someone's life, I'll just ask them not to die for a little while longer, so you can come watch!" Chris yelled angrily.

"Thank you!" Ditrina called happily.

"Four for forty-seven," Matt sighed.

The girl awoke a few minutes later after Chris had carried her outside. Cassy rigged up one of her short skirts and a shirt from her gear for the girl to wear. They stood around her, unsure of what to do with the child. Surprisingly, the clothes seemed only slightly too big for the small girl, saying volumes about Cassy's wardrobe.

"Well, now what?" Cassy asked.

"We could leave her here then head up the mountain. After we kill the dragon, we take her to the nearest village and drop her off," Matt proposed.

"That won't work. What if the dragon flies back down the mountain while we're at the top? It'll eat the girl before we can get to her," Sarah said.

When she mentioned the dragon, the girl gave a squeak of terror and scampered to Chris's leg, which she clung to for dear life.

"It looks as if she is afraid," Ditrina pointed out.

"Really? I hadn't noticed," Chris said with irritation.

"I detect sarcasm," Ditrina said flatly.

"Nice job, five for forty-eight," Cassy told her.

"Not the time, Cas," Chris said.

"Back to the matter at hand, we can't exactly leave her here, and we have to head up the mountain. I think we'll need to take her with us," Sarah said.

"You want to bring this girl to fight a dragon?" Matt asked in disbelief.

"Hey, I don't like the idea any more than you do but I don't see another option here," Sarah told him.

They turned to Chris.

"What's the plan?" Matt asked.

"I agree with Sarah," Chris said after a moment's consideration. "It's too risky leaving her here, and we do still have the dragon to deal with. She comes with us."

The girl clung tighter to his leg. Gently, Chris pulled her off and knelt beside her.

"What's your name, little one?" he asked kindly.

"Ever...Everi...Eve," the girl croaked.

Her voice sounded gravely and harsh, and Cassy winced upon hearing it.

"Eve? Your name is Eve?" Chris asked with a forced smile.

Eve nodded.

"We're going to help you Eve, but first we need to kill that dragon. We're going to head up the mountain, ok?" Chris asked softly.

Eve stared at him with huge brown eyes and nodded slightly.

"Don't worry, Eve; we'll keep you safe," Cassy said with a smile.

Eve saw Cassy's fangs and hid behind Chris's legs once more.

"Stop smiling, Cassy; you're scaring the poor girl!" Sarah scolded.

"Oh, that's not fair. I'm not that scary!" Cassy said, hurt by Sarah's assumption that it was her Eve was afraid of.

She walked around behind Chris and knelt beside Eve.

"See, I'm not going to hurt you," Cassy said, holding her hands out, palms up.

Eve took one look at Cassy's claws and shrieked, though it came out as more of a loud croak and sprinted toward Sarah. Sarah picked up the frightened girl and held her against her armored chest.

"I know, I know. The scary snake woman is mean, isn't she?" Sarah asked as she cradled Eve and gave Cassy a dirty look, made less effective by her full-face helmet.

"How is she not afraid of you? You're wearing all that spiky armor and, well…you're you," Cassy said.

"Do you want to expand upon that at all?" Sarah asked, giving her a vile look; again, useless behind her helmet.

"No, well…I just mean…Chris, help me out here!" Cassy said, looking at her brother.

She had put her faith in the wrong person.

"I have no idea what you're talking about. Sarah looks adorable in that armor," Chris said hastily, fearing his wife's barbed gauntlets.

"I think you're laying it on a bit thick," Matt said with a chuckle.

"Shut up, Matt," Chris said quickly.

They heard the dragon roar in the distance. Eve screamed and buried her face against Sarah's chest.

"Are you sure it is wise to bring her along? She seems quite frightened," Ditrina asked.

"Well, we're bringing you, aren't we? What's one more useless little girl to protect?" Matt asked.

"I may be young, but I hardly believe two hundred and ten qualifies me as a little girl," Ditrina pouted.

"Note she didn't dispute the useless part," Chris remarked.

"Oh no, I will likely be rendered catatonic when I see the dragon," Ditrina agreed.

"Great! You can watch Eve while we fight," Chris said, rolling his eyes.

Eve climbed off Sarah and walked up to Ditrina, looking at her curiously.

"What? Is she going to scream and run away from her, too?" Cassy asked, annoyed.

Eve smiled as well as she could with only half a face at Ditrina, more of a grimace than anything else, and made a choking noise that sounded like a cat being crushed slowly under a large rock.

"What in the name of the gods is she doing?" Cassy asked.

"I believe she is laughing," Ditrina said and knelt in front of Eve.

Eve pointed at her own eyes, then Ditrina's, and continued to make the horrible noise.

"Oh, look, she's laughing at Ditrina! She'll fit in just fine around here," Matt declared cheerfully.

CHAPTER THREE

They hiked slowly up the mountain. They had discovered a small path that seemed to lead farther up the cliffs, likely made by goats. The footing was treacherous, and the angle was steep, and as such, Eve quickly became tired and was forced to ride on Chris's shoulders.

"Doing all right up there?" Chris asked her when they stopped for a rest.

"Yes," Eve croaked, trying to say no more than what was absolutely necessary to spare her throat.

"All right then. If you need a rest, just let me know, and we'll take another break," Chris told her.

They pressed on. As they neared the peak, they became aware of a sound, like metal being scraped against stone.

"What *is* that?" Chris asked as they walked.

"It might be the dragon, maybe it's snoring?" Cassy proposed.

"What, like Matt?" Sarah asked.

"Hey, that's not fair," Matt complained.

"Yeah, we should probably be open-minded and give the dragon the benefit of the doubt here," Chris laughed.

Eve made the horrible choking noise again and pointed at Matt, whose face was scrunched in anger.

"That's right, Eve, Matt is funny looking, isn't he?" Chris chuckled.

"Short," Eve croaked before continuing with the horrible laughter.

"Traitor," Matt grumbled, but Chris saw he gave a small smile.

They reached the end of the trail, and the conversation died. Chris set Eve on the ground and peeked around the corner.

"What do you see?" Cassy hissed.

"It's the dragon, all right," Chris said grimly.

In his mind, Chris had pictured the dragon like the ones from his childhood fairy tales. The dragons of his youth were proud and majestic, standing tall on powerful legs with resplendent wings that filled the sky. A dragon's scales should be bright, and their appearance should be regal and awe inspiring.

The beast before him had obviously not read the same fairy tales.

"She's an ugly bastard, isn't she?" Sarah asked as she peeked around the rock with him.

Sarah was right; the dragon could hardly be called pretty.

It was around forty feet long and looked like a fat snake with wings. The dragon had two stocky legs at the base of its tail with powerful grasping claws. Its wings doubled as its front legs. The wings themselves were immense and leathery, folded against the beast's sides like an enormous bat. The wing's webbing ran down the creature's sides and stopped halfway down its tail. If Chris had to guess, he would have said the dragon's wingspan was easily thirty feet wide. Each wing had a massive hooked claw that Chris assumed the dragon walked upon. Its head resembled that of a viper, with the addition of two long horns sweeping back toward its neck, with a frill of spines that continued down its neck before tapering off around its shoulders. The dragon had a large webbed crest that ran along its neck and another such crest running the length of its tail. Rather than gleaming scales as Chris had expected, the dragon's scales were dull and molted, like those of a python.

Currently, the dragon was coiled, sleeping in its nest, which seemed to be made up of enormous uprooted trees.

"What's the plan?" Matt whispered.

"Ok, here's what we do. Ditrina, I need you to…" Chris trailed off.

Ditrina and Eve were currently huddled together, shaking in fear.

"Right, never mind. New plan. Matt, I need you to use your magic and keep it grounded. Sarah and I can't fight if it's flying all over the place. Cassy, help Matt as best as you can. Sarah and I will hack it apart while it's on the ground," Chris told them.

"Is everyone ready?" Sarah asked.

Matt nodded grimly, and Cassy set an arrow on the string of her bow.

"Right, let's go!" Chris said and drew his sword.

The blade burst into flames, and they charged. As they sped across the rocky clearing toward the nest, the dragon's scaly lids flicked open, and they found themselves observed by a huge eye, like that of a snake. Faster than they thought possible, the dragon uncoiled and spread its massive wings, letting out an earsplitting scream. Just as Chris reached the monster, it gave a beat of its wings, buffeting him with wind and launching itself into the sky.

"Matt, you're up!" Chris yelled.

"I'm working on it!" Matt yelled back as he frantically flipped through the pages of his book.

"Why didn't you do that earlier?!" Chris yelled as he nervously watched the dragon circle them.

"Ge would have probably shown me something about mountain hiking! You know how he is!" Matt argued as he read furiously.

"What do we do now?" Sarah demanded.

"Stall it!" Matt yelled.

The dragon dove, spewing fire from its jaws.

"Move!" Chris bellowed as they leapt out of the way, flames melting the rocks where they'd just stood.

"I'm going to try to ground it!" Cassy yelled as she began firing arrows at its wings.

The arrows flew true but seemed to have little effect. Many passed through the webbing without doing any serious damage, while others simply bounced off its armored scales. Suddenly, as if fate decided it wanted to humor her, she scored a lucky hit and put an arrow through the dragon's eye. The dragon screamed in pain and focused all of its rage on Cassy.

"Great job, sis; you got its attention!" Chris yelled.

"Lucky me!" Cassy screamed as she ran away from the dragon banking toward her.

Without warning, they heard a thunderclap, and the dragon was blasted out of the sky by a bolt of lightning.

"Hell yeah, go Matt!" Sarah yelled as she charged the fallen dragon, which was regaining its feet and shaking its head in confusion, smoke rising from its charred back.

Matt gave a weak thumbs-up and stumbled forward a pace; such a powerful spell had taken a lot out of him.

"The wings! Focus on its wings!" Chris yelled as he sprinted to his wife's side.

The dragon reared back to strike Sarah, but she bashed its nose with her shield, causing it to hiss and shake its head. Taking advantage of the confusion, Sarah slipped under the dragon's neck and began to hack away at the beast's wing. As Chris arrived, the dragon recovered and looked at him with its good eye filled with hate. Maddened by the pain, it misrecognized Chris as its source and screamed at him.

"Of course you have three rows of fangs; why wouldn't you?" Chris muttered to himself as he prepared to dodge.

Rather than strike as he had thought, the dragon reared its head back, and Chris saw an orange glow seeping from between its jaws.

"Shit," Chris said with terror as he realized he was too close to dodge.

He pulled his cloak around himself, preparing for the worst.

"Satrafi!" Matt yelled as the dragon's fire ignited the air.

There was a whooshing noise, and an explosion of steam as the dragon's mouth was filled with water. The dragon reared back and coughed violently, and Chris darted to its unoccupied side, hacking away furiously with his sword. The dragon shook its head and tried to snap at him and Sarah, but they used the size of its wings against it, hiding behind them whenever the dragon attempted to snatch them up and doing their best to stay in its blind spot.

The dragon grew tired of this game and spun violently, smashing into both Chris and Sarah with its tail, sending them flying across the clearing into a rock face. Stunned, but alive, Chris looked up in horror to see the dragon racing toward him, running on its bleeding wings in a strange combination of a bound and a slither. As it ran, Chris saw something else, a small figure racing toward the dragon.

It was Eve.

She was carrying a dagger, and Chris realized his own dagger was missing from its sheath. It clicked that she must have taken it when he wasn't paying attention.

"Eve, get back!" Chris managed to yell, but it was too late.

Eve reached the tip of the dragon's tail and plunged the dagger in up to the hilt. The dragon shrieked in pain and spun around, fixing Eve with its hateful glare. Eve backed away, looking around in terror for an escape route. Chris stumbled forward, still dazed from the dragon's blow but saw he was too far away to reach her in time. He looked and saw Sarah lying unconscious, and Matt's limp body being dragged clear by Cassy, his strength spent on magic.

"Run, Eve!" Chris yelled as he stumbled forward, but she was too afraid to move.

Like a bird frozen by the gaze of a snake, Eve stood before the dragon as it hissed at her. The dragon reared back its head, and Chris saw the deadly orange glow spreading once again between its jaws.

In an instant, there was fire everywhere, but not the dragon's.

"Get *away*!" Ditrina shrieked as she marched forward, hands outstretched, palms gushing fire.

Her flames blanketed the dragon, and it screamed in rage, launching itself into the sky on ragged wings. It only made it a few feet off the ground before Ditrina let out a scream to match its own and made a gesture like throwing her hands at the ground. The sky above them swirled red, and a pillar of fire streaked down and engulfed the dragon. Chris was blasted back by the force of the spell, smashing once more into the cliff face. Eve screamed and ran for the nearest cover, which tuned out to be the dragon's nest. Ditrina continued to scream, a mindless, wordless, declaration of fury as the dragon burned. It thrashed and shrieked within the inferno, but the force of the flames pinned it to the ground, making it impossible to flee. Suddenly the dragon was still, but Ditrina continued to scream, and the flames continued to burn away the dragon's body. It wasn't until only ash remained that Ditrina slumped to her knees and began to weep.

Chris sat stunned in mute horror after watching the incredible display of power. Looking across the rocky clearing, he saw Cassy was just as amazed. Slowly, he limped his way over to Ditrina, taking care to avoid the glowing section of stone where her flames had hit.

"Are you ok?" he asked her softly.

Ditrina continued to cry.

"Ditrina?" Chris asked softly and knelt beside her.

"It's all right, Di," Cassy said as she arrived, kneeling on Ditrina's other side.

Still sobbing, Ditrina buried her face in Cassy's shoulder. Cassy pulled her close and made reassuring noises, and Chris rested his hand on Ditrina's shoulder. They didn't move for some time.

"Chris, you were wrong," Ditrina sniffled eventually.

"What do you mean?" Chris asked.

"Killing a dragon did not help. I actually think I am more afraid than ever," Ditrina admitted.

Chris laughed softly.

"You know what, Ditrina? I think I'm a bit frightened of dragons now myself," Chris told her.

He stood up.

"If you're all right, Ditrina, I need to go check on Sarah. I think the dragon knocked her out," Chris told her.

"This is so weird. Usually, *you're* the one who gets knocked out," Cassy said.

"Yeah, well, there's a first time for everything," Chris grumbled as he walked toward his wife.

Eve cowered in the nest. She heard the sounds of battle raging outside and decided it was best if she remained put for the time being. The strange green woman with black eyes had started screaming, and Eve reached the conclusion that standing between her and the dragon was a bad idea, so she took shelter in the nest. In her hand, she still clutched the stolen dagger, blade slick with the dragon's blood. As she cowered, she noticed something—something small and pale. It was an oval, roughly the size of a small loaf of bread. Not knowing what to do, she picked up the strange oval and slipped it under her oversized shirt for further study. She found it was strangely warm to the touch.

From outside, she heard the dragon scream, but these screams seemed to be screams of pain, not of rage. She heard another scream as well, which she assumed to come from the green woman. Suddenly, it was quiet outside, with both screams dying abruptly, one fading after the other.

Eve stayed in the nest. When it was safe to come out, she knew the red-eyed man would come get her, but for now, the safest place was far away from the fire. She liked the red-eyed man. He had made her pain go away. She liked the short man too. He had helped with the pain as well. She wasn't sure what to think of the metal lady yet. She had comforted her when the creepy snake woman tried to eat her, but she was still a bit scary.

"Eve? Eve, are you all right?" she heard the red-eyed man call.

"Yes!" she called as loud as she could.

For some reason, her voice sounded funny and talking hurt, so she decided that that would have to be enough for the time being.

"Stay where you are, Eve; I'll be right there," the red-eyed man replied.

So, Eve waited, sitting patiently in the dragon's nest until she saw the red-eyed man's face appear above the lip of the nest.

"There you are. Come on out, Eve; it's safe now," the red-eyed man said with a smile, offering her his hand.

Carefully, Eve crawled out from within the nest. As she sat perched atop the lip, she had a good view of her saviors. The red-eyed man was beside her, of course, and appeared to be fine. The short man and the metal woman were sitting side by side and looked groggy, but otherwise unharmed. Snake woman was holding the green lady, and the green lady's eyes were puffy like she had been crying. Maybe the snake woman had tried to eat her as well?

"Oh, thank the gods, she's all right," snake woman said when she saw Eve standing beside the red-eyed man, having dropped down from the nest.

Eve flinched and hid behind the red-eyed man. She decided she was *not* going to give the snake woman another chance to try to eat her and readied her dagger.

"Oh, come on! I'm not *that* scary!" snake woman yelled.

"She disagrees," the red-eyed man said with amusement.

He knelt beside Eve.

"It's ok. I promise she won't hurt you," he said.

Eve looked at the snake woman. She seemed genuinely upset.

"Ok," Eve rasped, and began walking up to snake woman.

Eve believed that the red-eyed man wouldn't lie to her. He was nice, after all, but she still doubted the wisdom of what she was doing. If worst came to worst, she was still clutching the dagger. She had stabbed a dragon, after all. How hard could it be to stab the snake woman?

"See? I told you, I'm not going to hurt you," snake woman said and offered Eve her hand.

Cautiously, Eve touched it and felt the rough scales.

"My name is Cassy. Can you say Cassy?" snake woman asked.

"Casss…Cass…Cas," Eve croaked before settling on the nickname.

"It is ok, I call her Cas, too," the green woman said. "You seem to have trouble with long words, so you may call me Di."

"Di," Eve said.

She pointed to Cassy.

"Cas," Eve croaked.

"Good!" Cassy said excitedly.

"Green?" Eve asked, pointing at Ditrina.

"I am an elf; that is why I look different," Ditrina explained.

Eve pointed to Cassy.

"Elf?" she asked.

"No, I'm a naga," Cassy told her.

Eve nodded as if this explained everything, having no idea what either an elf or a naga was, and not really caring.

"Well, I'm glad to see she's making friends," the metal lady said.

She was walking toward them with the help of the red-eyed man, and the short man was following slightly behind them.

"Cas, Di," Eve said proudly, pointing at each of them in turn.

"Very good! My name is Sarah," the metal lady told her and pulled off her helmet.

"Red," Eve said, pointing at Sarah's hair.

"Sarah; come on Eve, *Sarah*," Sarah repeated cheerfully.

"Sarah," Eve croaked, then coughed.

"Well done, Eve. Those two are Matt and Chris," Sarah said, pointing to the men in turn.

Eve repeated the names and pointed at the men.

"Dragon?" Eve asked and looked around.

Not seeing a body, she feared it was still alive.

"Don't worry, Eve, Ditrina killed it," Chris told her.

Eve looked at him blankly.

"Di…Di killed it," Chris clarified.

Eve looked at Ditrina then back at Chris.

"I…don't think…I…should laugh…at her…anymore," Eve croaked before descending into a violent fit of coughing.

She only said what she felt was necessary, after all.

They returned to the burned-out village to get their horses. Too small to ride alone, and without a horse to spare, Eve rode with Chris. They decided to return to Glenord to spend the night so Ditrina could recover her strength before taking them home. That evening they sat around their fire, tents pitched and recounted the previous battle.

"I'd like to make a toast to this special occasion!" Chris called, raising his bowl of stew above his head.

"Really? What's so special it demands celebrating?" Matt asked with amusement.

"This is the first time that *I* survived a fight unscathed while *Sarah* got knocked out!" Chris said happily.

Everyone laughed, including Sarah, and spirits were high. Eve ate three bowls of stew, then stole one of Matt's, ravenous after being trapped in her home for so long. As the meal drew to a close, Chris felt a small tug on his sleeve. Looking down, he saw Eve offering him his dagger back.

"Sorry," she croaked quietly.

Chris smiled and ruffled her short hair.

"Keep it. All heroes need weapons," he told her.

Eve's eyes widened, and she clutched the blade close to her. Still smiling, Chris unbuckled its sheath and helped her fasten it to her hip like a tiny sword. Eve stood proudly and brandished the knife above her head, shrieking smugly. Sarah smiled.

"She's a fiery little one, isn't she?" Sarah asked.

"Chris, is that the old knife you bought all those years ago?" Cassy asked with amusement.

"Yeah, I bought it when I was eleven," Chris confirmed.

"You've been carrying that thing for seven years now?" Matt asked in amazement.

"Yeah, it was the first thing I ever bought with my own gold," Chris answered happily.

He paused as if lost in thought, and the others returned to their dinners.

"It was the last thing I still had from Shearcliff," Chris said quietly.

"Are you sure you want to give it away?" Matt asked.

"I'm sure. Eve got more use out of it when she stabbed the dragon than I ever did. Besides, it's just the right size for her," Chris said with a smile.

Eve ran happily around the fire, waving the knife above her head.

"Do you think we should let her keep doing that?" Cassy asked with concern.

"Please, she stabbed a dragon earlier today. It's a bit late to start acting responsible and concerned," Matt yawned. "I'm going to call it a night."

"Sleep well, Matthew," Ditrina said as she stood up. "I, too, am going to go to bed."

"Same," Cassy agreed, and they headed to their tent, leaving Chris alone with Sarah and Eve.

"We need to put Eve to bed," Sarah said. "Come here, sweetie; give me the knife," Sarah said as she walked toward Eve.

Reluctantly, Eve surrendered the weapon.

"You can have it back in the morning," Sarah assured her, and the half of Eve's face that could smile, did.

"So, what are we going to do with her?" Chris asked later that night.

He and Sarah lay in their tent, with Eve having crawled between them and fallen asleep.

"I think we should try to drop her off at the nearest village, and find a nice family to take her in," Sarah proposed.

Chris frowned.

"I'm not sure that'll work," he said.

"Why?" Sarah asked.

"Eve's face…her arm. I'm not too sure villagers will take kindly to the way she looks," Chris admitted.

"That's ridiculous! She's just a little girl!" Sarah said angrily, but Chris shushed her and gestured to Eve's tiny sleeping form.

"I'd like to agree with you, but I've seen firsthand what happens to a little kid who looks different in a small village," Chris told her quietly.

"You're thinking about your sister," Sarah realized.

Chris nodded.

"They drove her from her home. When she walked down the street, people walked the other way. They refused to speak to her or even look in her direction. And for what? Just because she had scales? I worry Eve will be in a similar situation because of her mutilation," Chris said.

"Maybe we could talk to Ophelia? Her kids are around Eve's age," Sarah proposed.

"Maybe, but you saw how frightened Eve was of Cas. I doubt sending her to live with a vampire is a good idea," Chris chuckled.

"So, what do we do?" Sarah asked.

Chris was quiet.

"What if she stayed with us?" he asked quietly.

"What?" Sarah laughed.

"I'm serious! Hear me out," Chris said hastily. "We've been talking about having kids; why doesn't she just stay with us? We can adopt her, and she can live in the valley. Nobody there will care how she looks, and the maids can look after her while we're away on missions."

"Do you think she'll like it there?" Sarah asked. "There're no other children for her to play with."

"Well, maybe we can do something to change that," Chris said with a small smile. "In the meantime, I think she'll be ok. I'm just worried about how she'll be treated if we just dump her someplace."

"We can ask her in the morning. Who knows; she might have family somewhere," Sarah said.

They went to sleep.

"Good evening, Chris!" Mi called cheerfully as the grey world expanded around him.

This night, like every night, Chris's mind was transported to a place between the physical realm and the astral realm so that he could speak with the spirits he was bound to.

"Hello, Mi," Chris said as he arrived.

"What's up?" Matt asked.

Like Chris, Matt was bound to a spirit and joined him in his nightly discussions.

"Congratulations on slaying the dragon, truly a feat to be proud of," Al said.

"Technically, it was the elf Ditrinadoma who killed the dragon. Chris merely assisted her," Ge said flatly.

"Nevertheless, it was an epic battle. Well done," Al praised.

"I had money on someone getting eaten. I'm disappointed," Mi admitted.

"You're joking, right?" Chris asked.

"Hell no! I had a bunch of other spirits over to watch the fight. The first King of Hailguard put up three-to-one odds that someone would die. How could I resist?" Mi asked.

"My life isn't some sporting event for you and your dead buddies to watch!" Chris yelled.

"I know! Besides, I had a side bet going that you would survive. You should be flattered!" Mi argued.

"Sometimes, I'm glad I can't return to the astral realm," Al said.

"Your wife says hello, by the way," Mi told him.

"Send her my regards," Al said sadly.

"It may interest you to know that Matthew and I have made no progress in the way of fixing your problem, Chris," Ge told him.

"Why would that interest me?" Chris asked.

"We do not want to get your hopes up," Ge told him.

"Not the best way of sharing, Ge," Matt chastised. "Anyway, Ge and I have work to do. We are still trying to find a way out of this for you," Matt said before both figures disappeared, leaving Chris and Al alone with Mi.

"So, what's this business with the girl about?" Mi asked.

"Yes, I believe you spoke with your wife about adopting her. Do you have much experience with children?" Al asked.

"You share my memories; you know the answer," Chris snapped.

"Exactly. So why are you determined to keep this child?" Al asked.

"You're a bit young to turn into a stay-at-home dad," Mi told him.

"I have no plans of stopping adventuring, and I'm not planning on asking Sarah to stop either," he said, anticipating Mi's next question.

"So, what? You're just going to give her to your maids to deal with? That's not exactly quality dad material," Mi taunted.

"Actually, I was planning on having her travel with us when she gets a bit older," Chris admitted.

"You want to drag a little girl around on your missions?" Mi asked skeptically.

"I understand where he's going with this," Al said.

"Really? Care to explain? Because I don't see how a six-year-old will be anything but a hindrance while out and about!" Mi yelled.

"This is why you never had kids, Mi. But as for your question, I share Chris's thoughts, so I know what led to this conclusion. I'll let him explain," Al said.

"When we were fighting the dragon, there was a point I thought I was going to get eaten…" Chris began.

"Really glad you didn't. I would have never heard the end of it," Mi cut in.

Chris and Al shot him withering looks.

"Sheesh, it was a joke. I didn't bet that much anyway," Mi muttered.

"*Anyway*, when we were fighting the dragon, Eve didn't just sit and hide; she actually attacked it. That little girl who had just lost everything charged at a forty-foot, fire-breathing monster and stabbed it in the tail. That says a lot about her," Chris said.

"Yeah, it says she's not right in the head," Mi told him.

"It says she's brave!" Al yelled. "Chris recognizes this child has potential and sees her as a worthy heir to his legacy, given some grooming. It is a wise choice," Al said.

"I think you're putting a bit too much thought into this," Chris told him. "I don't want her to end up kicked to the curb in some village somewhere, so I'm going to help her as best I can. As for the whole *inheritance* bit, I think you forget I'm not a king like you two. I'm just some adventurer living with his friends. Aside from my house, I don't have much to leave anyone, save a pocketful of gold," Chris told them.

"You have the artifacts," Al reminded him.

"I thought they would shatter if I died," Chris stated.

"Not if you pass them along first," Al told him.

"Fine, a house and two artifacts. Not the most impressive legacy," Chris told them. "What's with you two and me dying anyway? Every road leads to my death with you guys."

"To the dead, life is fleeting. I lived till I was eighty, but I've been dead ever since. That's eighty years compared to fifteen-hundred years. You tell me which has made more of an impact on me," Mi told him.

"That's a disturbing way of looking at things," Chris told him.

"You won't be saying that when you're dead," Mi said.

"Let's hope that's a long way off," Chris said.

"I agree. I've got a lot of money riding on you," Mi told him.

Chris gave him a dark look.

"Would it help if I bet on your friends living past fifty as well?" Mi asked.

"That's not the point, brother," Al sighed.

"Good, because I already bet against them," Mi said with relief.

As it turned out, Eve had no other family to speak of.

"Think, Eve. Do you have any uncles or aunts? Maybe grandparents living somewhere?" Chris asked the next morning.

Eve nodded.

"That's great! Where do they live?" Chris asked.

"Rooksberg," Eve croaked.

Matt winced.

"Nice going, Chris. I'm sure she just *loves* questions about her family right now," Matt called.

"I doubt it. They were all recently incinerated, so the topic is likely fairly sensitive," Ditrina commented.

"Five for forty-nine," Cassy sighed.

"All gone," Eve croaked.

Chris looked at her sadly, and Eve took it as a request for more details.

"Running...then fire. All gone," Eve repeated.

"I'm sorry, Eve," Chris said softly.

"Why? You helped," Eve said flatly. "Called Father...called Mother... no answer," Eve croaked before descending into a fit of coughing.

Once she had recovered, she continued.

"Pain...long time. You come...pain goes," Eve told him. "You come...dragon goes," she added, before sitting down, panting.

Speaking still proved difficult for the small girl.

"So, what do we do with her?" Matt asked.

"The most likely village to leave her at is Torville, but it is several weeks north of here," Ditrina told them. "Knowing how the villagers there like us, it is possible they might take the child."

"Actually, I talked to Sarah. We're thinking about keeping Eve," Chris admitted.

"What do you mean keeping Eve? Slavery is illegal in the kingdom," Matt said, perplexed.

"No! I mean we're thinking about adopting her! She has no family and nowhere to go. If we take her in, she can have a good life in the valley," Chris explained.

"You're serious?" Cassy asked bewildered.

"Well, yeah," Chris said.

"And you're ok with this?" Cassy asked Sarah.

"Why wouldn't I be?" Sarah demanded.

"You just don't strike me as the *mom* type is all," Cassy said with a nervous shrug.

"Oh? What makes you say that?" Sarah asked all too calmly, her hand edging closer to one of her short swords.

"Oh, I don't know. I guess it was just my imagination," Cassy said quickly.

"Does Eve wish to come with us?" Ditrina asked.

"What?" Chris asked.

"Does Eve wish to live with us? Have you asked her? Her voice may not function very well, but her mind works fine. Are you sure she wishes to go with you?" Ditrina asked.

"Well, not yet," Chris admitted.

All eyes turned to Eve.

"Yes?" she croaked with confusion.

"Would you like to stay with us, Eve?" Chris asked kindly.

Eve shrugged.

"Rooksberg...gone," she croaked.

"Yes, your home was destroyed. I'm sorry we didn't get there sooner," Chris said.

"Your home...nice?" Eve asked.

"Yes, it's very nice," Chris assured her. "It's in a big valley. You'll have room to run around and play and do whatever you like."

Eve shrugged.

"Everyone here...is dead. I...will come," Eve coughed.

Not feeling the need to complicate things further with more words, Eve returned to the tent to get her things, leaving the others alone.

"She seems strangely...uncaring," Matt said after a moment.

"You try watching your village get incinerated then half burn to death and see how well your mind works!" Sarah snapped.

"Hey, I'm just pointing out the fact that you're going to have to be careful with her. Little kid or not, if she starts seeing killing as something normal you're going to be in a world of trouble. Right now, she should be crying her eyes out over her family. Instead, she just decides to pack up and live with a group of strangers. That's not normal for a little kid!" Matt told them.

"What do you know about little kids?" Chris demanded.

"I have five little brothers, so trust me when I say that child's not right in the head. She charged a dragon, Chris!" Matt insisted.

"She's brave!" Chris argued.

"She needs close watching," Matt corrected. "I'm not trying to discourage you from taking her with us; I'm just warning you that you may be getting more than you bargained for. She's not just a scared little girl. She has the potential to be dangerous," Matt told him.

"She's six!" Sarah said angrily.

"And what happens when she's eighteen? If you don't make sure to teach her right from wrong, you're going to end up with a monster," Matt said firmly.

"You're overreacting," Chris refuted.

"I really hope so," Matt said.

Eve reappeared, her dagger once again at her hip.

"Hungry," she said simply, tugging on Chris's sleeve.

"I'll cook breakfast," Cassy sighed, grateful that the argument had been put on pause.

As they ate, Eve stared at Chris.

"Yes, Eve?" he asked when he noticed.

"I live...with you..." Eve croaked before trailing off, unsure of how to continue.

"That's right. If you want, Sarah and I will adopt you, so you can live with us," Chris told her.

"Adopt?" Eve asked curiously.

"It means Sarah and I would sort of be like your new mother and father," Chris explained.

"New father? Father died...everyone...died. Replace?" Eve rasped curiously.

She seemed totally at ease, not at all concerned with the death of her parents. Matt gave Chris a worried look but said nothing.

"Well, yeah," Chris said, slightly disturbed by the casual way Eve put it.

Eve shrugged.

"Ok, Father," she croaked before returning to her breakfast.

Sarah and Chris exchanged uneasy looks.

"Eve, it's ok to be sad about your village, you know," Sarah told her.

"Not sad...Mother. They died...I lived. I...am happy...I lived," Eve told her, coughing between words.

Sarah seemed just as surprised as Chris at the casual way Eve appointed them as her new parents.

"Don't you miss them at all?" Matt asked.

Eve looked at him strangely.

"I know...where...they are. They're...in Rooksberg. I'm not... missing anyone," Eve told him, confused by his question.

Matt had no response to that.

CHAPTER FOUR

Once they'd finished breaking camp, they gathered around Ditrina to go home.

"Drink this," Ditrina told Sarah moments before they departed.

"What is it?" Sarah asked, looking suspiciously at the green sludge Ditrina offered her.

"It is a potion I made last night; it should help with your nausea," Ditrina told her.

"Oh, thanks, Ditrina," Sarah said as she took the bowl from her hands.

Sarah drank the potion in one gulp, then gagged.

"Gods, Ditrina, I thought you said it would *help* with my nausea!" Sarah coughed.

"It will. It just does not taste very good is all," Ditrina informed her.

"You could have warned me, at least!" Sarah yelled, still coughing from the vile drink.

"I was planning to, but Cas told me you would enjoy the surprise. No need to thank me," Ditrina told her.

"Thank you?!" Sarah demanded in outrage.

"You are welcome," Ditrina said with a smile.

"Five for fifty," Matt called.

"No, that was outrage, not sarcasm. She's still good," Chris told him.

"Still five for forty-nine then?" Ditrina asked.

"Yeah, that sounds right," Chris told her.

"Good, my ratio this week is still my best yet," Ditrina said happily.

Sarah fumed.

"Can we get going? I just drank that stupid thing, so let's go before it wears off," Sarah said.

"Are you...ok, Mother?" Eve croaked tugging on Sarah's arm.

"I'm ok, Eve," Sarah reassured her.

"Why are...you upset?" Eve asked.

"Your Aunt Cas was just being silly," Sarah told Eve, giving Cassy a vile look.

"Aunt?" Eve asked in shock, looking at Chris suspiciously like he too was hiding scales somewhere.

"Yep!" Cassy said cheerfully, smiling at Eve.

Eve looked closely at Cassy's teeth, then at Chris.

"Teeth...claws?" Eve asked not understanding.

"Cassy is adopted, like you. She's my sister," Chris told her.

Eve shrugged.

"Don't...eat me," Eve coughed at Cassy.

"What?" Cassy asked in shock.

"Please...don't eat...me," Eve rasped again.

"I'm not going to eat you!" Cassy said with outrage.

"Teeth," Eve said simply.

"There're not for eating people!" Cassy insisted.

Eve shrugged.

"Sure," she said and gestured for Sarah to pick her up.

Sarah happily obliged.

"Don't...let her...eat me...Mother," Eve croaked quietly in Sarah's ear, trying to whisper in her broken voice.

Sarah laughed.

"I won't, sweetie," Sarah promised.

"If you're finished tormenting each other, can we go home now?" Matt asked irritably.

"I am ready," Ditrina told them.

They led their horses to Ditrina and linked hands, ensuring that everything that needed to be transported was touching in some way.

Several seconds later, after a brief spinning sensation, they were standing in front of their house in the valley.

"Well, what do you know? The potion worked!" Sarah declared happily.

"It's nice to not have anyone throwing up after we teleport," Matt agreed.

Eve tugged on his arm and looked uncomfortable.

"Yes, Eve?" Matt asked.

Eve puked on his shoes.

"Feel funny," Eve rasped.

"Gods damn it!" Matt cursed.

"Feel funny," Eve repeated before puking again, this time on the grass.

"It's ok, Eve, you'll feel better soon," Sarah reassured her.

"Fix…it," Eve demanded between heaves, still puking.

"It'll get better on its own," Sarah told her.

"I need to go clean up," Matt said angrily before walking toward the lake.

"Leader, may I please go rest? I have used more magic in the last few days than I am used to," Ditrina admitted.

"Sure, go ahead, Ditrina," Chris sighed. "And don't call me that," he added half-heartedly.

"Sorry, leader," Ditrina said before disappearing inside the house, Cassy on her heels.

"Your house?" Eve asked, seeming to either have recovered or run out of breakfast to throw up.

"Yep. This is where you will be staying," Chris told her.

Eve looked at it in amazement; it was the largest building she had ever seen.

"Pretty," she said finally.

"Do you want us to show you around?" Chris asked her.

Eve nodded eagerly.

"Come on, then," Chris said and took her by the hand.

Together, he and Sarah showed Eve the many rooms of the house, explaining what each one was used for. Along the way, they ran into the maids.

"Master Shearcliff, who is that child?" one of them asked nervously when they saw Eve.

"This is Eve. She will be staying with us for the foreseeable future. Eve's parents were killed in a dragon attack, and Sarah and I have decided to adopt her," Chris told them.

"Is she...?" one of them asked, looking at Eve's deformity.

Chris spoke before the maid had a chance to voice her concerns.

"She is my daughter and will be treated as such. Do I make myself clear?" Chris asked angrily.

"Yes, Master," the maids said hastily.

"Two?" Eve croaked.

The maids winced when they heard her voice.

"Two what, Eve?" Sarah asked.

Eve pointed at the maids with confusion.

"Same...but two. How?" Eve demanded.

"Flora and Fiona are twins. They look alike," Sarah explained.

"Twins?" Eve asked.

"Twins are siblings born at the same time. Sometimes they look the same," Chris told her.

"Have you never seen twins before?" Sarah asked.

Eve shook her head. Rooksberg had been a small village without much contact with the outside world.

"How do...you tell...them apart?" Eve asked before coughing violently.

"We, ah...well, we're actually having a bit of trouble with that," Chris admitted.

Eve appeared lost in thought.

"Hair," Eve said suddenly.

"What?" Chris asked perplexed.

"Hair," Eve repeated and gestured like letting her hair down, then pointed to one of the maids.

Comprehension dawned on Chris as he saw both maids wore their hair in tight buns.

"One of you two, let your hair down," Chris ordered.

"Why?" the maids asked.

"Because Eve just found a way to tell you two apart. Now, one of you, I don't care who, let your hair down," Chris told them.

One of the maids shrugged and let her blonde hair fall to her shoulders.

"Now which one are you?" Chris asked.

"My name is Flora; don't you recognize me, Master?" Flora said.

"How could I? You two look alike!" Chris yelled.

"What do you mean? Flora wears her hair down while I wear mine in a bun," Fiona told him.

Chris stared at them dumbfounded while Eve giggled. Sarah smiled.

"I don't have time for this. Come on, Eve," Chris said flatly as he led her away.

"One of you two run down to town and pick up some clothes suitable for a six-year-old girl. The other one of you needs to tend to the horses," Sarah said before following her husband.

The maids looked at each other and shrugged. Flora put her hair back into a bun while Fiona let hers spill around her shoulders with a smile. They took too much joy in tormenting their masters to be foiled by a little girl.

"This is your room, Eve," Chris told her as they stopped in front of the room in question.

The room sat directly across from their own so they could keep an eye on the girl.

"Mine?" Eve croaked eagerly.

"That's right. Why don't you look around?" Chris asked.

Slowly, Eve walked into the room. It was furnished simply: one bed, a table with two chairs, and a wardrobe. Eve looked stunned.

"Mine," Eve repeated softly.

"So, what do you want to do now, Eve?" Sarah asked her.

Eve looked lost in thought once more.

"Sleep," Eve rasped firmly.

Chris laughed.

"You've had a busy few days. You can take a nap if you want," he told her.

Eve nodded happily and flopped on the bed, making a contented sigh that sounded more like a gurgle. Chris and Sarah smiled and shut the door, leaving her to her rest.

"Well, Eve seems like she's settling in well. What do you want to do now?" Chris asked.

Sarah gave a wicked smile.

"Training," she told him.

Chris let out a groan.

"I'll make sure Matt's available," he said with resignation.

Eve lay with her face buried in her soft covers. She wasn't exactly sure what it was she did to earn such a massive room to herself, but she wasn't complaining. As she lay soaking in the softness, she felt her strange oval pressed against her stomach was warmer than usual. Checking to ensure she was still alone, she pulled out her treasure from under her shirt and stared at it.

"Smooth," she rasped to herself as she ran her hands over it, feeling its strange warmth.

Speaking still hurt, and she decided she would have to practice until it felt natural again.

"What...are...you?" she forced herself to ask, feeling her throat burn.

The oval twitched slightly.

Eve looked at it curiously, thinking her eyes may be playing tricks on her. Slowly, Eve reached over and tapped against the oval.

The oval made a small tapping noise in return and quivered on the bed.

Eve decided that there must be something trapped inside the strange oval and waited patiently. Whatever it was would have to show itself eventually, and when it did, it would be hers.

A sudden thought flew into Eve's head—a wonderful, horrifying idea.

"What if the oval is an egg? I found it in the dragon's nest so that would mean..." Eve wondered, but she was soon distracted.

The egg was hatching.

She was sure of it; small cracks could now be seen spider-webbing their way across its surface. She held her breath and waited, watching in awe as chunks of the shell fell away.

The baby dragon looked at her and chirped.

Eve felt a wave of terror wash over her. The creature before her was the spitting image of its mother, though the proportions were all wrong. Its head was far too big for its body, and its wings were far too small; so small, that Eve was convinced this creature couldn't fly. Its legs were small as well, but strong enough to hold the creature upright. With the way it was shaped, it looked even more snakelike than its mother.

Eve looked quietly at the dragon and reached slowly for her dagger.

The dragon looked at her with its red snakelike eyes and chirped in a strangely birdlike manner. It began to crawl and slither its way across the bed toward her, chirping excitedly.

Eve drew her dagger.

The dragon reached her and looked up happily, chirping a question she couldn't understand.

Eve prepared to stab but felt a flash of pity. Silently, she prayed that she could understand the creature, wishing she knew its intentions. It was so small, after all—so helpless.

"As you wish, it shall be," said a voice in Eve's head.

Eve recoiled in shock, not understanding. Those thoughts had not been her own, and the voice was that of a woman she didn't know. The voice had been beautiful, and the more she thought about it, the more she became sure that it hadn't been speaking common. Nevertheless, it had seemed familiar, like she had listened to it her entire life, and she had understood her just fine, the voice filling her with warmth and joy. It did not speak again.

Eve felt another presence in her mind, this time of an alien nature. It was hungry, and for some reason strangely trusting. Looking down, she saw the dragon giving her a weird look.

"Was that...you?" Eve croaked.

The dragon remained silent, but she felt the presence in her mind perk up. Eve concentrated and reached out to this bizarre intrusion to her mind. She felt it resist her momentarily before it yielded to her will, and suddenly she was met with a flood of images. New sounds, smells, and sights washed over her. It was a short sensation, lasting less than a second, but, in that time, Eve had seen herself for some reason, though she looked quite different than she remembered. Her face looked… broken. She knew her arm was scarred; she was reminded of that every time she opened her eyes, but she was unaware that her face looked the same. Stranger still, the images of her seemed to have been coming from the floor, because she looked massive. She fell back to reality.

The dragon chirped.

"You're hungry!" Eve exclaimed, coming out like a ragged cough.

For reasons she couldn't comprehend, she had understood the dragon. It wasn't so much that the dragon was speaking, but more so, she understood its intentions.

The dragon slithered up to Eve and crawled onto her lap. Sensing no hostility from the creature, Eve began stroking its back softly before transitioning her fingers to the edges of the crest on its neck and finally scratching it behind the horns. The dragon made a low rumble in its chest, and Eve sensed it was happy.

"I…wonder…" Eve croaked to herself.

Silently, she told the dragon to look at her.

The dragon looked up and chirped happily. Eve clapped her hands and squeaked in delight.

"You…understand…me!" Eve coughed.

The dragon hissed and thrashed its long tail, fixing Eve with its red stare.

"You…need food," Eve realized and stood up, sheathing her dagger.

The dragon chirped in agreement.

"Come on…then," Eve rasped and began walking toward the door.

The dragon crawled clumsily after her. Eve sensed it was having trouble moving quickly, so she turned around and scooped it off the bed. The dragon chirped gratefully and hooked its claws into her shirt. Working carefully as to not stab her with its talons, it crawled up to her shoulder upon which it perched, wrapping its long tail around her chest. The dragon was heavier than it looked, but Eve felt reassured having him up there for some reason. She didn't know how she knew the dragon was male; she just did. Similarly, she sensed the dragon knew she was a girl somehow, seeing her as its mother, its thoughts echoing her own. She felt the need to protect this creature like it was her long-lost child.

"Echo," Eve croaked. "You are...Echo."

Echo screamed his agreement into the sky and spread his tiny wings happily above her head.

Chris was drilling out in the yard with Sarah when they heard the scream. Matt, who had been standing by for first aid, stood up.

"Was that... Ditrina?" he asked in confusion.

"What is she going on about this time?" Sarah sighed.

"Maybe Cassy accidently mentioned a dragon," Chris chuckled, grateful for the distraction.

"Should we check on her?" Matt asked.

"She's fine; Cassy's with her," Sarah said dismissively.

They heard another scream. This time it sounded like Cassy.

"Gods damn it," Chris sighed as they raced toward the house. "What's wrong?" he yelled as he burst through the doors.

Ditrina came sprinting around the corner, obviously terrified.

"Dragon! There is a dragon in the house, and it is small, but I cannot kill it because you said no fire magic in the house but I—" Ditrina babbled, her words coming in a rush.

Chris clamped his hand over her mouth, and she continued to ramble on for several seconds before realizing she was muted.

"Calm down. Speak slowly. I'm going to let go, and when I do, please calmly explain what this business about a dragon is about," Chris instructed.

Ditrina nodded. Chris let go.

"There is a dragon on Eve," Ditrina said simply.

"What?!" Sarah demanded.

"There is a tiny dragon. It is riding on her shoulder," Ditrina explained quickly.

"Where is she?" Chris asked.

"In the common room," Ditrina stammered, pointing the way she had come.

"Let's go see what this *dragon* nonsense is all about," Matt sighed as he walked toward the corridor that led into the common room.

He peeked his head around the corner, looked back at Chris in shock, then looked around the corner again.

"She's got a baby dragon riding on her shoulder!" Matt yelled in disbelief.

"What?!" Chris yelled as he rounded the corner at full speed.

Eve was sitting on a sofa with Echo perched on her shoulder. Eve must have raided the kitchen because she had a large raw hunk of meat sitting on her lap that she cheerfully sliced off strips from using her dagger, before feeding them to Echo from her clawlike hand. Echo ate greedily, snatching whatever Eve offered him faster than Chris could blink, like a striking snake, but not once did he accidently bite Eve's fingers. Eve was humming happily to herself and seemed oblivious to them.

"Eve! What are you doing with that thing!?" Chris demanded as he ran toward her.

Eve looked up and smiled.

"Hello…Father!" she croaked happily. "Meet…Echo."

Echo screamed into the air upon hearing his name.

"Get away from it!" Chris yelled.

"Why?" Eve asked not understanding. "He needs…to eat."

Chris stopped a few feet away from her.

"Eve, very slowly take the dragon off your shoulder. I don't know what it's doing in the house, but it's *very* dangerous," Chris told her.

"Echo isn't…dangerous," Eve coughed. "He's sweet…and he's mine."

"What do you mean he's *yours*?" Chris asked suspiciously.

Sarah was standing beside him trying to think of a way to get the dragon off her daughter.

"I…took him…from…the nest," Eve explained in her rasping voice.

"How did we not see a dragon?" Matt asked with disbelief.

"Only egg," Eve told him.

"What?" Matt asked.

"Echo hatched…today," Eve explained.

"You stole a dragon egg!" Sarah said with disbelief.

Eve nodded happily. Echo nuzzled her face, smearing it with blood.

"Echo…likes it…here," Eve declared.

"Why is it so calm?" Chris asked Sarah.

"Maybe it imprinted on her; it might think Eve's its mother," Sarah proposed.

"That's…right," Eve croaked.

"How do you know that?" Chris asked her.

"Echo…told me," Eve coughed.

So much talking was starting to hurt her voice.

"He told you?" Chris asked.

Eve nodded.

"Do you understand him?" Sarah asked still looking at the dragon warily.

"He doesn't…use words. I understand…his thoughts," Eve wheezed.

Matt looked at Eve strangely, then muttered a spell.

His eyes grew huge.

"Chris, Eve is using magic!" he exclaimed.

"What?" Chris asked. "First, she's got a dragon, and now she's a cleric?"

"No, she's not using the power of a god…Eve is using her own mana!" Matt whispered in disbelief.

"I thought humans lost their magic during the crisis?" Chris asked.

"We did; that's why this is impossible. There's no way she should be able to do what she's doing. Somehow Eve's managed to cast a high-level clerical spell, a mind link. She and the dragon can understand each other's thoughts without the need for words," Matt said breathlessly.

"Well, how the hell did she do that?" Sarah demanded.

"Eve, what did you do once we left you in your room?" Chris asked as kindly as he could, doing his best to stay calm for the girl's sake.

Eve looked lost in thought.

"Laid…in bed," Eve croaked with a shrug.

"What next?" Chris asked, looking at the dragon which had coiled around her neck like a scarf and fallen asleep.

"Then Echo…hatched," Eve recounted.

"And then?" Sarah asked.

"Voice spoke," Eve told her.

"What voice, Eve? Be as specific as you can," Matt told her.

Eve was quiet as she thought about the best way to phrase it.

"I prayed…to understand…Echo," Eve said with a cough. "Voice spoke…woman's voice. It…made me…happy," Eve said with a smile on half of her face.

"What did the voice say, Eve? This is important," Matt demanded.

Eve thought for a moment.

"As…you wish…it…shall be," Eve rasped in an approximation of the voice she had heard.

Matt looked stunned.

"What is it, Matt?" Chris asked.

"I don't believe it," Matt muttered.

"What? What happened to Eve?!" Sarah asked angrily.

"I am…ok…Mother," Eve reassured her. "Echo is…ok, too."

"Eve was blessed," Matt whispered to himself.

"What?" Chris asked not understanding.

"Eve was blessed! A god spoke to her and blessed her with this ability! Something like this only happens once every few hundred years. A god spoke to your daughter!" Matt exclaimed.

"Why?" Chris asked, stunned.

"I don't know. This type of thing doesn't seem to have a pattern. Once in a while, I'm talking hundreds of years here, people just hear the voice of the gods and suddenly gain incredible abilities. It seems Eve has been bonded to that dragon," Matt said, still stunned.

"Well, what do we do? How do we get rid of it?" Sarah demanded.

"You don't! The gods have decided that Eve and that dragon are to be together. It would be very unwise for us to interfere with that," Matt cautioned.

"Echo is…mine," Eve repeated firmly, holding the dragon close against her.

"So, you're saying she has to keep the dragon?" Sarah asked.

"That's right. It's very important that she and that dragon stay together. I have no idea why the god did what they did, but what's done is done. The dragon stays," Matt said, shaking his head in amazement.

"Father…are you…ok?" Eve asked, concerned.

Chris looked like his mind had long since deserted him.

"Yeah, sweetie, I'm all right," Chris muttered quietly.

He shook his head.

"Matt, Sarah, go get the others. We all need to talk about this," Chris told them.

It took an hour to convince Ditrina to sit in the same room as the dragon, but, in the end, the promise of a new magical discovery proved too tempting to ignore. Still, she sat as far away from Echo as was physically possible and grew visibly nervous whenever he looked at her.

"Chris, why is the dragon still here?" Cassy asked nervously.

"I'll let Matt explain," Chris said, shaking his head.

"To put it simply, a god has blessed Eve by linking her soul to that of the dragon so they can communicate," Matt said.

A silence fell over the room.

"A god," Ditrina said simply.

"Or a being of equivalent power. Either way, the end result is the same. Eve is now producing enough mana of her own to fuel this connection," Matt told her.

"Mana?" Eve asked.

"It's what powers magic," Matt explained.

Eve nodded her understanding, not understanding at all.

"So, the girl has somehow been freed from the curse to some extent," Ditrina summed up.

"Yeah, she has," Matt confirmed grimly

"Why is this such a big deal?" Cassy asked. "You two use magic all the time; so, why is it so weird when Eve does it?"

"When I use my magic, I borrow the power of a god to do it, and the elves have inherent magical abilities of their own. No human is capable of producing their own mana to fuel a spell—not since the crisis. Even when Chris uses magic, he's borrowing some of Al's power. Humans can't perform magic on their own," Matt told her.

"But that's what you said Eve is doing," Cassy said.

"Exactly," Matt told her.

"So, what?" Cassy asked.

"So, what?! So, everything! This is huge! Eve is the first human to use magic completely on her own since the crisis! It may only be a little bit, and she may have no control over what it does, but the fact remains that she is producing and using her own mana. This will change the way the world looks at magic. It proves it's possible!" Matt said excitedly.

Ditrina looked like she might explode.

"This is it! This is what we have been looking for! Eve is the key to lifting the curse of the crisis!" Ditrina exclaimed.

"I…am not…a key," Eve rasped firmly.

"I need to report this!" Ditrina said excitedly. "I need to take Eve to the elven city!"

"Hold on, slow down. Eve's not going anywhere. What will happen to her in the elven city?" Sarah asked suspiciously.

"We will have our magic experts run tests on her to see how this phenomenon works," Ditrina told them.

"Will it hurt Eve at all?" Chris demanded.

"I do not think so," Ditrina told him.

"Think harder. Unless you are one hundred percent sure that she'll be unharmed, this information doesn't leave this room," Chris said firmly.

"But Chris!" Matt began, but Chris shot him a menacing look.

"If this is as important as you claim, we must be very careful about who we talk to. Eve's safety is our first priority," Chris told him.

"The elves will not damage your daughter," Ditrina assured them.

"If she comes to harm because of this, I will flay you alive," Sarah told her.

"You've got to be sure about this, Di," Cassy agreed.

"I am," Ditrina said firmly.

Eve looked at Cassy strangely, and Echo fixed her with his red eyes.

"Aunt Cas…what is…going on?" Eve croaked.

"We're going to go on a little vacation. How does that sound?" Cassy told her.

"Where?" Eve rasped.

"We're going to go see where the elves live. Do you want to see where Aunt Di was born?" Cassy asked her.

"Aunt?" Eve asked, looking at Ditrina in surprise.

Echo chirped in confusion and looked at Ditrina. Ditrina gulped.

"Yes, aunt sounds appropriate," she agreed.

Eve looked suspiciously at Chris.

"Adopted?" Eve asked, pointing at Ditrina.

Chris laughed.

"No, Ditrina is Cassy's girlfriend. She's not my sister," Chris told her.

Eve looked surprised.

"But…they are…both girls," Eve said, not understanding.

Sarah gave a small smile while Cassy giggled.

"Yes, Eve. We both prefer women to men," Cassy explained gently.

Eve looked at her strangely, then shrugged. She had already decided she liked Echo more than most people, so who was she to judge?

The next few days were a flurry of preparation. Unlike their trip to Glenord, they packed several weeks' worth of clothes and food, expecting to be in the city for some time. Ditrina told them that she could teleport them about two days away from the city. After that, they would have to ride.

While everyone else was preparing, Eve fell into a routine. She would wake up, feed Echo, then track down whatever family member was closest, be it her parents, one of her new aunts, or *Uncle S* as she had begun to call Matt and silently observe whatever it was they were doing. Matt's dignity refused to let him ask what the *S* stood for.

On that specific day, she had singled out Matt.

"Uncle S…" Eve rasped as she pulled herself into a chair beside him in the library, Echo perched on her shoulder as usual.

"What can I do for you, Eve?" Matt asked kindly, setting down his book.

"Can I...do that?" Eve asked.

"Do what? Read the book? Of course," Matt said as he handed it to her.

Eve stared at the pages for several minutes.

"How?" Eve asked suddenly.

"How what?" Matt asked.

"How do...you read?" Eve asked.

"You can't read?" Matt exclaimed in shock.

Eve shook her head sadly, and Echo let out a somber chirp.

"Well, bring the book here, and let's see if we can change that," Matt said kindly.

Eve smiled as much as she could with her mangled face and slipped out of her chair, crawling onto Matt's lap. Echo repositioned to the back of the chair like a scaly sentinel while Matt took the book from her hands and opened it to the first page.

"Good call, Ge," Matt said to himself, seeing a chart of the alphabet on the page before him. "Ok, Eve, this letter is A," Matt told her, and so Eve's education began.

A few hours later, her head hurting from far too many letters in far too short of a time, Eve stumbled out of the library with Echo. Uncle S had told her that she had made good progress on her first day and that she should go and play. Eve's favorite game at the moment happened to be watching her mother beat her father with a wooden sword, and to her disappointment, she saw them just sitting outside holding hands. Deciding this was boring and craving something fun to do, she looked for another family member. After a few minutes of searching, she came across a maid with her hair down.

"Hello, Young Mistress," the maid said with a curtsy, looking nervously at Echo.

"Hello...Fiona," Eve rasped.

"I am Flora, Mistress. Fiona wears her hair in a bun," the maid told her.

"No," Eve said, shaking her head.

"Mistress?" the maid asked with confusion.

"Echo says...you're Fiona. You smell...different," Eve croaked.

"It can tell us apart?" Fiona asked in alarm.

"Yes," Eve said simply.

"Excuse me, Mistress, I suddenly remembered something else I have to do," Fiona said quickly, hoping to warn her sister of this new development.

"Wait," Eve croaked.

"Yes, Mistress?" Fiona asked nervously.

"Play...with me," Eve commanded.

"What would you like to play, Young Mistress?" Fiona asked.

"Echo needs...exercise," Eve explained.

Fiona didn't like where this was going.

"And how do we give him exercise, Mistress?" Fiona asked cautiously.

"Too small...for fire," Eve croaked sadly.

Echo gave a low cry, lamenting his youth.

"Needs...target. For exercise," Eve explained in her rasping voice.

"A target?" Fiona asked nervously.

Eve nodded.

"Jump," she rasped and pointed at Fiona with her clawlike hand.

Echo raced along her outstretched arm and hurled himself at Fiona, gliding on his tiny wings. Fiona screamed in terror as Echo latched onto her, gripping her back with his claws and wings. Fiona ran screaming down the hallway, Echo still firmly attached.

"Echo!" Eve cried shrilly and raced after them.

She had told her he needed exercise. Why had she run away? This wasn't part of the game. She felt Echo's thoughts; he was frightened because he couldn't see her. Silently, she calmed him, assuring him she was on the way. She followed after Echo's thoughts and the desperate screams of the maid, searching through the corridors. She grew worried as she felt Echo getting farther away and heard the maid's screams growing fainter. She sprinted blindly around a corner and crashed into Cassy.

"Woah, slow down, Eve," Cassy said cheerfully.

"Aunt Cas! She...stole...Echo!" Eve cried.

"Wait, what? Who took Echo?" Cassy asked in confusion.

"Fiona! We...were playing...and she...ran off...with him! Help!" Eve rasped, begging desperately.

"Well, that would explain the screams," Cassy said with amusement. "Come on, little one, let's go find your friend," Cassy told her and led her down the hallway.

A few minutes of following Fiona's desperate cries later, Cassy opened a door and revealed Flora desperately trying to pull a terrified Echo off of Fiona. Fiona was screaming, and Echo was lashing his tail and snapping at Flora.

"Echo, come!" Eve rasped loudly.

Echo unlatched and threw himself toward Eve. Eve caught him and held him close, feeling him tremble in terror. She sent calming thoughts his way, and slowly Echo's heartrate returned to normal, and he made his way to his spot on her shoulder.

"Why did...you steal...Echo?" Eve demanded.

"I'd like to hear this as well," Cassy said with amusement.

"The little beast attacked me!" Fiona wailed.

"We were...playing!" Eve croaked angrily.

She tuned to Cassy.

"Eat her," she demanded, pointing at Fiona.

"What?" Cassy and Fiona asked together.

Flora was too shocked to speak.

"Eat her...Aunt Cas," Eve repeated still pointing at Fiona.

"I don't eat people!" Cassy insisted.

"Try!" Eve implored.

"No!" Cassy yelled indignantly.

"Fine," Eve grumbled. "Echo...eat her!" she rasped.

Echo looked at the maid and concluded that she was too big to eat all at once, and not wanting to waste food, decided against it. Instead, he coiled around Eve's neck like a scarf and fell asleep, neck and tail draping down her chest. Half of Eve's face frowned.

"Silly...dragon," she croaked disappointedly.

CHAPTER FIVE

"So, is everyone clear on what the plan is?" Chris asked as they ate dinner the evening before their departure.

Eve had elected to sit between him and Sarah, with Echo perched atop her chair like a sentry. From time to time she would toss up a tasty morsel to him, and not once did he miss.

"Ditrina will transport us somewhere outside the city. From there, we ride until we reach the gates," Matt said.

"It will be quite cold when we arrive; that far north, it snows all year long," Ditrina warned.

"Are there any other dangers we need to be aware of?" Sarah asked her.

"Nothing out of the ordinary. Roaming packs of dire wolves and the natives, of course, but neither should give us any trouble," Ditrina told them.

"Natives? What natives?" Sarah asked.

"There are primitive tribes of humans living far beyond the borders of Desgail. They speak a harsh language and are hostile to intruders, but they seldom show themselves unless you go into their territory, but as close to the elven city as we will be, we will not have to worry about them," Ditrina assured her.

"How cold will it be exactly; will I need to buy warmer clothes?" Cassy asked.

"You're asking this now?" Chris demanded in disbelief.

"Well, yeah. I didn't know how cold it will be!" Cassy argued.

"Unbelievable," Matt said, shaking his head.

"All week long you saw us packing warm cloaks; you even watched me line my armor with fur! How could you just now realize it's going to be cold?" Sarah demanded.

"You…picked out…my cloak," Eve rasped, remembering the little fur cloak she had brought her from the village.

"Well, yeah. I just thought that you wanted to get it for this winter, just in case. It's the middle of summer, for the gods' sakes!" Cassy yelled.

Echo hissed.

"You're right…Aunt Cas…is silly," Eve croaked in agreement.

Matt chucked.

"That dragon is smarter than it looks," he said.

Eve nodded proudly while Echo stretched his wings and shrieked from atop her chair. Ditrina looked uncomfortable and slid her chair a little farther away from the dragon.

"Cas, run down to the village tonight and pick up some warm clothes. You'll freeze to death if you dress like you normally do," Chris sighed.

"Hold on, dear. This is a perfect opportunity to learn if naga are warm blooded," Sarah said eagerly.

"I don't want my sister turned into a snake-sickle," Chris said with a hint of amusement.

"I say we put it to a vote. All in favor of watching her freeze, raise your hands," Sarah laughed, lazily raising her hand above her head.

"Snow…is fun," Eve declared and raised her hand proudly, not understanding in the slightest what was going on.

"I would rather not see Cas freeze," Ditrina said, nervously looking around, fearful of more hands.

"Really, Ditrina? They're kidding," Matt told her.

"Speak for yourself," Sarah muttered.

Cassy sighed.

"Whatever, I'll run into town and pick up clothes tonight," Cassy told them.

"Bring me!" Eve croaked suddenly.

"What?" Cassy asked, confused by the sudden request.

"I...want to...see...the village. Please...Aunt Cas," Eve asked, giving her an eager half-smile.

"How can I say no to a face like that?" Cassy asked with a toothy grin. "Aren't you worried I'm going to eat you?" she teased.

Eve shook her head firmly.

"Echo will...protect me. Not afraid...anymore," Eve rasped.

"Eve, you can't bring Echo to the village with you," Chris told her.

"Why?" Eve asked.

"Because he's a dragon; he'll scare everybody," Chris explained gently.

"Echo won't...scare anyone. Echo is...good," Eve said firmly.

"I know that, and you know that, but the people in the village don't know that," Chris told her.

"How will...they learn...if I...don't teach?" Eve coughed, her throat burning.

Echo made a low rumbling noise and looked at Eve.

"I'm...ok, Echo," Eve rasped.

Echo quieted.

"I don't see a problem with it actually. They're bound to find out eventually," Cassy told him.

"Eve will have enough trouble fitting in as she is now without the burden of a dragon," Sarah said firmly.

"Why?" Eve asked curiously.

"Oh, well..." Sarah trailed off, cursing herself for speaking without thinking.

"Is it...my face...Mother?" Eve asked.

"No, sweetie!" Sarah said quickly.

"My arm?" Eve croaked.

"Not at all!" Sarah assured her.

"My voice...then?" Eve coughed.

"Eve..." Sarah began but trailed off again, unsure of what to say.

"It's ok...Mother. I look...scary. If they...fear me...they will... respect me," Eve rasped firmly.

"That's messed up," Matt muttered under his breath, looking at the six-year-old with a shudder.

"You want them to fear you?" Chris asked in shock.

"No...I want...them...to like me," Eve croaked. "Fear is...next best...thing."

"Why do you say that, Eve?" Chris asked softly.

"If they...fear me...then I...can be...like Mother. If they...respect me...I can...be like you...Father," Eve said, then descended into a ragged fit of coughing, the sentence proving too much for her.

Chris and Sarah looked at each other, unsure of what to say.

"That's the spirit, Eve! If they don't like the way you look, screw 'em! You and Echo are more than welcome to tag along," Cassy said proudly.

"Cas, are you sure—" Chris began.

"Trust me, brother, I know what it's like to get those weird looks whenever I walk into town. Who better to teach her how to act than me?" Cassy asked.

"That's not very reassuring," Sarah told her.

"Listen, you can't shelter the girl forever. Sooner or later she's gonna go into a town, and like it or not, she's gonna get some weird looks. Best she learns how to deal with them now," Cassy told her.

"Aunt Cas...will teach me," Eve croaked happily.

"Cas, refrain from teaching her anything too vulgar," Ditrina warned her.

"What are you talking about, Ditrina?" Matt asked her.

"As it turns out, Cas knows all manner of interesting things. Just last night, for instance, she taught me how to—" Ditrina began.

"That's enough, Di! Really, they get the idea!" Cassy yelled quickly, her face the same shade red as Sarah's hair.

"I think I'm still a bit confused. Mind clarifying, Ditrina?" Matt asked innocently.

"Of course, Matthew," Ditrina said happily. "Cas taught me how to use my tongue to—"

"Shut up, Di!" Cassy screamed.

"Why? Matthew is confused," Ditrina said simply.

"Very confused," Matt agreed eagerly.

"I am...confused, too," Eve rasped, not understanding the conversation at all.

"We're leaving, Eve. Come on," Cassy said, dragging Eve out of the room by her arm, Echo chirping in protest.

Eve decided Echo was confused as well.

They rode down to the village together, with Eve wrapping her little arms tightly around Cassy's waist to stay on the horse. The sun had almost set by the time they arrived, and the town was alive with people walking between bars and laughing in the streets. Being heavily populated by smugglers, the town with no name saw its fair share of nonhumans, but be that as it may, Cassy still was exotic enough to draw interest from onlookers on any given day.

"Are they...looking at...me...or you?" Eve rasped as they walked through the town, having tethered their horse out front of the Lonely Elf.

"They're probably looking at Echo, to be honest," Cassy told her as they pushed their way through a crowd of drunks.

Echo looked around, fixing everything with his hungry red gaze. Eve sensed his desire to destroy, and his disappointment due to his size. Silently, Eve assured him that he could burn as many villages as he liked once he could fly, and that served to quiet him for the time being.

"Echo...is hungry," Eve croaked.

"Well, after we find what I'm looking for, we can stop by Sam's shop and get him something to eat," Cassy told her.

"Aunt Cas...who's scarier...me...or you?" Eve coughed.

"What a silly question! We're not scary, dear," Cassy assured her.

Eve shook her head.

"Echo smells...fear," Eve rasped.

"Maybe they're afraid of him?" Cassy proposed.

Eve shook her head again.

"More...than that...afraid of...us," Eve told her.

"People fear what they don't understand," Cassy explained. "I have my scales and claws, and that frightens people because they don't know what I am."

"Why do...they fear...me?" Eve asked. "I only...have scars."

"They see your scars and know that you must be very strong to have survived whatever gave them to you. On top of that, you have Echo. Any girl brave enough to carry around a dragon must be tough," Cassy told her.

Eve seemed pleased with this answer.

"I like…my scars. Make me…strong," Eve agreed, then coughed. "Just wish…voice worked," she wheezed, loud enough that people stopped to stare.

One evil glare from Cassy sent them on their way.

"Your voice will get better as time goes on. Who knows, maybe the elves can fix it for you?" Cassy proposed.

Half of Eve's face lit up.

"Really?" she rasped.

"Maybe," Cassy said with a smile. "Look, here's the tailor. Be a good girl and wait right here while I get what I need. I'll be right back," Cassy told her.

"Ok…Aunt Cas," Eve said and plopped herself in the dirt outside the shop.

"Echo…find fear," she rasped once she was alone, looking for something to pass the time.

Echo perked up and began scanning the crowd as it passed, searching for anyone more frightened than the rest. His red eyes settled on a young smuggler leaning against the bar across the street who had been staring at them nervously.

Eve stood up and walked over to him, and he quickly realized he had been noticed.

"What can I do for you, little one?" he asked awkwardly, feigning ignorance.

He looked no older than Chris and was sweating profusely. He had a short sword on his hip but was otherwise unarmed.

"You were…watching. Why?" Eve demanded.

"I don't know what you're taking about, kid. Why don't you run along—" he began.

"Liar!" Eve rasped loudly, and Echo screamed at him, thrashing his tail behind Eve like a whip.

The poor smuggler looked horrified at her voice and the enraged dragon. Eve pointed a clawlike finger at him.

"Why?" she demanded.

She liked this game. She'd made the man in front of her much more frightened than he had been originally. A small crowd had formed around her.

"My face?" Eve croaked angrily.

"No, I wasn't—" the hapless smuggler began.

"My arm?" Eve coughed, glaring at him.

"I wasn't staring!" the man insisted.

"Echo...then?" Eve rasped.

"What the hell? I don't know what you're talking about!" the man yelled.

"Echo! My...Echo! Were you...staring at...Echo?" Eve demanded, wheezing loudly.

Echo screamed shrilly from her shoulder.

"Listen, kid, I wasn't looking at you or your stupid dragon!" the man insisted, growing angry.

"Eve? Eve, where are you?" Cassy called from across the street.

Eve ignored her; she was having too much fun.

"Liar! Liar...liar!" Eve screeched at him. Echo was doing his best to make his displeasure known as well through sheer volume.

The crowd around them grew. The door of the bar burst open, and two drunk men stumbled out, one draping his arm around the young smuggler's shoulders, the other doing his best to simply stay upright.

"Marcus," the one with his arm around him began. "Who's...the girl?" he asked with a belch.

Cassy shoved her way through the crowd until she was beside Eve. Under one arm, she held a large bag of warm clothes.

"What's going on?" she demanded.

"This little freak won't leave me alone!" Marcus yelled, pointing a finger at Eve, almost losing it due to Echo's snapping jaws.

"He...kept staring," Eve rasped, giving him an evil look with half of her face, almost rivaling the scarred half in terms of menace.

"Is this true?" Cassy asked, giving the man an equally dark look.

"I hope not," the drunk standing beside Marcus burped. "I know you like 'em young, Marcus, but this one's just a tyke! Besides, have you looked at her?" he asked.

"This one's not half bad, though," the stumbling drunk mumbled, looking at Cassy hungrily. "Tell me, sweetie, do you have scales anywhere else?" he asked, reaching clumsily for her.

Cassy's claws flashed, and blood rushed from his face.

"Back away!" Cassy hissed.

Eve's eyes widened, and she couldn't help but smile. This game was getting better by the second.

"Bitch!" the wounded drunk screamed. "Kill her!" he yelled to his companions.

Marcus drew his sword with a flourish while the other drunk clumsily drew a long dirk from his hip.

"Eve, stay back," Cassy said quietly as she readied her claws. Her bow was back on the horse, and it wouldn't help in such close quarters anyway.

"Let...us help!" Eve said eagerly.

"No! Stay back, Eve!" Cassy yelled angrily, still looking at the men.

Slowly, Cassy and Eve tried to back away through the crowd, but by now, they were hungry for a fight and formed a solid wall behind them. The drunk with the dirk lunged at Cassy, and she planted a crushing kick to his chest, sending him flying into the wall of the bar with the power of her inhuman legs. Marcus approached her cautiously, twirling his sword.

He lunged suddenly, and if not for Cassy's superb eyesight, she would have been skewered. As it was, she had been watching to see his muscles bunch, so she could anticipate his strike. Marcus stumbled past her, his thrust meeting no resistance, and Cassy lashed out, raking his side with her claws.

"Get out of here," Cassy demanded, hoping the injury would serve to deter the smuggler.

To her dismay, he grimaced and raised his sword, still intent on gutting her.

"You're gonna pay for that," Marcus growled, but suddenly his eyes widened in shock, and he backed away a pace.

Cassy heard an earsplitting scream behind her. Realizing she had lost sight of Eve, she spun quickly and saw a scene of pure chaos.

Somehow, Eve had managed to climb atop the drunk Cassy had kicked into the wall and was clinging to the man's back. It appeared the drunk had regained his feet, and in order to maintain her precarious perch, Eve had thrust her dagger deep into his shoulder and was using it as a handle. The drunk stumbled around wildly, grabbing at Eve while screaming at the top of his lungs.

Contrary to the drunk's distress, Eve seemed to be having the time of her life and had one hand firmly clutching her dagger and the other holding a fistful of the man's hair all the while shrieking with joy. Echo held tightly onto Eve's own shoulder while flapping his tiny wings madly, adding his own harsh voice to the melody of pandemonium.

"Bruce!" Marcus yelled in shock, and Cassy remembered she was still in the middle of a fight.

While he was still distracted, she spun toward Marcus, delivering a savage kick to the side of his head. Marcus fell like a puppet with its strings cut.

Cassy heard Eve scream—this time in pain. Spinning once more, she saw Bruce had managed to grab hold of one of Eve's wrists and was crushing it in his strong grip. Before Cassy had a chance to act, Echo sprang to the rescue.

Sensing his mother was in danger, he scampered off Eve's shoulders and onto Bruce's chest, digging his claws into his flesh. In his drunken state, Bruce felt the pain but didn't recognize the threat the tiny dragon possessed until Echo sank his fangs into his throat. Bruce screamed, but this time it was more of a gurgle, and he began to beat furiously at Echo, trying to rid himself of the thrashing ball of spines, all thoughts of Eve forgotten. Echo held on tightly, sinking his tiny fangs in deeper and deeper, relishing in the blood that ran down his throat. Despite this, he was growing weary, and the drunk's blows were strong.

Eve felt Echo's excitement as he bit into Bruce and couldn't help but share in his primeval joy. It was as if they were sharing the sensation of biting him, feeling her fangs sinking into flesh, tasting the blood in her mouth, and she loved every bit of it. Still, she felt that Echo was in pain and couldn't stand to see her friend suffer for her sake. Twisting it sharply, Eve wrenched her dagger free of his shoulder and stabbed him again—this time in the side of the neck. Bruce collapsed to his knees, his strikes coming as little more than feeble waving of his arms.

Echo sank his fangs deeper.

Eve cackled with joy and stabbed again. And again. And again.

Bruce fell forward and lay still. Cassy stood in mute horror. The drunk she had slashed with her claws still crouched beside the bar holding his bleeding face, the combination of the pain and his own intoxication rendering him oblivious to the outcome of the fight. Marcus lay snoring beside her. The crowd stood in mute shock having witnessed Eve's primal display of violence. Eve now sat on Bruce's back, covered in his blood, while Echo had crawled out from beneath him and was now busying himself tearing large strips of flesh from his kill, which he ate greedily. Eve poked the body with the tip of her knife.

"Is…he dead…Aunt Cas?" Eve rasped curiously, seemingly content with the current situation.

Cassy nodded mutely.

Eve frowned.

"I wanted…to play…more," she pouted.

Cassy snapped herself back to reality and looked around. Scooping the discarded bag of clothes off the ground, she turned to Eve.

"Grab Echo, we're going home," Cassy said quickly.

"Ok. Don't need…to feed…him at…elf place. He's full," Eve announced happily and hopped off Bruce's corpse. "Echo, come," Eve rasped, and he crawled slowly back onto her shoulder, progress hampered by his bloated belly.

"We're going to run, Eve. Run to the horse," Cassy instructed.

"Why?" Eve asked.

"It's a game. Now, run fast!" Cassy commanded, and Eve took off, Cassy following behind.

She could have easily outpaced Eve but stayed right behind her in fear of the crowd. The town with no name had no guards, nor did it have any court system. Disputes were handled on the spot and often settled with violence, so technically, they hadn't done anything wrong; nevertheless, she didn't like the way the crowd was looking at Eve, nor did she like the way Echo looked at the crowd as he fed. For the safety of everyone involved, she had to get Eve out of the town as fast as possible.

"Oh, gods! What happened?!" Sarah demanded when she saw Cassy leading a blood-spattered Eve into the house.

"It's ok, it's not hers," Cassy said quickly and plopped into the nearest chair, burying her face in her hands.

"Eve, sweetie, are you ok?" Sarah asked rushing to the girl's side.

"I…am fine…Mother," Eve said happily. "I like…the village. It is… fun," Eve declared.

"What the hell happened down there?" Sarah yelled at Cassy.

"Aunt Cas…showed me…how…to play…a…new game," Eve said happily.

Echo chirped contentedly, belly full of Bruce.

"There was…we got into a fight," Cassy explained.

"How?" Sarah demanded.

"Eve got into an argument with a smuggler while I was buying the clothes. When I came out, they were shouting at each other," Cassy told her.

"He was…afraid," Eve added. "Wanted…to see…why."

"Then what happened?" Sarah asked.

"I went to get Eve away from him when his drunk friends showed up. One of them tried to grab me, and I sliced his face with my claws. They drew weapons and attacked," Cassy said meekly.

"Why did he try to grab you?" Sarah asked, puzzled.

"He…was asking…where else…Aunt Cas…had scales," Eve rasped, trying to be helpful.

Cassy blushed.

"I acted without thinking," she muttered.

"And the blood?" Sarah demanded. "Did you kill anyone?"

"*I* didn't kill anyone!" Cassy said quickly.

"Well, unless you wounded the entire village, that much blood says otherwise!" Sarah said angrily.

"Eve did," Cassy said, her voice practically a whisper.

"What?" Sarah asked, taken back by her words.

"Eve killed one of the smugglers. She got on his back and used her dagger," Cassy said, still not believing what she was saying.

"It...was fun. Echo...helped," Eve croaked happily. "Can I... have...a bath...Mother?" she added, looking at her blood-spattered clothing.

Sarah looked stunned.

"Sure thing, sweetie. Head to your room, and I'll bring the tub up. I need to talk to your aunt for a second," Sarah said in a daze.

Eve skipped off happily to her room with Echo.

"How?" Sarah asked quietly.

"She clung to his back like a spider and used her dagger like a handle. She was *laughing*," Cassy said with a shudder.

"And it sounds like she provoked the fight," Sarah said quietly.

"I didn't see it. I was in the shop...but yeah, I think she did," Cassy agreed somberly.

"Why did you leave her alone?" Sarah demanded.

"I left her sitting right outside! I was gone for less than three minutes! How was I supposed to know she would go and murder someone?!" Cassy wailed, physically shaking. "Little Eve. Our little Eve. She *killed* someone and laughed while doing it," she said with a large shudder. "Matt was right. She's not right in the head."

"It's not her fault! Her entire life was burned away in front of her! She just needs a little time to adjust is all," Sarah defended.

"And what? We're just supposed to ignore the fact she enjoys killing people?!" Cassy shouted.

"Don't act like a saint! You and I have both killed more people than we can count, so don't suddenly act like the walls are about to crash down! Eve just started a bit young is all!" Sarah yelled.

"We don't enjoy it!" Cassy screamed.

"Speak for yourself!" Sarah bellowed back.

A heavy silence fell over the room.

"Don't tell me that you don't feel that tiny bit of pride whenever you kill someone. That little nagging voice in the back of your head saying *good job, you were better. You don't have to die today.* I've seen your face when you do it. You have the same light in your eyes. Eve just needs to learn how to tune out that voice," Sarah said locking eyes with Cassy.

Cassy looked away.

"Once you start, you don't stop. I didn't, you didn't, and she won't. She's too young to be dealing with all this, Sarah," Cassy said quietly.

"We've been talking about Eve becoming an adventurer once she's older. Part of the job is killing people that need to be killed. She would've had to learn eventually," Sarah told her.

"She's six!" Cassy yelled.

"Well, maybe you should have thought about that before you left her alone in the village!" Sarah screamed. "This happened on *your* watch! You could have stopped this, but you didn't! It was *you* who insisted that she go into the village, *you* who said *you can't shelter the girl forever.* Guess what? She's not sheltered anymore! She killed a man! Don't mistake my rationality for acceptance. I will *not* forget what you did!" Sarah screamed, marching toward her with each word.

Cassy realized she was on the receiving end of Sarah's full fury, a very dangerous place to be. Sarah was currently unarmed, but Cassy knew all too well what she could do with her fists. Cassy did something then that she had never done before.

"I'm sorry," she said and sank to the floor.

"You're sorry? *You're sorry?*! Well, that makes it all better then, doesn't it?!" Sarah shouted at her, kicking her squarely in the chest.

Cassy crashed back against the wall but made no move to defend herself.

"I'm sorry," Cassy repeated, blood trickling from the corner of her mouth.

"Stop saying that! *Stop saying that*! You've never been sorry about anything in your life! You don't think! You just do what you like and let everyone else clean up after you! Well, guess what? *Sorry* won't fix this! *Sorry* won't bring that man back to life, and *sorry* won't unmake Eve a killer!" Sarah screamed, picking Cassy up by the neck.

Despite almost a half-foot difference in height, Sarah held her suspended in the air, legs dangling.

"I trusted you," Sarah hissed quietly. "And you let my daughter become a killer. No amount of *sorry* will ever undo that," she told her before tossing her to the ground where she crumpled in a heap.

Sarah left without another word, leaving Cassy sobbing quietly.

CHAPTER SIX

Ditrina teleported them the next day as they'd planned, and they arrived in a snowy forest. Before they departed, Sarah told the others what had transpired, and they had each, in turn, questioned Cassy about the events in the village. Deciding that what was done was done, Chris ordered the others to not bring it up and to be extra careful with Eve in the future. She was no longer allowed to be alone for any length of time, for any reason whatsoever.

Eve didn't seem to understand the reason for this new rule, but she didn't seem to mind, either. She saw it as a great way to spend more time with her new family. She hoped she would get a chance to play in the village again soon—maybe this time with her mother. She admired her mother's impressive array of weapons and decided they would be far more fun to play with than her own tiny dagger.

"Is everyone ok?" Matt asked as they appeared in the clearing, looking at Eve and Sarah specifically.

"Feel fine…Uncle S," Eve rasped happily, her scarred face peeking out from deep within her fur-lined hood.

"I'm good," Sarah muttered.

Each of them had drunk a healthy amount of Ditrina's potion before they departed.

Echo chirped and burrowed under Eve's heavy cloak for warmth.

"Give me a moment to get my bearings, and I will lead us toward the city," Ditrina told them as she stared into the night sky.

It had been early morning when they'd left, yet here it looked to be the middle of the night. Chris didn't recognize the stars in the sky.

"The city lies a little farther north from here. The city's glyph is designed to put you somewhere in the surrounding area, and we got lucky enough to land closer than I expected. If we hurry, we can make it to the barrier before sunrise," Ditrina told them after a moment.

"Let's get going then," Chris said and walked toward his gear-laden horse.

"Want to...ride with...Aunt Di," Eve declared when Sarah went to scoop her onto her horse.

"Do you mind, Ditrina?" Sarah asked her.

Eve looked at her hopefully, Echo's face poking out of her hood with her own. Ditrina shuddered.

"Would you not rather ride with your mother?" Ditrina asked nervously.

"Why...are you...afraid...Aunt Di?" Eve croaked, looking heartbroken.

"I am not afraid!" Ditrina exclaimed quickly.

"Echo says...you are," Eve croaked. "Do I...scare you?" she asked pitifully.

"Your aunt doesn't like dragons. She's afraid of Echo," Sarah explained kindly.

"He won't...hurt you," Eve assured her. "Please?" she begged.

"Very well," Ditrina said nervously and gestured for Eve to climb up behind her.

Eve squealed with delight and clambered onto the horse with Sarah's help, seating herself behind Ditrina. As she wrapped her arms around her aunt, she felt Echo testing the air and found that he thought Ditrina smelled delicious. Silently she flooded his mind with the way she saw Ditrina, her strong, brave aunt. She showed him how powerful Ditrina was, and how she wielded fire as well as any dragon. Echo's thoughts changed from hunger to excitement, and he began crawling out from under her cloak to be closer to his new favorite aunt.

"Echo...likes you," Eve declared as Echo began pulling himself onto Ditrina's back.

Ditrina's face drained of color, and she sat perfectly still as Echo positioned himself on her shoulder. Slowly, she looked to her left and saw Echo's red eyes staring into her own.

"Good dragon, nice dragon," Ditrina mumbled to herself.

"Yes...he is," Eve rasped happily in agreement.

"Please take him back," Ditrina begged, her voice a whisper.

"But...he likes you," Eve croaked.

Echo screeched in agreement and proceeded to nuzzle his snakelike head against the side of Ditrina's face.

"I am so glad," Ditrina mumbled before fainting and falling off her horse into a snowdrift, causing Echo to yelp in protest.

"We're off to a great start," Cassy muttered.

It took a few more minutes to revive Ditrina, and Eve agreed that it was for the best if she rode with someone else. Echo seemed displeased with this. After learning how the elf could control fire, he wanted to spend as much time with her as possible. Eve settled with riding with her mother after her second choice of Cassy was rejected immediately by Sarah. Echo tasted hostility between them that Eve didn't understand. So, perched behind her mother, she rode through the frozen forest, taking in the beauty of the spell-lit snow courtesy of Matt's magic.

After two hours of riding, Echo chirped loudly from Eve's shoulder. Eve sat bolt upright.

"People," Eve croaked.

"What's that, sweetie?" Sarah asked her.

"Echo smells...people. Angry people," Eve said as she coughed.

"Where?" Sarah asked quickly, drawing her sword and slinging her shield off her back.

Eve was glad she said something; this looked fun. She drew her dagger.

"Trees," she rasped, pointing with the knife.

Echo hissed.

"Everyone, form up," Chris commanded, and they dismounted, forming a barrier around Eve and the horses.

Matt prayed softly, and a faint blue pulse spread around them. As it passed through the trees, the silhouettes of birds and small animals glowed blue. They watched patiently until they saw the outlines of several men crouching several yards away.

"What's the plan?" Cassy asked.

"They don't know we know they're there. I say we ambush them," Sarah whispered.

"They could be friendly," Chris reminded her.

"Angry...rage," Eve told him. "Echo smells...danger."

"Ok, so, maybe not. Still, we don't need to fight them," Chris said.

"Looks fun," Eve rasped, sharing Echo's hungry gaze.

"It's best to avoid fighting whenever possible, Eve," Chris told her.

"Why?" Eve croaked.

"Because that way nobody has to die. Killing people is a bad thing," Chris said firmly.

"But...it's fun!" Eve protested. "Echo...likes it. I...like it."

"Well, you're not allowed to do it unless you're in danger. You don't go picking fights for no reason," Chris told her.

Eve frowned.

"In...the village...I killed...a man," Eve began.

"Why?" Chris asked.

Eve paused to think about it.

"We were...in danger," Eve told her.

"And why were you in danger?" Sarah asked, deciding to relieve Chris of the burden of the conversation.

Eve seemed confused.

"I...made the man...mad," Eve rasped.

"Why did you make him mad, Eve?" Sarah asked her.

Eve was confused. She hadn't put this much thought into what she did that night. She had just been having fun.

"Wanted...fun," Eve told her. "Made...new game."

"I don't want you playing that game anymore," Sarah told her.

"Yes, Mother," Eve rasped, nodding earnestly.

"I really hate to break up the mother-daughter moment, but we still have the problem of our guests," Matt hissed.

"They seem to be coming this way," Ditrina said.

She was right; the figures could be seen heading through the trees toward them.

"Ready up, but don't attack. They may want to talk," Chris said.

"We're outnumbered," Matt told him.

"All the more reason not to do anything rash," Chris told him.

The men stepped into view. There were fifteen of them in total, carrying an assortment of spears and axes. They all wore heavy furs that blended into the snow as they moved. Had it not been for Matt's spell, Chris would have had no idea they were coming despite only being feet away.

"You kill Higurd?" the leader of the bunch grunted.

He was built larger than the others—impressive, considering the average height of the men before them was around six feet. He carried a massive axe in each hand, but so far, showed no intent of using them.

"We haven't killed anyone; we just got here," Chris told him.

"We find Higurd dead. We find you nearby. You kill Higurd?" the man repeated, voice muffled by his massive, bushy beard.

"Listen, sasquatch, we didn't kill anyone. Now, why don't you move your hairy asses on home, or do I have to put my foot up them?" Sarah growled.

"Higurd killed by green beast. You no green beast," the man agreed.

"Well, I am glad we cleared that up," Ditrina said with a smile.

Upon hearing her voice, the leader looked among them more closely, and his eyes widened in rage.

"Green beast!" he bellowed and waved his axes above his head.

"I am not a beast," Ditrina said, perplexed, assuming he spoke of her green skin.

The brute charged.

"Move, Di!" Cassy yelled as she fired an arrow at the approaching brute's chest.

The power of Cassy's longbow proved more than a match for the fur armor the brute wore, and he soon found himself transfixed by a cloth yard shaft. He fell face forward into the snow, staining it crimson. His companions raised their weapons and charged to avenge him, screaming primitive battle cries. Chris drew his sword, but the blade felt heavy in his hands.

"Damn it! Sarah, sword!" Chris yelled, returning his sword to its sheath, realizing the blade refused to fight the men before him.

Sarah turned and tossed her long sword to him—which he caught—as the first of the barbarians reached them. Sarah herself opted to wield her short swords and discarded her sheild. Chris raised the blade and deflected the first of many crushing blows aimed at him. His opponents were strong, but Chris had studied under a harsh teacher. Together, Chris and his wife waded into the mass of opponents before them, fighting in sync. Matt stood behind them with Ditrina, sending blasts of magic into the crowd and doing their best to defend Eve. Cassy watched and picked off any that made it past Chris and Sarah with her bow.

Eve shrieked with joy as she watched the battle. Her family was right; this vacation was a great idea! Echo shrieked with excitement as he smelled the blood in the air. Deciding it wasn't fair that her parents got to have all the fun, Eve darted past her aunt and uncle and into the battle. Once inside, she realized, to her dismay, she was being ignored. The strange furry men ran right past her without so much as a second glance. Echo hissed his displeasure at being disregarded, and Eve wholeheartedly agreed. Eve decided to do something about this unforgivable transgression and stabbed the nearest man in the back of the knee. The man howled and fell forward, where Echo happily tore out his throat. Giggling, Eve ran farther into the fray, looking for more knees to stab.

"Where the hell is Eve?" Matt bellowed as he sent a group of barbarians reeling with a spell.

"She ran into the fight!" Ditrina yelled back as she cooked the fallen men with a blast of fire.

"She did what?!" Sarah screamed as she lopped off the nearest man's arm.

"You were supposed to watch her!" Chris yelled as he put the man out of his misery.

"Well, it's difficult to fight and babysit at the same time!" Matt called back as he scanned the crowd for his self-proclaimed niece.

He noticed from time to time a man would fall for no apparent reason, and after watching carefully, he caught a glimpse of Eve racing through the crowd, unnoticed by their assailants.

"She's taking care of herself!" Matt told them.

"Get her out of there!" Chris bellowed.

"She is actually helping quite a bit," Ditrina admitted as she set yet another man on fire.

Chris heard Eve's hysterical laughter drift over the din of battle. Out of nowhere, Eve raced passed his legs, and he snagged the hood of her cloak with his free hand.

"What are you doing?" Chris demanded, parrying a blow with his sword while holding Eve to his side.

"Helping!" Eve croaked gleefully.

Echo screamed and looked for more targets.

"Eve, get back by your aunts and let your mother and I handle this," Chris instructed, pulling Eve low to the ground to evade a spear thrust.

"But I...wanna play...too!" Eve rasped.

"Not now, Eve!" Chris yelled before suddenly being knocked off his feet by an axe blow to the back.

His cloak spared him from being cut in half, but nevertheless, he was driven to the ground with a cry of pain.

"Father!" Eve screamed.

Chris's assailant stood triumphantly over him and raised his axe high above his head when suddenly he found a furious six-year-old clinging to his chest.

"Leave...Father...alone!" Eve screamed as she plunged her dagger between the man's ribs.

Echo reared back and let loose the first blast of fire of his life directly into the man's face. Eve felt a surge of pride flow through her as she smelled the char of burning flesh.

Chris tried to stand but found he couldn't feel his legs. He was vaguely aware of Eve dispatching the barbarian, and his wife appeared to be pulling her own swords free of the final standing attacker.

"Your back has been broken," Al informed him.

Chris was unable to form an intelligent enough thought for a reply, his mind clouded by the pain.

"Stay still; Matt's on his way," Al said calmly.

Sure enough, Matt was racing his way across the battlefield toward him, the words of a prayer already on his lips. Sarah hurried away from her newest kill to his side while Cassy and Ditrina followed close behind.

"What happened!?" Sarah yelled as she knelt beside him.

"It looks like a spine injury," Matt replied as he gently set his hands on Chris's back.

Chris felt the magic flowing through him and the uncomfortable sensation of his bones shifting inside him.

"Father was…hit by…an axe," Eve croaked nervously.

"Gods damn it, Chris! I just want one fight where you try not to get yourself killed, *just one*! Is that too much to ask?" Sarah demanded.

Chris yelped in reply as his spine snapped back into place.

"He's fine," Matt announced as he stood up.

"I don't feel fine," Chris muttered as he rose unsteadily to his feet.

"You need to thank Matt," Sarah commanded.

"He knows I'm grateful," Chris grumbled.

Sarah folded her arms and waited. Chris decided it was best to retreat rather than risk another injury.

"As usual, thanks for stopping me from dying," Chris told his friend with a nod.

"That wouldn't have killed you, actually. You would have just been paralyzed for the rest of your life," Matt informed him with a smirk.

"Yeah, yeah; don't rub it in. We get it, you keep us from ruining our lives on a regular basis. We would be lost without you," Chris said with a roll of his eyes.

"Just nice to hear you say it out loud once in a while," Matt chuckled.

"Is anyone else hurt?" Chris asked.

The others shook their heads.

"Figures," Chris muttered and went to take a step forward, only to find a heavy weight attached to his leg.

Eve was firmly latched to him and showed no intent of releasing her vicelike grip.

"Is everything all right, Eve?" Chris asked.

"Were you...dead?" Eve rasped without releasing him.

"No, I was just hurt really bad," Chris told her.

"But...if you died...Uncle S could...bring...you back...right?" Eve coughed, hopefully.

"Once you're dead, you stay dead. Nobody can bring you back from that," Sarah told her.

Eve looked up at him with horrified disbelief.

"Now, do you understand why we don't want to fight unless we have to?" Chris asked her softly.

Eve nodded mutely.

"If you...don't...come back. How do...they?" Eve asked pointing to the fallen barbarians.

"They won't," Chris told her.

"What about...the village man?" Eve rasped fearfully.

"He will never come back," Sarah told her.

"Rooksberg?" Eve croaked quietly, the color draining from her marred face.

"Their souls have departed for the astral realm. They will never again walk this earth," Matt said somberly, playing the priest.

Eve sat with a small thud into the bloodstained snow. Chris sat beside her, and Sarah joined him in holding her close. Eve said nothing. Her face showed no emotion. For a time, they feared she would simply accept this as she had casually accepted everything they had told her so far when they noticed a tear trickling from the corner of her eye. It seemed that only one of her eyes could produce tears, and a steady stream of moisture ran down the right side of her face.

"It's ok to miss them, Eve," Sarah told her softly.

Eve's expression didn't change. Her face showed no emotion, save the tears she shed. It was Echo who expressed their collective grief.

He didn't understand the reason for what he felt. Echo saw no more reason to lament the fate of the people of Rooksberg than he felt to not eat the fallen barbarian whose face he had roasted earlier. Still, through his connection with Eve, he was drowned with sorrow. It overwhelmed him, smothering him. He felt all the pain, the sadness, the horror that Eve had hidden away all at once. Echo screamed into the sky. It was a long, somber sound. He screamed for the pain Eve felt, for the mother he had never known, and for a thousand other things no dragon should ever understand. He was the first of his kind to know grief, to know regret, and he wanted the world to know.

"Leader…" Ditrina began after a few minutes, her voice barely heard over Echo's anguished cries.

"Not now, Ditrina," Chris told her.

"We need to figure out why those men attacked us," Ditrina continued.

"Ditrina, not now!" Chris said angrily.

"She's right. I know this is an important moment for Eve, but there might still be more of these savages around. We need to know why they attacked us and what it is they have against *green beasts*," Matt agreed.

"Eve will be all right," Cassy told them.

Eve sniffled.

"I am…ok…Aunt Cas," she croaked.

Echo stopped his song of lamentation.

"Are you sure?" Chris asked her.

"I…understand. I…don't want…to play…this game…anymore," Eve coughed, looking pitiful.

"Sometimes, you have to play," Sarah told her as they stood. "But not for a long time. For now, we'll keep you safe."

"Let's find out who this Higurd fellow is," Cassy told them, and began walking the way the barbarians had come.

As it turned out Higurd was an unremarkable looking man who seemed to have been killed by a sword wound to the neck. They found his body lying in a snowdrift half a mile in the direction the barbarians had come. For some reason, his body seemed to have been partially burned.

"So, the elves did this?" Cassy asked as they inspected the body.

"This man was not killed by my people," Ditrina said firmly.

"How can you be sure?" Chris asked.

"The elves don't use weapons; we have no need for them. If he had been killed by an elf, he would have been killed by magic," Ditrina explained.

"What about the burns?" Chris asked.

"Those burns did not come from an elf," Ditrina told him.

"She's right. I can't detect any trace of elven magic on him," Matt confirmed. "That was something else."

"So, who killed this man?" Sarah asked.

"Could it have been a rival tribe?" Cassy proposed.

"Perhaps. The local human tribes do fight for resources from time to time, and they do have a few spell casters among them, but it is unheard of to see them so close to our city. I will have to inquire with my father when we arrive," Ditrina said, lost in thought.

"How far from the entrance are we, Di?" Cassy asked.

"Not far now. We should reach the signal point within the hour. Follow me," Ditrina said and led them farther into the forest.

Eve felt Echo alert her to more people hiding in the forest, but she said nothing. She didn't want to play *that* game for a long time. Still, she found it strange that these people felt no fear; rather, they seemed excited and hungry. As they traveled closer to the city, their hidden watchers followed, out of sight, but never far behind.

"Here we are," Ditrina declared a short while later.

Chris was unsure of where *here* was. This stretch of the forest looked no different to him than any other stretch of the forest they had ridden through in the last few hours. Cassy put his uncertainty into words.

"Are you sure about that, Di? There's nothing here," she said, glancing around in confusion.

"Trees," Eve declared, looking around the snowy forest for any sign of irregularity.

Matt jolted upright suddenly.

"No! Ditrina's right! This is it!" Matt said excitedly.

"So, you can feel it as well, Matthew?" Ditrina asked happily.

Matt nodded breathlessly.

"What is it he's feeling?" Sarah asked, pulling off her helmet.

"The magic. There's so much magic," Matt whispered in awe, mostly to himself.

"I just need to send the signal, so they lower the barrier," Ditrina said before launching a flare from her hand into the air.

It flew high into the night sky before exploding, showering them with golden sparks. A ripple passed through the air before them, and suddenly they found themselves looking at a very different place.

"How...what is this?" Chris asked as he stared through the hole in existence.

It was like an invisible door had opened to a new world. Around him, Chris could still see the frozen forest, and looking behind the opening, the forest seemed to stretch on as far as he could see. Despite this, the doorway that opened before him showed Chris miles of farmland bathed in the summer sun. Looking farther, he was able to make out a massive city rising in the distance.

"Please hurry; the gateway will not stay open for long," Ditrina told them.

Without further delay, Chris urged his horse through the door, followed by his companions.

As she passed thought the gateway with her mother, Eve felt strange, as if she had traveled a very long distance in a short time. Through Echo, she learned that the mysterious people who had been following them could no longer be smelled. Satisfied she could avoid any unwanted games, for the time being, she looked around this new paradise, her eyes filled with wonder.

The farmland was well maintained, and without a house or farmer in sight. Chris wondered how it was that anything was accomplished until he saw a tree uproot itself and begin walking toward the city, branches laden with fruit.

"The farms take care of themselves," Ditrina explained, seeing his amazement.

"This is incredible!" Sarah said as she soaked in the sites.

Looking behind them, they saw the doorway to the frozen forest still stood open, but behind that, they saw farmland stretching as far as the eye could see.

"How does this work?" Matt demanded as he rode up beside Ditrina.

"Well, fifteen hundred years ago, right after the gods cast the curse of the crisis, the various elves of the world decided to pool our collective power and resources to create a sanctuary of learning in the hopes of breaking the curse," Ditrina began.

"I know that; that's why you and the rest of the Rikes are out exploring Targoth all the time. I want to know how this paradise is in the middle of a frozen forest," Matt said irritably.

"I am getting to that, Matthew," Ditrina chided. "As I was saying, we decided to make a sanctuary for all of elvenkind. With this in mind, we recognized that it may take more than one generation to break the curse, and as a result, prepared for a sudden drop in our population. All of the elves moved to the city you see before you in anticipation of this so that we could continue to find fertile mates. As for the city itself, it was created by folding reality. To the far south, there is a massive prairie that lies uninhabited. To the untrained eye, it looks no different than any other grassland, but with the proper spell, you would find yourself in the middle of a frozen forest, much like what we just did. It is like we created a copy of a place and put it inside of another place. Does that answer your question?" Ditrina asked.

"A little," Matt replied.

"How did you get anything out of that?" Chris asked in amazement.

"Well, the concept is something I'm familiar with, I've just never heard of it being done before," Matt told him.

"I'm still stuck on the part where an entire species moved into one city. How did you all fit inside?" Sarah asked.

"What do you mean? The city was built to house over a billion people. The elves fit without any difficulty. These days, less than a million elves live on Targoth, and most of them are out exploring. The city is a very lonely place," Ditrina told her.

"That is…very sad," Eve croaked.

"We keep the hope that one day the city will be filled again and that we will have to build new cities," Ditrina told her with a smile. "Let us hurry, it has been a long time since I have visited my family," Ditrina said eagerly, spurring her horse onward.

As they hurried toward the city, the gateway closed behind them, but not before several figures slipped inside. They glanced around and set their hungry eyes on the city.

It took longer to reach the city than Chris expected. The farmland seemed to stretch on for miles around them, and Chris was amazed each time a seemingly mundane object would spring to life and begin working on its own.

"Leader, you do not have to stare at the farm equipment. It is not going to hurt you," Ditrina told him.

"It's just so incredible; I can't help it," Chris told her.

"Still, you have spent the last ten minutes studying the shovels and hoes as they work. You do not have to act so shocked," Ditrina argued.

"I always try to study the hoes whenever I can, if you know what I mean," Matt piped in with a cheesy grin.

"Really, Matthew? I did not know you had an interest in agriculture," Ditrina said happily.

Matt sighed.

"Not the point, Ditrina. Does anyone know what that puts her total to for this week?" Matt called.

"I've lost track," Chris admitted.

"Same," Sarah sighed.

"Wait, what? No! I was doing so well this week," Ditrina pouted as she realized she had missed the point yet again.

"Don't worry, Di, we'll keep better track next week," Cassy assured her.

"Anyway, Ditrina, you said that city was built to house a billion people?" Sarah asked, changing the subject.

"That is right," Ditrina agreed.

"Impossible. That city is at most three times the size of Draclige. While large, that could hardly house a billion people; hell, it would barely hold over five hundred thousand," Sarah argued.

"You forget the elves have magic at their disposal. You will see what I mean when we arrive," Ditrina told her.

It took another two hours to reach the gates, which Chris found as impressive as everything else he had seen. They seemed to be made of solid stone and stretched far enough into the sky he was forced to crane his neck to see the top. Chris could see no indication that this was a gate at all. Actually, it looked no different from the surrounding walls, though the lone guard watching them approach said otherwise.

"He's not armed," Sarah commented.

"Still, he could most likely kill you before you could draw your sword. So, behave yourself," Matt warned her.

"Shouldn't you be telling that to Ditrina? She's the one who's likely to say something stupid," Sarah replied.

"This is her home, remember? She's royalty here," Matt reminded her. Sarah snorted.

"I'll believe it when I see it," Sarah scoffed.

"How can you still doubt the fact that she's royalty after seeing how Sam treats her?" Chris asked.

"I've known Ditrina for a while now, so I feel safe saying that that girl has never wielded power a day in her life," Sarah argued.

"I assure you, I am indeed a princess, though you are correct about my lack of power. Aside from being of royal blood, I have little influence," Ditrina agreed.

"Well, I wasn't completely wrong," Sarah chuckled.

"You're just jealous that Di was raised as a princess and you had to live as a soldier," Cassy taunted.

"I tried the life of a noble. It wasn't for me," Sarah said.

"What are you talking about, Sarah?" Chris asked.

"Well, if you recall, I ran away from home when I was twelve and joined a mercenary company," Sarah told him.

"Yeah, you said it was called the Band of the Boar, but they were wiped out in a battle on the coast years ago," Chris said, remembering the story of his wife's past.

"Well, before I ran away, I was the daughter of a nobleman, Duke Morgson," Sarah told him.

"I've heard of him. He has land on the western side of the Godspine," Matt said.

"Why did you leave?" Chris asked.

"It was all court dresses and dancing lessons. It wasn't for me. I wanted to be like the soldiers I saw around the castle, but my father wouldn't even let me have a dagger of my own. He even went so far as to promise me to some son of a noble I had never heard of once we had both come of age. To him, I was simply a way to expand his power," Sarah spat.

"My father has tried to marry me off before for political reasons," Ditrina said with a dreamy expression on her face.

"You look more cheerful than I would expert about that," Cassy said warily.

"Oh! Forgive me, I was just remembering the size of the explosion I set off in the castle when my father did not take *no* for an answer. It was truly some of my best work," Ditrina said with a smile.

"And suddenly, it makes sense why they didn't try to bring the Fire Princess home," Chris sighed.

"Please, do not call me that," Ditrina said immediately.

"Why do you hate that nickname so much?" Chris asked.

"You will see why once we are inside the city. I doubt I will have the luxury of privacy for long," Ditrina sighed.

"I thought you were excited to return home?" Chris asked.

"My home is in the valley with all of you. This is a trip to see my family," Ditrina corrected. "Here, I am the crown princess. Everything I do is seen by thousands of people, and everything I say has to be premeditated and well thought out. I never liked it here very much. In the valley, I am surrounded by all of you. I get to spend time with my girlfriend and her family. I have Matthew to discuss spell craft with, and I trust that Sarah will keep us safe. I have the honor to say I am part of Shearcliff and Company, under the leadership of Christian Shearcliff himself. I am grateful that you all tolerate me," Ditrina said seriously.

"What do you mean *tolerate* you? We all love you, Di!" Cassy assured her.

"Since when am I some bigshot? '*Christian Shearcliff himself.*' Ha! As if..." Chris muttered under his breath.

"I know it may come as a shock to you all, but some of my mannerisms could be considered strange by some, and I have difficulty understanding basic social conventions at times," Ditrina said, completely deadpan.

"What the hell?! *May come as a shock*... Ditrina, you're one the weirdest people I've ever met!" Matt yelled.

"Zero for one," Ditrina said simply.

"What?" Matt asked.

"That was sarcasm. You failed to recognize it. Your weekly total is now zero correct for one attempt. Try harder to recognize it in the future, Matthew," Ditrina told him.

"Did...did Ditrina just try to make a joke?" Matt demanded.

"Chris, I'm afraid," Sarah whispered.

"Me too," Chris said, looking at Ditrina in horror.

"Echo smells...terror," Eve declared, looking around with confusion.

"I think we should hurry inside. The guard is starting to look restless," Cassy said, trying to move past Ditrina's attempt at humor.

"That may be for the best. I would hate for you all to be vaporized for being mistakenly recognized as intruders," Ditrina said, riding toward the guard.

"Vaporized?" Chris asked in disbelief.

He looked to his right and watched a wheelbarrow push itself across a field before deciding it wasn't worth finding out what else the elves could do with their magic. He hurried after Ditrina.

CHAPTER SEVEN

As they approached the guard, he issued a challenge in elvish, which Chris failed to understand.

"For the sake of my companions, please speak common," Ditrina replied.

"Who seeks to enter the city?" the elf replied.

Like the two elves Chris had met so far, he had blue hair and green skin. His eyes were mirrors of Ditrina's own. Despite being a guard, he wore no armor and carried no weapon. Regardless, he had an aura of danger about him, and the official looking robe he wore labeled him as a guard.

"Princess Ditrinadoma Figinoma Rike, here to give my report along with Shearcliff and Company. They are my escort," Ditrina told the guard.

"Princess! Forgive me, I didn't recognize you. Please excuse my poor manners," the guard said as he bowed deeply.

"It is fine. I look quite different from when I last stood in the city. Open the gates," Ditrina commanded.

Chris looked at his friends in disbelief. Ditrina played the princess quite well. The guard hurried to the wall and placed his hands on it. Chris watched as a seam appeared, running from the very top of the wall to the ground. Without a sound, the walls swung open, giving them their first look into the elven city. It was composed of tall identical buildings made of stone. Not a soul could be seen.

"It's...empty," Cassy said bluntly.

"Not for long. Word will spread of my arrival, and the people will flock to the streets. For now, it seems there are just no elves in our vicinity," Ditrina told her.

"Enjoy your stay, Fire Princess!" the guard called from behind them. Ditrina sighed.

"Let us hurry," she told them as they rode deeper into the city.

The walls closed silently behind them.

"I still don't see how you could fit a billion people into this city," Sarah said as they rode.

"Look inside one of the buildings," Ditrina told her as she stopped her horse.

Sarah complied and slid gracefully off her mount. She walked toward the nearest building, a five-story monolith made entirely of stone, and peeked inside.

"What the hell?" Sarah yelled and stumbled back out of the door.

"Do you understand now?" Ditrina asked.

"It's an entire city block!" Sarah yelled.

"What?" Matt asked.

"Behind that door is an entire city block. Roads, buildings, trees, you name it! Somehow they fit an entire block into one building!" Sarah said in amazement.

"It is like how the city is in the forest and in the prairie. We folded reality to make extra room," Ditrina explained.

"Is every building like that?" Sarah demanded.

"Well, some hold areas as large as Draclige. That building is actually fairly small," Ditrina told her.

"Princess?" a voice called from down the street.

Looking in the direction it had come, they saw an elf woman standing in amazement.

"Oh no, it begins," Ditrina sighed.

"It's the Fire Princess! She has returned!" the elf woman cried before vanishing with a small pop.

"Where has she gone off to?" Chris asked.

"Most likely to fetch as many other elves as she can. They, in turn, will gather more elves, and before we can make it to the end of the street, the entire city will be here," Ditrina said sadly.

"Should we run?" Sarah asked looking for escape routes.

"Too late," Ditrina sighed as another elf popped into view a few feet away.

"Fire Princess!" he cried, waving his arms wildly above his head.

"As if somehow, we missed him popping out of thin air," Sarah grumbled.

"Please protect me," Ditrina said suddenly.

"What?" Chris asked, not understanding the nature of the request.

"It seems they are more fanatical than I remember. I fear they may try to pull me from my horse in their excitement," Ditrina told him.

Sure enough, several more elves appeared and began running toward them, calling madly:

"Fire Princess! Fire Princess, over here!"

"Shearcliff and Company, form up! Protect Ditrina!" Chris bellowed over the crowd.

Quickly, they arranged their horses around Ditrina, so she was encased by her friends. Matt and Cassy took her sides, while Chris took the lead. Sarah slipped her helmet back on and positioned herself directly behind Ditrina to deter any would-be flankers. The crowd grew larger by the second, with elves pouring out of buildings or popping out of thin air.

"Why are they so obsessed with you?" Chris demanded as he carved a swath through the crowd with his horse.

"I am unsure," Ditrina replied, looking around nervously.

"Are you…upset, Aunt Di?" Eve rasped.

"No, dear; just a little nervous is all," Ditrina told her.

"Is it…because of…them?" Eve asked pointing to the crowd.

"In part," Ditrina admitted.

"Can Echo…eat them then? He is…hungry," Eve croaked.

"Echo can't go around eating people, Eve," Sarah scolded.

"But they…are upsetting…Aunt Di!" Eve coughed angrily.

"No eating anyone!" Chris called from ahead of them.

"Fine!" Eve pouted.

Silently, she gave Echo the bad news, and he screeched sadly from her shoulder.

"You can tell your friend that there will be plenty to eat in the palace," Ditrina assured her, trying to silence the tiny dragon.

"That is…good," Eve rasped happily.

Echo quieted.

"Make way for the Fire Princess! Make way for Princess Ditrinadoma!" called the guard from before, appearing suddenly in front of them.

Quickly, he was joined by more guards, and they formed a wall around the horses—a living barrier. The crowd parted reluctantly around them.

"Make your way to the palace, Princess. Your father is waiting for you," the guard told her before their escort began marching forward in lockstep.

"Well, this in an impressive welcome," Matt said.

"It will only get worse," Ditrina said with a sigh before turning to the crowd and giving a halfhearted wave.

The crowd lost its mind and cheered so loudly Chris feared he would go deaf.

"It has been many years since I have seen a royal welcome. This is refreshing," Al said within Chris's head.

"Perhaps for you, but Ditrina looks unhappy," Chris thought back.

"Regardless, the crowd is enjoying itself. Keeping the people happy is part of ruling. Watch Ditrina. Despite the fact she is unhappy, she is waving to the crowd and smiling as much as she can. It's good for appearances," Al told him.

"What's the point of all this if she's unhappy, though? She's said it herself, she will never sit on the throne because she is a Rike. Why bother with the display?" Chris wondered.

"She must maintain a certain image for the sake of her family. If only Mi had tried as hard as Ditrina," Al grumbled.

"How far away is the palace?" Sarah called to the guards.

"We are close, *human*," one of the guards replied.

"How close?" Sarah asked.

The guard shrugged.

"It matters little to you. Stay on your horse and stay silent," the guard ordered.

"What the hell is your problem?" Sarah demanded.

The guard ignored her.

"Sarah asked you a question," Ditrina said firmly.

The crowd fell silent immediately.

"Princess, you can't possibly expect me to…" the guard began.

"You were asked a question, soldier," Ditrina replied angrily.

"By a human. I don't understand why you even brought these things into our city, to begin with," the guard spat.

Ditrina's expression hardened.

"And why is it that my companions should be treated as second-class citizens?" Ditrina demanded.

"They are outsiders. The only reason they were allowed inside the gates was because you ordered the gate guard to open for them. Had you not been with them, they would have been killed on sight," the guard told her.

"Since when is it our way to attack travelers without reason?!" Ditrina yelled.

"Much has changed since you departed, Princess. Things are not as they once were. Your father will explain more," the guard told her. "Until then, your companions will be allowed to remain in the city, but they will be removed as soon as possible," the guard sneered.

"They are here by my invitation! I will not have my friends treated as criminals!" Ditrina yelled.

A low murmur ran through the crowd.

"As I said, things have changed. Outsiders are not welcome in the city," the guard told her.

"Then I will have to ensure that they are not outsiders anymore," Ditrina said angrily.

"What are you doing, Di?" Cassy hissed.

"I am sorry, my friends, but I must ask you all to dismount," Ditrina told them.

"Ditrina? What's going on?" Chris asked skeptically.

"Please, just trust me," Ditrina told him.

Chris looked at his companions and shrugged. Together they dismounted and stood awkwardly around Ditrina. The guards held their barrier around them, and the crowd remained silent.

"What are you doing, Princess?" the guard hissed.

"In ages past, it has been the custom for the Princess to appoint her champions. I have decided to select mine," Ditrina said loudly, so the entire crowd could hear. "Please kneel," she told her friends.

Deciding it was best to play along, Chris knelt before Ditrina, and his companions followed suit. Even Eve knelt beside him, looking around in confusion.

"Remove your hoods," Ditrina commanded.

One by one, they cast back their hoods so the crowd could see their faces better. Sarah pulled her helmet off and set it on the ground before her. The crowd gave a gasp upon seeing Cassy's face and claws clearly for the first time.

"She's a half-breed! The Princess brought a half-breed into the city!" they heard one outraged voice cry.

"Silence!" Ditrina yelled, startling her friends.

"What the hell is a half-breed, and why do I feel like they were talking about me?" Cassy hissed under her breath.

"In recognition for their bravery while fighting by my side, and as thanks for accepting me into their ranks, I hereby grant Shearcliff and Company the honor of being my champions! Christian Shearcliff, Sarah Shearcliff, Eve Shearcliff, and Matthew Bleakstar, rise and bear your rank proudly!" Ditrina said, placing her hand on each of their heads in turn, shuddering when Echo licked her as she placed her hand on Eve's brow.

One by one they stood and noticed that only Cassy had failed to be called out.

"Cassy Shearcliff," Ditrina called.

The crowd looked uncomfortable and murmured quietly.

"You have proven yourself every bit as capable as those who stand before you, but you are far more to me than a simple champion. Rise, Cassy Shearcliff, Royal Consort!" Ditrina yelled.

The crowd let out an enraged bellow and pushed against the wall of guards.

"What have you done, Di?" Cassy demanded.

"I have formally acknowledged you all as my champions. You now all carry the honorary title of Gel and are above the laws of the city. As for you specifically, I have claimed you as my consort. This gives you the official rank akin to my fiancée, as well as the status that entails. I hope that is all right?" Ditrina asked her nervously.

"Gods, Di, give us a little warning next time you wanna do something like that!" Cassy laughed.

"So, it was ok then?" Ditrina asked.

"You're fine, Di," Cassy said, giving her a small kiss, causing the crowd to yell louder.

"Princess! You must hurry to the palace! Your actions have enraged the crowd!" one of the guards yelled over the mob's angry cries.

"We should hurry," Ditrina agreed and headed toward her horse.

"Am I...a knight?" Eve rasped hopefully.

"Ask your aunt; I'm not exactly sure what that was," Chris told her as he pulled her onto his horse.

"Are we...knights?!" Eve screeched excitedly to Ditrina.

"Of a sort. *Technically*, you are now my personal knights. You answer only to me, but seeing that I answer to our leader, Chris, nothing has really changed," Ditrina told her.

Eve only heard the part that said she was a knight.

"We're knights!" she shrieked before cackling madly, her harsh laughter echoing over the crowd.

Echo decided now was a good time to scream as well, and together they added their voices to the chaos.

Sarah sighed.

"If Ditrina starts trying to give me orders, I'm going to tie Echo to her back," she told Chris.

Chris smiled.

"I don't think we'll have to worry about that," he assured her.

"Please do not do that," Ditrina begged as they hurried toward the palace.

"Well don't go around shouting things like 'knights, attend me,' or anything like that. I was a knight once, and I've had my fill of serving nobles," Sarah warned her.

"Do not worry. I answer to Chris, same as you," Ditrina promised.

"For reasons I fail to understand," Chris sighed as they rode.

"Cas told me it was a good idea," Ditrina explained to him.

"Of course she did; why wouldn't she?" Chris grumbled.

"Relax, leader. You're doing a good job so far!" Matt called happily.

"I'm going to hurt you, Matt!" Chris called back.

Matt laughed.

"The words came from your mouth, but I heard Sarah talking! You're turning into your wife!" Matt cackled.

"And what's wrong with being like me?" Sarah demanded.

"Oh, nothing. It's just you have a tendency to threaten to murder those who displease you," Matt told her.

"I want…to be…like mother!" Eve croaked happily.

"Start by feeding Matt to Echo, sweetie," Sarah said with a smile.

"But…we like…Uncle S!" Eve protested. "He…shows us…words!"

"That's right, Eve. You see? You don't want to be *completely* like your mother," Matt told her.

Eve seemed to ponder this for a while and fell silent.

"Here we are. Escort the Princess inside, *champions*," the guard spat, gesturing to a squat stone building.

"This is the palace?" Chris asked skeptically.

"It is much nicer on the inside," Ditrina assured him.

"If you say so," Chris said as he dismounted.

Chris walked through the stone doorway and into a new world.

"I admire their throne room. It's quite regal," Al admired from within Chris's head.

Chris was forced to agree; the throne room was impressive. Tall, marble pillars held the roof impossibly high, and multiple balconies stretched around the room. A large throne sat in the center of the room, and atop it sat a very old elf wearing a gold crown resembling branches intertwining around his brow. He was the first elf Chris had seen with a beard, and what a beard it was. Like a blue bolt of cloth, it hung from his chin to his waist. As he noticed him, the King called something in elvish Chris was unable to understand. Deciding it was best to play the part he had been given, Chris straightened up.

"Now presenting the Princess Ditrinadoma!" Chris called, hearing his voice echo around the room.

Behind him, Sarah and Matt entered the room, taking positions on either side of the door, before Ditrina entered with Cassy on her arm. Eve trailed behind her aunts and decided to stand beside her mother, holding her hand.

"Hello, Father," Ditrina said happily, waving with her free hand.

The Elf King said something in his language they couldn't decipher.

"Please, for the sake of my companions, use the common tongue," Ditrina requested.

"You have returned, my daughter," the King said simply.

His accent was thick, and Chris found him difficult to understand. It was as if every word he said was a song, and his deep voice rumbled throughout the room.

"It is good to see you," Ditrina said as she dropped to a knee, momentarily releasing Cassy.

Chris and the others quickly followed suit—Eve with the prompting of her mother.

"Who are your companions? How were they allowed within the city?" King Figinoma asked.

"These are my champions and my friends," Ditrina said as she stood. "Allow me to present Shearcliff and Company. The man beside me is my leader, Christian Shearcliff. The ones beside the door are Matthew Bleakstar and Sarah Shearcliff. The young girl is my niece, Eve Shearcliff," Ditrina told him, gesturing to each of them in turn.

"And what of the half-breed?" King Figinoma asked, raising a bushy blue eyebrow.

"This is Cassy Shearcliff, my consort," Ditrina told him.

The King laughed, but it did not reach his eyes.

"I truly hope this is a jest, though it would be in poor taste. How could you bring a half-breed into the city, and how could you dare to claim it as your consort?!" King Figinoma demanded.

"I'm getting tired of being called a half-breed. I've been called a lot of things by a lot of people, but that one's new to me. Care to explain what it means, blue beard?" Cassy asked angrily.

The King ignored her.

"I was willing to condone you remaining unmarried, and I was even willing to accept your desire to explore Targoth. Both of these things were well within your rights as a Rike, and I lack the power to deny you those, but this? How could you possibly bring this *thing* before me?" the King yelled.

Cassy opened her mouth to say something vile, but Ditrina proved her tongue was faster.

"She is my chosen consort and will be treated as such unless you wish to try to deny me the right to choose my partner. The right to choose is the greatest honor a Rike can bear!" Ditrina yelled.

"She's an abomination!" King Figinoma yelled.

"What the hell are you talking about?" Cassy screamed.

She began marching toward the throne.

"What's your problem with me? Why do you hate the naga? What the hell is a half-breed?!" Cassy demanded as she approached.

The Elf King flicked his hand dismissively, and a bolt of blue light flew toward Cassy. Before she had a chance to react, Ditrina waved her hand in an arc, and a shimmering wall of light materialized between Cassy and the spell. The blue bolt smashed into the wall with a deafening boom and showered sparks across the room.

"You dare defy me?" the King demanded of Ditrina.

"They are Gel! They have been publicly acknowledged as my champions, and she has been chosen as my consort! You cannot harm them!" Ditrina screamed.

Slowly, Ditrina began rising off the ground, a miniature whirlwind of fire around her feet.

"You *will* acknowledge their rights as Gel; you *will* allow them to remain in the city as long as they wish, and you *will* apologize to my friends for trying to vaporize them, or so help me, I will blast this entire building down around our ears!" Ditrina shrieked, flames swirling around her fingers.

The King looked at his enraged daughter and to her terrified companions. Each of them trembled at this display of power, save the little girl. She seemed to be having the time of her life and hopped from foot to foot, clapping with joy. Her tiny dragon screeched excitedly and sent a small gout of fire into the air in an attempt to be useful.

"Fine," the King said with a lazy shrug. "I'm sorry for trying to kill you."

Ditrina returned to the ground. The fire disappeared, much to Echo's disappointment.

"Go to your quarters. I will have a room prepared for your friends. We will discuss the reason for your return over dinner tonight. For now, you must be weary from your travels. Rest," King Figinoma told her before vanishing into thin air, leaving them alone in the throne room.

"Di, what the hell was that all about? Why do all the elves hate me?" Cassy demanded, walking angrily toward her.

"I may have forgotten a small detail about your species and the elves. I will explain more when we are in private," Ditrina told her.

She reached out and pulled her companions into a circle and teleported them somewhere deeper within the palace. They spun briefly, then popped out onto a balcony. Sarah and Eve promptly vomited over the edge.

"So sorry. I forgot that happens to you," Ditrina said quickly.

"You've forgotten quite a lot, apparently. Start talking!" Cassy demanded.

"Follow me," Ditrina told her.

She led them inside, revealing a dusty looking room filled floor to ceiling with books. A comfortable looking chair could be seen hiding behind a table stacked high with tomes of all shapes and sizes. The walls were completely covered by bookshelves bursting to the brim, and several doorways could be seen buried in the corners. Ditrina clapped her hands, and several sofas appeared, flying to arrange themselves around the table as the table itself was cleared of books, tomes zooming back to their spots on the shelves. The dust vanished instantly, and Ditrina sat in the chair and gestured for them to take seats.

"You were right, Ditrina; I totally get the whole Fire Princess thing now that we're in the city," Chris told her with a weak smile.

"Yes, yes, Di likes to burn things to smithereens. Now, what the hell is a half-breed, and why do they keep calling me that? I've gotten used to racism from the humans, but the elves too?" Cassy demanded with outrage.

Ditrina let out a weary groan.

"I have to apologize for the way all of you were greeted. I have no idea what is going on or why the elves seem so hostile to outsiders at the moment, but I should have anticipated my father's response to Cas," Ditrina sighed.

"What's wrong with being a naga?" Cassy asked angrily. "Why is it that everywhere I go I'm hated for being a naga?"

"It has to do with your race's origin. Unlike the normal races such as the elves, humans, dwarves, and orcs, the naga are not a natural-born race; rather, they are the product of the gods' experimentation. During the time in the years after the crisis, the gods found themselves faced with a lack of worship due to the low population. To combat this, the gods formed a hierarchy, with the ten you all worship presiding over the others so that none of the gods would go hungry. They receive the worship as it is given and distribute it among the other, now lesser, gods. This was how the angels were created. They are, in fact, just gods who lack worshipers of their own," Ditrina explained.

"Why is it that the churches don't know this? We were taught that the ten gods saved Targoth from the events of the crisis. First, you told me that it was the gods themselves that caused the crisis, and now you're telling me that the only reason we worship the gods we do is so the angels don't starve?" Matt demanded in outrage.

"Exactly. Your entire religion is based on a lie," Ditrina said cheerfully before returning her attention to Cassy. "As I was saying—" she began.

"Wait just a moment! You can't just go saying something like that then blow me off! Why the hell don't people know about this?" Matt demanded.

"Matthew, there will be time to discuss theocracy later. Right now, I am explaining to Cas why the elves consider her a disgusting abomination!" Ditrina said irritably.

"Wow, you really know how to make a girl blush, Di," Cassy said with a roll of her eyes.

"As I was saying, the gods appointed ten representatives to ensure that the worship was evenly distributed. For a time, they walked among the people spreading their names and what they stood for—gathering worshipers. After a while, the people prayed to them and them alone, the crisis only a distant memory of generations past," Ditrina told them.

"Fascinating, but what does that have to do with me?" Cassy demanded.

"I am getting to that!" Ditrina protested. "While most of the gods were satisfied with this distribution of power, some felt that they should be the ones prayed to instead. These gods were not satisfied with the amount of worship they were allotted and sought followers of their own. At this point in history, most of the races were teetering on the edge of extinction due to the slow removal of the curse of the crisis. This meant that the worship the ten received was closely monitored, and with this in mind, these rogue gods knew that trying to steal followers from the ten was suicide. So, rather than start a war among the gods, they decided to create worshipers of their own," Ditrina told them.

"How is it the elves know all of this?" Matt demanded.

"We are on our third generation since the crisis; in fact, my grandfather was alive for the event itself. While none alive remember the moment the gods were born, many recall the tales their parents told them about that fateful day. The other races may have forgotten the treachery of the gods, but the elves will always remember," Ditrina told him.

"That's wonderful, Di, but you still haven't told me about the naga!" Cassy said angrily.

"But she has…" Matt said in disbelief.

"What do you mean?" Cassy asked skeptically.

"The rogue gods decided to create worshipers of their own, so they gave birth to a multitude of new races. Giants, arakne, and the naga, just to name a few," Ditrina told her. "Each god fashioned a people to serve them and warped their appearance to claim them as their own. These races lack the inherent magic of the other races, so the gods held no fear of rebellion. Sadly, most of these races did not last very long—all but two are now extinct. Without knowledge of the world around them, many perished within a few short years or were wiped out by clashes with the old races. Some, like the arakne, disappeared completely from Targoth for reasons we do not know, while others like the giants were converted by the ten original gods and folded into common society. The rogue gods eventually perished from lack of worship or returned to kneel before the ten. Only one race managed to withstand the test of time and carve its own place upon Targoth: the naga. The naga captured the lands to the far east across the desert, and there they worship their rogue god. They call her Semel, and it is said hers is a harsh and dark religion," Ditrina said sadly.

"So, that's it, then? The elves hate me just because I'm a *new* race or something?" Cassy asked angrily.

"Not exactly. The elves harbor no ill will toward the giants for what they are. It is the naga in specific that are despised," Ditrina told her.

"Why?" Cassy demanded.

"It has to do with the naga culture. Naga society is quite different from that of the elves and, to an extent, the humans. While the society of the elves and the other races was founded on magic, the naga never had a taste of this power aside from what their dark god has gifted to them. So, while our societies place importance on expanding the mind and acquiring power through intellect, the naga pride themselves in their ferocity and cunning. The law of the land is red in tooth and claw, and the only hard rule is *might makes right*. The envoys we have sent to them over the years have all been killed, and relations with the naga are tense, at best. It is good for both parties that we live on opposite sides of Targoth," Ditrina said.

"You know about my people?!" Cassy exclaimed in disbelief.

"Yes..." Ditrina said, looking uncomfortable.

"Why haven't you told us this before?" Chris asked in shock.

After all, he was just as eager to learn about his sister's species as she was.

"When I first met Cas, I was afraid," Ditrina admitted. "Everything I had learned about the naga told me that she would be a cruel and vicious monster, so when I spoke to her, I was amazed by how kind she was. It was like she took everything the naga stood for and turned it on its head. She was eager to be accepted into society and willing to help me fit in with the rest of you. She proved to me that the naga are not inherently evil; rather, it is the result of Semel's corruption that has twisted them so," Ditrina said softly.

"Why didn't you tell me any of this?" Cassy asked quietly.

"You are always so eager to prove that you are not a monster, that there is more to you than your fangs and claws. I thought it would upset you to learn that what most people see when they see you is an accurate representation of your species," Ditrina admitted.

"Tell me everything you know about the naga. Leave nothing out," Cassy ordered.

"Very well," Ditrina sighed. "I warn you, much of what you hear will upset you," Ditrina told her.

"Everything," Cassy repeated firmly.

"The naga, as you now know, are an artificial race created by Semel after the crisis. They live to the far east in a massive city built atop the world's largest natural spring, allowing them to thrive despite the desert's harsh conditions. They seldom interact with the other races with the exception of their slaver parties. The naga society is built on the backs of their slaves, and they are always looking for fresh stock. Despite a lack of government within their civilization, a basic hierarchy has emerged. Their society is matriarchal, with the brood-mothers ruling their family houses. Any breeding female is considered to be of higher rank than even the most accomplished male, and to harm a female is akin to a declaration of war. A female's status is determined by the strength of her sons. The more powerful warrior sons she raises, the more powerful her house becomes. Male naga are often considered to be expendable, and the concept of marriage is foreign to them. Females often trade their sons for the purpose of strengthening bloodlines and forming alliances. Another way a house can gain prestige is through their slaves. The number of slaves a house has is a direct reflection of its status. The houses strive to acquire the most exotic house slaves possible and the strongest warrior slaves for the arena. That is all I know. If you wish to learn more, you will have to inquire with the librarians. As I said, we have tried on several occasions to negotiate with the naga, but they have proven unreceptive," Ditrina told her.

Cassy was silent.

"Are you all right, sis?" Chris asked.

"Di, can you show me my room? I need a little time to think about this," Cassy said softly.

"Of course. For now, you can use my room. It will give you privacy until a room of your own is set up," Ditrina told her.

Cassy shook her head.

"I'd rather stay with you…if that's all right?" Cassy asked.

Chris had never seen his sister look so pitiful.

"Of course, Cas; anything you ask," Ditrina said with a small smile before leading Cassy though one of the doorways, leaving the others alone.

"Well, that wasn't what I expected to hear today," Sarah said bluntly.

"So, Cassy's descendent from bloodthirsty slavers. I'm absolutely shocked," Matt spat.

"What's your problem?" Chris demanded.

"What's my problem?! Oh, I don't know, maybe it has something about the religion I've dedicated my *entire life to* being nothing more than an elaborate ruse to feed some astral assholes who enjoy cursing people!" Matt bellowed. "Why haven't the elves told the temples this? If they know so much, how come they're not sharing this knowledge?!" Matt demanded.

"Think, Matt. The elves are battling extinction. If they were to come out and declare the gods as false idols, the temples would rally against them, or worse still, the gods themselves. I'm sure once the elves have their own situation under control, they'll try to warn the world about the evils of the gods, but for now, they're just not ready for that fight," Sarah told him.

"Besides, regardless of its origin, the power of the gods is real. Have they ever ignored one of your prayers, Matt?" Chris asked.

"That's not the point!" Matt yelled. "That's not the point," he repeated softly. "We are taught that the gods are an absolute good and that they exist to protect the people. I was taught that the gods saved us from the crisis, but over the last few months, I've learned that they were the ones who caused it! Fine, whatever, I can accept that. After all, the crisis is shrouded in myth and legend, and nobody really knows what happened all those years ago. What I can't accept is that the only reason we have for praying to the gods is to feed them! They're nothing more than glorified parasites! How can I worship a creature like that? They're not really gods at all! You heard Ditrina. Some of them starved to death! How can *anyone* pray to something like that?!" Matt demanded, growing increasingly agitated as he spoke.

"I can't answer that for you, Matt," Chris responded. "For now, all I know is that the magic of those so-called *gods*, for lack of a better term, has saved my life more times than I care to remember. Perhaps they're not as bad as Ditrina's making them out to be? You know the elves hold a grudge against the crisis, still," Chris told him.

"I'm taking a page from Cassy's book. I need some time to think," Matt said before departing to the balcony.

"Why is...everyone mad?" Eve rasped fearfully.

"Everyone is just a little tense right now, sweetie. Things will be ok," Sarah assured her.

Eve nodded and hoped that this had nothing to do with the strange people Echo kept smelling because, at that moment, he warned her of their presence once again. Eve debated saying something but decided that everyone was already angry enough. She decided it was probably just more elves she hadn't met yet and pushed it from her mind.

"You know, I think Ditrina may have mentioned the whole gods-feeding-on-our-worship thing before," Sarah said after nearly an hour of sitting in silence.

"What? When?" Chris asked.

"It was right after I met her. You all were incapacitated, and I was talking to her about what was wrong with Matt. I think she might have said something about the gods feeding on our worship, but I didn't put much thought behind it. After all, what else are the gods supposed to do with it? It sorta just made sense," Sarah admitted.

"I wouldn't go saying that around Matt," Chris warned her.

"Who are...the gods?" Eve rasped curiously.

"Do you not know the ten?" Chris asked in surprise.

Eve shook her head.

"I know...Yorken," Eve replied proudly.

"Well that makes sense, most villages pray to Yorken. He is the god of the harvest, after all," Chris mused.

"Do you want us to tell you the names of the other gods?" Sarah asked her.

Eve nodded eagerly, and half of her face lit up with excitement.

"Well, to start, there's Balgast, god of soldiers and battles. He protects the good soldiers as they fight," Sarah told her.

"Of course you would start with him," Chris chuckled.

"What? He's important!" Sarah argued.

"Who...else?!" Eve rasped excitedly.

"Well, there's Fienox, she guides souls from the physical realm to the astral realm after they die," Chris told her.

"You already know Yorken. He watches over farmers and ensures they have a good harvest," Sarah added. "Along with him, there's Hikara. She's the goddess of extravagance and plenty."

"Then there's Migol. Migol is the god of nature, and he protects the wild places all across Targoth. Sometimes he's called the father of all because it's said he created all the wild beasts," Chris told her.

"Like Echo?" Eve croaked.

"Not exactly," Chris told her. "I'll get back to Echo."

"Those are the five good gods, but they each have an opposite. The five evil gods rule over Targoth as well, and it's important to pray to them, too, so they stay away," Sarah told her.

"First there's Gorgana, the goddess of war. She spreads chaos and violence wherever she goes. It's important to always pray to her so that she'll stay far, far away," Chris explained.

"Next there's Gith. Gith is the god of torment and rules over hell. He takes the souls of the wicked from the astral realm and punishes them forever," Sarah said.

"Why?" Eve asked curiously.

"Because, if you're a bad person in life, you have to pay for that after you're dead," Sarah cautioned. "That's why it's important to be as good as a person as you can be so Gith won't take you," she explained.

Eve nodded earnestly.

"Gith and Gorgana aren't the only dark gods though. There's also Vielven, Niles, and Jainaka," Chris told her. "Vielven is the god of calamity. He causes natural disasters and tragedies. Then there's Niles. He's the god of poverty and greed. It is said that Hikara and Niles are in a never-ending cycle of balance. Together they stop anyone from becoming too rich or too poor."

"In theory," Sarah muttered.

"Who is...Jainaka?" Eve rasped.

"Jainaka is something of an oddity. Unlike the other gods, she isn't inherently good or evil, though most consider her to be a dark god," Chris began. "Much like how Migol created the wild creatures and watches over the wild places, Jainaka is said to have created the monsters and seeks to protect them. She and Migol share the duty of protecting the wilds, with each tending to their own creations," Chris told her.

"Echo?" Eve croaked hopefully.

"Yes, Jainaka created the dragons," Chris told her happily.

"You don't know that," Matt muttered as he entered the room.

"What do you mean?" Chris asked, surprised Matt had returned without warning.

"It's most likely all bullshit," Matt snarled.

"Matt, what the hell's gotten into you?" Chris demanded.

"You heard Ditrina! It's all a lie! The gods, the stories, all of it! Why bother teaching her something that's not true?" Matt asked angrily.

"Matt, this morning you believed these stories wholeheartedly!" Sarah argued.

"That was before the great and all-knowing Ditrina decided to enlighten me with her elvish wisdom!" Matt mocked.

He turned and stormed back out to the balcony. Chris looked at Sarah in confusion.

"I'm gonna go talk to him," Chris told her and walked outside to where Matt sulked.

"Matt, talk to me," Chris said softly as he stood by his friend's side.

"How many times have I healed you with my magic?" Matt asked quietly.

"More than I care to remember," Chris told him. "Earlier today, in fact."

"Every time I used magic to save you, or one of the others, I was convinced that I was enacting the will of the gods; that their intention was for you to live and continue to do good in this life. I was *so* sure that I was their tool, that they worked their will through me and that I was doing the right thing. The more I learn, the more I see, each time I use my magic, I become more and more sure that I was wrong. The gods don't care what I use my power for so long as they get fed," Matt said, his voice barely more than a whisper.

"How long has this been troubling you, Matt?" Chris asked. "This can't all be from what Ditrina told you in there."

Matt sighed.

"Remember that night when Sarah almost killed you?" Matt asked.

"How could I forget?" Chris chuckled, looking at the large scar on both sides of his wrist.

"That night I cast a dark spell, one that falls under the domain of Gith. Ge showed it to me in the book, and I panicked and cast it when I couldn't think of any other way to save you. The problem is, I shouldn't have been able to cast that spell. A spell like that should be reserved for a cleric of Gith's order and should be impossible for anyone else to cast. They teach us that the only spells a cleric can cast are those of their god, with the exclusion of very minor cantrips like I usually cast. After I cast that spell, I got curious and started testing out what else I can cast. While nothing I've been able to cast has been very powerful, I've learned that I am not bound by the laws the temples taught me. Anybody with power can cast any spell they like. The gods have nothing to do with it," Matt said pitifully.

"I hardly think that's proof that the gods are false," Chris argued.

"You don't get it! It's not that the gods aren't real; it's that they aren't gods! They don't have spheres of influence. Gith isn't some god of hell, and Yorken isn't the god of harvest! They're just these beings who have set themselves up as deities, and we blindly worship them!" Matt yelled.

"Even if that's true, so what? They get fed, you get power, and everyone wins!" Chris argued.

"How can you say that?! I've spent all nineteen years of my life praying devoutly to those *things* every single day, begging for magic to use! Now I learn that all I've been doing is filling their bellies. Billions of people pray to the gods every second of every day. If this worship really is their food *and* their power, then they should have more than enough to spare. With that in mind, explain to me why when I ask for just a little more power than they gave me, they were going to let me die! I was fighting to save my friends, who also pray devoutly to the gods, may I add, and they were willing to just let us all die!" Matt screamed.

"Purevein," Chris said softly, remembering the disastrous fight in the mine when Matt had almost died from using too much magic while they fought a hoard of monsters.

"Oh, but it gets better," Matt ranted. "They've stopped answering me!"

"What?" Chris asked perplexed.

"After thinking about all of this and listening to what Ditrina told me in there, I came out here to pray. Instead of begging for power like I usually do, I issued a challenge. I demanded that the gods answer me, that they deny these claims made against them, and they prove to me my faith hasn't been misplaced. They answered Eve, after all, why shouldn't they answer one of their clerics?! Do you know the response I got? *Nothing.* They said nothing, but they heard me. Do you know how I know? Because I felt my magic abandon me. The connection I've had with the gods since I was six years old, the thing that makes me a cleric, is gone," Matt snarled.

"Your magic is gone?" Chris asked in shock.

"Luminita," Matt said and held out his hand.

Rather than the glowing ball of sunlight Chris had come to expect when Matt cast that simple spell, he saw nothing. No glow, not even a flicker of light.

"Do you see? The *gods* have finally decided that I'm no longer fit to be a cleric. My prayers will be just as ignored as everyone else's, and I will be unable to use my magic," Matt said in defeat. "I'm not the godless cleric anymore," he laughed sadly. "I'm nobody."

CHAPTER EIGHT

"It can't be as bad as you're making it out to be," Sarah told him once Chris coaxed Matt back inside to share the bad news.

"What do you mean? I can't cast spells anymore, and I can't heal you guys because of it!" Matt yelled.

Sarah shrugged.

"I've never had any magic before, and I've done just fine," she told him.

"That's because you're proficient in removing people's limbs with big sharp sticks! I don't share your talent!" Matt snarled.

"Unless you want me to demonstrate my talent, watch your mouth," Sarah warned. "I still say you're making too big a deal out of this."

"I agree with Matt on this one. Losing his magic is a pretty big deal, and I say that we find a way to get it back as soon as possible," Chris said.

"Impossible," Matt said firmly.

"How so?" Chris asked.

"The only way for a human to use magic is through a god, and that option is closed to me. I'll never be able to use magic again," Matt said quietly.

"Well, what if you apologized to the gods? Maybe they'll forgive you?" Sarah proposed.

"Even if that would work, which it wouldn't, I couldn't do it. I'm never praying to those *things* ever again," Matt said with a tiny shudder.

"We should talk to Ditrina about this. Maybe there's another way for you to use magic that we don't know about?" Chris asked hopefully.

"I will...find her," Eve rasped happily and slid off Sarah's lap, with Echo hopping off the back of the chair and onto her shoulder.

"It's all right, Eve; you don't have to go looking for anyone," Matt said with a small, sad smile.

"I want...to help," Eve declared. "You...are sad. Aunt Di...can help."

With that, Eve walked across the room to the door Ditrina had escorted Cassy through earlier and peeked inside. She stood there for almost a full minute without saying a word, but Chris could see she was confused about something.

"They're...wrestling," Eve rasped eventually.

"What are you talking about, little one?" Matt asked curiously.

"It looks...like wrestling...but not..." Eve said with confusion, trailing off due to her uncertainty.

"What?!" Matt yelled as he sprinted toward Eve.

As soon as he reached her, he clamped a hand over her eyes and pulled her away from the door, Echo squawking in protest.

"Let...go!" Eve protested as she tried to squirm out of his grasp.

"No! This isn't for you!" Matt said immediately as he maneuvered her farther away from the door.

"Matt, what the hell is going on over there?" Sarah asked suspiciously.

"Nothing! Nothing at all!" Matt said hastily, though Sarah saw that he himself had yet to leave the doorway and was staring intently at something.

Sarah stood up and walked over to the doorway. Her eyes widened, and she wheeled around to fix Matt with a look of disgust.

"You're a pig," Sarah snarled.

"I'm distraught!" Matt said quickly. "You were right, Ditrina's cheering me up already!"

Sarah pulled Eve from his grasp.

"Go explain that to Ditrina then," Sarah said and shoved him through the doorway, slamming it behind him.

Chris heard nothing for several seconds as Sarah led Eve back to the table, hushing her eager questions until a shrill scream echoed from behind the door followed by a dull boom that shook it on its hinges. The seconds dragged out, and they heard several smaller explosions go off until the door opened releasing a cloud of smoke. A soot-stained Matt stumbled out.

"What have we learned, Matt?" Sarah asked happily.

Matt looked at Chris with a stupid grin.

"Worth it," he mumbled before falling on his face.

Ditrina and Cassy, looking to have dressed hastily, raced into the room.

"What the hell?!" Cassy demanded.

"I…have questions," Eve rasped.

"No, you don't!" Sarah said quickly.

"I'm just going to pretend that I don't know what the hell just happened and try to get…*this* out of my head," Chris said, gesturing vaguely at his assembled friends.

"Which one of you two screamed? That sounded pathetic," Sarah said with a laugh.

"That was Matthew," Ditrina confirmed.

"Of course it was," Sarah chuckled.

"Why did you push him inside?!" Cassy demanded.

"So Ditrina would blow him up," Sarah told her like it should have been obvious.

"I nearly killed him before I recognized him as a friend. That was unwise," Ditrina said simply.

"Why were you guys doing peeking inside our room anyway?" Cassy asked angrily.

"I was…looking for…Aunt Di," Eve croaked.

Cassy looked horrified.

"She saw?" Cassy asked with terror.

"I…have questions," Eve repeated with a cough.

"Oh gods, she saw!" Cassy wailed.

"I have…questions!" Eve repeated for the third time, irritated by being ignored.

"No, you don't!" Cassy and Sarah screamed at the same time, horror written across their faces.

"Can we please try to focus on Matt?!" Chris yelled.

"I did not hit him that hard," Ditrina told him.

"That's not what I'm talking about," Chris said with exasperation. "Matt's lost his magic."

"What?" Ditrina asked with mild surprise.

"Your little comments about the gods shook him bad enough he had a crisis of faith. He challenged the gods and demanded an answer. As a result, the gods severed their connection to him, and he lost his magic," Chris explained quickly.

"That is wonderful!" Ditrina exclaimed. "He has finally freed himself from those parasites."

"How can you say that? He's lost his ability to use magic!" Chris yelled.

"True, but he is also free now. He is no longer beholden to the gods for anything," Ditrina told him.

Matt groaned from the floor.

"Wake up," Cassy said, giving him a small kick with a clawed foot.

"I don't want to," Matt mumbled into the floor.

"Matt, get up so we can talk about your magic," Chris ordered.

With a moan, Matt pulled himself into a sitting position and did his best to wipe the soot off of his face.

"What's there to talk about? I had magic, now I don't. End of story," Matt spat.

"See? Nothing to concern yourself over," Ditrina told them.

"I hate to bring it up, but what *can* you do, Matt? Other than magic and looking at things that aren't any of your business, I mean," Cassy asked angrily.

"Well, I can read some of the older languages used in the holy books, maintain a library…oh, and I'm not too bad at scribe work," Matt said, listing off his skills.

"What about useful things? Like, can you use any weapons?" Sarah asked.

"No, why would I? I've always fought with magic," Matt said irritably.

"What else? Can you cook?" Chris asked.

"I mean, I've made my fair share of meals as I've traveled but nothing worth writing home over," Matt admitted.

"So, you cannot fight, and there is nothing useful you can do that would benefit our group," Ditrina summarized.

"That's a rather blunt way of putting it, but yeah," Matt said angrily.

"Don't get the wrong idea, Matt; we're not about to ditch you or anything, but we're just trying to figure out what you can still provide without your magic," Chris told him.

Matt was silent. He looked lost in thought.

"Don't worry, Matt; we'll find something for you to do," Sarah said, trying to cheer him up.

"I'm not a fighter," Matt said quietly.

"So, what?" Chris asked.

"So, everyone else here is! Ditrina can burn things to ash with her magic; Sarah's a walking armory; you have your magic sword; Cassy's an expert marksman. Hell, even Eve can fight pretty well with Echo backing her up! When I *had* my powers, I could keep up with you all, but even then, just barely. Maybe it's time for me to give up all this adventuring nonsense and just settle down. I could watch Eve while you're away on missions and teach her to read and write. The only things I'm any good at besides magic are scholarly pursuits, and I doubt that those'll help me on the battlefield. I think it may be time for me to be done," Matt said slowly.

"Matt, you can't be serious!" Chris exclaimed.

"Of course, I'm serious! You all just pointed out how useless as an adventurer I'd be without my magic, and frankly, you're right! All I would do is slow you down. At least as Eve's tutor, I can still earn my keep," Matt told him.

Chris readied himself to argue further, but then Sarah spoke.

"He's right," she said simply.

She looked at Matt.

"Not trying to insult you or anything, but you're right. You're likely to get hurt if you travel with us. We would have to take the time to watch after you to try to keep you safe, which, in turn, would distract us from our fights. It's safer for everyone if you remain behind," Sarah said quietly.

"I can't believe you're encouraging this!" Chris yelled.

"Think, Chris! Matt could get seriously hurt or worse if he travels with us. Do you think he could have survived that dragon fight without his magic? Do you think we would have survived if we had been worrying about watching Matt the entire time?" Sarah demanded.

Chris said nothing but looked angry.

"Listen, Chris, I don't like losing our healer either. From a tactical perspective, it puts us at a disadvantage, and on top of that, I've grown to enjoy Matt's company, but it's just not safe for him to stay with us. At least, this way, Eve can get a proper education, and it gives her a familiar face to play with while we're away," Sarah told him.

Matt finally stood up from the floor.

"I'm going to wash this stuff off me. Call me when it's time for dinner. Let's get this trip over with so I can go home," Matt said, before wandering off in search of a place to clean up.

Chris slumped back into his chair, and Sarah sat beside him.

"It'll be all right, Chris. Matt just needs some time to get used to this. It's better for everyone if he's not in danger for a little while," Sarah told him.

Ditrina turned to look at Eve.

"Are you excited? You are going to get a proper education!" she said cheerfully, trying to lighten the mood.

Eve frowned.

"I still...have questions," she rasped in frustration.

An elf fetched them from Ditrina's suite a little while later for dinner. Matt reappeared, having cleaned the last of the soot off his face and changing into a fresh set of robes after their travel bags appeared in the common room—courtesy of elven magic. They each wore the nicest of the clothes they'd brought, and to Chris's shock, Sarah elected to wear a dress.

"Are you feeling all right?" he asked her as she reappeared, having changed.

"Uggg, getting Eve into a dress was harder than I expected. She's totally fixed on bringing Echo to dinner. I don't know how to stop her! That little monster keeps trying to bite me whenever I separate them, and I'm not talking about the dragon!" Sarah grumbled.

"I'm not talking about that! You're wearing a dress! What gives?!" Chris asked in shock.

"Does it look all right?" Sarah asked nervously. "I'm not sure how the blue suits me."

"It looks great, but Sarah…" Chris trailed off, unsure of what to say.

"What's the problem, Chris?" Sarah asked, bemused.

"You're wearing a dress!" he said again as if stuck on repeat.

"Ditrina! I think something's wrong with Chris!" Sarah called down the hall.

"No! It's just, you never wear dresses; in fact, I think this is the first time I've seen you in one!" Chris explained.

"What, did you think I was going to wear my armor to dinner with the King?" Sarah asked with amusement.

"Well, you wore your armor to our wedding, so yeah, a little," Chris admitted.

Sarah only laughed.

"What is wrong with Chris?" Ditrina asked as she raced down the hall.

"False alarm. He's just an idiot," Sarah said still laughing.

"Well, we knew that. It hardly warrants an alarm," Ditrina told her.

Sarah continued to laugh.

"What happened to '*Christian Shearcliff himself*'?" Chris asked irritably.

"You are a good leader, but as Cas puts it, you are an imbecile at times," Ditrina told him.

Chris raised an eyebrow.

"Cas called me an imbecile?" Chris asked skeptically.

"Well, actually, she used a different word, but I do not feel comfortable repeating it," Ditrina admitted.

"That's more like her," Chris said with a satisfied nod.

Matt appeared leading an irritated-looking Eve shoved into a small yellow dress. Her dagger was clutched tightly to her chest, and Echo sat atop his usual perch.

"No weapons, Eve," Sarah chided.

"I...want it," Eve rasped angrily.

"You can have it back once dinner's over, but for now, leave it here," Sarah ordered. "Nobody gets to bring weapons to dinner."

"Now you know how I feel," Chris muttered, thinking of how many times he had had this conversation with none other than Sarah herself.

Cassy poked her head out of a door down the hallway.

"Is all this really necessary, Di?" she asked with exasperation.

"Yes," Ditrina replied firmly.

"I feel silly," Cassy called back.

"Stop yelling from down the hall and get out here!" Sarah bellowed.

Cassy meekly stepped into the hall. Chris let out a low whistle.

"I don't think I've seen you wear something that...concealing in a while Cas," Chris laughed.

"Shut up! I can barely move," Cassy hissed as she teetered down the hall.

She was wearing a massive hoop skirt and was adorned with so much jewelry that she looked tired just carrying it all. Dozens of necklaces pulled her forward, and she had several rings on each finger. A massive gold belt that looked to weigh several pounds was draped around her hips.

"What's with the getup?" Sarah asked Ditrina.

"She is my consort; as such, she must look the part," Ditrina told her.

"She looks ridiculous," Sarah told her. "Have you ever attended a court function before?"

"Well, not really. My father usually let me stay here for all the boring official stuff. The few things I have been to have taught me that the more important you are, the more jewelry you wear," Ditrina told her.

Sarah sighed.

"So, naturally, you forced her to wear every piece of jewelry you could get your little green hands on," Sarah summarized.

"Exactly," Ditrina said proudly.

"Cassy, get back in the changing room. Let's get you something that doesn't make you look like a walking treasury," Sarah ordered as she led her back down the hall.

For the next several minutes they heard Sarah barking orders to Cassy as she had her try on other clothes, punctuated by Sarah occasionally yelling:

"That doesn't belong to you; get that necklace out of your bag!" followed by Cassy's indignant protests and claims of innocence.

"She does know those were all mine, right? Cas can have whatever she likes," Ditrina said with confusion.

"Be quiet, or else she'll walk out with half the city's gold in her bag," Chris chastised.

"Well, she could; she is a Gel," Ditrina said, not understanding.

"Just because she can doesn't mean she should," Chris said, confused he needed to explain this.

Echo began screaming from Eve's shoulder, and she hushed him quickly.

"He can eat soon," Ditrina said quickly, taking a step away from the tiny dragon.

Eve nodded and thought to herself that perhaps she should say something about the strange people Echo kept smelling when her mother reappeared with her aunt.

"There, much better," Sarah declared, leading Cassy out before them once more.

Chris had to agree she had changed for the better. The gaudy hoop skirt had been replaced with a slim, green dress that shimmered like liquid as she moved, and it matched the scales on her arms. The only jewelry she wore was a gold armband wrapping around her upper arm, standing out against her dark skin, and a single necklace.

"How will people know she is my consort with so little jewelry?" Ditrina asked, perplexed.

"I've been trying to tell you, that's not how it works, Di," Cassy said with annoyance etched across her face.

"Besides, she's the only naga in the entire city. People will recognize her," Matt said with slight amusement.

"I still can't believe you were watching us, Matt," Cassy said with disgust.

"Well, I can't believe you let my daughter murder someone. Get over it," Sarah growled as they began walking toward the banquet hall, following their elven escort.

"You're still mad about that?" Cassy asked in shock.

"Mad? No, I'm far beyond mad. I'm so beyond mad, that if you weren't Chris's sister, I would have chopped you into pieces days ago," Sarah told her.

"Please, do not do that. I like Cas in one piece," Ditrina said in alarm.

"Oh, don't worry, I know *exactly* how you like Cassy," Matt said with a vile grin.

He suddenly found himself bouncing off a nearby wall, courtesy of none other than Cassy herself.

"Shut up! Eve's right here!" she yelled.

"It's a bit late to act concerned for Eve's innocence, Cassy. You let her kill a man then play with his corpse," Sarah said irritably as she pulled her off Matt. "At least Matt had the decency to shield what innocence Eve has left when he saw her watching you do gods knows what to Ditrina."

"I know what," Matt snickered.

"And Sarah did push him inside. It is not completely his fault, after all," Ditrina commented, much to Cassy's horror.

"See! I'm a saint!" Matt yelled. "Besides, if you should be mad at anyone, you should be mad at Eve. She was the one who watched the longest. I only saw a few seconds. I'm actually a bit jealous," Matt said cheekily.

"At least Eve has no idea what she was looking at," Cassy said with a shudder.

"Wrestling," Eve rasped.

"That's right, Eve; we were wrestling," Cassy assured her.

"Aunt Di...was winning," Eve added with a croak.

"Please, stop talking about this. I'm trying *very* hard to get the image of Ditrina defiling my sister out of my head, but you guys are making it so, so difficult," Chris moaned.

"Funny, because I'm trying to see *more* of Ditrina defiling your sister," Matt said with an evil grin.

"Dude!" Chris exclaimed in disgust.

"What? She's not *my* sister," Matt told him.

"Enough is enough. Shut up, Matt," Sarah told him.

"But...my questions!" Eve croaked pitifully.

"Don't worry, Eve, as your private tutor, I'll answer *all* your questions," Matt said with a savage smile directed at Sarah.

"Sooo, should I kill him now...or do you want me to wait so we can take turns beating him to death with his own arms?" Sarah asked Chris.

"Dibs on his left arm," Chris told her.

"I didn't think it was possible, but somehow Matt's *more* of an asshole when he's upset!" Cassy exclaimed.

"I'm not upset, I'm just a victim of unfortunate circumstance!" Matt said with a forced laugh.

"Echo smells...despair," Eve croaked.

"Echo is confused," Matt told her.

Eve shook her head.

"He is...showing me. You are...in pain," Eve said, looking at Matt strangely.

"As I said, he's confused," Matt said, turning away from Eve.

Eve launched herself at Matt's legs without warning and wrapped him in a tight hug.

"Don't...be sad. We...all love you...so...don't be sad...Uncle S," Eve said in her horrific voice, giving him the biggest smile half her scarred face could muster.

Matt gently pulled her off his legs.

"I told you that dragon was confused," Matt said quickly and hurried through the doors into the banquet hall.

"He's...sadder now," Eve said quietly and walked slowly to Chris's side, taking his hand.

The poor elf who had escorted them silently all this time looked between them in a combination of horror and disgust.

"Princess," he began, "we have reached the banquet hall. If you require more assistance, please, I beg you, find another elf," he said before disappearing into thin air.

"I really hope he's getting paid well," Chris muttered to himself.

"Let's just get this over with," Cassy grumbled before following behind Matt.

One by one they proceeded into the banquet hall and saw that the King had yet to arrive despite the table being laden with food. Ditrina seated herself beside the head of the table, which Chris assumed was reserved for the King himself, and Cassy took her place beside Ditrina. Chris sat across from Ditrina and placed Eve beside him. Sarah sat on Eve's other side to ensure she wouldn't do anything too outlandish in front of the King. Matt sat beside Sarah. They waited in silence for several minutes, until with a small pop the King appeared sitting at the head of the table. Still, no one spoke for some time after that.

"You are looking well, Father," Ditrina said after a while.

"Spare me the tedious small talk and tell me why you have come. What was so important that you saw it fit to bring a half-breed and a group of humans into the city?" King Figinoma asked.

"I'm not like them," Cassy said angrily.

"What?" King Figinoma asked with disinterest.

"I'm not like the other naga. Hell, I've never even met another naga! Can you please stop acting like I'm some beast?" Cassy asked impatiently.

"You expect me to believe you've never met one of your kind? I'm sure I don't have to remind you that the only place naga live is in the city of Gishkar, across the desert. Logically, it is the only place you could have come from," the King told her.

"That's not true!" Chris said suddenly.

The King fixed him with his black-eyed gaze.

"Explain," he said simply.

"I found her wandering the woods by my village when we were children. Her scales hadn't grown in yet, so we had no idea what she was. We took her in and raised her. She's my sister," Chris told him.

"Interesting," King Figinoma said. "So, they can be trained to act like civilized beings. I hardly think this qualified a full report, however. A simple letter would have sufficed," the King said, now speaking to Ditrina.

"Cas actually has nothing to do with the reason for my return. I returned to tell you about her," Ditrina said, pointing at Eve.

The King looked at the scarred girl, who was currently reaching up to scratch the chin of the dragon who was perched above her with a boney hand.

"What of her?" King Figinoma asked with mild interest.

"She has been blessed," Matt told him simply.

"Blessed. You mean to tell me a god blessed *her*?" the King asked with disbelief.

"She is producing her own mana, enough to fuel a mind link around the clock with that dragon," Matt explained.

The King grew excited.

"This in unbelievable! She has somehow overcome the curse of the crisis!" King Figinoma exclaimed.

"Which is why I saw the need to bring my niece before you," Ditrina explained.

"Your niece? What relation do you have to this child?" the King asked in shock.

"Her parents were killed in a dragon attack; therefore, Chris and Sarah adopted her after slaying the monster. Cas is Chris's sister, making her the child's aunt. Because of my relationship with Cas, I have become something of an aunt to the child myself," Ditrina told him.

The King said nothing but looked at Eve with renewed interest.

"How much do your companions know about the crisis?" King Figinoma asked eventually.

"I told them all of the important details: how the gods came to this world and forced the people to bow before them, how the elves managed to keep our magic by refusing to negotiate, and why our population is still so low," Ditrina told him.

"And you, cleric, knowing this, you still kneel to them?" the King asked with a small smile.

"Father, were you listening in my room again?" Ditrina demanded.

"I have no idea what you're talking about," King Figinoma said, feigning ignorance.

"Ex-cleric," Matt muttered.

"I see," the King said with a small smile. "Allow me to show you all the curse in a way you can understand, so that you may better see the evil of the gods."

"What do you mean?" Chris asked with curiosity.

To answer, the King waved his hand across the table, causing the air to shimmer.

"Look at Ditrinadoma, and you will see. This spell reveals the aura the curse leaves upon its victims," the King told them.

Sure enough, Ditrina was encased in a dark miasma, slowly twisting around her like a snake crushing its prey.

"That's...unnerving," Chris admitted.

"Usually, this is invisible to mortal eyes, but this spell allows us to view it as if it were a physical substance," the King explained.

"Isn't that cool, Sarah?" Chris asked, still staring at Ditrina.

She did not reply.

"Sarah?" Chris asked looking at his wife.

Sarah sat looking at her hands in stunned silence. Slowly encasing her was a dark cloud, a mirror of Ditrina's own.

"What the hell? Why is Sarah covered in that stuff?" Chris demanded.

"Can it spread?" Matt asked nervously.

Eve played with Echo, oblivious to all that was transpiring.

"Relax, it cannot spread," the King told them. "It seems she is one of the few humans still affected by the curse. This is a rare find. Less than one percent of the human population still suffers from the curse," King Figinoma said with mild interest.

"What does the curse entail again?" Sarah asked quietly.

"It is very simple, it just ensures that the cursed individual can never bear children," Ditrina explained.

Sarah sat very still and said nothing.

"It'll be ok," Chris said quietly, resting his hand in hers.

Again, Sarah said nothing, but she gripped Chris's hand tightly. Chris did his best not to wince, seeing how Sarah's definition of tightly was much more severe than most.

"As for the child," the King began, not seeming to care much for Sarah's distress. "We will study the nature of this blessing and see if it can be replicated. If so, this may be the first step to lifting the curse of the crisis, at least the part that blocks the other race's magic. While not very influential for us elves, it does pave the way for breaking the rest of the curse. You have done well bringing this girl here," the King told Ditrina.

"She will not be harmed, I trust?" Ditrina asked.

"The spells we will use will not injure the girl, though I must ask, what is the nature of her injuries?" King Figinoma inquired.

"Dragon...fire," Eve rasped with a cough.

Realizing they were talking about her, she had begun to pay attention.

"Her voice is horrific, bring her here," the King commanded.

"Why?" Cassy asked with suspicion.

"So I can fix it, you fool. If we are to be studying this girl, we will have to communicate with her, and the way she speaks now simply will not do. Bring her here," King Figinoma repeated with irritation.

Eve didn't wait for one of her family to escort her. When she heard her voice was going to be repaired, she leapt up and sprinted toward the King, Echo barely managing to latch onto her shoulder to avoid being left behind.

"Stand still," the King commanded as he placed his hands on the sides of Eve's head.

Echo grew excited as a glowing nimbus of light encased Eve. Nothing happened for a time, with the King simply holding her in place as Echo began to scream. Eve stood perfectly still. The King sat back with a sigh, and the glow that encased Eve faded.

"The damage was more severe than I had anticipated; however, her voice should be repaired," the King told them.

"Mother! Mother, he fixed my voice! Can you hear it? He fixed my voice!" Eve yelled happily.

Her once harsh voice had softened, though one could hardly call it pretty. Rather than the horrid rasp that she had once possessed, her voice now sounded more like she was recovering from a cold, like a sore throat she couldn't escape from. Still, it was a vast improvement over the old, and Eve was happy with the progress.

"There was too much scar tissue that could not be healed; however, this should make communication much easier," King Figinoma said. "Now, come here, girl, and I'll see what I can do about that horrific face of yours. Perhaps I can hide some of the damage with an illusion..." he began but was quickly drowned out.

Echo was screaming louder than ever, flapping his wings madly while shrieking into the air. Despite Eve's best attempts to silence him, he seemed intent on carrying on in this fashion.

"Will you silence your beast?" the King asked angrily.

"He's still angry about the strange people!" Eve said as she wrestled with her dragon, trying in vain to calm him.

"Strange people?" Chris asked in confusion.

"He's been smelling strange people ever since the forest! I keep telling him it's just elves we haven't met yet, but he won't settle down!" Eve complained as she tried to soothe him.

"There were no other elves outside the city when you arrived. Does he still smell these people now?" the King demanded.

"Yes! And he won't settle down!" Eve yelled as she managed to clamp Echo's mouth shut, cutting off his shrill shrieks.

"Intruders! Intruders in the palace!" the King bellowed, but it was too late.

Around the edges of the room the air rippled, and figures that had once been hidden came into view. There were eight of them in total, each standing around nine feet tall. They resembled snakes that had somehow grown long, muscular human limbs. Their hands were enormous and sported talons that made Cassy's look downright pathetic, and their feet were just as massive. They wore very little—what looked to be a leather kilt around their waist and a harness across an otherwise bare chest, though their thick scales and rippling muscles looked as if they would provide fair armor on their own. Despite their snake-like appearance, they lacked tails, though their necks were longer than one would expect and sported large cobra-like hoods. Though their claws were impressive in their own right, they carried massive, curved swords, easily six feet long.

One creature stood out, wearing strange priest-like hooded robes and carrying no weapons they could see. While most of the creature's scales were shades of green, this one's were dark blue.

"Take them!" the robed creature yelled, his voice a rasping hiss.

The creatures sprang forward, reaching for them with outstretched talons. Sarah didn't hesitate and produced a dagger from somewhere under her dress, springing toward the nearest assailant. Chris was well aware of Sarah's superb speed and near superhuman strength. He had no doubt that she would dispatch her target with ease, despite its size, which is why he was so horrified when the creature's hand flashed out faster than he could track and gripped Sarah by the neck. Before she had a chance to bring her dagger to bear, the creature flipped her though the air and slammed her into the ground. When it lifted her again, her body was limp, and her dagger clattered to the floor.

"Sarah!" Chris yelled as he snatched a knife off the table, moving to defend his wife, but the creatures were too fast.

Before Chris had a chance to make it from his chair, Matt was snatched up by another one of the monsters, hoisted into the air and bitten on his side. As it turned out, the creatures had fangs like a snake as well, and as soon as they sunk into Matt, he screamed and fell still. One of the creatures made the mistake of reaching toward Ditrina because in an instant it was reduced to a smoldering pile of ash.

"Get the elf!" the robed one hissed, and several creatures lunged toward her.

None made it. With an angry hiss, the robed creature reached out and grabbed the two monsters that held Sarah and Matt. Only one creature stood away from the group, and it hurried toward them.

"Get back here!" Cassy screamed as she hurdled herself toward the lone creature, hoping to take a prisoner of her own.

To her shock, the creature stopped dead in its tracks, and she smashed into it. The robed creature's eyes widened when it saw Cassy and realized what she was. Before her captured creature could escape, the robed figure disappeared, along with its companions.

Matt and Sarah vanished with them.

CHAPTER NINE

"What the hell just happened?" Chris screamed as he raced toward his sister, who was still straddling her captured creature.

"I have no idea!" Cassy yelled. "What are you? Why did you attack us? Where are my friends?!" Cassy yelled at the creature.

"It's a naga! You brought these things into my city!" the King bellowed as he reappeared holding Eve.

As soon as the battle had begun, he had snatched the girl and teleported to safety.

"How can this thing be a naga? It looks nothing like me!" Cassy yelled.

She hauled the creature to its feet.

"What are you?" she demanded.

"I am yours to command, Mistress," the creature replied, placing a clawed fist over its heart.

"What the hell are you talking about?!" Cassy screamed.

"You ordered me to remain, and I lack orders at the time. I am yours to command," the creature replied.

"These are naga slavers; they must have slipped through the barrier when you entered the city! You planned this!" King Figinoma yelled, pointing a finger at Cassy.

"She had nothing to do with this!" Ditrina yelled at the King.

"Where is Mother? Where is Uncle S?" Eve asked, looking around nervously.

"Where did you take them?!" Cassy screamed, shaking her prisoner.

"Back to the city, of course. Mistress Tinacee desired an elf as a house slave and sent us here to acquire one. We went to the palace to find an elven princess to please her, but we were unaware that this was your hunting ground. Please, forgive us," the creature told her.

"Where is my wife?!" Chris yelled.

The creature ignored him.

"Well, where is she?" Cassy demanded.

"I have already told you; the slaves we took have been brought back to the city," the creature explained like it should have been obvious.

"What city?" Cassy asked.

"He is referring to the naga city, Gishkar, across the desert," Ditrina explained.

"Mistress, have you forgotten your homeland?" the creature asked in disbelief. "Have the elves worked their foul magic on you?!" he asked with alarm and bared his claws.

"I'm not like you monsters," Cassy hissed firmly. "I am no one's prisoner, and nobody has *worked magic on me,* as you put it."

Ditrina did something unexpected. She reached out, gripped the naga by the arm and disappeared. Before they had a chance to wonder where she had taken him she reappeared, this time alone.

"Where did you take him?" Chris asked quickly.

"I moved him into a cell down in the dungeons so that we may speak in private," Ditrina told them.

"Why? How's he going to tell us how to get Sarah and Matt back if he's down in a cell?" Cassy asked angrily.

"Ditrinadoma's actions make sense. It seems there is some level of confusion surrounding you in this creature's head," the King told Cassy.

"What do you mean?" Cassy asked in confusion.

"Male naga are completely subservient to the females within their society. When the slaver party saw that you were here, they likely feared that they had somehow interrupted something important and fled with their captives. You gave an order to that one, telling it to come to you.

147

Because of that, when the others fled, it remained. It likely believes that you have captured it from its old master, making it obedient to you. Females stealing males from one another is not that uncommon among the naga," Ditrina explained.

"So, what? This thing is going to follow me around now?! I don't want that monster anywhere near me!" Cassy said angrily. "Why does it look like that?"

"Male and female naga have very different physical structures. The naga were created by combining snakes and humans. Female naga tend to appear more human while the males more like snakes," Ditrina explained.

"Great, so why did you take it away? We still have questions for it!" Chris yelled.

"Where did they go?" Eve repeated quietly.

"If the male naga believes that Cas is an enemy, it will clam up and say nothing. I believe that we can convince him that Cas is in charge and that we are her slaves so it will lead us to the city so that we may rescue Matt and Sarah," Ditrina proposed.

"Hold on, who said anything about you going anywhere? I will not permit my daughter to go to that savage city!" the King yelled in outrage.

"I am not asking. My friends are in danger, and I will rescue them," Ditrina said firmly. "They are Gel. This attack cannot go unanswered."

"The lives of two humans are hardly worth the life of my daughter! I forbid you to go after them!" the King yelled.

"I named them my champions, and as such, they have been given all the rights that go along with that. Would you ignore this attack if elves had been taken prisoner?" Ditrina demanded.

"They may bear the title of Gel, but do not deceive yourself into thinking they share the same importance! They are outsiders!" the King bellowed.

"They are my family!" Ditrina screamed back.

"One of them isn't even a Gel by our standards! She is as much of a Rike as you are!" the King yelled.

"If you care so little for the lives of Rikes, then you should not care that I am going after them!" Ditrina told him.

"You are the crown princess! I cannot allow you to endanger yourself in such a way! You have duties to uphold!" the King yelled.

"Just like how I left to explore Targoth, I will leave to save my friends. You do not have the right to hold me here!" Ditrina snarled at him.

"I have every right! As your father and your King, I have the authority to keep you here!" King Figinoma bellowed.

"You may have the authority, but you lack the power," Ditrina said menacingly, smoke beginning to drift from her hands.

She tuned back to Cassy.

"I will bring him back. When I do, we will all play the part of your slaves. Order him to escort you to the city. Once we get there, he may prove useful in navigating the unfamiliar territory," Ditrina told her.

"I will not act like anyone's slave!" the King yelled.

"Then leave," Ditrina said with a hint of malice in her voice, fire now swirling between her fingers.

Chris had never seen Ditrina so determined before—or so angry. Usually, her emotions were hidden behind an unreadable mask or bubbling over in an overt attempt at making them known. This quiet intensity was something new, a side of her he'd never seen before. He found it somewhat frightening. It appeared the King thought much like Chris did because he vanished with a small pop.

"I will bring him now," Ditrina told them before disappearing only to reappear with the naga a moment later.

The naga seemed angry and looked as if it was preparing to attack Ditrina when Cassy spoke.

"What is your name?" she asked irritably, falling into the role of slaver.

The naga paused its plans for vengeance.

"I am called Jasheir, Mistress," he hissed.

"Do you have any idea what you have interrupted here?" Cassy demanded.

"I am sorry, Mistress, I was simply following Mistress Tinacee's orders," Jasheir told her.

"That is no excuse," Cassy yelled. "You interrupted a very important meeting, and worse still, you stole two of my favorite slaves."

Jasheir's eyes widened, and he dropped to a knee.

"We meant no offence, Mistress. Please forgive our transgression," he pleaded.

"Your companions disobeyed my orders to remain, fleeing with my property. Only you proved loyal enough to obey, thus only you will be spared. The other's lives are forfeit," Cassy declared.

"As you command, Mistress, I will serve," Jasheir promised, now groveling at her feet.

"Where is Mother?" Eve yelled angrily.

"Quiet, Eve," Cassy told her.

"Where was she taken?!" Eve shouted.

Echo screamed in rage from her shoulder.

"Your Mistress ordered you to be silent!" Jasheir hissed as he rose suddenly to his feet.

He stalked toward Eve who, to her credit, held her ground against the nine-foot-tall monster, each glaring at the other. Jasheir raised back his clawed hand to strike.

"Halt!" Cassy yelled, her voice echoing around the banquet hall.

Jasheir froze in place.

"As punishment for your transgressions, you will serve as my slave. You are not above those around you and will follow the orders as each of my other slaves as if they were my own. You are nothing," Cassy snarled.

Jasheir fell to his knees once again.

"You are most merciful, Mistress. Semel smiles upon you. Please, tell me your house so that I may spread your name to all the corners of this world!" Jasheir begged.

"Slaves should not address the Mistress directly!" Ditrina yelled. "If you wish to speak, speak to me."

"Who are you?" Jasheir inquired.

"I am Ditrina, most senior among Lady Shearcliff's slaves. If you displease the lady, you will answer to me," Ditrina told him, gesturing to the piles of ash that had once been naga warriors.

"Yes, Ditrina," Jasheir said meekly. "I have never heard of this house Shearcliff before, and the name sounds strange. What is our lady's lineage?"

"Lady Shearcliff's house is new, and her linage is none of your concern. Do not ask questions; simply obey," Ditrina ordered.

"Yes, Ditrina," Jasheir said in his hissing voice.

"Return him to his cell. I do not wish to see this failure more than necessary. We leave for the city in the morning," Cassy said haughtily.

Ditrina nodded and disappeared with Jasheir once more. When she returned, she turned to Cassy.

"I took the role of your head slave to spare you the need to speak, seeing that I know more about the naga culture than you do," Ditrina explained.

"You play the slaver part pretty well," Chris commented.

Cassy rounded on him.

"Don't say that! I'm nothing like those monsters. Don't *ever* say that!" Cassy hissed.

"Relax, sis, I was just impressed by your acting. No need to get upset," Chris told her.

"Where is Mother? Where is Uncle S?!" Eve yelled, thoroughly frustrated from being ignored so long.

"Some bad people took them away. We're going to rescue them," Chris told her.

"I will kill them," Eve said as a statement of fact. "I will kill them all."

"Shouldn't we leave her behind? I don't think it's a good idea to bring her where we're going," Cassy said nervously.

"Echo's sense of smell will prove useful in finding the others. I believe she should come," Ditrina said.

"If it's so useful that Ditrina is backing the dragon, then I agree. Eve should come," Chris said, smiling at his daughter.

"We will save Mother," Eve said firmly. "We will save Uncle S."

"We will leave tomorrow morning; we need time to gather our supplies. This is going to be a dangerous journey," Ditrina told them.

Sarah awoke in a cell. It was a dark, filthy thing. She had barely enough room to stand and not quite enough room to lie down properly. To make matters worse, she felt the presence of another in the cell with her, squishing her against the cold iron bars.

"Oh, good, you're awake. Mind getting off me? I've lost the feeling in my legs," Matt grumbled from beneath her.

"Sorry," Sarah muttered as she shifted her weight off of her hapless friend. "Where are we?"

"Nowhere good," Matt told her. "I woke up a little while ago, but what you see now is all I've had to look at. It's so dark I have no idea what's outside our cell, and nobody's come to check on us."

"Where are Chris and the others?" Sarah asked nervously.

"I don't know," Matt said quietly. "I don't know where *we* are, to be honest."

Sarah fell into a long silence. Neither of them had any idea what had happened, nor did they see a reason to fill the silence with mindless chatter. They had no means of escape, so, for the time being, they concentrated on making themselves comfortable—difficult as that may be.

Suddenly the room was flooded with light when a door behind them opened. Sarah turned in her cell and saw Cassy silhouetted in the doorway.

"Cassy! Good to see you. Get us out of this cell!" Sarah called.

The figure stepped closer, and Sarah realized something was very wrong. Cassy's scales were emerald green; this naga's scales were blood red.

"Who is this Cassy?" the naga asked with mild surprise.

At first glance, she and Cassy had appeared similar, with the same basic body type and smooth caramel skin, but the longer Sarah looked, the more alien this woman appeared. Her scales were red, and her hair brown. Her eyes were cold and uncaring as if she was looking at a bug she had found on the floor.

"Who are you?" Sarah demanded.

"Shock them, Narfus," the naga said, and the robed naga with blue scales from before appeared.

Before Sarah had a chance to protest, Narfus reached out and muttered a prayer, resting his hand on the bars of the cage. Lightning arced from his fingers and electrified the iron bars. Within the cramped cage, Sarah and Matt had nowhere to go, and were forced to writhe and scream until finally, the naga woman said:

"Enough."

Sarah had many choice words she wanted to share with her captors, but at the moment, her body refused to answer her, and she twitched uncontrollably.

"I told you to bring me an elf," the naga woman said to Narfus irritably.

"We tried, Mistress, but the elf's magic proved too much for us to combat. In the end, we were forced to flee with the few humans we had captured," Narfus said, gesturing to Sarah and Matt.

"If I had wanted more humans, I would have sent you to fetch more of those barbaric north-men. These two are useless to me!" the naga woman yelled.

"There is more, Mistress Tinacee!" Narfus said quickly. "There was another female there, though what she was doing I do not know."

"Another female? What was her house?" Tinacee demanded.

"I do not know," Narfus admitted. "It seems that these two were slaves of hers, and the elf also seemed to answer to her. She may be powerful."

"If these two are really her slaves, then I doubt that she will let this be forgotten. She will come for them, or risk looking weak. When she comes, we will take her elf from her. An elf would prove most useful as a house slave," Tinacee mused.

"The elf I saw was an impressive fighter. Perhaps she would be better suited for the arena?" Narfus proposed.

"And risk her dying to some stray arrow? I think not. An elf is far too valuable to risk in that blood sport. These two, however, you may use as you see fit. I have no need for *more* humans in my home," Tinacee said angrily.

"I will bring them to the arena pens. Their sacrifice will bring you glory in the eyes of Semel," Narfus assured her.

"Yes, yes, whatever you say, cleric. Just get them out of my pens. I don't want to waste food feeding them," Tinacee told him.

Narfus smiled, a ghastly sight, revealing his long fangs. He reached out and electrified the cage once more. Sarah fell back into darkness.

"So how long will it take us to return to the city, Jasheir? My elf can get us as far as the desert, but we will be forced to ride from there," Cassy told her prisoner.

They had spent the night in the elven city, leaving Jasheir in his cell. They had awoken early, gathered the supplies Ditrina said would be needed for a trip through the desert, and now stood ready to depart.

"There will be no need to ride, Mistress. We will take a barge to the city. It is only proper," Jasheir told her.

"And once I arrive, where will I find my friends?" Cassy demanded.

"Mistress?" Jasheir asked in confusion.

"My slaves. Where will I find my stolen slaves?" Cassy corrected, silently cursing her breach of character.

"They will likely be working within Lady Tinacee's estate, or they will be fighting in the arena for the glory of Semel," Jasheir told her.

"What currency will the bargemen accept?" Ditrina asked.

"Gold, or slaves, depending on what you have to offer. How many slaves does Mistress Shearcliff own?" Jasheir asked.

"She only has the slaves you see before you. Our lady values quality over quantity," Ditrina explained.

"All the more reason to recover our Mistress's property," Jasheir agreed.

"Di, are you ready to go?" Cassy asked.

"Whenever you want," Ditrina told her.

"Everyone, gather 'round," Cassy commanded.

They formed a circle and linked hands. Echo sat on Eve's shoulder. With the promise of a barge, they decided the horses would just be one more thing to teleport, so they decided to leave them in the stables.

"Has Eve drank her potion yet?" Cassy asked, remembering how the poor girl suffered from teleporting.

"Yes, Aunt Cas," Eve confirmed happily.

She hadn't quite understood the need to act like a slave and was still acting like normal. Jasheir looked at her strangely but said nothing.

"Let's go then," Cassy said.

Ditrina nodded, they spun briefly, and then they were somewhere else, somewhere with sand as far as the eye could see. Heat rose in waves off the ground, and a dry wind shifted the dunes.

"This is the glyph the elves use whenever we send envoys to the naga," Ditrina explained. "Once, there was a prosperous town here."

"You are quite knowledgeable; I see why you are her head slave," Jasheir told her.

"How far from the barge are we?" Cassy asked.

"The river is about a mile north of here," Ditrina told her.

"Gods, it's hot," Chris complained.

"Sand. Lots of sand," Eve said, looking around in amazement.

"Slaves should not make idle chatter," Jasheir hissed.

"You're not in charge of anything," Chris warned him.

"I serve the Mistress, and you are being disrespectful," Jasheir said, drawing his sword. "No human has the right to speak so freely around a naga."

"Let's teach him a lesson," Al said in Chris's head, and Chris was inclined to agree.

"Stand down, Jasheir!" Cassy yelled angrily.

"Yes, Mistress," Jasheir said quickly and lowered his blade.

"Hold on a sec, Cas. We're going to be traveling with this idiot for some time. It would be best if he learns his place quickly," Chris told her.

"Suit yourself," Cassy said with a shrug.

"You dare question the Mistress's orders?" Jasheir said in a combination of rage and disbelief.

"I dare much more than that. Our Mistress is a greedy idiot who's too impulsive for her own good," Chris said as he drew his sword, sending a small wink his sister's way.

Jasheir howled and threw himself at Chris faster than he thought possible, curved sword flashing. Thankfully, Chris's sword decided a creature like Jasheir was perfectly suitable for fighting and burst into flames, moving to intercept Jasheir's blade. They met with a ringing crash, and Jasheir stood stunned, unsure of how the human had stopped the strike from his massive sword.

"What trickery is this?" Jasheir demanded as he swung yet another blow at Chris.

Despite the sword being longer than Chris was tall, he again blocked it with casual distain. Chris flicked his wrist and sent Jasheir's blade spinning through the air, landing in the sand several yards away. Chris didn't wait to see if Jasheir would surrender; rather, he channeled as much magic into his fist as possible and landed a crushing blow under Jasheir's snake-like chin. There was a small explosion, and Jasheir's eyes glazed in his head as he was thrown backward with a thud into the sand.

"Do not forget your place, Jasheir; among those around you, you are by far the least dangerous. Even young Eve could kill you with her dragon if she wished," Cassy told him.

That last part had been a bit of an overstatement, but after seeing the power of the cloaked swordsman with red eyes, Jasheir was in no mood to test her words. Instead, he turned and knelt at Chris's feet.

"Forgive me, Master. I had no right to challenge our Mistress's personal bodyguard, for what else could you be with such skills?" Jasheir told him.

"Oh, get up and drop the gracious servant act. We all see the disgust in your eyes whenever you look at us. We don't like you, and you don't like us. All you have to do is what you're told," Chris said irritably as the red glow faded from his eyes.

"Of course," Jasheir hissed.

He started to stand but felt a weight on his back. Turning his long neck, he saw Echo standing on his shoulders. Snake eye stared into snake eye, each testing the other. Echo let out a low growl, and smoke began rising from between his small jaws.

"He doesn't like you," Eve declared.

"Why should your pet's opinion concern me?" Jasheir asked her irritably.

"Because he's starting to wonder what you taste like, and I'm getting curious myself," Eve told him as she pulled Echo off his back. "But for now, you're useful in finding my mother, so we'll have to wait," she told him as she walked away.

"Was one of the slaves stolen the girl's mother?" Jasheir asked Chris as he stood.

"Yes, my wife," Chris told him.

"Humans are strange, choosing a singular mate," Jasheir said with a shake of his head as he stood.

"Lead the way to the barge. You've humiliated yourself once already today. Don't do it again," Cassy told him.

"Yes, Mistress," Jasheir said reverently as he began hiking north toward the river.

When Sarah awoke again, she was in another cell, but thankfully, it was much larger than the previous one. Just like before, Matt lay in the cell with her, his once white robes soiled with dirt and blood. Sarah looked and saw that her dress has seen better days.

"I see you have awoken," Narfus hissed from outside the cell.

"Let us out of here," Sarah demanded, rising to her feet.

Narfus laughed, which sounded more like a hacking hiss than anything else.

"You will be free of these bars soon enough, but that is not why I am here. Change," he ordered, tossing two shapeless rough-spun tunics into the cell.

Sarah stood defiantly, refusing to move until Narfus's hands crackled with lightning once more. Seeing no reason to get shocked into a stupor again, she reluctantly began to undress under Narfus's watchful gaze. He waited patiently as she pulled on the tunic and pushed the discarded dress aside.

"Are you happy now?" Sarah demanded.

"The ring," Narfus commanded.

"What?" Sarah asked in confusion.

"Give me your ring," Narfus repeated, pointing to Sarah's wedding ring.

"Not happening," Sarah said angrily.

Narfus cast back the cowl of his robe, exposing his face properly.

Like the other male naga Sarah had met, he had a large hood like a cobra, but it seemed he had gotten the edges of his pierced. Dozens of glittering gold and silver earrings lined the edge of his hood, dangling off the edges. She looked closer and recoiled in horror. Not earrings, but rings. Human rings. Wedding bands, signet rings, and many more simple things. They stood as gruesome proof of the number of slaves he had taken.

"It will be a fine addition to my collection," Narfus told her as he stepped inside the cell.

"The only way you're getting this ring is over my dead body," Sarah assured him as she crouched low, readying herself to fight.

"That will not be necessary," Narfus said with a small smile.

Sarah found herself sailing through the air and slammed into the bars of the cell. Narfus had moved so fast she hadn't realized he had attacked her. Before she had a chance to stand, Narfus gripped her by the hand and pinned it to the ground. He produced a wicked looking dagger from within his robe.

"Wait!" Sarah yelled, but it was too late.

With a quick cut, Narfus severed Sarah's left hand at the wrist.

Sarah screamed and clutched at her bleeding stump. Matt was awakened by Sarah's cries and sat up in confusion. Narfus continued to kneel beside her, still clutching her arm, and chanted quietly. A nimbus of light encased the stump, and the skin grew over it quickly.

"We can't have you bleeding to death before your debut in the arena tomorrow, now can we?" Narfus said, hissing laughter.

He turned his attention to Matt.

"Give me that book, then put on the tunic," he commanded.

Matt looked at the book that was still on his hip and at Sarah's severed hand.

"I can't; it's magic," Matt said hastily.

"Fool, I am a cleric of Semel. Do you think you can lie about..." Narfus began, but he trailed off.

"What is that?" he asked softly, sensing the power of the book.

"I didn't lie. It's enchanted," Matt said quickly.

Narfus reached for it but found he couldn't take it from him. He hissed in frustration.

"Give it to me," Narfus commanded, pointing at him with the dagger.

Reluctantly, Matt surrendered the book, and Narfus turned to leave but found he could not. It was as if an invisible barrier held him within the cell.

"It can't be stolen," Matt told him.

"What if I just kill you then?" Narfus asked, turning with the dagger.

"Then it would explode and kill us all!" Matt lied hastily.

Narfus hissed in frustration again and threw the book at Matt, not wanting to test what else the strange artifact could do.

"I will take it from your corpse once you die in the arena," he spat before storming out of the cell, locking them inside.

Narfus took Sarah's hand on the way out, plucking the ring from its finger. Matt hurried to her side.

"Sarah, oh gods, what happened? Are you ok?" Matt asked hastily.

"That bastard!" Sarah screamed. "I'll skin him alive! I swear to the gods, I'll get that ring back!" Sarah bellowed.

"Aren't you hurt?" Matt asked nervously.

"Forget that! That filthy son of a whore stole my ring!" Sarah screamed as she pounded her stump to the ground.

"Easy Sarah, hurting yourself won't help us get out of here! We need a plan to escape!" Matt told her.

Sarah sat up and looked at him.

"We're surrounded by giant monsters that are physically superior to us in every way, and on top of that, some of them have magic. You have no fighting skills to speak of and no magic. I have no weapons and, as of now, one hand. How can you possibly think we have any chance of escape?" Sarah demanded.

"I don't know! I thought you'd have an idea!" Matt yelled.

"Here's one. Try not to die in that arena. Hopefully, we'll get weapons, then maybe we can try something. Until then, sit tight," Sarah told him.

"Do you think the others will come for us?" Matt asked.

"I'm sure they'll try," Sarah sighed.

"I'll try talking with Chris when I'm asleep. I couldn't reach him while we were unconscious. He must have still been awake. I'm not sure how long it's been since we were captured, actually," Matt told her.

Sarah shrugged.

"Hours? Days? Your guess is as good as mine," Sarah admitted.

"Are you sure you're all right?" Matt asked, gesturing to her missing hand.

"His magic stopped the pain. Once we get out of here, I'll have Ditrina bring me to the elves so they can grow me a new hand," Sarah told him.

"Sarah, you know that's not how it works, right? Magic can't just regrow limbs. Once the wound has closed or scarred over, magic can't do a thing, and on top of that, your hand is gone, so they can't reattach it. The elves can't help you," Matt told her.

"Wow, Matt! You should become a counselor! With skills like those, I'm sure you'll be able to cheer entire cities up!" Sarah yelled.

"Listen, I'm just being realistic!" Matt yelled back.

"Leave me be, Matt," Sarah told him and turned away.

Matt looked around the sparse cell and tried to judge the time. Hoping vainly that Chris would be asleep wherever he was, Matt curled up on the stone floor and did his best to doze off.

"Oh, thank the gods you're here!" Chris yelled as Matt appeared in the grey world they used to speak with the brothers.

"I'm not in the mood to thank the gods for anything, but it's good to see you," Matt said happily.

"This really sucks," Mi said as he popped into view.

"I agree the situation is dire," Ge told them as he joined them.

"I'm sure we can think of some way around this," Al said.

"Let's start from the beginning. Where are you guys? Is Sarah all right?" Chris asked quickly.

"We're in a dungeon somewhere, and I'm fine, thanks for asking," Matt said irritably.

"Yes, yes, I guessed that because we're talking! What about Sarah?!" Chris demanded.

"Your wife seems to have lost a hand," Ge said flatly.

"What the hell! What happened?!" Chris yelled.

"She stood up to one of our captors when he decided he wanted her ring. He took the whole hand with it," Matt explained.

"Knowing your wife, she's gonna be pissed," Mi chuckled.

"Really, man? That's what you decide to say right now?!" Chris asked with rage boiling in his eyes.

"Calm down, buddy, just trying to lighten the mood a little," Mi told him.

"Do you know what they want with you?" Chris asked Matt.

"They keep saying something about fighting in an arena. Other than that, we don't know," Matt told him.

"Stay alive. We're coming to get you, but you need to survive," Chris told him.

"We'll do our best. What have you guys done so far?" Matt asked.

"We captured one of the naga that attacked us, and it's convinced that it needs to serve Cas now. It thinks we're all her slaves and is escorting her back to the city. We're on a barge right now floating down the river. We should get there in a couple hours by Jasheir's calculation," Chris told him.

"Who's Jasheir?" Matt asked.

"He's the naga we captured," Al told him. "We kicked the crap out of him."

"You two took down one of those monsters?" Matt asked in shock.

"Yeah, I'm getting better at using magic," Chris said sheepishly.

"Good, use it to get us the hell out of here," Matt told him.

Matt looked like he was going to say more, but suddenly he disappeared.

"Where did he go?" Chris asked quickly.

"It seems his captors have woken him up. I should go," Ge told them and faded from sight.

"This is bad," Chris said to himself.

"I know! If you get yourself killed on this rescue mission, I stand to lose a lot of money!" Mi agreed.

Chris gave him a withering look.

"I should probably go, too—spirit stuff to do and all. Bye!" Mi called before fading as well, leaving Chris alone with Al.

"We will find a way to save your wife, and your friend," Al assured him.

"I can't believe this happened," Chris said quietly.

"Do not despair. Once we reach the city, I'm sure you will see a way to rescue your loved ones. Until then, concentrate on the matter at hand, which is playing the part of the loyal slave," Al reminded him.

"I know. It's just hard to call my sister Mistress," Chris said with a weak laugh.

"I wouldn't have any problems with *that*, if you know what I mean," Mi said, reappearing suddenly wearing a cheesy grin.

"*Really?*" Chris demanded.

"Oh right, I'm hypothetically supposed to be busy. Carry on!" Mi called cheerfully as he vanished again.

"How have you kept your sanity with that one?" Chris asked Al.

"He has his moments. This is not one of them," Al told him.

"I'm just going to rest for a while. We should be able to see the city in a little bit," Chris said and faded from the grey world into a dreamless sleep.

Al sighed, and several seconds later his brothers reappeared.

"Matthew is currently being beaten by his captors, so I have a few moments I can spare," Ge told Al flatly.

"Do your best to keep them alive. If they were to die, I fear for Chris's sanity," Al told him.

"Understood," Ge replied.

"I tried to take his mind off of what was happening, but he didn't seem in the mood," Mi said despondently.

"I know, keep trying whenever you see him. These coming days will be hard on him, and we need to make sure more than his body survives," Al told him.

"I'll do my best," Mi said before fading away.

Al sighed again and settled in to wait until Chris decided to wake up. These days he found he had very little to do.

CHAPTER TEN

"Matt, Matt wake up," Sarah said, gently shaking her friend.

Matt groaned and forced his swollen eyes open.

"Sarah? Wow, you look like shit," Matt muttered, looking at her smashed face.

Two black eyes and a large gash across her forehead proved that Narfus had not been content with simply beating Matt unconscious, rather he had decided to take the time to abuse them both.

"You don't look much better, but you have to get up. I heard one of the guards talking; they're about to shove us into the arena," Sarah told him as she pulled him to his feet.

"After a beating like that, they expect us to fight?!" Matt asked with disbelief. "We'll be killed for sure!"

"I think that was Narfus's point," Sarah said with a grimace. "I don't understand, though. If he wants us to die so badly, why doesn't he just kill us and be done with it?"

"I think it's a religious thing. If he just kills us, then nobody cares; but if we fight in this arena and die, our sacrifices have some sort of significance. On the other hand, if we win, that Tinacee woman gains prestige," Matt told her.

"How does dying in the arena have any significance?" Sarah asked.

"Ask Narfus. Maybe he'll share the tenants of his faith the next time he's beating us to a pulp," Matt said with a small smile.

"Funny, you're funny. I see why Chris keeps you around," Sarah said, rolling her bloodshot eyes.

"Get against the wall," one of their guards commanded as he walked toward the cell.

He was a hulking specimen, with dull brown scales. A multitude of scars across his face and hood proved that he was either tenacious or bad at ducking.

"What's the point of all this? We all know that we can't overpower you," Sarah said angrily as the guard pulled the cell open.

This earned her a backhand from the guard that opened a large gash across her cheek.

"Stay silent," he hissed.

Sarah looked at him with hate-filled eyes but stood silently beside Matt in the back of the cell. They heard clawed footsteps approaching slowly down the corridor. Tinacee stepped into view and stood behind the guard. She looked them over with an appraising eye, taking stock of their wounds.

"Bring them with me," Tinacee commanded, and the guard stepped inside the cell, grabbing them roughly by the arms.

She began walking down the hallway, with the guard dragging them behind her. They passed many cells, some empty, others containing wretched looking souls. A multitude of species looked out at them as they passed, but despite the variety, all the eyes they saw looked the same. They were hollow and seemed to look past them. Silently, Sarah decided that they would either escape or die before they ended up like that.

"In here," Tinacee ordered and pointed to a doorway.

The guard pushed the door open and shoved them through. Sarah was surprised; this seemed to be the way out of the prison. She found herself looking at a long corridor, but this one lacked cells. Tinacee led them farther away from their cells and finally motioned for them to be placed in another room. It was furnished with a comfortable looking sofa and several chairs. The guard released them and stood beside the door while Tinacee reclined on the sofa.

"I find spending too much time in the pens unpleasant. The smell is a bit much," Tinacee told them.

"What do you want with us?" Sarah demanded, earning herself a blow to the back of the head from the guard.

"You are interesting to me. Everything I have heard points toward you being this...*Cassy's* slaves, but you lack discipline. Either Cassy has no idea how to discipline her stock, or you are something else entirely. Sit," Tinacee ordered, pointing at the chairs.

Reluctantly, Sarah and Matt chose seats across from the naga.

"If you are simply slaves, I do not care one way or another what happens to you. Hundreds of slaves die in the arena every day, and you are nothing special. I, however, believe that you are more than slaves. Somehow, you have convinced this *Cassy* that you are her friends based on how you speak about her in such a familiar manner. I want you to tell me everything you know about this Cassy. Who is she? Where did she come from? I have found no record of any female with such a strange name anywhere in the city. I am also interested in how she managed to convince the elves to let her into their city," Tinacee told them.

Sarah thought quickly. If she told this woman about Cassy, they might be spared fighting in the arena. If she could somehow convince her that they were valuable, they may be protected and used as hostages rather than fodder. It wasn't much better than their current situation to be sure, but they were far less likely to be killed. As she was busy planning how to best spin this in their favor, Matt spoke.

"We don't know our Mistress's origin, and we are no more than her humble slaves. We beg that you return us to her," Matt told her.

"Perhaps I have put too much thought into this," Tinacee sighed. "Take them away," she told the guard.

A few seconds later, Sarah and Matt found themselves back in their cell.

"Matt, what the hell?! That was our chance to get out of this mess!" Sarah yelled.

"Clam down. Before Narfus woke me up to beat us senseless, I was talking to Chris," Matt said quickly.

"Why didn't you tell me?" Sarah demanded.

"I didn't get a chance. I was too busy getting dragged off to talk to Tinacee!" Matt shot back. "He told me that they're coming to rescue us and that they're posing as Cassy's slaves. If they get here and we've already told everyone that Cassy isn't really a slaver, how do you think they'll treat her?" Matt asked quietly, fearful of listening ears.

"Fine, I get it. Still, this means that we'll have to survive the arena," Sarah reminded him.

"I think we'll be all right. Even with only one hand, you're a fantastic fighter," Matt told her.

"And how do you plan to stay alive?" Sarah asked him.

"I'll be standing behind the fantastic fighter," Matt said solemnly.

"Look, Mistress, the jewel of Semel, the city of Gishkar!" Jasheir exclaimed, pointing from the front of the barge.

The barge was a large thing, powered by slaves rowing below deck. The bargeman, an aged looking naga male, had given them passage in return for three gold coins each. For many long hours, they had drifted down the river, looking at the palm trees growing on the banks or sitting under tarps to try to avoid the heat of the sun. Cassy had been treated with reverence by the bargeman, while the others were ignored. He had seemed interested in Jasheir at first until he learned his station.

The city itself was a massive thing, seemingly made up of square sandstone houses stacked atop one another, like a giant child had dumped their blocks in a haphazard pile. The largest structure was by far the large arena rising from the center of the city.

"It has been a very long time since our lady has visited the city. You will have to guide her to your old Mistress," Ditrina told him.

"I would be honored," Jasheir told her, bowing deeply.

"I'm just happy we're finally getting off this boat," Chris said.

An afternoon spent drifting down the river had taught him that watercraft was not his preferred method of travel.

"Not as happy as Eve, I bet," Cassy said with a small smile.

They turned and saw the small girl leaning over the edge of the boat, heaving violently. Chris added boats to the list of travel options to avoid with her, right behind teleportation.

"Where is the dragon?" Ditrina asked nervously, not seeing Echo on his usual perch.

Eve looked up from her seasick misery.

"Flying," she said simply before returning to her private hell.

Their eyes turned to the sky, and sure enough, they saw Echo gliding above the stern like a seabird, happily surveying the river with red eyes.

"He's growing fast," Chris said with amazement.

"I'd say he's six inches longer than when he hatched," Cassy agreed. "How fast do dragons grow, Di?"

"Too fast," Ditrina muttered, stepping closer to Cassy.

"Mistress, if I may, I have counsel I wish to give," Jasheir said to Cassy.

"For the gods' sakes, if you have something to say, just spit it out. I'm growing tired of all this groveling," Cassy snapped.

"That is what I wish to speak about. As I have traveled with you, I have realized your relationship with your slaves is…different than most. I am not one to judge your wisdom, but I wish to warn you that many will see this as strange. If you wish to avoid too much attention, then I recommend that you adopt a sterner approach with us when you are inside the city," Jasheir told her.

"I agree, you are acting too much like a friend and not enough like a master," Ditrina warned.

"I'll try harder," Cassy told her.

Jasheir looked at them quizzically.

"Mistress, what will you do once your slaves are returned to you?" he asked.

"I will leave this place as fast as possible," Cassy told him.

"Where will you go? Naga are not welcome in most places to the west, and the only thing to the east is barren desert," Jasheir told her.

"It seems that you haven't gone far enough west yet," Cassy said dismissively.

"Mistress, the barbarians to the west do not practice slavery. How is it you have kept these?" Jasheir asked cautiously, gesturing to those around him.

"That is none of your business!" Ditrina said angrily, but Cassy held up a hand.

"It would be better if he was in on the plan," Cassy told her.

"Are you sure?" Chris asked cautiously.

"I think it'll be ok. He's already suspicious," Cassy told him.

She turned to Jasheir.

"As I'm sure you already suspect, I'm not normal," she began.

"Some of your mannerisms seem strange, and you lack the basic knowledge all naga are taught from birth," Jasheir told her.

"That's because I wasn't raised in this city. This is actually my first time coming here. I was raised by humans far, far away from here. When you attacked the elven city, I saw another naga for the first time. I have no slaves, and I have no house. These three are my family, and I'm looking to get my friends back," Cassy told him.

"How is this possible?" Jasheir demanded.

"I don't know how I ended up on the other side of the world, but that's where I was found. A man named Samuel Cogwell took me in and raised me, just like how he had taken in Chris a few years prior," she said, gesturing to her brother.

"Why do you tell me these things?" Jasheir asked.

"Because you already doubt me. I can see it when you look at me, hear it in your voice. I suspect your plans are to bring me before this Tinacee woman then betray me with the hopes that she will forgive your failure. That is why I have decided to be honest with you. If you decide to betray me, know that we will kill you, but if you help me get my friends back, I will let you go and forgive you for attacking us, to begin with," Cassy told him.

"And if I decide I want nothing to do with you?" Jasheir asked.

"We can't risk you telling others what you know," Chris said.

Jasheir was quiet.

"This place you live, the place with no slaves. What is it like? Who rules?" Jasheir asked.

"It's a place where anyone can make a life for themselves if they are willing to work. Someone like you could easily make a living as a warrior. We are ruled by King Patel, but his influence is fairly weak and doesn't affect how we live our lives," Cassy told him.

"What house do you serve then?" Jasheir asked.

"We have nothing like that. We have rulers, but we are not bound to them," Cassy told him.

"If I help you, will you bring me to this place?" Jasheir asked.

"You want to leave?" Cassy asked with surprise.

"Those who failed to capture an elf are likely dead now. Mistress Tinacee does not tolerate failure. If I return to her, I will likely be killed, so I decided my best chance of survival was to stay as your slave. Now I learn that you are an outsider and seek to leave this place as soon as your business is concluded. Without your protection, I will be forced to return to Tinacee empty-handed, which seals my fate. If in this western land I may survive, then I seek to go there," Jasheir said.

"If you help us rescue our friends, then we will take you with us," Cassy told him.

"What is this land called?" Jasheir asked.

"It's called Desgail, but everyone just calls it the kingdom. We like to keep it simple," Cassy told him, and he nodded.

"If it is possible for me to live in this *kingdom*, then I will help you. If you believe that I can start anew there, then I will come," Jasheir told her.

"There are basically no naga that far west and many people will not recognize you. You will have to be tolerant," Chris warned.

"I will adapt," Jasheir told him.

"Until then, we shall continue to play the part of slaves and master, simply to avoid detection," Cassy told them all.

"Eve still hasn't really gotten with the program yet," Chris warned.

"Do your best to cover for her, then," Cassy said.

Chris nodded and walked over to his daughter, who was currently trying to stop puking, and Jasheir walked off to sit under a tarp, leaving Cassy and Ditrina alone at the bow. Neither spoke for several minutes.

"Is everything ok, Cas?" Ditrina asked without warning.

"What are you talking about, Di? Matt and Sarah are prisoners! Of course I'm not ok with that!" Cassy said angrily.

"I am not talking about that," Ditrina told her.

"Care to explain what you *are* talking about then?" Cassy asked with irritation.

"You do not seem to be doing well. When you are around naga, you are acting like a slaver, and as such, obviously are not yourself, but even when you are alone, I have noticed that you are not behaving like you usually do. Is there anything I can do to help?" Ditrina asked.

Cassy sighed.

"I just want to go home, Di. I just want all of us to go home," she said quietly.

"We will," Ditrina told her.

Cassy looked at her for an explanation.

"Statistically, we have a good chance of success. With you as our cover, we should be able to move without suspicion, and Chris will not give up on finding them. Sarah will fight to her last breath in order to survive, and Matt is smart enough to stay alive. As soon as we manage to get close to them, I will teleport us home. I suspect this will work," Ditrina said.

Cassy smiled.

"As always, you know what needs to be said, though your delivery could use some work," Cassy told her.

"Why? I said everything that was significant," Ditrina said.

"Yeah, but…never mind. It's not important," Cassy told her.

"Very well. If it makes you feel better, I want to return to the valley as well. This has proven to be my worst trip to the elven city ever," Ditrina said.

Cassy laughed.

"I thought this was your first visit since you left home?" Cassy asked.

"It is, and that makes it the worst trip ever," Ditrina said seriously.

"Wouldn't that also make it the best trip ever?" Cassy asked with amusement.

"Yes, but if I told you that, I doubt it would cheer you up," Ditrina told her.

Cassy continued to laugh.

"You really need to work on cheering people up, Di; you're horrible at it," Cassy said as she laughed.

"I disagree. You are laughing and seem much happier," Ditrina told her.

"Whatever you say, Di," Cassy said with a smile, her laughter fading with a content sigh.

"If you are still unhappy, I believe I have something else that may cheer you up," Ditrina told her.

"Oh really, what's that?" Cassy asked, bemused.

"When we return to the valley, we could get married, if you like," Ditrina told her.

Chris was busy consoling his poor daughter when Jasheir walked over from where he sat under the tarp.

"I have come to the realization that you are likely the one in charge here. Is that correct?" he asked.

"Yeah, that's right," Chris said as he patted Eve gently on the back.

Eve heaved over the edge of the boat. Echo squawked and dove to her side, nuzzling her leg in an attempt to cheer her up.

"Is it truly possible for me to live among this *kingdom?*" he hissed.

"I don't know. That really depends on you. You see if you—" Chris began, but a sudden scream cut him off.

"What was that?" Jasheir asked, looking around in panic, his snakelike tongue tasting the air.

Chris, who recognized that sound, sighed.

"Well, this should be good. What's the problem, Cas?" Chris called to his sister.

Her reply was simply another excited squeal.

"Nobody has any idea what that means, Cas!" Chris called back.

"Cas is having trouble making words at the moment. I believe that is my fault," Ditrina told him. "I may have broken her."

"What did you do?" Chris asked cautiously.

"I simply suggested that Cas and I get married when we return home. I have no idea why she has been rendered senseless," Ditrina said, gesturing to Cassy who was currently making small excited giggles and hand motions, but nothing that could be mistaken for intelligent thought.

"We're hundreds of miles from home, surrounded by bloodthirsty creatures that wish to enslave us and have us fight to the death, two of our best friends are prisoners, and you decide that now's a good time to propose?" Chris asked with disbelief.

"That is an accurate assessment of the situation, yes," Ditrina said happily.

"Is it normal for females to take other females as their mates in this kingdom?" Jasheir asked.

"Relatively normal, yeah. Nobody really cares," Chris told him.

"How strange. This behavior would never occur within Gishkar," Jasheir told him.

"Why?" Chris asked.

"Females who do not breed have no sons. Without strong sons, how can their house flourish? And if males were to sire no children, how would their strength be passed on?" Jasheir asked.

"Like I said, in Desgail, nobody cares. It's not an issue," Chris told him.

Jasheir shrugged.

"It seems I have much to learn about this kingdom. Once we are situated within the city, you must tell me more," Jasheir said.

"If you insist," Chris said.

"Is Aunt Cas getting married?" Eve asked suddenly, her seasickness at bay for the moment.

"That is the current plan," Ditrina told her.

"We need to get Mother then. She will want to be there," Eve said seriously.

"I still do not see the need for choosing a single mate. It seems... boring," Jasheir hissed, settling on the proper word.

"Di is not boring!" Cassy yelled suddenly, Jasheir's words rousing her from her stunned stupor to defend her betrothed.

"You never did reply before you descended into mindless rambles," Ditrina told her.

"Yes! Of course, it's a yes!" Cassy said hastily.

"Good," Ditrina said, nodding happily.

"I hate to be the one to break this up, but it looks like we're almost at the docks. Everyone, get into character," Chris told them.

Sure enough, the bargeman could be seen walking the length of the barge toward them, stopping along the way to speak with the few other scattered passengers.

"Time to find them," Chris said quietly, and the others nodded their agreement.

A couple hours later, the guard with brown scales returned to bring Sarah and Matt to the arena.

"It is time for you to fight," he hissed.

"At least tell us that we get weapons?" Matt asked hopefully.

The guard laughed.

"You will find plenty of weapons within the arena; do not worry. Now, walk," he commanded, opening their cell.

Reluctantly, they were led down the corridor, past the doorway that Tinacee had brought them down, and past many more cells. There were fewer slaves than they remembered. As they continued down the hall, they became aware of a sound, like a dull roar. At the end of the corridor, they saw a massive door bound in iron.

"Through there," the guard ordered.

Sarah led the way and pushed open the door slowly with her good hand, revealing yet another, larger door. Before she could ask what the point of two doors was, she was shoved inside, with Matt receiving the same treatment. The door locked behind them. The roar grew louder.

"Do you think we could just stay here?" Matt asked, looking around the confined space.

"I doubt that's going to fly with these monsters," Sarah replied.

She reached out to open the door, but before she could touch it, a voice boomed out over the roar.

"Now fighting for the glory of Mistress Tinacee, Sarah Shearcliff and Matthew Bleakstar!" Narfus called, his voice echoing around them.

"We never told him our names," Sarah said quietly.

"He may have read our minds," Matt told her.

"He can do that?" Sarah asked with concern.

"Only if we are willing or too weak to resist. That may be the true reason for the beating earlier," Matt said angrily.

"Damn him, that means he knows about Cassy!" Sarah exclaimed.

"Maybe not. Things we don't want to be known are harder to extract, and mind reading is fairly difficult, to begin with. He may have only learned very basic information about us. Still, be careful around him. Assume he knows everything you do," Matt told her.

"I'm going to kill that bastard. He has no right to dig through my mind!" Sarah yelled, but slowly a thought entered her head. "Hey, Matt…" she began.

"Yes, Sarah?" Matt asked nervously, afraid of the glint in her eyes.

"You said clerics could do that mind reading thing, right?" she asked cautiously.

"Powerful ones, yeah," Matt told her nervously.

"Oh, thank the gods. I was worried you might have been able to do something like that," Sarah said with a sigh of relief.

"Ok, I may not be a cleric anymore, but that still hurts," Matt told her.

The doors in front of them swung open revealing the arena.

"I'll worry about your feelings later, assuming we survive today," Sarah told him as she ran out into the sun.

The arena was impressive. Ten stories tall with a two-hundred-yard sand pit for fighting, it was easily one of the largest buildings either of them had ever laid eyes on. It looked like every seat was filled with a screaming naga, mostly males, but with the occasional female scattered among them. Several skyboxes protruded around the top of the arena, and directly across from them, Sarah thought she saw one occupied by a female naga with red scales, and a robed figure, but at that distance, it was too hard to tell for sure.

They wished they had more time to look around at the arena, but a battle was already raging around them. Men and women, old and young, members of every race Sarah knew, fought for their lives in the sand. They watched in horror as an orc boy, barely older than Eve, was cut down from behind by a woman old enough to be Sarah's grandmother, only to see her speared through the back seconds later. A giant, twenty feet of rage and muscle, stormed across the sand tossing bodies around like playthings, and small bands of armed men huddled together for survival.

"This is a nightmare," Matt declared.

"I've seen worse," Sarah said, looking around for some type of weapon.

Her eyes lit up.

"Follow me!" she yelled before charging across the bloodstained sand.

Matt followed, unsure of what Sarah was doing until he saw her target. Kneeling beside the fallen orc boy was what looked to be his sister.

While not as common as humans or dwarves, the orcs made up a large chunk of the world's population. Slightly larger than the average human, and with a subtle underbite and grey skin, they were unmistakable among the people of Targoth.

"Sarah, what are you doing?" Matt called as they hurried toward the child—who was still oblivious to them—blinded by her grief.

Sarah reached the boy's corpse and pried his weapon from his hands—a crude short sword. Matt reached the girl and knelt beside her.

"Are you all right?" he asked kindly.

The girl looked up at him with large tearstained eyed and stifled a sob. Without warning, she lunged at him with her own short sword.

"Easy!" Matt yelled as he jumped away from her clumsy swing.

The girl continued to advance, swinging her sword wildly, all the while sobbing loudly.

"Calm down, we'll help you, you just need to..." Matt started, but his words died off as the girl's head suddenly fell from her shoulders.

He stared in horror at the girl's head, which now lay in a pile of bloodstained sand several feet away from her body, the last of her tears running down her cheeks. Sarah shook as much of the blood off her sword as she could.

"What the hell!" Matt screamed at her.

"I could ask you the same thing! Do you want to die here?" Sarah demanded.

"You just murdered that little girl!" Matt screamed in horror.

"Listen to me! Every single person in this arena wants to kill you! The only way we are going to survive is if we kill them first! I don't know about you, but I *will* see Chris and Eve again! Fight if you ever want to see our family again!" Sarah screamed at him and shoved the bloodstained sword against his chest.

As if in a trance, Matt took the weapon from her and held it with uncertainty. Sarah plucked the second sword from the girl's limp hand and turned to him.

"We'll keep to the edges and avoid fighting as much as possible. If it comes to it though, don't hesitate. I need you," Sarah told him.

Matt nodded mutely and looked at the sword in his hands, blade still slick with the girl's blood.

"Follow me," Sarah commanded and led him to the edge of the arena.

"What do we do now?" Matt asked nervously.

"We do our best not to look weak, and most importantly, we stay alive. I refuse to have to explain to my husband how his best friend got killed on my watch, or to Eve why her favorite uncle isn't coming home," Sarah told him.

"These people are in the same boat we're in," Matt said quietly.

"Exactly. Just like us, their choices are fight or die. Most are going to die, and some of them are going to die because we're gonna kill them. I will not die here; I still have to get my ring back," Sarah snarled over the din of battle.

"We have company!" Matt yelled suddenly, pointing behind Sarah.

Three ragged looking men armed with an axe, a spear, and a sword approached quickly, pointing at them.

"I'll deal with the spearman and the swordsman. You get the one with the axe," Sarah said as she crouched low, sword at the ready.

"I don't know how to fight with a sword!" Matt yelled.

"It's not that complicated! Stick them with the pointy bit!" Sarah yelled as the men reached them.

"Get lost!" Sarah yelled, but they looked at Matt's unsure face and her missing hand with hungry eyes.

The spearman lunged toward Sarah, but she dodged nimbly to the side and cut the spear in half with her sword. The spearman, meeting no resistance, stumbled and fell face first in the sand. A quick thrust from Sarah and he didn't rise again. Matt wished he had time to admire her prowess, but the axeman aimed a wild swing at his head forcing him to duck.

"Die!" the axeman bellowed as he aimed another wild swing at Matt, but once again, Matt managed to jump aside and avoid being cut in half.

While he was still off balance from his last swing, Matt rushed toward him, clutching his sword in both hands, screaming in an incoherent combination of rage and terror. Matt felt the blade meet momentary resistance as it sank deep into the man's side, followed by the sickening sensation of cutting through muscle and a jolt as he hit a bone. Matt stumbled back in horror, revolted by the feeling.

"What's the issue, Matt? I've seen you kill before," Sarah yelled as she pulled her blade from the swordsman's lifeless corpse.

"I've always used magic," Matt muttered before he retched violently.

"Get a hold of yourself! This is no different, you just feel it a bit more! Did Chris start puking the first time he killed someone with a sword?" Sarah demanded.

"He was possessed! He didn't know what he was doing! On top of that, he always has the spirits patting him on the back whenever he does something vaguely heroic! This is different! I'm killing people who are fighting for their lives!" Matt screamed.

"You *are* fighting for your life! What do you not understand about that?" Sarah screamed back. "Would it make you feel better if you were blasting them with magic where they can't fight back? Are you that much of a coward?"

"I am not a coward!" Matt bellowed.

Sarah looked at his bruised face and saw his eyes were streaming tears. She made her decision.

"Prove it," she snarled.

Matt's face morphed between several emotions quickly: betrayal, hurt, anger, and then rage. He gripped his sword tightly, and for a moment Sarah wondered if perhaps she had pushed him too far when suddenly he howled and charged toward the center of the arena where the fighting was the thickest.

"Oh, shit," Sarah cursed, realizing her decision could have used a little more thought.

With a sigh, she charged behind him, determined to protect her friend.

Now off the barge, Chris stood and took in all that was Gishkar. It was unlike any other city he'd ever seen. Massive structures made of wood and sandstone sprawled before him without any real sense of organization. Colorful stalls and booths lined the streets from which slaves hawked their master's wares. Powerfully built naga males strolled down the street, talking with one another or admiring what the slaves sold. From time to time they would see a female being escorted by a group of males down the street or being carried on a litter by slaves. The city was vibrant, chaotic, and very much alive.

"We must acquire transportation," Jasheir told them.

"Can't we just walk?" Cassy asked.

"It is not customary for a female to walk the streets with so few guards. We need a litter," Jasheir told her.

"There's not enough of us to carry one of those; Eve's too small," Chris told him.

"We will rent one then," Jasheir told them before leading them into the city.

Several quick turns later put them standing outside a dimly-lit shop.

"What is this place?" Chris asked.

"It is a place where one may rent a litter that I know. Tinacee used it on several occasions," Jasheir explained.

"Do they provide slaves to carry it?" Chris asked.

"Yes," Jasheir confirmed.

"I don't like the idea of being carried by slaves," Cassy told them.

"This is an important part of your appearance. You will survive," Jasheir told her.

Cassy muttered darkly but protested no further.

"Where are they keeping my mother?" Eve asked irritably.

Echo squawked from her shoulder in agreement.

"She is likely in Tinacee's home or fighting in the arena," Jasheir told her.

"Hurry," Eve said angrily.

Cassy sighed.

"Just go get the damn thing," she told him.

Jasheir disappeared within the shop. The others stood in the busy street for several minutes, unsure of what to do while they waited. Chris noticed Eve looking around for something to *play* with and took her hand in an attempt to stop her. He felt Echo rubbing his head against his arm and scratched the dragon behind the horns with his free hand.

"He likes that," Eve told him happily.

"My lady, I require thirty gold. I have acquired transport and must pay," Jasheir told her, having returned from within the shop.

"Here," Cassy told him, handing him the sum in question from her coin purse.

A few seconds later several slaves walked around the edge of the building carrying a large litter, adorned with a silk curtain and comfy looking pillows.

"Where does the lady wish to go?" one of the slaves asked politely.

"Bring us to the estate of Mistress Tinacee," Jasheir told them.

"Of course, please have your lady climb aboard then," the slave told Jasheir.

"Why doesn't he just tell me to get on?" Cassy asked.

"It is not the place of a slave to speak to a female directly," Jasheir told her.

"I hate this city," Cassy muttered as she climbed up onto the litter.

"I wanna ride with Aunt Cas!" Eve yelled suddenly, breaking away from Chris and jumping onto the litter.

"Get her down from there!" Jasheir said angrily.

"Oh, shut up. It's fine. She can stay here with me," Cassy said as she sat Eve between her legs.

Eve leaned back against her aunt and sighed contently while Echo curled up on a pillow and fell asleep. Jasheir looked at Chris with concern, but Chris merely shrugged.

"Do you really want to be the one to disobey the lady's orders in public?" Chris asked with a smirk.

"You are learning about this land a little too quickly, I fear," Jasheir told him.

"Let us get going. Every moment we spend here is a moment wasted," Ditrina reminded them.

"Of course, let us depart," Jasheir told them and ordered the slaves to begin their march.

They picked up the litter with practiced grace and set a steady pace toward the estate. Jasheir walked in front to clear the way, while Chris and Ditrina walked on either side to ensure Cassy and Eve were well protected.

"Look at that!" Eve exclaimed, pointing at the arena as they rounded a corner and got a good view of it.

"Given the time, there is likely a match going on as we speak. Perhaps after we speak with Tinacee, we can watch a bout or two. We will likely be in the city a few days," Jasheir told them.

"I wonder what's fighting in there now?" Eve asked eagerly.

"Matt, duck!" Sarah screamed as she threw a spear over his head.

Short as he was, Matt only had to lower his head a little, and he watched as the spear impaled the man in front of him. Matt focused on the next combatant and attacked the dwarf with the axe he had found, his sword long discarded. As he fought, Sarah engaged the dwarf's companions, and several seconds later they found themselves gifted with a moment of reprieve; the other fighters lying still on the ground.

"How long do they expect us to keep this up?" Matt panted.

"I'm not sure. Maybe we're just expected to fight until we die," Sarah replied breathlessly.

"While we have a few moments, let's catch our breath and see what's going on," Matt told her.

Sarah nodded and smiled to herself. After they survived Matt's suicidal charge through the center of the arena, Sarah had seen the last of his moral resistance crumple. To her relief, he began to fight without remorse and obeyed her orders to the letter. All in all, she decided that, given a little training, he could make a pretty good soldier.

"I see three groups fighting near the center, and there's still the giant to worry about, but other than that, I think they've stopped releasing new slaves," Matt said.

"You're right. The numbers are thinning. I bet this is some sort of last man standing type battle," Sarah realized.

"Shouldn't we stay here then and wait for the others to pick each other off then kill the winner while they're tired?" Matt proposed.

"That's a plan I can get behind," Sarah said with a smile.

"What do we do until then?" Matt asked

"We rest. We try to get our strength back. Stay awake, though," Sarah told him.

"All right," Matt said as he sat with a thud in the sand.

Sarah sighed and sat beside him. Together they watched the other fighters butcher each other and listened to the cheers and jeers of the crowd.

"Do you think they'll get to us in time?" Matt asked quietly.

"To be honest, I'm not thinking about that at all right now. Keep your thoughts on the current problem," Sarah said, gesturing around them.

Matt sighed.

"You're right. What weapons do you have?" he asked.

"I have two daggers and a longsword. I lost the short sword fighting the man with the mace and the shield. It's a shame. If I had my other hand, I really could have used that shield," Sarah said irritably.

"I would have taken it, but I need two hands for this axe," Matt told her, gesturing to the massive war axe he carried, a souvenir from his dash through the center.

"Nice job taking him down, by the way," Sarah said proudly, referring to the massive axeman Matt had killed to claim the weapon.

"Thanks; you've done really well yourself," Matt told her.

"I think I've gotten two for every one of yours," Sarah said proudly.

"It's not a competition," Matt reminded her.

"You're just saying that because you're losing. Step up your game," Sarah said with a laugh.

Matt joined her, and for a moment they laughed together, letting the stress of the battle fall away. Matt's face clouded after a while, and his laughter died in his throat.

"That was wrong. I shouldn't be laughing at this," he said quietly.

"You're not going to get all ethical and uptight again, are you? Because if you do, I'm leaving you for the giant," Sarah warned him.

"Don't be ridiculous. I want to survive as bad as you do, but that doesn't change the fact that I shouldn't be enjoying this," Matt told her.

"But you are enjoying this, aren't you," Sarah told him.

It wasn't a question; it was a statement of fact.

"I don't understand why," Matt muttered to himself.

"It's your body's way of congratulating you on surviving. Every time you go toe to toe with somebody and come out on top, you feel that little sensation, like your brain is giving you a pat on the back," Sarah told him.

"Exactly! I hate it," Matt said with a shudder.

"Get used to it. You lost your magic, and with that your ability to kill at a range. You no longer have that disconnect that let you kill with a clean conscious. Learn to live with this, because if you ever want to adventure with us again, want more in life than teaching Eve how to read and write, then you're going to have to practice fighting with weapons like everyone else," Sarah told him.

"I'm not doing too badly today!" Matt protested.

"That's because you're fighting other slaves who have likely never touched a weapon before in their lives. If you had to fight a trained warrior, you'd be history," Sarah said.

"Thanks for the vote of confidence," Matt said dryly.

"If it makes you feel any better, you're much better at fighting than

Chris was when he started. Do you remember how clumsy he was the first time he held a real sword?" Sarah asked.

"Yeah, and I seem to remember you cutting his arms off a few seconds later," Matt said with a chuckle. "I don't understand how he puts up with you sometimes."

"Hey, I wasn't trying to cut his arms off. He was just a lot clumsier than I expected, and I didn't realize it in time. Besides, you put them back on so fast that he didn't even get a scar. No harm, no foul," Sarah told him.

"Still, I'd hardly call that normal behavior for newlyweds," Matt teased.

Sarah was oddly quiet.

"He understands that I'm trying to help him, right? He doesn't resent me, does he?" Sarah asked quietly, suddenly much more serious than before.

"Sarah, where is this coming from? Chris loves you, and he really doesn't mind you making him train. He's smart enough to realize that you're trying to keep him alive in the long run," Matt told her, surprised by Sarah's sudden question.

The battle raged on, the sounds echoing around them.

"It's just, sometimes I worry that he regrets marrying me. He proposed right after he woke up from his coma, and I was so excited that he was ok that I accepted right away, but looking back on it, I worry he wasn't thinking clearly. He had a lot to worry about, after all, and two sets of thoughts rattling around his head. We had only known each other for a couple of months, and I almost killed him when we first met. How could he have honestly wanted to marry me?" Sarah asked quietly. "Now to top it all off, I learn that I can never bear him any children. I'd hardly call that an endearing quality; wouldn't you agree?"

Matt didn't know what to say. This uncertainty was a side of Sarah he didn't know existed, and he was unprepared to deal with it. Still, he knew he had to say something.

"Sarah, I can't begin to pretend that I know what goes on in Chris's head. I can't say why he proposed to you when he did or why he lets you beat the hell out of him on a daily basis. What I do know is that he's traveled halfway across the globe to rescue you. I have never once heard him complain about you or show any sign of regret about marrying you. He loves you. That's really the only thing that matters, isn't it?" Matt asked kindly.

Sarah stared at the bloody sand and said nothing. She stood and picked up her sword.

"Forget waiting. I need to kill something," she told him with frustration.

"Are you sure? The giant's the only one nearby," Matt warned her.

"Good, I can stab him a couple dozen times before he dies," Sarah said as she marched toward the massive man.

Looking to be an abnormally muscular human who had somehow grown to twenty feet tall and given nothing but a filthy loincloth to wear, the giant turned his large brown eyes toward them as they approached. He hefted his massive club and bellowed at them.

"Oh, shut up!" Sarah yelled back as she charged him.

"Sarah, be careful!" Matt yelled as he ran close behind her, but it seemed his warning was not necessary.

As the giant swung the club at Sarah, she ducked low and without breaking her stride, sliced the behemoth's wrist. The giant howled and stumbled back a pace as Sarah continued her advance, peppering the giant's legs with cuts and slashes. To their surprise, the giant jumped back a pace, which for him was almost five yards, his landing shaking the ground on which they stood. The crowd roared.

"We need a plan," Matt told her.

"Distract him," Sarah yelled as she charged again.

"That's not a plan!" Matt called as he raced after her.

As they neared the brute, Sarah split off and ran to the right, leaving Matt at the center of the giant's attention.

"Hello!" Matt called nervously.

The giant roared loud enough to set Matt's ears ringing.

"Not in the mood to talk...got it," Matt muttered as he circled the monster cautiously.

Deciding that he found Matt's stature enough to judge his combat skill, the giant charged forward, swinging his club around his head.

"I can't dodge like you, Sarah. *Help!*" Matt screamed as the giant charged him, looking around in terror for the deadly woman.

As if summoned by his pathetic cries, Sarah was there, running up behind the giant. As the giant stopped to crush Matt with his club, Sarah sliced behind his knee. The giant screamed a long, heartbreaking sound, and fell to the ground; propped up on his good knee and club. Without waiting for him to recover, Sarah took a few steps back before charging forward, leaping onto the giant's back. With only one hand, she was forced to stab the sword into the back of her victim for balance before she began scampering up his back toward his head. Matt watched in awe as Sarah appeared, standing atop the giant's shoulders before she plunged her sword deep between his eyes. The giant fell forward into the sand, and Sarah was tossed clear of the massive corpse. She landed in the sand at Matt's feet.

"I've never killed a giant before," she mumbled from the ground.

"The next time you decide you wanna talk about your feelings, *don't*," Matt said, looking at the fallen giant in horror.

Sarah stood up.

"Actually, that really helped, Matt, thanks," she said, thumping him on the back with her stump.

"Uh, you're welcome…I guess," Matt said slowly.

"It looks like there are a few survivors left; let's kill them, too, and end this match!" Sarah said all too cheerfully as she strode toward the nearest group of fighters, who stared at her in awe and terror after watching her kill the giant.

"I swear, I am *not* becoming a counselor," Matt muttered.

CHAPTER ELEVEN

"We have arrived. Behold, the estate of Mistress Tinacee," Jasheir told them, pointing toward a massive sandstone complex.

"That's rather impressive," Chris said.

"Most prominent females make their primary estates on the edges of the city, but Tinacee decided to make hers near the center. It is a symbol of her power," Jasheir told him.

"Just who is this woman?" Cassy asked.

"Tinacee is a young female who has gained considerable prestige through the arena. She has a reputation of fielding the fiercest fighting slaves and, as such, commands respect. Lately, she has been looking to branch into exotic house slaves, though I do not know why. Interestingly enough, she has yet to lay a clutch of eggs, and many strong warriors seek to gain her favor," Jasheir explained.

"Is that why you served her?" Cassy asked with distaste.

"There is no higher honor than siring a strong clutch of warriors," Jasheir told her.

"Do *not* get any ideas," Ditrina warned, stepping close to Cassy's side as she helped her off the litter.

"I would never dream of such a thing," Jasheir told her, but Chris saw his snakelike eyes narrow.

"Let's just go in and try to find Sarah and Matt," Chris told them, deciding to end this line of conversation.

"Eve, you need to be quiet for a while," Ditrina told her.

"Yes, Aunt Di. Echo and I will be quiet," Eve promised.

"Let's go," Jasheir told them and led them inside the massive estate's doorway.

They had made it no more than ten steps before they were challenged by a guard hefting a massive sword, much like Jasheir's.

"Who enters the land of Mistress Tinacee?" the guard demanded.

"Lady Shearcliff and her slaves," Jasheir declared. "We seek an audience with the Lady Tinacee."

"On what grounds?" the guard hissed.

"Tinacee has taken Lady Shearcliff's property. She seeks to reclaim it," Jasheir told him.

"The Mistress is away at the arena. Come back later," the guard told them.

"I would have thought with an estate as grand as this that the Lady Tinacee would have accommodations for guests. I guess the reports of her wealth were over exaggerated," Jasheir said with a shrug as he turned to leave.

"Wait," the guard hissed.

"Yes?" Jasheir asked impatiently.

"If you are weary from your travels, then I could escort you to the guest wing. I merely thought your lady had better things to do than lounge around the estate," the guard told him.

"My lady thanks you. This is a matter of the upmost importance. As soon as the Lady Tinacee arrives, tell her of our presence. She will wish to speak with us," Jasheir told him.

The guard snapped his clawed fingers, and a slave rushed around the corner.

"He will escort you to the guest wing," the guard told them.

"Thank you," Jasheir told him. "Take us," he ordered the slave.

The slave bowed deeply and began to walk down one of the corridors. After many twists and turns, he showed them inside a large open-air room, with gauzy silk curtains and a fountain gurgling in the center. Several sofas were scattered around in a semicircular pattern.

"Does this please the lady?" the slave asked nervously.

His accent was thick and slightly familiar.

"This is fine; you may go," Jasheir told him, but Cassy held up her hand.

"Wait," she said quickly.

"My lady," the slave said, quickly dropping to a knee.

"Where are you from?" Cassy asked him.

The slave looked around nervously.

"I do not understand…" he stammered.

"Where were you taken from? Where is your home?" Ditrina clarified.

The man's eyes widened.

"You are one of the summer folk!" he exclaimed.

"What are the summer folk?" Chris asked with confusion.

"That is the name the north men have given to the elves because of the nature of our city. While we do not interact with them much, we have occasionally conversed over the years," Ditrina explained.

"If they have taken the summer folk, then all is lost," the man wailed, falling to the ground.

"Have the naga been preying upon your people?" Chris asked.

"Yes, the green beasts have been taking away my people for some time now. I was on the way to beg the summer folk for help when I was taken," the slave told them, looking up from the floor.

"When they were yelling about green beasts, I thought they were talking about Ditrina," Chris muttered.

"This explains why we saw north men so close to the city and why the elves were so hostile to outsiders. They do not like to be disturbed," Ditrina told them.

"How do we stop them?" Cassy demanded.

"Not our problem. Once we get Sarah and Matt, we leave. I don't want to get caught up in all this," Chris told her.

"That is wise," Jasheir agreed. "Leave us," he told the slave.

"How long do you think it will be before Tinacee arrives?" Ditrina asked.

"That depends on how long the arena fight drags out. Given what day it is, I'd say that today is a last house standing match. Those can take some time," Jasheir told her.

"How do those go?" Chris asked.

"The fight ends when only slaves from the same house remain. Then victors are declared, and glory is given to their master," Jasheir told them. "It is truly a sight to behold."

"We have a victor!" Narfus's voice cried out over the cheers of the crowd. "Fighting for the Lady Tinacee, Sarah Shearcliff and Matthew Bleakstar! Glory to Tinacee!"

The crowd exploded, rising from their seats like a wave, cheering and stomping their clawed feet as Sarah pulled her sword from the last opponent. She looked at Matt and saw that while he was exhausted, he was alive.

"Wow...that sucked," he panted between deep breaths.

"I told you to let me handle this last group. You got tired for nothing," Sarah chastised.

"Yeah, but I stopped the guy with the halberd from taking your head off. That's reason enough for me to be tired," Matt panted.

"Thanks for that; I really don't wanna die in this horrible place," Sarah said, looking around.

"We're in this together," Matt said with a smile.

Sarah turned and clasped his arm.

"Together," she agreed.

"Survivors, proceed to a gateway or prepare to be killed," Narfus's hissing voice warned them.

"Let's get moving," Sarah said, walking briskly toward the gate they passed through.

As they approached, the gate swung open like the jaws of a massive beast, welcoming them back inside. They shut with a boom behind them, sealing them between the two doors again.

"Drop your weapons," a hissing voice told them.

Realizing that the doors before them would likely not open until they did, they let their weapons fall to the stone floor with a clatter.

The door before them swung open quickly and they found themselves faced with two burly looking naga armed with spears.

"Walk slowly ahead of us," one of them ordered.

Sarah and Matt walked cautiously forward, and the guards directed them with light prods from their spears until they found themselves standing in their cell once more.

"You'd think that we'd at least get a blanket or something for winning," Sarah mused, sitting back against the stone wall, looking at the iron bars that confined them.

"Do you think it's safe to sleep?" Matt asked.

"Safe or not, that's what I'm doing," Sarah told him as her eyes slid shut.

Matt decided that Sarah had the right idea and shut his eyes, wondering if perhaps he would be able to talk to Chris.

Chris and the others sat in the guest room for nearly three hours before they saw another living being. Remarkably, Eve kept her vow of silence the entire time. To their surprise, when they were finally disturbed, it was not a slave, rather a female naga with yellow scales, wearing a short silk dress.

"The Lady Tinacee has returned from the arena and requests your presence over dinner," she told them.

She looked a lot like Cassy in many ways, from her scales to her proportions, but in other ways, she was different. To start with, she was blonde, with her hair trailing down to the center of her back, and her eyes were shockingly blue. Her skin was also slightly darker than Cassy's, and her curves more apparent. Her eyes were filled with distain as she looked over the *slaves*, but apprehensive as they rested on Cassy.

"Let us be going then," Cassy said, rising from the sofa, gesturing to her friends.

"They will not be needed. Lady Tinacee has plenty of servants to care for you," the yellow scaled naga told her.

"They stay with me," Cassy said firmly.

The yellow scaled naga looked at her with mild surprise but shrugged.

"As you command," she said before leading them down a corridor.

"Here we are," she told them as they arrived at a large balcony on the second floor. Behind several colorful gauzy curtains, they could see another female naga sitting at a table.

"Thank you, sister," the naga on the balcony said without looking at them.

The yellow scaled naga bowed and left quickly. Cassy pulled aside the curtain and stepped onto the balcony, with the others following close behind her. The naga, who they assumed to be Tinacee, looked to be a clone of her sister, with the exception of her scales and hair, which were blood red and brown, respectively. She looked to be slightly older than Cassy, but it was difficult to tell her exact age.

"Why did you feel it was necessary to bring your slaves with you to dinner?" Tinacee asked, still not having taken the time to look at them.

"They are my guards; would you wander into a hostile estate unguarded?" Cassy asked as she sat across from Tinacee.

"Hostile? Why do you say that?" Tinacee asked with a slight smile.

Chris and Ditrina took positions on either side of Cassy's chair, with Jasheir standing behind her. Silently, Eve climbed into Cassy's lap with Echo on her own. Tinacee raised an eyebrow but said nothing.

"You have some things that belong to me," Cassy told her, cutting right to the chase.

Tinacee looked at Ditrina and smiled. She ignored Cassy's statement.

"For you to choose these slaves to guard you, they must be exceptionally skilled. I see you let the human carry a sword freely. They must be very well trained," Tinacee hissed with a small smile.

"Very," Cassy said curtly.

"Let's see just how well," Tinacee said with the same small smile.

She snapped her clawed fingers. Four naga males armed with swords rushed through the door and without a word, hurled themselves at Cassy. While they were quick, Chris and Ditrina proved their match. With the aid of his magic, Chris drew his sword faster than humanly possible, and as the blade was bursting into flames, he cut down two of the charging naga. Ditrina proved faster still. The other two naga didn't make it past the curtains before they were incinerated. Chris leveled his sword at Tinacee's chest and stared at her with glowing red eyes, and Ditrina stood with flames crackling around her fingers. Tinacee began to clap slowly.

"Very impressive. For them to best naga in combat is a feat to be proud of. You have chosen your stock well," she told Cassy.

"Why?" Cassy demanded.

"As you said, you are in a hostile house. I have some things that belong to you, and had these two failed to protect you, I would have kept them," Tinacee told her.

"So, what happens now?" Cassy demanded, her friends still at the ready.

"Dinner!" Tinacee said cheerfully as slaves carrying platters of meat and strange looking fruit walked onto the balcony.

They stepped over the fallen naga without breaking their stride and set the platters on the table. Cassy looked at the food cautiously. Chris slowly lowered his sword, and the flames in Ditrina's hands died out. Seeing her hesitation, Tinacee took a large bite out of a hunk of meat before passing it to Cassy.

"It's not poisoned. I've made my attempt to kill you, and you survived. Now we can eat and discuss your missing slaves," Tinacee said happily.

Cassy reached out slowly and took the chunk of flesh from Tinacee. Catching the alluring scent of the strange meat, she threw caution to the wind and tore off a large hunk with her fangs. Her eyes lit up.

"It's good, isn't it?" Tinacee said happily.

"Very, what is it?" Cassy asked, still chewing.

"My dear, have you never tried dwarf before? I would have figured one of your status would have sampled all of the lesser races by now," Tinacee said with mild surprise.

Cassy gagged, and a large chunk of chewed dwarf fell onto the table.

"What's wrong, my dear? Is the dwarf not to your taste? Try some orc instead. It's a little gamey for my liking," Tinacee said, sliding another platter toward her.

Tinacee picked up a small cube of meat and popped it into her mouth.

"I find that one cannot beat the simple taste of human, lightly seasoned and cooked rare," she said as she savored the flavor.

Chris's face paled under his hood. Ditrina set her hand on Cassy's shoulder and squeezed tightly. Echo did his best to discreetly steal the discarded dwarf off the table. Cassy steeled herself and looked at Tinacee.

"You said you have my slaves," Cassy told her.

"Right to business, I see. Yes, I have the two slaves my men took from you," Tinacee told her.

"I want them back," Cassy told her.

"I'm sure you do. They are skilled fighters. They won the last house standing match in the arena earlier today. Very impressive for first timers," Tinacee told her.

"If you will not give them to me, what is your price?" Cassy asked irritably.

"I see that you have claimed Jasheir as one of your warriors. You may keep him; I have no use for failures. That seems like a fair trade to me," Tinacee told her.

"They were not for trading, to begin with. They are quite valuable, and I want them returned to me," Cassy told her.

"Well, while they may not have been for trading, to begin with, they are now. In exchange for your slaves, I want her," Tinacee said, pointing at Ditrina.

"My elf? Do you really think I would trade an elf for two humans?" Cassy demanded angrily, managing to maintain her façade as a slaver a little while longer.

Ditrina's hand remained firmly grasping Cassy's shoulder.

"I have no idea what you did to acquire such an exotic slave, or how it was that the elves allowed you inside their city, but you must tell me. An elf would make a fine addition to my stock," Tinacee said with a greedy glint in her eyes.

"She's not for sale. One way or another, I will leave here with all of my slaves, including the two you stole," Cassy hissed angrily.

"I see. In that case, why not a wager?" Tinacee proposed.

"Of what kind?" Cassy asked cautiously.

"Of the simplest kind. The two slaves you seek have currently been entered into a tournament. I do not expect them to survive, but they will likely win me much prestige all the same. I bet that the two of them die in the arena. If neither of them makes it past the final round, you will give the elf to me. However, if either of them manages to win the tournament, they will be returned to you the same day. How does that sound?" Tinacee asked as she popped another cube of human flesh into her mouth.

Ditrina squeezed her shoulder twice quickly. Cassy glanced up at her, and she gave the slightest, indistinguishable nod, noticed only by Cassy's heightened senses. Cassy tuned her eyes back to Tinacee.

"Very well, I accept your wager," Cassy told her.

"Wonderful!" Tinacee exclaimed and clapped her hands together. "Let's shake on it then," she hissed as she extended her hand to Cassy.

Cassy reached across the table and clasped her hand, red and green scales scraping against one another.

They returned to the guest wing while a room was prepared for Cassy. Tinacee's sister escorted them, and nobody spoke until they were alone. As they heard the footsteps retreat down the hallway, Cassy's face crumpled, and she began to shake violently.

"Cas, are you ok?" Chris asked as he rushed to her side.

Cassy continued to shake uncontrollably. Eve tugged on Ditrina's arm with a claw-like hand and whispered something in her ear when she knelt down. Ditrina nodded.

"You can talk again, Eve. Well done," Ditrina told her kindly.

Eve rushed to Cassy's side.

"It's ok, Aunt Cas, I know you don't eat people," Eve said as she hugged her.

Cassy opened her mouth like she was going to speak but vomited instead. Slowly, she fell to her knees.

"Echo wants to know what dwarf tastes like, by the way," Eve added, his efforts to steal it from the table having failed.

Cassy continued to puke on the floor.

"Easy, Cas, deep breaths," Chris told her.

Cassy began to sob, her cries intermingled with her retching. Ditrina walked to her and pulled her into a hug. Quietly, so only Cassy could hear, Ditrina began to sing. Chris felt the presence of magic and recognized what Ditrina was doing. Despite only hearing the faintest traces of the song, he began to feel sleepy and saw that Eve was swaying where she stood. Cassy's head slumped against Ditrina's shoulder, and Ditrina stood, cradling her sleeping form.

"Good call, Ditrina," Chris said with a grateful nod.

"She needs rest. This has been taxing for her," Ditrina told him and carried Cassy to a sofa, laying her down gently.

Ditrina sat next to her, resting Cassy's head on her lap.

"I guess the fangs were for eating people, after all," Chris muttered to himself, looking at Eve nervously.

To his relief, Eve didn't seem to be frightened by Cassy, and she climbed up next to Ditrina, sharing her signature half-smile from her mutilated face.

"When will Aunt Cas wake up, Aunt Di?" Eve asked curiously.

"Not for a while. She is tired and needs rest," Ditrina told her.

"Can you sing for me, too?" Eve asked eagerly, excited by the magic she had witnessed.

Ditrina looked at Chris, and Chris gave her a small nod. Ditrina began to sing once again, letting her magic work its way into Eve's mind. Eve's eyes closed slowly, and she slumped against Ditrina, her short hair falling in front of her face. Echo gave a tiny yawn, exposing his rows of razor sharp fangs and coiled up on Eve's lap, snoring lightly. Ditrina looked at him uncomfortably.

"Thank you," Chris told her as he sat next to Eve on the sofa.

"They all could use the rest," Ditrina told him.

"Why was the Mistress so upset?" Jasheir asked nervously.

When Cassy fell into despair, he had watched in stunned silence, unsure of what to do.

"In the kingdom, it is taboo to eat another intelligent creature. When she ate that dwarf, it upset her greatly," Ditrina explained.

"I find this strange, but then again I was raised on healthy servings of orc. What do they eat in the kingdom?" Jasheir asked.

"Basically, anything but that," Chris told him.

"Interesting. If I may be excused, I will check the room they are preparing for traps or assassins. I would not put it past Tinacee to strike while we are asleep," Jasheir told them as he walked out of the room.

"You should sleep as well, leader," Ditrina told Chris.

"Don't call me that," Chris muttered half-heartedly.

"I am being serious. Try to get some rest," Ditrina told him. "I can guard you all while you sleep."

"I couldn't sleep with everything that's going on," Chris told her.

Ditrina began to sing softly, but Chris clamped a hand over her mouth.

"I appreciate it, but I'd rather stay awake," Chris told her as he pulled his hand away.

"As you wish," Ditrina told him.

They sat in silence for a while.

"I'm shocked that you're sitting next to Echo without crying," Chris said after a while.

"I am growing more accustomed to him. It helps that he is loyal to Eve," Ditrina told him. "I still do not wish to touch him; he terrifies me."

Chris chuckled, and they fell back into silence.

"Ditrina, I have a favor to ask of you," Chris told her after a while.

"Anything. Say it, and it will be done," Ditrina told him earnestly.

"There's a good chance we are going to fail," Chris said quietly. "If we do, if Cassy and I go down fighting to save Sarah and Matt, I need you to take Eve. You're the only one who can escape at a moment's notice. I'm not going to sit idly by and watch my wife die in that cursed arena; if it looks like she's in danger, I will fight to reach her side, and I know that Cassy will be right behind me. I'm asking you, if we don't make it, to leave. Don't try to avenge us; don't try to recover our bodies; just take Eve and run. I'm trusting you to raise her in the absence of Sarah and me," Chris told her.

Ditrina looked at the sleeping girl.

"I will protect her with my life," Ditrina swore. "If you fall, if they are lost, then I will raise her as best as I can."

"Thank you," Chris said gratefully. "I never got the chance to ask him before he was taken, but I was going to see if Matt was willing to be her godfather. I'd like you to be her godmother," Chris told her.

Ditrina smiled and brushed Eve's short hair back so she could see her scarred face. She smiled lovingly at the girl.

"I will never be able to have children of my own. I will do everything I can to keep her alive," Ditrina promised.

Chris sighed contently.

"That has been troubling me for some time now; thanks," he told her.

"I will make sure it does not come to that," Ditrina told him.

"What do you mean?" Chris asked.

"I will burn this entire city down around us to keep you all alive. We will make it home to the valley," Ditrina told him.

"Well, let's hope you don't have to," Chris laughed.

"It has been a long time since I have been able to unleash my magic to its fullest extent. I actually hope I get to here," Ditrina admitted.

"What about the fight with the dragon? You really cut loose there," Chris reminded her.

"Oh no, that was simply me panicking and throwing fire around. It has been almost a hundred years since I used as much magic as I could," Ditrina told him.

"Who knows, maybe you'll get to while were here then?" Chris said with a small smile.

"Really?" Ditrina asked with an excited smile. "Do you promise?"

"Only if we rescue everyone," Chris laughed. "Or, if the plan falls apart, we'll call that plan B. You distract them while we get Sarah and Matt."

"I will do my best," Ditrina said, nodding seriously.

"So, how did your negotiations go?" Narfus asked Tinacee as he sat on the balcony.

"She is strange but well-guarded. The warriors I ordered to kill them never stood a chance. You were right, the elf is dangerous, but the swordsman is also interesting. He would do well in the arena," Tinacee told him.

"What steps have you taken to secure the elf?" Narfus asked.

"Relax, Narfus, relax. She was not willing to trade the elf directly and seemed to take stock in her counsel, from what I can tell. However, she has agreed to a wager. All we need to do is ensure the other two slaves die in the arena tomorrow, and the elf will be ours," Tinacee told him.

"I will make it so," Narfus told her.

"Just remember, they must die fighting, and it must look somewhat believable. Do not injure them so badly that it is overtly apparent from the stands," Tinacee told him.

"I would never dream of it, Mistress," Narfus told her.

"You are a good priest, but remember, you can always be replaced," Tinacee warned.

"I will not fail," Narfus promised.

"Matt, wake up; I hear footsteps," Sarah told him, shaking him awake.

"What's going on?" Matt mumbled as he opened his bleary eyes.

"Hello, *champions*," Narfus hissed as he stepped into sight. "Congratulations on surviving today. You have impressed the Mistress so much that she has seen it fit to enter you in a tournament," Narfus told them.

"Well, if you want us to fight, we need something to eat," Sarah snarled at him.

Narfus laughed.

"Let the hunger fuel your fighting spirit. We do not waste food on green slaves," Narfus laughed.

"Have you come just to mock us?" Matt demanded.

"I would never dream of it," Narfus hissed as he fingered a familiar ring hanging from the front of his hood.

Sarah's eyes narrowed in anger.

"What do you want?" she demanded.

"Well, because you asked…" Narfus said as he opened the cell and stepped inside.

Matt and Sarah backed against the far wall, fearful of what Narfus was planning.

"Matthew, come here," Narfus said, beckoning him forward.

Reluctantly, Matt stepped forward. Sarah watched as Matt stood awkwardly in front of the hulking cleric. Narfus smiled at him.

"This will hurt," he told him before reaching out and grabbing Matt by the sides of the head, with his palms covering his eyes.

Lightning flashed between Narfus's hands, and Matt screamed. With a shove, Narfus sent Matt sprawling in the cell and walked out without a word, locking them back inside. Matt lay on the floor clutching his face, moaning.

"Matt! Matt, what's wrong?" Sarah yelled as she knelt beside him.

"Sarah? Sarah, where are you? I can't see you!" Matt said with terror, his eyes looking around without seeing a thing.

Sarah stifled a tiny gasp. Matt's blue eyes were now burned completely white.

"Sarah, what's happening? Where are you?" Matt whimpered, feeling around blindly.

Sarah reached out and clutched his hand.

"I'm here," she promised, squeezing tightly.

"I can't see," Matt sobbed.

"It's going to be all right," Sarah lied. "You're going to be ok."

Much later that night, Chris decided it was finally safe for sleep. Ditrina had just awoken from a nap and was now standing guard. As she stood up, Eve nestled up against him, and Chris allowed himself to drift off. He was greeted by the three brothers huddling around Matt.

"Matt! What's going on? I heard you fought in the arena!" Chris called as he jogged over to them.

Matt pushed through the brothers and looked at Chris.

"It's good to be able to see you," he said with relief.

"What's that supposed to mean?" Chris asked with a nervous laugh.

"Matthew has been rendered blind by his captors," Ge told him.

"What?!" Chris yelled.

"He came into our cell, blinded me with lightning, then left. I have no idea why. We didn't do anything!" Matt yelled.

"You can see me now, though?" Chris asked.

"In this place, physical wounds have no effect on you," Ge told him.

"You need to get us out of here as soon as possible. They said something about a tournament we're supposed to fight in tomorrow. They took one of Sarah's hands and my sight. We haven't had anything to eat or drink since we got here, and we're exhausted. There's no way that we can survive the tournament," Matt told him.

"Cassy made a deal with your captors. If you win, she gets you two, and you can come with us," Chris told him.

"That's a shitty bet. When we die, what do you stand to lose?" Matt asked.

"Ditrina," Chris told him.

"Not such a bad bet, after all," Matt said with a forced laugh.

"I need you two to fight as hard as you can. We'll find a way to get you out," Chris told him.

"Please hurry," Matt begged.

"Don't worry; we will not fail," Al assured him.

"Yeah, I'd hate to lose a stupid bet like this," Mi agreed.

He tuned to Ge.

"Isn't there some magic stuff you can do to fix all this? Something that would let Matt see or maybe blow stuff up with spells?" Mi asked hopefully.

"I am afraid that the only way to do that is to create a situation similar to that of Chris and Al. I would be forced to sever my connection to the afterlife and tear out a chunk of Matthew's soul to make room for myself. Given that this would likely prevent either of us from ever returning to the astral realm, and the statistical chance that Matthew will die tomorrow anyway, I do not think that is a good plan," Ge told them.

"Well, that cheered me up," Matt grumbled.

"I detect that you are being sarcastic," Ge told him.

"What god did I piss off so badly that I'm cursed with two Ditrinas?" Matt demanded.

"Just be thankful that they will never meet," Chris told him. "One might get jealous."

"I would actually like to speak to Ditrinadoma very much," Ge told them.

"Nobody cares, Ge," Mi said.

"Back to saving Matt and Sarah, how is the arena laid out? Is it possible for us to grab you during your match?" Al asked.

"It's massive, and there are clerics of Semel running the place. I don't see how you could get to us during a fight," Matt admitted.

"Well, in that case, try not to die, and I'm sure Chris will think of some way to get you out of there," Al told him.

"We may not have a plan yet, but we have enthusiasm!" Mi yelled.

Matt looked at Chris.

"We're all going to die in this horrible city," Matt declared sullenly.

CHAPTER TWELVE

The next day, Tinacee invited Cassy to watch the tournament with her. Eager to see her friends again, Cassy accepted, with the condition that her guards accompany her. Tinacee had told them that the skybox could not hold all of them, so Jasheir reluctantly volunteered to remain at the estate. So, Chris and his family found themselves sitting in a skybox in the arena, looking down over the massive show floor.

"I believe the match we are interested in is third, but for now, we can enjoy some of the other qualifying matches," Tinacee told Cassy as they waited.

Narfus walked out from behind the doorway and sat beside Tinacee.

"This is Narfus. He is a cleric of Semel and, as such, oversees the arena. He has pledged himself to my service and will be acting as my announcer for today," Tinacee explained when she saw Cassy looking at him suspiciously.

"We've met. He was the one who stole my slaves from me," Cassy said angrily.

Narfus looked over at her and smiled smugly. His eyes drifted to Chris's ring.

"I see you allow your slaves to wear adornment...how unusual," Narfus said, still staring at the ring.

"It is a small thing to allow, and it keeps them happy," Cassy told him.

"I have a ring just like that one, right here," Narfus said, pointing to Sarah's wedding ring hanging from the edge of his hood. "Would you be so kind as to give me that one? I would love to have a matching set," Narfus said hungrily.

Chris's expression hardened.

"It's not for me to give; it's his," Cassy told him.

"How absurd. Of course it's yours to give," Tinacee told her.

"If Narfus wants the ring so badly, then he can try to take it, though I would not recommend it," Cassy told them.

"I have heard that before," Narfus said with a hissing laugh.

He lunged for Chris's hand, but Al was waiting and fueled Chris with magic, heightening his strength and reflexes. To Narfus's surprise, Chris's eyes glowed red as he grabbed him by the wrist and twisted sharply. They heard the snapping of bone.

"I did warn you," Cassy said with amusement.

"Let's break his other arm next; he's more than earned it," Al told Chris.

"We need to stay in character," Chris thought in reply.

Narfus looked at him murderously as he pulled away. He muttered the words of a prayer and his arm healed itself.

"Her guards are more capable then they look," Tinacee said with amusement.

"So I see…" Narfus hissed angrily.

"You should recover your wife's ring while you have the chance," Al told Chris.

"As much as I would love to, now is not the time. I doubt I could get away with taking it from him," Chris thought irritably.

"You might," Al told him.

"Not now," Chris thought firmly.

"When do the matches begin?" Eve asked.

"Soon, I expect," Ditrina replied.

"My, they are talkative," Tinacee commented.

"At times. I find allowing them to speak freely is better for their efficiency," Cassy told her.

"How interesting," Tinacee said with a small smile. "Perhaps I will try that with some of my house slaves."

"Echo smells mother!" Eve said suddenly.

"Where?" Chris demanded.

"He can't tell, but he caught her scent," Eve confirmed.

"Now I see, they are a family!" Tinacee said cheerfully. "Now I understand why you want these two slaves back so much."

"They are much more effective as a group," Cassy confirmed, doing her best not to strangle Tinacee.

"And the girl with the dragon, how did you tame such a creature?" Tinacee asked eagerly.

"That's a secret, I'm afraid. If everyone had dragons, she wouldn't be valuable," Cassy told her through gritted fangs, her grip on her persona slipping.

Tinacee laughed.

"You are not wrong. I look forward to seeing the girl's reaction to seeing her mother. It will be entertaining, to say the least," Tinacee giggled.

"These are vile creatures; we should wipe them off the face of this earth," Al seethed in Chris's head.

"I agree, but now is not the time," Chris thought.

"Oh look, the first match is starting. It looks like it's slaves versus monsters today! This will be entertaining," Tinacee said excitedly.

Despite being deep under the arena, Matt and Sarah could hear the faint sounds of battle drifting down to them, punctuated by the occasional bestial scream or growl. They had learned to ignore the sounds of the crowd by now, and the ever-present roar fell on deaf ears.

"Do you think we'll have to fight soon?" Matt asked quietly.

"Maybe, I can't really tell," Sarah admitted.

Matt sat silently for some time and eventually fumbled around until he pulled the book out of its hip case. He began running his hands over the pages.

"What are you doing?" Sarah asked quietly.

"It turns out that the book can show you braille," Matt explained.

"That's fantastic!" Sarah exclaimed. "At least this means that you can still read!" she said trying to cheer him up.

"It's a shame that I can't read braille," Matt said with disgust as he snapped the book shut.

"Maybe you could learn?" Sarah asked with forced cheerfulness.

"Are you going to teach me? It's not exactly like we have long now anyway," Matt told her.

"Not if you think like that!" Sarah said angrily, her cheerful façade failing.

"I'm just being realistic," Matt replied, his sightless eyes looking past her.

"We've both lost something in this hellish place, so don't play the pity card!" Sarah yelled.

"Sarah, I really don't see the point in trying to get pity from anyone at the moment. The only two people who care about us in this place are sitting in this cell. You are still a fantastic fighter even with one hand, but do you really think you can protect both of us?" Matt asked.

"I will try," Sarah said firmly.

"Just worry about yourself. As things stand now, I'm dead weight," Matt replied.

His white eyes continued to stare at her.

"Turn your head; that's creeping me out," Sarah told him.

"How considerate of you," Matt said as his face swiveled away.

They sat in silence once again—for how long, they couldn't tell.

"Get up!" the guard hissed from outside the cell.

Sarah's eyes snapped open, and she realized that she had drifted off to sleep in the dark cell.

"It is time for you to fight," the guard told them.

"Lucky us," Matt grumbled as he stood, using the wall to maintain his balance.

"What is wrong with that one? Were you two fighting?" the guard demanded, looking at Sarah.

"No, he's blind," Sarah told him.

The guard laughed.

"This will be fun to watch," he said as he opened the cell door, pulling Sarah from within.

"Could we perhaps have something to drink? We haven't had any water since we got here," Matt asked hopefully.

"Stupid night shift, always forgetting to feed the slaves. Fine, drink before you die," the guard told him, handing him a water skin from his belt.

Matt's hands fumbled with the cap, and he drank greedily before handing the skin to Sarah, who finished it off.

"Thank you," Matt said gratefully, shocked that the guard had actually let them drink.

"Shut up and march. You have a match to fight," the guard replied, shoving them forward with the butt of his spear.

They proceeded down the corridor, with Matt holding on to Sarah's stump for guidance until they reached the large doorway once more.

"You know the drill," the guard hissed as they stepped through the gateway.

The door shut and sealed them inside.

"Why do you think he let us drink?" Sarah asked.

"Well, there has to be more to them than the monsters we see. Maybe he has a compassionate streak?" Matt proposed, but his voice had a note of uncertainty.

"Ugg, you make it sound like they're people," Sarah snarled.

"Cassy's a person," Matt reminded her.

"As far as I'm concerned, Cassy's not a naga," Sarah said firmly.

"Maybe I should have asked for food, too; I'm starving," Matt mused.

"We're about to die, and the last thing you decide to think about is food. How typical," Sarah taunted as the doors before them swung open.

"Fighting for the glory of Mistress Tinacee, Sarah Shearcliff and Matthew Bleakstar!" Narfus's magically amplified voice boomed.

Blinding sunlight streamed over them, and Sarah shielded her eyes.

"Are the doors open yet? Is it time to start?" Matt asked nervously.

"Hold onto me," Sarah ordered as she led him out into the sun.

Together they walked into the center of the arena and waited for their opponent.

"Their opponent, captured in the burning canyons…" Narfus began before trailing off, giving the crowd a chance to cheer.

"Oh gods, this is bad," Sarah said as she saw the gate on the far side of the arena open.

"A griffin!" Narfus yelled.

"That's not good," Matt said, looking around sightlessly.

Sarah stared at her opponent. She had never seen a griffin up close, but she still recognized it. With the head of an eagle and a feathered lion's body, it was unmistakable. As the griffin stalked out of the gate on its talon-clad feet, it stretched its large wings in the air and screamed, a combination of a lion's roar and an eagle's cry.

"Well, the good news is, it looks like it's wings have been clipped, so I don't think it can fly," Sarah told Matt.

"Sarah, I grew up in Hailguard. I've seen the griffin riders before, and I know what those monsters can do. There is *nothing* good about this!" Matt yelled.

"We need a weapon," Sarah muttered to herself.

"Do you expect them to fight it unarmed?" Cassy demanded as she saw her friends standing in the sand.

"Of course, that's part of the fun. Why would I give them weapons when I want them to die?" Tinacee asked with a laugh.

"You're interfering with our bet!" Cassy yelled.

"You never said I couldn't rig the match," Tinacee said with a smug smile.

"Fine, two can play at that," Cassy said angrily. "Eve!"

Eve was leaning so far over the railing that Chris was forced to hold the back of her shirt to stop her from falling. She was waving madly to her mother, but Sarah had failed to notice her so far.

"Aunt Cas, it's mother!" Eve yelled.

"Aunt?" Tinacee asked in confusion.

"Eve, how strong is Echo?" Cassy demanded.

"Very," Eve assured her.

"Chris, your sword," Cassy ordered.

Understanding flashed across his face, and he drew the blade. It burst into flames due to the proximity of their hosts.

"Eve, I need Echo to take this to Sarah. Tell him to carry it," Chris instructed.

Eve looked at the burning three-foot sword and the small dragon. She smiled, and Echo's head snapped toward Chris.

"Throw it," Eve told him.

Chris hurled his sword out of the skybox toward the arena floor. As soon as it left his hand, the flames died. Eve held out her claw-like hand and Echo launched himself into the sky like a hunting falcon. With a beat of his small wings, he raced toward the plummeting blade. He folded his wings against his sides and dove, falling after the sword. Mere moments before the sword would have landed, Echo's wings snapped open, and he snatched the sword out of the air. It was lighter than it looked but still difficult for the small dragon to hold. Awkwardly, he flew toward Sarah, hampered by the weapon.

Sarah looked up as a small shadow passed over her and, to her surprise, saw a sword falling toward her face. Instinctively, she snatched it out of the air, and the shadow passed over her again. She saw Echo circling her, looking for a place to land. She looked at the sword again and recognized its distinctive rubies. She smiled.

"We're going to be fine, Matt," she called to her blind friend.

"Oh, why do you say that?" Matt asked nervously.

Echo decided to land and chose Matt as an appropriate perch. Matt felt claws grasp onto his shoulders and panicked, flailing around.

"Sarah, the griffin got me! Get it off! Sarah! Sarah, save me!" Matt screamed as he thrashed.

"Relax, Matt; its only Echo!" Sarah yelled as she tried to calm her companion.

The griffin looked at them with confusion from the other side of the arena and decided that these two would make a fitting lunch. It began to pace forward lazily.

"What do you mean, it's Echo? Isn't Echo always with Eve?" Matt asked as he calmed down.

Echo nuzzled the side of Matt's face and wondered why he panicked when he landed.

"Yeah, he is…" Sarah began as the gears in her head turned.

Her head searched the arena for Tinacee's skybox, and as she feared, she saw her daughter waving madly to her. Sarah's face became clouded with rage.

"Christian Shearcliff, you *did not* bring our daughter to this horrible city! When I get up there, I'm going to beat you within an inch of your life, *I swear to the gods!*" Sarah ranted as she shook the sword in his direction.

"Please don't kill him; that would be bad for me, too," Al told her.

Sarah almost dropped the sword in surprise.

"Mother saw me! Look, she's waving back!" Eve exclaimed gleefully.

"Your wife's going to kill you," Mi said cheerfully in Chris's head.

"What the hell are you doing?" Chris wondered in horror.

"Calm down, calm down. You've gotten so used to having a voice in your head; I thought that you might get lonely without Al clucking around like a mother hen. It'll be our little secret," Mi told him.

"Where is Al?" Chris wondered.

"Right not, he's convincing you wife not to kill you. It's a full-time job," Mi explained.

"How is he able to talk to her?" Chris wondered. "I thought you guys could only talk to me."

"No, no, no—easy mistake to make. We're *bound* to you, but we can talk to whoever's holding the artifact at the time. We usually just choose not to," Mi told him.

"I hate all this spirit stuff. You know that, right?" Chris thought irritably.

"Now's not the time to complain; now's the time to watch your wife butcher that griffin! I've got odds of three to one on Sarah!" Mi cheered.

"Are you Al?" Sarah thought in amazement.

"Yes, my name is Al," he replied.

"You're one of those spirits possessing my husband!" Sarah thought angrily.

"We are not possessing him…we're just sharing his body a little. It's harmless!" Al protested.

"You broke his soul!" Sarah yelled in her head.

"What's going on? Have we won yet?" Matt asked as he stumbled around blindly.

"You can lecture me later, but for now, use the sword to kill that griffin!" Al told her.

"We are going to have a long talk later," Sarah promised him as she charged toward the approaching griffin, leaving Matt wandering aimlessly with Echo, asking what was happening and getting no response.

The griffin saw her charging and quickened its pace, letting out a fearsome screech.

"How does this sword work?" Sarah demanded as she neared the monster.

"Just fight, and my skill will work alongside yours!" Al told her.

"That doesn't make any sense!" Sarah screamed aloud as she swung the sword at the griffin.

The blade burst into flames, and the griffin sprung backward, narrowly avoiding the attack.

"You are not allowed to interfere with a match in progress," Tinacee told Cassy angrily.

"Oh, but *you're* allowed to rig the match?!" Cassy demanded.

"Yes! That's how this works!" Tinacee insisted. "You act like you've never seen an arena fight before!"

"That's it! I'm done with this!" Cassy shrieked, the slaver act finally proving too much for her to bear.

"Well, with that, your plan fails," Mi told Chris. "Try not to die and remember your magic!" he said with a laugh.

"What are you talking about?" Tinacee asked, thoroughly confused.

"Chris, I tried, but I can't stand these people! It's too much!" Cassy screamed, finally pushed to her wits' end.

"Oh, hell, Ditrina! Plan B!" Chris yelled as he sprung to his feet.

"Really?" Ditrina asked excitedly.

"Burn it all!" Chris bellowed.

"Whooooo! This is gonna be cool!" Mi cheered.

"What are you people talking about?" Tinacee demanded. "Plan B?"

Ditrina reached over and palmed Tinacee's face. White hot fire burned between her fingers, and before Tinacee had a chance to scream, they heard a sound like fat popping in a fire. Tinacee's body slumped forward, her face a smoldering charred mess. Narfus's eyes widened, and he vanished from sight, teleporting to safety.

"You were very rude to Cas," Ditrina told the corpse.

"I'm sorry, Chris. I tried, I really did," Cassy sobbed.

"It's all right. You did your best. Find a weapon," he told her.

"I'll meet you down on the arena floor. Go get Sarah and Matt," Cassy told him as she raced away from the skybox.

"Can I go now?" Ditrina asked eagerly, looking around with excitement.

"Once you've done as much damage as you can, meet us down on the arena floor. Remember, that's where we are, so don't accidentally kill us," Chris warned her.

"Got it!" Ditrina yelled cheerfully before disappearing.

"Where have my aunts run off to?" Eve asked Chris.

"They're going to help us escape," Chris told her.

"You should put the cloak on Eve, so she doesn't get hurt," Mi told him.

"Good thinking," Chris thought back and unclasped the cloak, beckoning Eve to come closer.

"What is it, Father?" Eve asked happily.

"I need you to wear this. It will protect you," Chris told her as he fastened the cloak around her.

To his shock, the cloak seemed to shrink to fit her tiny frame. Eve smiled at him, then cocked her head as if she was listening to a voice only she could hear. Chris realized what was happening, but it was too late.

"Mi, don't!" Chris yelled, but he was too slow.

Eve disappeared.

Chris concentrated on seeing his daughter, but with everything that was going on, he found he couldn't focus enough to see through the enchantment.

"I'm going to kill you, you undead bastard," Chris muttered, looking around for the fastest way down to the arena floor.

In the distance, he heard a low boom and saw smoke rising above the lip of the arena.

Ditrina rose slowly into the air, suspended in a vortex of fire. She had returned to the estate of Tinacee, near the center of the city, and now she contemplated how best to destroy everything she could see. This was a once-in-a-lifetime opportunity, after all, and she didn't want to waste it. A squad of naga bowmen let loose a volley at her, but she waved her hand, and archer and arrow alike turned to ash. Most of the city was built of sandstone, so she doubted simply setting things on fire at random would have much effect. An idea rushed into her head, and she made her decision. She decided it was finally time for her to earn her nickname.

Sarah lunged backward to avoid the griffin's snapping beak. Despite the sword's speed, the griffin proved too fast to kill outright. They had engaged in a strange dance, dodging and weaving around one another as they avoided each other's blows.

"Sarah, am I safe here?" Matt asked as he bumbled toward them.

"Matt, get back, you blind idiot!" Sarah screamed as the griffin fixed him with its yellow eyes.

The griffin decided the one without a flaming sword would be a far better target and leapt over Sarah toward Matt, gliding on its clipped wings.

"Matt, hit the deck!" Sarah yelled, charging after the griffin.

"Why?" Matt asked as the griffin landed directly in front of him.

The griffin shrieked triumphantly as it reared back to slice Matt with its talons, but to its surprise, it was hit in the chest by a tiny ball of scales and anger. Echo latched himself firmly to the griffin's chest and began to tear into its neck with his short fangs. The griffin stumbled back in surprise and attempted to rake Echo off with its talons, but to no avail. Echo managed to reposition himself on the griffin's back and promptly lit the feathers on its head on fire. The griffin screamed in rage and reared farther back trying to toss him off.

"Thanks, Echo!" Sarah yelled as she sliced the legs out from under the distracted griffin.

The beast landed in the sand and shrieked in pain. Sarah thrust quickly and put it out of its misery. The crowd cheered madly, still oblivious to the destruction outside the arena.

"What just happened?" Matt asked as he stumbled forward blindly, proceeding to trip over the griffin's corpse.

"Take a left up ahead," the voice in Eve's head told her.

She didn't know who this strange invisible man was or why she could hear him, but she didn't care. He had told her he was one of her father's friends, and he had begun to speak to her right after she had put on her father's cloak, so she was inclined to believe him. He had told her many things, like how to stay hidden using the cloak and, more importantly, ways to have fun she had never imagined.

"Why are we running?" Eve asked.

"Because you don't have much time left in this city. Don't you want to have a little fun before you go?" the man asked her.

"Who are you?" Eve asked.

"Call me, Mi," Mi told her.

"I'm confused," Eve admitted, not understanding the difference.

"That's ok! We're going to play a game now," Mi told her.

"I like games!" Eve exclaimed.

"I know, your dad told me. Now, do you still have that little dagger?" Mi asked.

"Yeah," Eve answered, not understanding.

"Wonderful! Now, do you see that guard up ahead?" Mi asked.

Ditrina looked around her and saw naga running wildly below her, like ants with their hill disturbed. Calmly, she let her magic flow through her, building her strength. When she was ready, she released it all, no direction, no aim, only power. It felt wonderful. She found that she couldn't help but laugh as the air around her became fire, rushing madly through the city streets. Gauzy curtains vanished in puffs of smoke, and the stone streets glowed with heat. Several buildings crumbled into dust. Had it not been for the screams, Ditrina would have sworn she had found her way to heaven.

She looked toward the arena and nodded happily seeing that, while scorched, it was intact. Her friends were fine. There was a sudden blinding light and a crack of thunder, and she was falling. Regaining control, she used her magic to slow her descent, and she landed lightly, nursing her injured shoulder.

Marching down the street toward her, seemingly oblivious to the scorching flagstones, were three naga dressed in the robes of clerics. They chanted, and another blast of lightning flashed toward her. Ditrina summoned a wall of energy, and the lightning exploded against it.

"Go away! I am trying to have fun here!" Ditrina yelled angrily.

The clerics replied with more lightning. Ditrina sighed.

"Fine, if you are that eager, I will deal with you first," she told them as she marched down the blazing street, her blue hair flying around in the scorching wind.

"Lady Shearcliff!" Jasheir yelled as he raced through the arena entrance toward her.

"Jasheir? What are you doing here? I thought you were back at Tinacee's estate?" Cassy asked.

"I ran here right away. It's Ditrina! She's gone mad! The entire city is in flames!" Jasheir yelled.

"Don't mind her, she's just letting off a little steam before we go home," Cassy told him with a dismissive wave. "By the way, where can I find a bow? I left mine back in the elven city to avoid suspicion,"

"She's killing everyone!" Jasheir pleaded.

"No, she's killing *most* everyone. She agreed not to destroy the arena floor. Head there if you want to live," Cassy told him.

"I need to stop her!" Jasheir yelled, rushing back out of the arena into the city.

"Your funeral!" Cassy called after him.

She sighed and looked out into the burning city. She felt a pang of guilt.

"Gods damn it," Cassy muttered, charging after Jasheir.

Chris looked around in horror. The dead guards seemed to have been killed by a dagger, but that wasn't what concerned him. What worried him was the mutilation of the bodies. It looked like most had been killed with the first cut, but for some reason, the killer had decided to continue to slice away at the bodies long after they had died. He sighed.

"Mi, what the hell are you telling my daughter?" he asked as he inspected one of the guard's massive swords.

Deciding that it was far too big for him to wield, he discarded it and raced to find a way to his daughter. After all, Sarah had Al to look out for her.

"Sarah, where the hell are we going?" Matt protested as Sarah dragged him along, Echo riding on his shoulder.

"It looks like Chris set Ditrina loose, which means we're leaving the city soon. I need to get my ring back!" Sarah told him as she let go of Matt to pull open the massive arena doors.

She wasn't quite strong enough with only one hand.

"Matt, help me open this door," Sarah told him.

"I can't see!" Matt protested.

"You don't have to see to pull!" Sarah yelled as she placed his hands on the door. "Pull!" she ordered and slowly the door opened before them.

"Great, now what?" Matt asked.

"Now we open the second door," Sarah told him.

Matt groaned.

"Quit your complaining. We need to get through here," Sarah told him.

"How do we know Narfus is down here?" Matt asked.

"I just have a gut feeling that we should head this way; trust me on this," Sarah replied.

"Just don't let me run into any walls," Matt muttered as he fumbled toward the door.

"Why are we going under the arena?" Eve asked as Mi led her deeper through the tunnels.

"They keep all the gold from the bets down here. Wouldn't you like a little souvenir for the trip home?" Mi asked in reply.

"I don't want gold. I want Echo," Eve told him.

"Well, the dragon isn't here right now, so just keep going, and you can have the next best thing," Mi told her.

"No, I'm going to find Echo," Eve told him as she stopped running.

"Fine. If you're so insistent on finding that little beast, go find him. I'm warning you, though, you're missing out on a great opportunity to get rich," Mi told her.

"Gold is heavy," Eve replied as she ran back the way she had come, trusting her connection to the dragon to lead her to him.

Like a compass, it guided her through the tunnels. She began to hear quick, heavy footsteps.

"Ok, Eve, stop!" Mi said suddenly.

"Yes, Mi?" Eve asked.

"Focus on hiding, and see who's coming," Mi instructed.

Eve followed his orders to the letter and peeked out around the corner.

"Wonderful!" Mi exclaimed, seeing the person in question.

Narfus was walking quickly down the corridor, carrying a large sack that sounded suspiciously like it was filled with coins.

"Eve, that's the person that took your mother away," Mi told her softly.

Eve tensed up and readied her dagger.

"Wait, do you want to make your mom *really* happy?" Mi asked her.

"Yes!" Eve said quickly.

"In that case, we're going to play another game, but this time, there are some rules. Listen closely," Mi began.

"Where is Ditrina?" Jasheir yelled as he looked around.

They saw a large explosion in the distance.

"That way!" Cassy yelled as she raced down the street.

By now, those in the arena had begun to panic, and a river of bodies raced from the gates behind them out into the burning city.

"Kinda funny, the safest place for them was actually right where they were," Cassy said as they ran.

"How is this amusing to you?" Jasheir demanded.

"I've spent the last few days violating everything I hold dear. I've been forced to use slaves; I've been forced to eat *people*; and worst of all, I've had to act like the monster most people think I am! If you are looking to me for mercy, you're going to have little luck," Cassy snarled at him.

Jasheir was silent for several blocks.

"I was wrong. Perhaps you are more like us than I thought," he said quietly.

Cassy chose to ignore him.

Ditrina waved her hand, and the sky began to rain fire. Smoke from burning buildings began to block out the sun, and the brightest thing in the city was her flames. She giggled in delight and stepped over what was once a cleric of Semel, blasting a nearby building to smithereens.

"And they said you should not destroy buildings," she laughed.

Several naga raced toward her, though she saw they were unarmed. Two males and one female, they stopped a few yards away.

"Why?" the female called.

"This city is a foul place, filled with foul creatures. It deserves to burn," Ditrina called back.

"What do you want? Slaves? Gold? We'll give you anything, just please stop!" they begged, tears streaming down their faces.

"I have no interest in stopping. Thank you for your offer, though," Ditrina told them with a cheerful smile.

She waved her hand, and they vanished into flames.

"I am so glad Chris told me this was ok. I must remember to pay him back somehow," Ditrina mused as she walked down the street, casually destroying buildings in the flaming rain.

CHAPTER THIRTEEN

"Look, there she is!" Cassy called as she sprinted toward Ditrina.

"Perhaps we should be cautious?" Jasheir proposed.

"Why? Di would never hurt me. Come on!" Cassy called as she ran toward the destructive elf. "Di! Di, over here!" she called as she ran.

Ditrina turned, and suddenly Cassy saw a giant ball of fire rushing toward her. She froze in fear, but at the last second, the spell broke apart into sparks. Even so, Cassy felt the searing heat wash over her scales.

"Cas! You snuck up on me!" Ditrina called as she ran toward her, embracing Cassy with a large hug. "I almost cooked you," she giggled.

"Di, are you feeling all right?" Cassy asked nervously, still shaken from her near incineration.

"I feel wonderful! Look!" Ditrina yelled as she detonated a massive fireball in the building next to them.

Sandstone melted, and wood turned to ash, leaving them coughing in the dust.

"I am having so much fun!" Ditrina yelled as she spun in a circle, arms outstretched.

"You still have enough power left to get us home, right?" Cassy asked cautiously.

"Yes, of course," Ditrina said with a smile as she fell backward into Cassy's arms.

"Let's head back now, Di. You're not acting like yourself," Cassy told her as she returned the elf to her feet.

"Do we have to?" Ditrina pouted.

"What is wrong with her?" Jasheir asked nervously.

"There is nothing wrong with me!" Ditrina yelled with sudden anger.

Flames burned in her hands.

"I am perfectly normal! I am the Fire Princess!" Ditrina cackled.

"Di, you've always hated that nickname," Cassy reminded her.

"Did I? Maybe because I felt like I never really earned it," Ditrina told her with a hungry gleam in her black eyes.

"You're starting to scare me, Di. Let's head back," Cassy said nervously.

"Ok, ok, fine, just one more," Ditrina told her.

"Di, I *really* think we should head back…" Cassy began.

Ditrina didn't hear her. She was too busy launching herself into the sky on a pillar of fire. Cassy and Jasheir stumbled back under the sudden wave of heat, and they were gifted a large explosion that set their ears ringing. Small chunks of rubble fell around them, and Ditrina floated gently back down to the ground.

"We can go back now," she said contently.

Chris heard muffled explosions in the distance and recognized them as Ditrina's handiwork. Following the trail of bodies, Chris searched for his daughter. Finally, he found a set of bloody footprints to follow. They seemed to lead deeper under the arena.

"Mi, where are you taking my daughter?" Chris muttered as he jogged down the corridor.

"Come on, Matt, he's gotta be right ahead," Sarah said as she dragged her blind friend along.

"Slow down, Sarah!" Matt yelled as he stumbled behind her.

"He's getting away with my ring!" Sarah yelled back.

"How do you know he's down here? He probably fled with everyone else once the explosions started," Matt told her.

"That scum is probably grabbing as many slaves to take with him as he can. Do you think a monster like him would leave empty-handed?" Sarah demanded.

"I hear something up ahead," Matt told her suddenly.

Sarah stopped and listened as well. Coming from around the corner were reptilian hisses of pain and familiar giggling. Sarah pulled her stump free from Matt's hand and readied Chris's sword as she rushed around the bend. She discovered something bizarre.

"What is this!?" Narfus screamed as his snakelike eyes scanned the corridor for his assailant.

Sarah watched in awe as a deep cut appeared behind his knee, and he fell to the ground. Narfus healed it quickly and rose to his feet once again, only to have another cut appear on his stomach. He screamed in rage and shot a lightning bolt at random down the hall. For a moment, it seemed as if the attacks had stopped, but suddenly Sarah heard a giggle, and Narfus found himself sporting a long cut on his back.

"This is Mi's treachery," Al told Sarah.

"You mean Chris is doing that?" Sarah thought.

"No, Chris is elsewhere, though he is close. I don't think you're going to be happy," Al warned her.

"Why?" Sarah wondered cautiously.

"I led you toward my brother so that you could find Chris, but it seems Chris has given the cloak to another," Al told her.

"Oh, gods," Sarah said as she realized what was going on.

"Please don't kill your husband; I'll die too," Al pleaded.

"Eve?" Sarah called cautiously.

Narfus's head snapped toward her, but he was cut behind the knees again. He fell to the floor howling.

"Hi, Mother!" Eve called excitedly, looking to have appeared out of thin air. "I'm playing a game with the snake man! Mi said you would be happy if I kept him here for you. Are you happy?" Eve asked excitedly.

Sarah looked at the wounded naga and saw her ring dangling from his hood.

"Very happy, sweetie. Go stand by your uncle now. I have something I need to do," Sarah told her.

221

Eve skipped happily over to Matt and pulled Echo off his shoulders. "Your eyes look funny," she told him.

"I can't see anymore," Matt told her.

"That's ok. You don't need to see to be my uncle," Eve said cheerfully as she took his hand.

"Hello, Narfus," Sarah said as she walked toward him, twirling the sword.

Narfus snarled and blasted a bolt of lightning at her, but Al moved quickly and deflected it with the blade. Sarah continued to walk forward slowly.

"You have something that belongs to me," she said, smiling sweetly.

"Slave filth," Narfus spat as he rose to a knee.

"If you'll excuse me for a moment," Sarah told him before the flaming sword flashed in front of him.

Narfus screamed as his hands fell to the floor.

"Fair is fair," Sarah said, nodding seriously.

"You cur!" Narfus wailed as his blood ran across the ground.

Sarah pressed the edge of the sword against the back of his head, and Narfus went very still.

"I'll be taking this back," Sarah told him, and with a flick of her sword, her ring fell from the edge of his hood, along with a sizeable chunk of the hood itself.

Narfus shrieked and attempted to crawl away on his stumps.

"Matt, what was it I said I was going to do to this piece of scum?" Sarah asked as she strolled casually after him.

"You...you said you were going to skin him," Matt said, unsure of whether or not he was glad to be blind at the moment.

"That's right! I did say that, didn't I? Eve, sweetheart, can I borrow your dagger?" Sarah asked sweetly.

Chris heard an inhuman scream echo through the stone corridors.

"I really hope Eve didn't have anything to do with that," he muttered as he quickened his pace to a full sprint.

Deciding to try something new, Chris attempted to tap into Al's magic. He had never tried this while they were separated before;

nevertheless, he was pleasantly surprised to find the power awaited his command. He drew it out and let it fuel him. His eyes began to glow. His speed increased, and soon he was running far faster than humanly possible. Details blurred around him, and he shot down the hall until he skidded around the corner. Halfway down this new corridor, he saw a grizzly sight.

"Sarah!" Chris yelled in shock and disgust.

His wife was completely covered in blood and was currently straddling a large chunk of unrecognizable flesh pinned to the floor by his sword. She held a dagger in her single hand and was currently scraping the last of the skin off the edges of the carcass.

"Look, Chris! I got my ring back!" Sarah called, waving her bloody hand high, the gold ring smeared with gore.

"What are you doing?" Chris asked as he ran down the hall toward her.

"Just teaching Eve how to properly skin a naga," Sarah said with a smile as she stepped away from the body, a ragged skin draped over her arm. "It's good to see you," she told him as she stepped in for a hug.

"Let's wait until after you've cleaned up," Chris said, backing away hastily.

Sarah looked at herself and seemed to notice the blood for the first time.

"Oh yeah, that would probably be for the best," she laughed.

"Look, Father! Uncle S is blind!" Eve called excitedly. "Isn't that cool?"

"I wouldn't say it's cool," Matt said with a frown.

"Is everyone all right?" Chris asked, looking at the three of them.

"Well, I lost a hand, and as Eve just said, Matt's blind. I'd say that qualifies as not all right," Sarah told him.

"Allow me to rephrase. Is anyone about to die?" Chris asked.

"Well, you are, unless you have a damn good reason for bringing our daughter to this city," Sarah said as she pointed the sword at him.

To his relief, it became too heavy for her to hold and the tip clanged to the floor.

"This is why magical weapons suck! They never work when they need to!" Sarah ranted as she struggled with the sword.

Her eyes widened as she looked past Chris.

"Look out! More naga!" Sarah yelled as the sword once again became light as a feather.

Chris turned and saw Jasheir running toward them.

"Relax, it's just Jasheir," Chris told her.

"Who?" Sarah asked.

"He's one of the naga who tried to capture you; he's on our side now," Chris explained.

"Bullshit," Sarah spat, but she made no move to attack.

"What's going on, Jasheir?" Chris asked.

"It is Ditrina. She is refusing to come into the arena. Something about her work not being done yet or something like that. Cassy is trying to lure her inside, but it is not working!" Jasheir hissed with frustration.

"What's gotten into her?" Matt asked with confusion as another dull boom shook the arena.

Dust fell from the ceiling above them.

"I may have told her that she could cut loose on the city," Chris said sheepishly.

"You're an idiot," Sarah told him as she handed his sword back.

"Eve, can I have my cloak back?" Chris asked kindly.

"Can I still talk to Mi?" Eve asked cautiously.

"Not right now," Chris told her.

"Nope," Eve said before vanishing from sight.

Sarah looked at him irritably.

"You gave a six-year-old the ability to hide whenever and wherever she wants, with an irresponsible voice in her head and a dragon. You deserve the parent of the year award!" Sarah snarled at him.

"Weren't you just teaching her how to *skin people?*" Chris yelled back.

"No, I was teaching her how to skin *naga*. It's easy to mistake these monsters for people, but don't let them fool you," Sarah said, looking at Jasheir.

"Can we please stop the elf?" Jasheir begged.

"Fine, come on, Eve," Chris called as they set off down the hallway.

"Coming!" Eve called from wherever she was hidden.

"How come Echo got hidden as well?" Sarah asked as they ran down the hallway.

"Probably because he was riding on her shoulder?" Chris proposed.

"But I thought the cloak only worked on one person at a time?" Matt said as he was dragged along by Sarah, remembering the disastrous time he and Chris had tried to share the cloak to avoid a pack of dire wolves.

"Why is that what you guys are worried about right now?" Chris asked as they ran.

"Just curious," Sarah replied.

"You've never had the slightest interest in magical artifacts before," Matt pointed out.

"Well, I had also never *used* a magical artifact before, so shut up, blind boy or you're going to end up running into a wall," Sarah warned.

"Shutting up now," Matt agreed.

Eve's laughter echoed around them.

"Eve, please stop hiding," Chris told her.

"Mi told me to say no!" Eve called gleefully.

"Of course he did," Sarah sighed.

"It's times like these I hate my brother," Al told Chris.

"You and me both," Chris thought in reply.

"I got a glimpse of what goes on in your wife's head," Al said.

"Do tell," Chris thought with mild amusement.

"It was frightening," Al said, and Chris was sure he felt him shudder in his mind.

"Pansy," Chris thought back.

"There is only so much bloodlust I can stomach at one time," Al told him. "She did some dark things in that arena."

"Look, it is Cassy!" Jasheir yelled from the front of the group.

"Oh, thank the gods, you found them! I was worried that…what is that?" Cassy asked, noticing what Sarah was carrying.

"Narfus," Sarah said cheerfully.

Cassy did her best not to gag.

"Where is Ditrina?" Chris demanded.

"Up there," Cassy told him, trying to tame her rebellious stomach.

Chris looked to the sky and saw Ditrina suspended atop a vortex of flames. Her long blue hair whipped around her face, and her black eyes gleamed in the firelight.

"I thought it was daytime?" Eve asked with confusion, unable to see the sun through the massive clouds of smoke.

"What has she done?" Sarah asked with horror.

They heard Ditrina's insane musical laughter and saw a nearby building vanish in a ball of fire.

"This is why Echo likes Aunt Di," Eve's voice confirmed.

"Ditrina! Get down here!" Chris yelled up at her.

Ditrina's face turned to them, and they saw madness in her eyes.

"What the hell is wrong with her?" Chris demanded.

"I don't know! The more stuff she's destroyed, the worse she's gotten! It's like she's forgetting who she is!" Cassy told him nervously.

"Listen to me, Ditrina! We need to go home now!" Chris called up to her.

"Go home, then!" Ditrina yelled back before gleefully destroying another building.

"You need to come with us!" Cassy screamed up at her, her voice barely audible over the roar of the flames.

"That won't help," Matt told them.

"What do you mean?" Chris asked.

"She's not in her right mind. Logic won't help you here," Matt explained.

"Do you know what's happening to her?" Cassy asked hopefully.

The sounds of insane laughter and explosions drifted around them.

"When you use magic, it feels good..." Matt began.

"What? No, it doesn't," Chris interrupted.

"Shut up and let me explain!" Matt snapped. "When you use enough magic, your body begins to experience a slight euphoric effect because of the residual mana coursing through your system. If you use too much, then that effect is intensified. It usually doesn't happen to clerics because we are only given the bare minimum amount of magic to fuel our spells, but from time to time, I've heard of it occurring. With as much magic as Ditrina's used, she's likely drunk on the power. If this goes on, she'll lose all reason and eventually burn herself out by casting more than she's capable of," Matt told them.

"What happens then?" Cassy demanded.

"She dies," Matt told her bluntly.

"This is bad," Jasheir said, looking up at the insane mage.

"We need something to shock her out of this, something she really likes or is afraid of," Matt told them.

"Well, she's not listening to me!" Cassy yelled indignantly.

"She probably can't hear you very well; don't take it personally," Matt told her.

"We need something she's afraid of…" Chris mused to himself.

He realized what had to be done.

"Eve! We need Echo again!" Chris yelled suddenly.

"Mi says you're trying to trick me," Eve's voice told him.

"Tell Mi to shut up, then come here!" Chris yelled, his voice raising in anger.

"Sorry," Eve said meekly as she appeared in front of him.

"It's ok. In fact, if you help us, you can keep the cloak a while longer," Chris promised her.

"What do I need to do!?" Eve asked with excitement.

"Tell Echo to go say hello to Ditrina. She's feeling a little lonely up there all by herself," Chris told her.

"Are you sure? I don't think Aunt Di likes Echo very much," Eve said with uncertainty.

Her head cocked to one side like she was listening.

"But Mi is saying that this is a good idea. And he's laughing. I guess this will be ok," Eve decided.

She was silent for several seconds, and suddenly Echo's face appeared from within the cloak. His red eyes fixed on his favorite aunt, and he sprang into the air, disappearing into a cloud of smoke.

"I hope this works," Jasheir said, looking at the destruction nervously.

Ditrina continued her assault on the city, all the while giggling like a lunatic until they saw a small flash of scales plunging toward her. Ditrina was too focused on destruction to notice until Echo crashed into her chest, latching onto her robes with his talons and licking her face with his long, snakelike tongue. Ditrina screamed, and the spell that held her aloft died. She plummeted toward the ground.

"I got her!" Cassy screamed, racing forward on powerful legs, springing off a large chunk of rubble and grabbing Ditrina out of the air.

She landed lightly and set Ditrina on the ground.

"Get him off! Get him off! Get him off!" Ditrina shrieked while trying to pull an excited Echo off of her chest.

Eve raced forward and snatched Echo away from her.

"Why are you always cruel to Echo?" Eve protested, stroking the dragon lovingly.

"He attacked me!" Ditrina shrieked as she scampered behind Cassy.

"Ditrina!" Chris yelled.

"Yes, leader?" Ditrina asked.

"Are you done playing Fire Princess?" he demanded.

"Please do not call me that," Ditrina said quickly as she stood up.

"Hold on! She was just insane! Are we just ignoring the fact she destroyed a city?" Sarah demanded.

"Chris told me to," Ditrina told her like it made everything better.

"You are all mad," Jasheir said, looking at them in horror.

He was ignored.

"Ditrina, can you take us home now?" Matt asked.

"Of course," Ditrina said, dusting herself off. "Everyone gather around me please."

One by one, they formed a circle and linked hands. Chris double checked to ensure that Eve was between him and Sarah before he gave Ditrina the nod. They spun quickly and found themselves standing in a frozen forest in the middle of the night.

"Ditrina, what the hell? We were supposed to go home!" Chris yelled.

Sarah and Eve were too busy being ill to voice their complaints, while Matt had no idea where they were, only that it was cold. Cassy and Jasheir were looking around in shock.

"I am sorry, but we must stop here first. There is a small chance that Matthew's vision can be repaired by the healers in the city, and many of our belongings are still here. The elves also wish to conduct their tests on Eve, and if we were simply to return to the valley, we would be forced to leave again soon. I want to get this over with so that I never have to return here again," Ditrina told him.

"Fine, let's just make this quick," Cassy said, shivering in the cold.

"We will hurry," Ditrina agreed as they set a quick pace toward the entrance of the city.

"I'm cold," Eve declared as they walked, shivering despite the warmth of the cloak she still wore.

The cloak seemed to shimmer around her, and suddenly it was lined with fur.

"I didn't know it could do that," Chris thought with surprise.

"Knowing my brother, it can probably do quite a lot," Al told him.

"I wonder why he never told me," Chris thought.

"Likely because you never needed it. He likes to always have a surprise at the ready," Al told him.

As they continued to walk, Ditrina stumbled.

"Are you all right, Di?" Cassy asked.

"I am fine, just tired," Ditrina told her with a weak smile.

"We need to keep moving," Jasheir hissed, looking around the frozen forest nervously. "We are unprepared for this weather."

"It will take several hours to reach the city," Ditrina told them.

Her breath was coming in ragged gasps.

"Di, you need to rest. You've used too much magic," Cassy told her.

"Do not worry about me," Ditrina told her. "I can keep moving."

They set out once more, trudging through the snow.

Half an hour later all, save Eve, were violently shivering.

"Sarah, I swear if you let me walk into a tree one more time we're going to have a problem," Matt warned her, nursing his face.

"We are going to freeze to death," Jasheir hissed, looking around angrily.

"How did you make it through the forest the first time?" Cassy asked him.

"Narfus used his magic to keep us from freezing," Jasheir told her.

"Well, he's doing his best to keep me warm now," Sarah told him, gesturing to the bloody skin draped around her shoulders.

"You are not amusing," Jasheir told her.

"I can try to warm us up with magic," Ditrina proposed.

"It's too risky for you to use any more magic at the moment; you could pass out," Cassy told her.

"Either way, we need to warm up. Jasheir's right, at this rate we won't reach the city," Chris told them.

He looked at Ditrina.

"If you send off that flare, will they come to you, or does it only open the gate?" he asked.

"It can be seen from the other side, so if I sent it up from this far away, they will likely investigate to see what the problem is," Ditrina told him.

"I hate to ask this, but would you cast it?" Chris asked gently.

"Of course. I keep telling you all that I am fine," Ditrina said as she stretched her hand above her head, sending a golden flare into the sky.

She smiled at them to prove her point, then her eyes rolled up into her head, and she collapsed into the snow.

"Fine, my ass," Cassy muttered as she picked Ditrina up out of the snow.

"Let's make a fire and hope the elves find us. We need to get warm," Chris told them.

"I'll get wood," Jasheir hissed as he walked off into the woods a way.

"I'll help," Sarah said, placing Matt's hand in Eve's. "Watch your uncle," she told her before following the naga.

"Mi is telling me to lead you into more trees, but I won't because I like you," Eve told him cheerfully.

"Glad to see I'm loved," Matt said as he sat carefully in the snow.

Eve promptly sat on his lap and leaned back against him. A few seconds later, she was asleep.

"I'm not surprised; she's been through so much these last few days," Cassy said, kneeling beside her niece, still cradling Ditrina.

"Matt, if you like, you can get some rest, too," Chris told him.

"Just because I'm blind doesn't mean that I'm useless, you know," Matt said angrily.

"Ok, how would you like to help?" Chris asked him.

Matt opened his mouth to reply, but no words came out. After several seconds of thinking, he said:

"I'm watching Eve."

Chris laughed.

"Watching her?" he asked innocently.

"Metaphorically!" Matt said angrily.

Cassy sat beside him, laying Ditrina across her lap.

"It's all right, Matt. Being blind has its benefits, you know," Cassy told him.

"Like what?" Matt asked cautiously.

"Well, for starters, Ditrina and I never have to worry about you peeking ever again!" Cassy said happily.

"How is that a benefit?" Matt asked crossly.

"I never said they were benefits for you," Cassy replied.

"I hate you all," Matt said with a shake of his head, but Chris saw him smile a little bit.

"We found enough wood," Sarah called as she walked back toward them with Jasheir, arms laden with firewood.

Even with one hand, Sarah carried a sizeable amount.

"Great, let's get a fire going before we all die," Matt snapped.

"Echo will help," Eve declared, roused from her brief nap by their return.

The little dragon slithered out from under the cloak. He looked at Eve and the pile of wood then sent a little gout of fire into the center. As it turned out, dragon fire burns hot enough to ignite even frozen wood, and soon they were all huddled around a roaring fire. Echo returned to Eve's side, and Eve returned to her rest.

"So, what happens now?" Jasheir asked once they could all feel their fingers once again.

"Well, you heard Ditrina's plans for once we reach the city," Chris told him.

"Yes, and what comes after? What is to become of me?" Jasheir asked.

"Don't know, don't care," Sarah told him.

"Your concern warms me more than the fire," Jasheir told her with a grim smile.

"I'm still a little confused. Who the hell are you?" Matt asked.

"Do you remember the naga that bit you on the side?" Jasheir asked.

"How could I forget? That hurt like hell!" Matt yelled.

"Yes, naga venom is quite painful," Jasheir mused. "Anyway, I was the one to the left of him."

"One of the slavers? How did you end up freeing us then?" Matt asked.

"Cassy told me to," Jasheir explained like that was a reasonable answer.

"Sorry, but anytime a story begins with *Cassy told me to*, it never ends well. Gimme more details, please," Matt told him with an amused smile.

"Well, at the time, I thought that Cassy was an important naga house leader, and as such, I was afraid that she wielded some type of authority. I was mistaken, but by then I was already assisting her and had passed the point of no return," Jasheir told him.

"See, that was your first mistake—thinking Cassy had any authority." Matt laughed.

"Believe me, I know," Jasheir sighed.

"I'm right here, you know!" Cassy said indignantly.

"Are you? I didn't see you there," Matt said, smiling sightlessly in the direction of her voice.

"A new era of mockery has dawned. Leave it to Matt to find a way to make blindness insulting." Sarah laughed.

"I try," Matt said, smiling in her general direction.

"Anyway, now that we've gotten away from that horrible place, we're going to go home, rest for a while—" Chris began.

"A long while," Cassy cut in.

"Then get back to work," Chris finished.

"Where do you recommend I try to find employment?" Jasheir asked.

"Well, what can you do?" Chris asked.

"I am a skilled swordsman and slave catcher," Jasheir said proudly.

"Slavery is illegal in Desgail," Chris reminded him.

"I am still a skilled warrior. Is there a need for such people?" Jasheir asked.

"Yeah, people are always looking for a skilled blade. Slaying monsters, guarding caravans, exploring reaches unknown, it's really up to you," Sarah told him.

"What do you all do?" Jasheir asked.

"Whatever we get paid to do. Killing monsters, for the most part, but we're open for really anything," Chris told him.

"Where do you find work?" Jasheir asked.

"We've found a place where jobs come to us. It's a little off the beaten path, but you see some interesting people around there," Cassy told him.

"Could you bring me to this place? From there, I will find my own way, but this seems like a good place to start," Jasheir told them.

"I don't see a problem with that," Cassy agreed.

"Just don't come showing up on our doorstep," Sarah warned.

"Do not worry; I wish to be on my way. That little girl frightens me," Jasheir told them.

"Why is everyone so mean to my daughter!? I swear, it's like the entire world is out to get her!" Sarah yelled.

"I watched her laugh while stabbing a man to death," Cassy told her.

"That was one time!" Sarah argued.

"I had to follow the trail of bodies she left behind in the city," Chris told her. "They were pretty gruesome."

"How could you take their side on this?" Sarah demanded.

"It's not a matter of what side I'm on, I'm just pointing out the fact that Eve's killed a lot more people than your average six-year-old," Chris told her.

"She's killing my legs right now," Matt muttered as he shifted his weight under the girl.

"Sorry, Uncle S," Eve said as she readjusted her position.

"Eve! I thought you were asleep," Matt said with surprise.

"I was. Echo woke me when he heard my name," Eve told him. She looked at Chris.

"How many people do normal kids kill?" she asked.

"What do you mean? You're perfectly normal," Chris assured her.

"I have a baby dragon and half of my body is covered in scars. For whatever reason, you all keep saying I'm something called a *blessed*, and I've started to realize that when the nine-foot-tall snake man is scared of you, that you are not normal," Eve replied.

"That's right; you're just as weird as the rest of us," Matt said cheerfully as he gazed sightlessly into the fire.

"Good," Eve said with a content sigh.

She was silent for several long moments.

"Is she asleep again?" Jasheir asked cautiously.

"No," Eve said from deep within the hood of the cloak, her face hidden.

"You should try to rest, sweetie," Cassy told her.

"But what if someone attacks us, and you kill them before I wake up? That would be boring," Eve told her.

"See, no child should talk like that," Jasheir told them.

"Echo still wants to eat you. I told him not to because you helped rescue mother and Uncle S, but I can still change my mind," Eve assured him.

"I do not fear your tiny lizard," Jasheir hissed.

"You should," Eve warned him as two little red eyes glared out from within the hood.

"New topic! One that doesn't involve killing each other!" Chris said quickly.

"Mi is calling you a bunch of words I don't recognize," Eve told him.

"As soon as we get back to the city, I'm taking that cloak back," Chris told her. "Mi is a bad influence."

"He says that he's a good role model, and he did tell me to grab this," Eve said as she produced a massive leather sack from under the cloak.

She set it in the snow with a clunk. How she carried it as far as she did or kept it concealed was a mystery to them.

"What is that?" Cassy asked nervously, fearing a trophy similar to Sarah's.

"I don't know, but Mi said that you would like it," Eve told them.

"I'm concerned," Al told Chris.

"As am I," Chris thought while pulling the bag toward him.

When he opened the drawstring at the top, he was greeted by a massive amount of gold glittering in the firelight. All were shocked, save Matt and Eve.

"Well, what is it?" Matt asked angrily.

"Eve, where did you get this?" Sarah asked with amazement.

"The naga you skinned was carrying it. I picked it up while you were working," Eve told her.

"What is it?" Matt demanded.

"It's a unicorn, Matt," Cassy said sarcastically.

"Seriously, whatever that is was heavy! Eve's so much lighter now!" Matt exclaimed.

"It's not nice to make fun of the disabled," Sarah said, scolding Cassy.

She looked at Matt.

"It's a sack filled with all the stupid things I've heard you say over the past few days, which I'm sure is why it weighed so much," Sarah told him.

"*Really?*" Matt said angrily.

"Come on, guys. It's not like it's a secret or anything. Matt, the bag is filled with rocks. Nothing but rocks," Chris told him.

"I hate you," Matt told him.

"Some of the rocks are smooth if it makes you feel better," Chris said.

"Just like the rocks between his ears," Cassy chimed in.

"Sarah, why didn't you let me die in the arena?" Matt asked.

"Mi is telling me to tell you that the bag is full of..." Eve began but trailed off as she listened to him. "I don't know what that word means," she said finally.

Her head tilted to the side as Mi explained.

"That's gross. I'm not saying that," Eve said before falling quiet once again.

"Good try, sweetie," Chris told her.

"It is truly a wonder that you have not killed each other yet," Jasheir said, looking at them with awe.

"Well, some of us try to from time to time," Cassy said, looking at Sarah.

"Some of us are about to try right now," Sarah warned her.

"Truly a wonder," Jasheir repeated with disbelief.

CHAPTER FOURTEEN

The elves found them an hour later. Ditrina had yet to wake up, and the others were doing their best to stay warm around the fire.

"Name yourselves!" cried a songlike voice from within the trees.

"Shearcliff and Company returning Princess Ditrina to the city!" Chris called quickly.

Several elves walked into the firelight. The leader looked at them huddled around the fire and Ditrina's limp form.

"I am Kaleian Figinoma Rike. I was sent to investigate why the royal gold flare was sent up so far from the gate. Care to explain why the princess is unconscious in the middle of the forest surrounded by half-breeds?" he asked.

"She used too much magic, and now she's passed out. She needs to get back to the city as soon as possible!" Cassy told him.

"And who might you be, half-breed?" Kaleian sneered.

"My name is Cassy Shearcliff, Royal Consort!" Cassy told him angrily.

"Oh, so you're my sister's pet! I've heard quite a lot about you from my father," Kaleian taunted.

Cassy's clawed hands tightened into fists, but she managed to keep her temper in check.

"We need to get to the city or else your princess is going to freeze," Sarah told him angrily.

"And we will bring her to the city, but I fail to see a reason to bring the rest of you," Kaleian told her.

"And who said we were just going to hand her over? We're her champions and, as such, must protect her," Chris told him.

"And what a wonderful job you are doing! Gaze upon the mighty champions, freezing in the snow! An inspiration to the people everywhere. They will sing songs of your heroism!" Kaleian mocked.

"We go with her, or she stays with us," Chris said firmly.

"Do you think you can stop us from taking her?" Kaleian asked as the other elves approached.

"No, but do you think you'll be able to calm your sister down once she realizes you left us here?" Matt asked.

Kaleian looked unsure.

"She would understand. Outsiders are not permitted within the city these days, not with all the slavers on the loose," Kaleian said looking at Jasheir.

"I have seen her destroy one city today. I do not think she would hesitate before destroying another," Jasheir hissed.

"What is he talking about?" Kaleian demanded.

"Gishkar isn't much of a city anymore," Cassy told him.

"What have you done?" Kaleian asked, the color draining from his green face.

"He told me I could," Ditrina mumbled from Cassy's lap, her eyes still closed.

"Sister, what did you do!?" Kaleian demanded.

"It was just a little harmless fun…" Ditrina muttered.

"I estimate death toll was a combined total of fifteen thousand naga and slaves, but those numbers could be much higher," Jasheir said.

"Why?" Kaleian asked, looking at them in horror.

"He told me I could…" Ditrina mumbled once more before lapsing once again into unconsciousness.

"It was cool! I saw her blow up a building!" Eve exclaimed.

"Forget what I said, you are all coming with me. You are coming with me right now!" Kaleian yelled.

"I thought you didn't want us in your city?" Sarah asked innocently.

"Shut the hell up! Do you have any idea what you have done?" Kaleian demanded.

"We saved Mother and Uncle S?" Eve told him, not understanding the nature of the question.

"You likely just started a war!" Kaleian screamed.

"Unlikely. The naga are probably fighting amongst the rubble over what little they have left. It is doubtful that they will field a unified fighting force for many years to come," Jasheir told him.

"I don't care, just come with me!" Kaleian yelled.

Chris looked at the others and signaled for them to stand. They set off once more toward the elven city.

"What happened?" King Figinoma demanded when he saw Cassy carrying Ditrina into the throne room.

"She used too much magic too fast," Matt explained from Jasheir's arm.

Without his sight, he had grabbed hold of one of the naga's large arms and allowed himself to be led along. Sarah had offered at first to guide him, but his face still hurt from one too many trees, so he politely declined.

"Explain yourselves!" the King demanded.

"Chris told me to!" Ditrina mumbled, waving an arm aimlessly above her.

"What happened!? You were gone less than a week!" the King bellowed, looking between their assorted injuries.

"Mother skinned a snake person!" Eve yelled excitedly.

"Quiet, Eve," Chris said hushing the girl.

As promised, he had reclaimed the cloak as soon as they had entered the city.

"Why is Ditrinadoma unable to stand!?" King Figinoma yelled.

"Because she used too much magic. We told you that already!" Cassy said angrily.

"Do you have any idea the amount of magic she would have to use to be rendered in such a state? You're lying!" the King bellowed.

"She destroyed an entire city!" Jasheir hissed.

"Ditrinadoma would never do such a thing!" the King insisted.

"He said it was ok…" Ditrina said weakly.

"She told me she wanted to use as much magic as she could, and I let her," Chris explained.

"Get her to the healers!" the King said quickly, and an elf rushed forward, teleporting Ditrina and Cassy away.

"I will go with them," Kaleian told the King and vanished as well, leaving the King alone with Chris and the others.

"Tell me exactly what went on in that city," the King said quietly, his black eyes burning holes through them.

"We did what we went there to do. We rescued our friends," Chris told him.

"And how did that involve destroying a city?" the King asked.

"Sometimes these things just happen!" Eve said with an overdramatic shrug. "It was only one city, after all."

"*Quiet, Eve*," Chris said sternly, hushing the girl yet again.

"Why are your companions so injured?" the King asked, looking at Sarah and Matt.

His eyes narrowed when he saw what Sarah was carrying.

"And why is she carrying *that*?" he added.

"Well, as for our injuries, a slaver named Narfus saw it fit to torture us. As for the skin, meet Narfus," Sarah said, admiring the bloody blue scales proudly.

"After the nature of her departure, I did not expect Ditrinadoma to come back for some time, let alone with guests. Why have you returned?" the King asked.

"Ditrina thought that your healers may be able to help restore Matt's vision, and Eve's blessing still needs to be investigated. There is still much that needs to be done here," Chris told him.

The King sighed.

"You likely have caused more problems than you could possibly imagine, but that is a discussion for another day. For now, I must thank you for returning my daughter safely to me," King Figinoma told them.

He snapped his fingers, and another elf appeared.

"Take the blind human to the healers and see what can be done," the King ordered.

The elf bowed and walked quickly to Matt's side, teleporting him away without a word. Jasheir vanished as well, seeing as he was still in contact with Matt.

"What about my hand?" Sarah asked hopefully.

"It appears that the wound had already closed; in addition, the missing limb is not here. I'm sorry, but no amount of magic can restore your hand," the King told her.

Sarah let out a sigh of resignation.

"I figured as much, but it was worth a shot," Sarah said with a small smile.

"Could we perhaps be given quarters to stay in? We're all very tired," Chris told him.

"And risk you running off to the other side of Targoth again? I think not. We will settle the matter of the girl now, then you may rest," the King told them.

"But you already fixed my voice, and I don't want to lose my scars!" Eve said quickly, stepping behind Chris.

"What an odd thing for a child to say," the King said with slight amusement. "Do not fear, little one; I will not change how you look."

"What are you going to do to her?" Sarah asked cautiously.

"To start, I will examine her memories and try to learn as much as possible from her interaction with this mystery god. From there, I will use magic to sense the nature of the spell she is casting and see if it can be duplicated through more mundane methods," the King explained.

"Forget I asked," Sarah said, baffled by the King's explanation. "Just don't do anything that will hurt her, or you'll answer to me," Sarah added darkly.

"Do you really think you could harm me? I have powerful magic at my disposal!" the King laughed.

"So did he," Sarah said smugly, gesturing to the skin draped over her arm.

The King's laughter died.

"I will do nothing to harm your daughter," the King promised them. "Please bring her here."

Chris and Sarah exchanged a nod, and each of them took one of Eve's hands, leading her toward the King.

"What are we doing?" Eve asked cautiously. Echo scanned the room for escape routes.

"The King is going to use a little more magic on you," Chris told her.

"He did fix my voice, but he's still rude. I don't like him, I don't want to," Eve declared, planting her feet on the ground.

"Eve, we need to do this, it's important. Besides, this man is Ditrina's father. If you help him, it's sorta like you're helping her. Don't you wanna help Aunt Di?" Chris asked her.

"Well, yes," Eve admitted.

"It's ok if you're frightened," Sarah told her.

"I'm not scared!" Eve said quickly.

Sarah smiled to herself.

"If you're not afraid, then go up there," she told her.

Eve pulled her hands free from her parents' and marched defiantly up to the King.

"I am not afraid of you," Eve declared.

"Good, then come here," the King said, gesturing to the foot of his throne.

Eve plopped herself at the King's feet and glared up at him with Echo.

"I'm going to read your mind now. Is that ok?" the King asked her.

"I'm not afraid of you. Do whatever you like!" Eve said angrily.

"Try to relax, this may be strange for you," the King told her as he rested his hands on Eve's head.

Eve's eyes began to glow with white light, and she slumped forward, held up only by the King. Echo's eyes fixed on the King as he worked his magic, ensuring that his mother was well taken care of. The King sat silently with Eve for some time, reading her memories like a book. When he finally pulled his hands away, he had tears in his eyes.

"She has been through so much for one so young," the King said quietly.

Eve yawned as if waking from a slumber, and the light faded from her eyes.

"Everise, thank you for allowing me to look into your past," the King told her.

"Everise?" Sarah asked with confusion.

"Your daughter's full name, it is Everise Longbrook," the King said, not understanding her confusion.

"Eve, why didn't you say something? We never knew!" Chris exclaimed.

"I am not Everise," Eve said firmly.

"What are you talking about? Everise has been your name since birth. I have seen as much," the King told her.

"Everise Longbrook lived in Rooksberg with her family. She laughed with them, played with them, and loved them with all her heart. She died with them, bathed in dragon fire. I am Eve Shearcliff, mother of Echo, slayer of men!" Eve yelled, and Echo screamed his agreement.

"She has quite the dramatic flair, wouldn't you agree?" Sarah whispered to Chris.

Chris smiled.

"She gets it from you," he replied.

"In any event...Eve," the King said, looking at the girl with concern.

Her eyes snapped to him.

"It should please you to know that there are no side effects from the blessing, other than your soul being tethered to that dragon of yours. The bad news is, I have no idea what form of magic is being used here. It is as if what you are doing is as natural as breathing. There are no spells in play that I can detect," the King admitted.

"I thought Matt said that this was a mind link?" Chris asked.

"Yes, and while the end result is the same, the process is different. It is as if she is getting the benefit of the spell without actually casting it. All I know for sure is that Eve is powering it with her own mana. Everything else is alien to me," the King told him.

"That didn't make any sense to me," Sarah said crossly.

"He is confused," Eve summarized.

She looked at him with knowing eyes.

"He is afraid of what he doesn't understand," she said softly.

"What are you taking about?" the King demanded.

"I saw your fear, and Echo smells it now. You hide it well, but not well enough," Eve said with a little giggle.

"Eve, what are you saying?" Chris asked cautiously.

"As he read my mind, I read his," Eve said with pride.

"What?!" the King bellowed.

"You have lived a boring life, Garin," Eve told him.

"Who is Garin?" Chris asked.

"My name, it is Garinlina. I never told any of you that," the King whispered.

"How did she do that?" Sarah asked with confusion.

"I wanted to, so I did!" Eve declared proudly as she skipped back over to her parents. "Echo helped."

The King took a deep breath and managed to collect himself.

"The only explanation that I can come up with is that Eve is still resisting the curse of the crisis, and she is winning. Slowly, but surely, she is recovering more of her natural mana, and with that, the ability to control it. When I created our connection, she used some of her mana to reach out to me as well," the King summarized. "I don't understand how she did that, though—to force herself into my mind without me knowing would take a remarkably strong will."

"Echo helped," Eve repeated.

"What about two wills?" Sarah asked.

"What?" the King asked with confusion.

"Well, I don't really understand any of this magic rubbish, but from what I've heard, Eve and Echo share a mind. Could that mean their wills are united, stronger together?" Sarah asked.

"Perhaps. This requires further study," the King said eagerly. "I invite you to remain in the city as long as you like while we examine your daughter. She has much to teach us."

"So long as she is unharmed and is ok with you studying her," Chris told him.

"Would you do us the honor of teaching us your secrets, Eve?" King Figinoma asked kindly.

"I have a condition," Eve declared.

"A condition?" the King asked with confusion.

"I want a banelance," Eve said with a smug grin.

"What's a banelance?" Sarah asked.

"Absolutely not!" the King yelled.

"Then no," Eve said with a half smirk.

Echo hissed with amusement, laughing at the King's plight.

"Hey, Garin, what the hell is a banelance?" Sarah demanded.

"It is a weapon," the King said, looking uncomfortable.

"What does it do?" Chris asked with caution.

"It does whatever the bearer wishes. It is borderline sentient. The main purpose of the banelance is to act as a conduit for mana, letting the wielder use magic without physical limitations, such as Ditrinadoma is suffering now. In addition to that, they are immensely dangerous melee weapons, capable of penetrating magical defenses with ease. There are only three banelances in existence," the King told them.

"Why do such weapons exist?" Chris asked, dreading the answer.

"The elves one day hope to overthrow the tyranny of the gods. The banelances were one of our first ideas, but they proved too difficult to create, making an arsenal of them impossible. Their production was stopped after only three were created, and their existence has been a closely guarded secret," the King told them.

"Until Eve read your mind," Sarah pointed out.

"And demanded one as payment, yes," the King sighed.

"Eve, why don't you ask for something a little more your style? You could get a new dress or maybe a pretty necklace?" Chris asked sweetly.

"It's a magic lance that can kill gods! It's exactly my style!" Eve yelled with an excited giggle.

"She's not wrong," Sarah pointed out.

"Quiet. Just because you want one, too, doesn't mean you should encourage this!" Chris told her.

"I never said I wanted one!" Sarah said hastily.

"I saw that look in your eyes," Chris told her with dry amusement.

"I'm waiting," Eve said impatiently.

"Fine, you can have one of the banelances. Don't destroy anything too important," the King told her.

"Wait, no!" Chris yelled.

"Deal!" Eve yelled happily and shook the King's hand, half of her face lighting up with a smile.

"What have you done!?" Sarah asked with shock.

"I'm sure you'll do just fine. With the proper supervision, she should have nothing to worry about," the King said with a dismissive wave of his hand. "Come now, Eve; let us begin," he said before teleporting away with their daughter.

"I didn't think he'd actually agree to give her one," Sarah said with horror.

"He must really wanna know what's in Eve's head," Chris said.

"I've seen her head. It's a wonderful place," Mi told him. "So much ferocity in such a tiny package, and don't even get me started on Echo!"

"Mi! What are you doing! You're not supposed to talk to Chris while he's awake!" Al yelled.

"Relax, brother. It's just for a little bit. You do it all day long, after all. Relax," Mi told him dismissively.

"Get out!" Al yelled.

"Nope," Mi said cheerfully.

Chris groaned and fell to his knees, clutching his head.

"Suck it up, buttercup; it's just an extra voice. You've gotten used to one, two shouldn't be an issue," Mi told him. "I'm tired of being left alone with Ge all day anyway."

"Chris? Chris, what's wrong?" Sarah asked nervously as she knelt beside him.

"Both of you shut up!" Chris screamed.

He looked at Sarah nervously.

"Not you, sweetheart," he assured her.

"I don't really feel like it," Mi told him smugly.

"Mi, I'm going to kill you," Al growled.

"How? I'm already dead!" Mi laughed.

"Get out!" Chris yelled again.

"Sheesh, I'll pipe down. No need to get so upset. I'm not leaving though. I'll just be silent," Mi told him.

"Why?" Chris thought in horror.

"I believe it is as he said. He became bored. I'm sorry, it looks like you may have a second set of thoughts to deal with now," Al told him.

"Think of it as a reward for a job well done!" Mi exclaimed.

"Both of you, no talking unless I directly *and specifically* address you first," Chris thought desperately.

"Or what?" Mi taunted.

"Or I'm going to jump off one of those balconies!" Chris thought angrily, looking at the balconies high above them.

"Oh, let's not do that. That would be bad for us, too. Shutting up now," Mi said hastily.

Chris's thoughts were once again his own.

"Chris, what the hell just happened?" Sarah asked softly, terrified by Chris's sudden collapse and apparent lunacy.

"Long story short, Mi is an asshole, and now I have two spirits nagging me around the clock," Chris sighed as he stood up. "Thankfully, they're quiet now."

"We need to get those things out of your head; you're going to go insane," Sarah said with concern. "But for now, let's find someplace to rest. I don't think we'll see the others for a while."

"Sounds like a plan I can get behind. Lead on, Sarah," Chris said with a smile.

Sarah began to wander toward the nearest doorway and pushed it open with a bloodstained hand, leaving a red, sticky handprint

"We really need to get you cleaned up," Chris mused.

"You can help give me a bath then," Sarah said, shooting him a wink over her shoulder.

"Another plan I can get behind. See, this is why you're our tactician," Chris said eagerly as he followed behind her.

It took almost an hour, but eventually, Chris and Sarah found themselves in what appeared to be guest quarters of some kind—bed, bath, and all. They would have found it faster if they had directions from one of the palace staff, but they didn't see a single soul as they wandered.

"Now what?" Chris asked, looking around the richly furnished room with an appraising eye.

"Now I do my best to get this blood off me," Sarah said with amusement. "Would you mind drawing the water for my bath?"

"Not at all," Chris said as he walked toward the massive tub set into the floor.

Large enough to almost be considered a small pool, equipped with several faucets, it was easily the largest bath Chris had ever laid eyes upon. It was so large he decided he could probably swim in it if he so wished. He tried turning one of the faucets at random. Hot water filled the tub, and soon the room was filled with steam. He tried another faucet and soap was added to the water, covering the surface with bubbles.

"I'm impressed that this place has plumbing. I wonder how the drain works with each building being separated by magic?" Sarah mused.

"Likely, as you just said—magic," Chris replied with a laugh.

Sarah plucked the bloody remains of Narfus off her shoulders and hung him over the back of a nearby chair.

"Tomorrow, I'm finding a tanner," she announced.

"I think you wearing anything made from that will upset Cassy," Chris warned her.

"Has that ever concerned me?" Sarah replied.

Chris laughed.

"No, forget I brought it up," he said with a chuckle.

Sarah reached down and pulled the bloody slave tunic she still wore up over her head and dropped it in a heap on the floor. Chris's eyes flicked over her, admiring her muscular body.

"You know, with one hand, I doubt I'll be able to get all this blood off. Mind getting in and helping me?" Sarah asked innocently as she walked toward the bath.

She slid into the water with a contented sigh, sinking in up to her neck. Her red hair spread out over the surface of the water like a crimson fan.

"More than happy to help," Chris said as he pulled off his cloak, tossing it onto the bed.

The rest of his clothes followed quickly, and he joined her in the water. Sarah tossed him a brush she had found and turned her back toward him. Chris set to work removing the blood and grime that had been caked on her over the last few days.

"Losing a hand was a small price to pay for this," Sarah said with a content sigh as Chris worked.

"Many would think differently," Chris said with amusement.

"Well, they would be incorrect," Sarah said with a smile, sinking deeper into the hot water.

"I can't exactly help you clean up like that," Chris laughed, addressing the part of his wife he could see, which at that moment consisted only of her face poking through the bubbles.

"What's the rush?" Sarah asked with a smile.

She sat up, allowing her shoulders to crest the water.

"I've got nowhere to go. Do you?" she asked.

Chris smiled.

"Wherever you are, I'll be," he replied.

Sarah closed her eyes and suddenly disappeared under the bubbles. Chris looked around with bemusement, searching for signs of his wife. He heard a splash behind him and felt an arm wrap around his waist. Sarah's chin rested on his shoulder. She pulled him back against her, and for a time they relaxed in the water together, enjoying each other's company after so long apart.

"Matt was right," Sarah said after a while.

"What do you mean by that?" Chris asked with confusion.

"Nothing at all," Sarah said with a smile, allowing herself to float away from her husband.

"I feel like that's a rather strange thing to say without reason. After all, Matt's never right." Chris laughed, watching her drift across the tub.

"Come on, hurry up and finish getting me clean," Sarah said suddenly, deciding to change the subject.

"Why the sudden rush?" Chris asked.

"Because I'm feeling the need to get dirty again," Sarah said with a mischievous grin, splashing water in his direction.

That was all the motivation Chris needed.

Ditrina awoke in her bed with no idea how she got there. She remembered the strangest dream. In it, she had destroyed a city, then fled with her friends to the frozen forest. Everyone had been there, and it had been a wonderful dream, despite Echo's presence.

She looked around her room and saw Cassy slumped across the foot of her bed, fast asleep.

"What a strange place to fall asleep," Ditrina mused.

Cassy's eyes snapped open.

"Di!" Cassy squealed, throwing herself across the bed at her.

"Hello, Cas," Ditrina said with a smile. "What are you doing here?"

"Di, don't you remember? You brought us back to the elven city after you destroyed Gishkar," Cassy reminded her.

"That cannot be right, I just dreamed about destroying a city! You must be confused with that," Ditrina told her.

"Di, how would I know what you dreamed about?" Cassy asked.

"Fair point, but that still begs the question: if I did not destroy that city, who did!?" Ditrina exclaimed.

"Di, you did destroy that city!" Cassy said with exasperation.

"But you just said that..." Ditrina began.

"Ditrina!" Cassy yelled.

Ditrina fell silent.

"It looks like you're still a bit mixed up. That dream you just had, where you destroyed a city? Two days ago, that actually happened! You burned the naga city of Gishkar to the ground. Don't you remember?" Cassy asked.

"That seems familiar, but why would I do that?" Ditrina asked.

"Chris told you you could," Cass reminded her.

"Oh! Why did you not say so? That makes it all better then," Ditrina said with a content sigh. "I was worried for a moment I might have done something wrong."

"Destroying cities *is* wrong!" Cassy shrieked.

"But you just said yourself that Chris told me I could. How could it be wrong if he told me it was ok?" Ditrina asked.

"Do you think that everything that Chris does is good? Just because he told you to doesn't make it right!" Cassy yelled.

"Then did I do something wrong?" Ditrina asked nervously.

Cassy sighed and buried her face in her hands.

"I'm happy you're ok. You used too much magic and ended up drunk on the power for a while. The healers treated you, but you have to be more careful in the future. Do you understand?" Cassy asked her.

"Yes, Cas. I am sorry I worried you," Ditrina said seriously.

"It's ok; you had no idea what you were doing. Your mind was clouded," Cassy told her.

She sat beside her silently.

"Cas, are you feeling all right?" Ditrina asked her.

"I'm fine," Cassy snapped.

Ditrina's eyes widened slightly, and her mouth closed quickly, unasked questions dying on her lips.

Cassy sighed.

"I'm sorry, Di, I'm just a little shaken up right now," Cassy said quietly.

"Have the elves been giving you difficulties? Who was it? I will burn them!" Ditrina said quickly.

"No! It's nothing like that," Cassy said hastily.

"So, the elves have been treating you better then?" Ditrina asked hopefully.

"What? No, they're just as big a bunch of assholes as ever. I've just learned to tune them out," Cassy told her.

"What is wrong then?" Ditrina asked with concern. "Have I done something to upset you?" she asked cautiously.

"It's nothing, I swear. You didn't know what you were you doing," Cassy muttered.

"Is this about me massacring most of your species?" Ditrina asked nervously.

"No, no, no! They deserved what they got! You'll get nothing but respect from me over that," Cassy assured her.

"What happened then?" Ditrina asked.

"Do you remember when I found you in Gishkar?" Cassy asked quietly.

"Vaguely. I believe that I was burning something at the time, and you snuck up behind me," Ditrina recalled.

"What happened next?" Cassy prompted.

"I believe I...oh," Ditrina said as she remembered what happened.

Cassy waited for her to say it.

"I believe I almost incinerated you," Ditrina admitted.

"Like I said, you weren't in your right state of mind. It wasn't your fault," Cassy said quietly.

"Cas, I am so, so sorry," Ditrina said in a panic. "What do I have to do for you to forgive me?"

"I told you, I'm not mad. It just shook me up a little to see you turn your magic on me is all," Cassy told her.

"So, we are ok?" Ditrina asked cautiously.

"We're fine, Di," Cassy assured her.

They heard a knock at the door.

"Go away!" Cassy called.

"You messed up. That was your big chance to put Ditrina in your pocket," Matt said as he opened the door slowly.

"What are you doing here, Matthew?" Ditrina asked curiously.

"What? Do you think I'd stop irritating you two just because I lost my vision? I have a reputation to uphold," Matt told her as he fumbled his way across the room, eventually bumping into the bed.

"Does Di have to blast you with magic again?" Cassy asked angrily.

"For what? You two could be doing it right now, and I wouldn't know." Matt sighed as he sat on the edge of the bed.

"I take it the healers were unable to restore your eyesight?" Ditrina asked sadly.

"It *looks* like it," Matt said with a chuckle.

"I've heard that when you go blind your other senses get better. Try improving your sense of humor," Cassy said with a giggle.

"Ouch, that cuts deep," Matt said with mock despair.

"So sorry, Matthew. I believe Cassy was just teasing you! Please do not take offence!" Ditrina said quickly.

"Really, Ditrina?" Matt asked with disappointment.

"I assure you!" Ditrina insisted, looking at Cassy to come to her aid.

"Di, he wasn't insulted in the first place!" Cassy yelled.

"I am sorry! I was too busy committing genocide to practice my sarcasm!" Ditrina yelled with a smile, looking at them expectantly.

Cassy looked at her with shock, and Matt let out a low whistle.

"Was my joke not funny?" Ditrina asked nervously.

"Too soon, too soon," Matt said with a chuckle.

"Leave the jokes to the professionals, sweetie," Cassy said kindly.

"I'll give you points for the attempt," Matt told her.

"How many points?" Ditrina asked with excitement.

"Figure of speech," Matt sighed.

"Aww, I really thought I won something that time," Ditrina said, pouting.

CHAPTER FIFTEEN

"Let's check out this building next!" Eve said excitedly, pointing to another doorway.

Chris and Sarah smiled as they led Eve into the shop. They had been in the city for a week now, and the elves had spent almost every second of that time studying Eve. Still, they recognized that she was a child and made sure that each day she had enough time to herself to get her impulses out. They learned the hard way that Eve's impulses were more violent than most and often accompanied by dragon fire. So, in the evenings, Chris and Sarah had taken to exploring the city with their daughter.

On occasion one of the others would accompany them, but for the most part, they were alone. Matt's blindness slowed them down considerably, not that Chris and Sarah minded, so he decided not to tag along usually. Ditrina spent most of her time in the palace, catching up with her father or brothers or giving various reports to the other elves studying Eve. Ditrina herself volunteered to head up the study, given her expertise on soul transmutation, the field that Eve's condition seemed to most fall under. Cassy rarely left Ditrina's side. Strangely, Chris hadn't seen Jasheir since he had teleported away with Matt, and Matt was unsure of where he had gone.

All agreed that it was for the best that Ditrina lead the study. Aside from her knowledge on the subject of souls, Eve liked her and was willing to follow her directions. This alone was enough for the king to approve her position, after his disastrous attempt to get Eve to do what he wanted. In retrospect, it would have been better to give her the banelance *after* they were done with their research, but as the king put it, *live and learn.*

"Father, can I please have that?" Eve said with awe, looking at a strange shining talisman hanging behind the counter.

"Do you know what that is, little Eve?" the elf behind the counter asked.

By now, news of Eve had spread across the city, and the scarred girl with the dragon had become something of a local celebrity.

"It's shiny!" Eve said with excitement. "Echo wants it!"

"Ah, I see your dragon is growing old enough to want a hoard. I do not recommend that talisman. Its enchantment is a little mundane, I'm afraid," the elf admitted.

"But it's so shiny!" Eve said, staring at the glittering talisman, Echo perched on her shoulder, bobbing his head with excitement.

"What does it do?" Chris asked.

"It makes the wearer more appealing to the opposite sex," the elf explained.

"No, we don't need that," Sarah said firmly, irritated by the way Chris's eyes lit up upon hearing the elf's words. "I didn't know that dragon's made hoards, I thought that was just part of the fairy tales," Sarah said, changing the subject.

"Oh yes, dragons are like magpies, they covet shiny things. Swords, coins, random pieces of metal junk, it's all the same to a dragon," the elf explained.

"The one we killed didn't have a hoard," Chris said.

"Yeah, but the one we killed was new to the area. Maybe it hadn't started making one yet?" Sarah proposed.

"You killed a dragon?" the elf asked with amazement.

"Yes," Chris said simply.

"To kill a dragon without magic is an impressive feat. I am amazed," the elf admitted.

Chris was about to point out that Ditrina actually finished off the beast herself with magic, but Sarah had other ideas.

"Why, thank you. We *are* world renowned adventurers, after all," Sarah said, puffing out her chest proudly.

"Yeah, right, of course!" Chris said, deciding to play along.

"I stabbed it!" Eve said excitedly.

"Really? You fought the dragon as well?" the elf asked with surprise.

"Yes!" Eve said joyfully.

Echo chirped happily, so overwhelmed by Eve's pride that for the moment he forgot that he was a dragon himself.

"Why in the world would you let a little girl fight a dragon?" the elf asked Sarah with shock.

"We actually didn't want her fighting it, but she had other ideas," Sarah said, ruffling Eve's short hair proudly.

Eve's scarred face beamed up at her mother, and Echo launched himself onto Sarah's arm, scampering up to her shoulder. He began licking her face.

"Eve, please get him down," Sarah said with cheerfulness forced through gritted teeth while Chris laughed.

Outside the shop a few minutes later, Chris decided to question Sarah.

"So, why did you tell him that we killed it ourselves?" Chris asked.

"Because padding our reputation can't hurt and, as Ditrina's knights or whatever, our reputation is supposed to be the best," Sarah explained.

"Isn't that lying?" Eve asked with large eyes.

"Well, no. Ditrina killed the dragon to be sure, but Ditrina serves under Chris. As the leader, he can take credit for anything we do. And we never did claim to kill the dragon without magic. The elf said that. We just didn't correct him. Do you see what I did?" Sarah asked her.

"Yes!" Eve said with excitement.

"I feel that wasn't a lesson she needed to learn right now," Chris said with a disapproving frown.

"I've given up sheltering her. Every time I try that, someone ends up getting killed," Sarah sighed.

"People get killed when she's not sheltered as well," Chris pointed out.

"Not the point," Sarah said crossing her arms.

"Yeah, not the point!" Eve said, crossing her arms beside Sarah, adopting a mirror pose.

Chris couldn't help but smile.

"Come on, Eve; I have something to pick up," Sarah said, leading the girl away by the hand.

She looked back over her shoulder.

"Coming, Chris?" she called.

"Right behind you," Chris assured her as he caught up with his family.

Taking his daughter's other hand, they made their way through the city, enjoying every moment of it.

"So, when you said you were going to find a tanner, you weren't kidding, were you?" Chris asked with mild shock, seeing their destination.

"Not in the slightest. I had that scaly bastard tanned and tailored into something special," Sarah said proudly as they walked into the shop.

"What did you get, Mother?" Eve asked excitedly.

"After a lot of thought, I realized *what could be better than putting my sword through that snake time and time again*? As such, I present to you..." Sarah said proudly as she held out her hand to the elf running the shop.

The elf looked at Chris uncomfortably but eventually reached under the counter and pulled out a package wrapped in brown parchment paper and handed it to Sarah. While Sarah was busy tearing away the wrapper like a child on holiday, the elf mouthed the words *I'm sorry* to Chris.

"Ta-da!" Sarah yelled, brandishing her new sword sheath above her head.

Chris had to admit, it was a beautiful piece of workmanship. Despite the harsh conditions the skin had been subjected to as Sarah dragged it along with her, the elven craftsmanship proved good enough to keep the leather supple. Seemingly studded with blue scales, polished until they gleamed cobalt, it was truly a wondrous thing. Chris would have been envious had he not spoken to the man that had become the sheath only the week before. As it was, he found it unnerving.

"It's so pretty, Mother!" Eve said with awe.

"I'm glad you think so, sweetie, because I have something for you, too!" Sarah said, kneeling before the young girl.

Sarah pulled an identical sheath from where she had concealed it. This sheath was much smaller, however—sized for a dagger.

"I had him make one for you, too," Sarah told her.

Eve squealed in delight and ripped her old leather sheath off her hip as fast as possible, pulling out her dagger.

"Can I have it now? Please?" Eve begged.

Sarah smiled.

"Of course," she told her as she helped fasten the new sheath to Eve's hip.

Eve slid her dagger into it and found it was a perfect fit.

"Thank you so much, Mother!" Eve exclaimed as she threw herself at Sarah.

Sarah caught the girl and wrapped her in a hug.

"Now you have the dagger from your father, and a place to put it from me!" Sarah laughed.

Chris did his best to hold back a joke for his daughter's sake about storing his dagger in his wife's sheath. To Al's relief, and Mi's disappointment, Chris bit his tongue.

"It must have been tearing you up inside that I gave Eve her first weapon," Chris teased.

"I don't know what you're talking about," Sarah scoffed, but Chris saw her wink at him.

"Do I get one for my banelance, too?" Eve asked with excitement.

"Sorry, Eve. Narfus didn't have enough skin to cover that," Sarah told her sweetly.

"Well, what if we skin some more naga? Could we get more skin?" Eve asked hopefully.

"That's my girl!" Sarah said proudly.

"Absolutely not!" Chris said quickly.

Eve pouted.

"Fine," she said quietly.

Eve fixed the shopkeeper with her big brown eyes.

"Thank you for turning Narfus into something so pretty, elf man," Eve said seriously, and Echo let out a low, slow chirp.

"Of course, any time..." the elf trailed off uncomfortably.

"Come on, Eve, let's head back to the palace. I'm sure Aunt Ditrina has more questions for you," Chris told her.

"Can I have my banelance back after that?" Eve asked.

The weapon had been taken from her after she had destroyed a large chunk of the palace *accidentally,* as she claimed.

"Maybe if you behave," Chris told her.

"Parent of the year. *You can have the superweapon back after dinner, sweetie,*" Mi mocked.

"Shut up," Chris thought irritably.

"Father, look!" Eve exclaimed.

"Yes, Eve?" Chris asked, looking around, not seeing what she was talking about.

"It's Aunt Cas!" Eve exclaimed.

Sure enough, Chris caught sight of his sister walking outside the shop's window.

"I wonder what she's doing here," Sarah mused.

Eve didn't wait to find out.

"Aunt Cas!" Eve squealed as she raced back out of the building.

"Oh! There you are, Eve!" Cassy said happily. "Di sent me to find you. It's time for more tests."

"Look what Mother gave me!" Eve cried, showing off the sheath proudly.

Cassy was confused for a moment before recognition flooded across her face. She became pale.

"Well...that's nice," she said nervously.

"Echo says you're scared. What's wrong?" Eve asked with concern.

"Nothing, nothing at all," Cassy lied, forcing a smile. "It's a beautiful gift. I wouldn't go showing that to Jasheir though. He may not like it," Cassy warned her.

"Where has he been anyway? I haven't seen him since we got here," Chris said.

"Didn't you hear? The elves agreed to send him to the nameless village. He left soon after we arrived. I wonder what he's doing now?" Cassy asked with curiosity.

"Don't know, don't care. Good riddance to the scaly bastard," Sarah sneered.

"You could be nice. He did help us, after all," Cassy told her.

"Cassy, I love you like a sister, so don't take this the wrong way, but I've decided naga are filthy monsters. I'll be happy if I never see another naga as long as I live," Sarah admitted.

"That might be a little harsh," Cassy said with a frown. "They're not all like him," Cassy said, gesturing to Sarah's sword sheath.

"That's right. I'm sure some of them are wonderful people just like you, but I really don't have the patience to sift through the shit to find the diamonds. As far as I'm concerned, they can stay in what's left of their city, and I'll stay here, and we never have to bother each other again," Sarah told her.

"I think you two should have this discussion another time," Chris said looking at Eve's face, which was intently focused as she listened to the debate, considering the merits of genocide.

Sarah caught on.

"Right, of course. Another time," she agreed.

Cassy looked like she was going to say something else, but she realized what was going on and held her tongue.

"Right. Let's head back to the palace," Cassy told them.

They returned to the palace and went their separate ways. Cassy escorted Eve to Ditrina while Chris and Sarah returned to the guest room they had claimed. So far, nobody had told them they couldn't use it, and they had no intention of leaving. They had gone to watch the first few times Eve was experimented on, but after realizing it consisted mostly of her standing still surrounded my muttering elves, they realized their presence wasn't needed.

"Do you really think it was a good idea to give Eve that sheath? I'm concerned she's slipping closer to madness," Chris told her as they relaxed in their bed, preparing to sleep for the evening.

"What are you talking about? She loved the present. Slipping how?" Sarah asked.

"I know she liked the gift, and that's part of what troubles me. That thing is made of the skin of an intelligent creature. Wouldn't it bother you if you saw something like that made of human skin?" Chris asked.

"I see what you're saying, but Narfus was a monster. He deserves what he got, or have you forgotten what he did to me?" Sarah demanded, brandishing her stump.

Chris raised his hands in surrender.

"You're missing the point of what I'm trying to say. Eve shouldn't think something like that is normal, yet she seems to think it's perfectly ok. When we fought those north men the first time, we were in the frozen forest. Remember how I almost died?" Chris asked.

"You dying while fighting is hardly a noteworthy thing these days," Sarah said with a small smile.

"But you remember how Eve responded. She was crying and seemed to see the impact of death for a moment. At the time, I really thought that that was the perfect thing for her to go through because I actually hoped that she had a chance to be normal," Chris told her.

"Yeah, it was a good learning experience for her. What of it?" Sarah asked.

"Well, it seems that her trip to Gishkar pushed it from her mind. The things she saw in that city, combined with whatever Mi told her, pushed her right back over the edge. She's a sociopath," Chris said bluntly.

"How could you say something like that?!" Sarah said with outrage.

"Face the truth, Sarah!" Chris yelled back.

Sarah looked at him with flames in her eyes, but she was silent.

"I love our daughter with all my heart, do not misunderstand me, but she's dangerous. If we were to let her loose in a town, she would likely kill someone within twenty-four hours and brag about it. The fact that her mind is linked to that bloodthirsty creature she carries around only makes it worse. She needs constant supervision just to be allowed in public, and when she gets older, she's going to be very dangerous. Think about it; in a few years, she's going to have a fully-grown dragon under her command and one of the most dangerous weapons ever created in her hands. When she gets to that point, I don't think stern words will be enough to curb her murderous tendencies. We need to start seriously teaching her right from wrong," Chris told Sarah.

She said nothing.

"I don't think I'm the right person to be telling anyone what's right and what's wrong," Sarah muttered.

"What are you talking about?" Chris asked. "Eve looks up to you more than anyone, and you're a wonderful person. Who better to help teach her?"

"Oh, wake up, Chris! I'm just about the most horrible person on Targoth! I don't know what part of that sword tells you who's good and who's bad, but it must have broken when you pointed it me!" Sarah yelled angrily.

"What the hell are you talking about?" Chris asked with confusion.

"If you were to draw your sword and point it at me right now, I guarantee that this time it wouldn't spare me," Sarah sneered.

"Sarah, losing a hand doesn't make you any worse of a person," Chris assured her.

Sarah began to laugh, horrible sad giggles that made Chris's skin crawl.

"You have no idea what I'm talking about, do you? Matt never told you, did he?" Sarah laughed.

"Told me what? You're not making any sense, Sarah!" Chris told her.

"I did things in that arena that no person should be proud of, but for some reason, I am. If I could go back and do it again, I would, and I'd do it with a smile. Matt saw it then; I'm just as much of a monster as the beasts that imprisoned us. I fit right in. I skinned a person alive, for the gods' sakes! How could you possibly think I'm a good person?" Sarah demanded.

"Because I know you, Sarah," Chris said softly.

"You're blinder than Matt," Sarah snarled.

"If you really were as horrible as you claim, do you think you could have wielded the sword in the arena?" Chris pointed out.

"Get up," Sarah ordered, slipping off the edge of the bed. "I have an idea."

"What?" Chris asked cautiously.

"Get up and draw your sword!" Sarah commanded.

"Sarah, I think you're making more of this than you need to..." Chris began.

"Get up!" Sarah screamed.

Chris reluctantly got out of the bed.

"Pick it up," Sarah said quietly, pointing at his sheathed sword propped in the corner of the room.

Chris walked slowly to it and drew it from its sheath with a small hiss.

Sarah dropped to her knees in the middle of the room and lowered her head.

"Now we'll see for sure. Just like Kelti, you remember?" Sarah asked with a small giggle, madness gleaming in her eyes.

Chris recalled the night he had killed Kelti, how he had told her if she was innocent then his sword would not harm her. It had been Sarah who held her down as Chris held trial.

"Sarah, this isn't how to go about this," Chris told her.

"I need to know!" Sarah screamed.

Chris took a deep breath and tightened his grip on his sword. Slowly, he walked over to his wife. He gave the blade a small twirl with one hand, showing how light the blade was.

"Do it," Sarah whispered.

Chris raised the sword high above his head and swung toward Sarah. The blade flashed through the air toward her neck, but at the last moment, the tip plummeted toward the ground where it clanged off the stone floor. Chris struggled to raise it, but Sarah saw he was unable to do so. He released his grip on the hilt and let the sword clatter to the stones.

"Do you see now? You're a good person, Sarah," Chris assured her as he knelt beside his wife.

Sarah's eyes were wide with disbelief.

"I don't understand," she muttered.

"Whatever you did in that arena didn't taint you. You did what you had to do to make our family whole again. Don't let it trouble you," Chris told her as he helped her to her feet. "Why don't you lie down? We'll rest for a while, and you'll feel better in the morning," Chris assured her as he led her back to the bed.

Sarah slipped under the covers as if in a trance and lay there staring at the ceiling. Chris slipped into the bed beside her and placed his hand in hers, reassuring her. Sarah closed her eyes and did her best to go to sleep.

"Why did you lie to her?" Al asked Chris quietly.

"Go away, Al," Chris thought angrily.

"The blade was going to kill her, but you made it look like it was too heavy for you to hold. Why didn't you show her the truth?" Al asked again.

"Because that would involve chopping my wife's head off!" Chris screamed in his own mind.

"If she's the type of person you can harm with the sword, then perhaps that would be the best," Al said quietly.

"How dare you?" Chris wondered with quiet menace.

"She is the woman you have entrusted your daughter to. She is the one you will fight beside and be judged by. Do you really want someone like her by your side?" Al asked.

"When I met her, the sword refused to fight her. After everything she's been through, the blade changes its mind. Who's to say it won't change its mind again?" Chris wondered.

"It is easy to fall from grace but hard to rise again," Al cautioned.

"She is strong. I know who Sarah is, and she's a good person," Chris thought.

"I truly hope you are correct," Al said before falling silent.

"I find the notion of good and evil overrated. People are just people. Sometimes they do good things, and sometimes they do bad things," Mi told him.

"I was in her mind; I saw her memories. She butchered children in that arena," Al said quietly.

"So, she did a little bad. Who cares? She also protected Matt. There's a little good to balance it out," Mi said.

"The sword still decided to kill her," Chris thought quietly.

"And you lied to her about it," Al reminded him.

"That's rich coming from you," Mi sneered at Al.

"What are you talking about?" Chris wondered.

"Well, let me put it this way. Ge controls his book and shows Matt things he thinks are important. When you wear my cloak, it's my power, my choice that hides you if you want to be hidden bad enough. Do you really believe that the sword's enchantment is completely autonomous?" Mi asked.

"Quiet, brother!" Al said angrily.

"Shut up, he deserves to know!" Mi yelled. "I'm *not* losing my bet because he gets sad and kills himself or anything like that. Chris is worth more than your pride!"

"What are you talking about?" Chris wondered cautiously.

"Come on, do I have to spell it out?" Mi asked with exasperation.

Chris saw the brothers appear before him and realized he had drifted off to sleep as they argued. Mi and Al stood glaring at one another, while Ge and Matt were nowhere to be seen.

"Don't say another word, Mi!" Al yelled.

"He needs to know!" Mi shot back.

"Tell me!" Chris demanded.

"The sword doesn't choose anything. Al makes the choice!" Mi yelled.

"Damn you, Mi!" Al bellowed.

"Explain what the hell you're talking about!" Chris demanded, looking at Mi.

"Al uses his magic to look into the hearts of those around you, seeing the good and bad things they've done in their lives. In the end, he makes a choice whether or not to let the sword kill them," Mi explained.

"You told me that the sword was enchanted and did that on its own—an impartial and perfect judge. You never said *you* were the one calling the shots," Chris told Al with quiet fury. "You lied to me."

"And you lied to your wife. We all lie from time to time," Al told him.

"Do you know how many times I've nearly died because that sword—no, because *you* refused to let me fight!" Chris screamed.

"Better you die than corrupt yourself!" Al yelled.

"What type of stupid logic is that!?" Chris screamed.

"I'm looking out for your best interests!" Al yelled.

"No, you're trying to live again through him!" Mi yelled.

"I'm mentoring him!" Al yelled.

"You made us swear to stay out of his everyday life. You told us we needed to let his choices be his own. The next thing we knew, you had torn his soul apart and latched yourself to him, chatting all day long! You did a good job of acting like it was some horrible tragedy that you and Chris were stuck together, but don't forget, it was your choice to do that!" Mi yelled.

"I was protecting him. He would have died without my help!" Al yelled.

"Oh, so now you care if I die?" Chris said angrily.

"My goal is not for you to get killed!" Al insisted.

"Then why do you never let me fight? I'm so tired of being in life or death situations only to find the sword *I can't get rid of* can't be used!" Chris screamed at him.

"What would you have me do?" Al yelled.

"Let me use the sword however I like. No more picking and choosing who I can fight, no more controlling my decisions like a twisted puppeteer," Chris said firmly.

"Or what?" Al spat, enraged by Chris's demands.

"Or I'm going to start carrying another sword. Sarah's trained me well enough I'll get by. Then again, maybe I won't, and we'll die together!" Chris sneered. "Besides, I've figured out that I can use magic without your permission. Simply put, I don't need you anymore."

"How can I just sit back and let you kill innocent people?" Al demanded.

"What type of person do you think I am? Have I ever shown any desire to kill people?" Chris yelled.

266

"Well, no," Al admitted.

"Then what in the gods' name is your problem!?" Chris screamed at him.

"He's paranoid," Mi told him. "He fears that you'll go mad with power if you can use the sword freely and try to take over the world or something."

"How could I possibly do something like that?" Chris asked, stunned by the mere idea.

"Well, if you haven't noticed, when you're using the sword and magic together you're basically invincible. Al is afraid of what anyone other than him will do with that power," Mi told him.

"Power corrupts even the best people!" Al yelled.

"Al, I have no desire to rule anything! I just want to go home to the valley and live with my family. I'll take enough contracts to make sure that we never lack gold, but I have no dreams of power. I have everything I ever wanted already," Chris told him.

"I still do not wish to relinquish control of the sword," Al replied.

"Well, if you ever want the sword to get used again, then you will, else I'll find another weapon," Chris promised him.

Al looked conflicted.

"Just give it up, you megalomaniac!" Mi yelled.

"Fine! I'll stop controlling the sword. Chris can use it however he likes," Al said quietly.

"Good evening, guys. What's going on?" Matt asked as he appeared with Ge.

"Nothing. We were just finishing a discussion," Al said, looking at Chris.

"Yeah. I think we're done here," Chris agreed, giving Al a harsh look.

"You two are acting weird," Matt said suspiciously.

"Don't they always?" Mi asked cheerfully.

"Fair enough." Matt chuckled.

"Chris, it may interest you to know I have discovered a way to separate your soul from Al's," Ge told him.

"Really? How!?" Chris asked excitedly.

"You need to be blessed by a god," Ge told him proudly.

"What?" Chris and Al asked blankly.

"It is simple. As proven by young Eve, the gods have the power to bend reality as they choose. All you need to do is get a god to bless you in such a manner so that your souls are restored to their original states," Ge said proudly.

Chris was surprised. This small amount of pride was more emotion than he had ever seen Ge show. It almost made him feel bad for what he said next.

"Ge, that doesn't help me at all. You know the chance that I get randomly blessed is basically nonexistent, right?" Chris asked.

"I never said it was likely. I only said I had found a way," Ge corrected.

"Ge, in the future, only share likely options with him, ok?" Matt instructed him.

"Very well," Ge said with a nod.

"So, how is the city, Matt?" Mi asked, trying to keep the subject moving.

"Oh, it's just great. The art, the incredible views, the stupidly high number of tables for me to smash my shins into, I'm loving every moment of it," Matt said, rolling his eyes.

"Matthew, if I remember correctly, you despise this city," Ge told him.

"Thanks, I had forgotten," Matt sighed.

"Any time, Matthew," Ge responded.

"Don't feel bad. Soon, you'll be home! Think about it! You can bump into *your* tables for a change!" Mi said happily.

"Yes, very amusing. Goodnight, gentlemen," Al said before fading away.

"What's his problem?" Matt asked.

"We had an argument. Don't worry about it," Chris assured him.

"It's a bad sign when you're arguing with the voices in your head," Matt said with a smile.

"It'll be worse if he starts listening to them," Mi piped in, and Matt laughed.

"Yeah, much worse," Chris said quietly.

CHAPTER SIXTEEN

"Goodbye, elf people!" Eve called happily as she waved from the back of Chris's horse.

After two weeks in the city, the elves had concluded that they had learned all they could from Eve, and they were finally about to return home. A large crowd had gathered to see the princess and her champions off. It was quite the celebration. Chris found it interesting that they seemed much happier to see them go than to see them arrive.

"Does everyone have everything they need? We're not coming back for a long time, so double check," Chris called.

"Yeah, I see all my stuff is right where it should be," Matt called.

"Shut up, Matt," Sarah called.

She had returned to wearing her spiked armor, with a leather cup attached over her stump. While in the city, she had had a smith fashion her a strange cross between a short sword and a shield, thin near the point like a blade and wide like a shield near the base over her arm. It was bizarre looking, and all the edges were very sharp. It was attached to her arm by a complex series of straps and buckles, but Sarah swore it would let her fight just as well as before. Chris was in no mood to test that theory, having seen Sarah sharpen the strange device all week. Other than that, she looked normal, with the exception of the new sheath on her hip.

"I believe we have everything we need," Ditrina said, looking at her equipment and Cassy's.

"Yeah, I'm ready," Cassy confirmed, her pockets filled with jewelry Ditrina had unknowingly *gifted* to her.

"Does Eve have her banelance?" Matt asked.

"Why would you bring that thing up?" Chris asked with exasperation.

"To torment you," Matt said smugly.

"I have it!" Eve said happily.

Chris looked at her and saw, aside from the dagger she carried, she had no weapon.

"Where?" Chris asked.

Eve was dressed in rather rugged garb, with a leather vest over a white shirt, styled after her father. She wore a short red skirt, and Chris could see no way for her to conceal the massive weapon. Her only adornment was a large feather tucked into a leather headband, and of course, Echo perched on her shoulders.

"Right here, Father," Eve said as she pulled the feather free from her hair.

Chris watched as the feather transformed into a long ivory staff, with a brilliant golden blade sticking out from the end, glittering in the sun. It was easily the most beautiful weapon he had ever seen—his sword unable to compete with such radiance.

"Why does it turn into a feather?" Cassy asked with amusement.

"Because I told it to," Eve said simply as if that explained everything.

She twirled the massive weapon with one hand, allowing the magic to do all the work, and it returned to feather form. With a half-smile, she tucked the feather into her headband.

"Won't it fall out if there's wind?" Sarah asked cautiously.

"Nope, it's magic!" Eve said happily.

"Remember, Eve, no using that in the house," Chris told her.

"I know, I'm only allowed to vaporize things outside," Eve said solemnly.

"Chris likes to make unfair rules like that," Ditrina told her with a wink.

"Enough chatter. I want to go home before the potion I drank wears off!" Sarah yelled.

"Right, of course. Come here, everyone!" Ditrina said cheerfully.

They gathered their horses around her and linked hands. There was a brief spinning sensation, and suddenly the cheers of the crowd were gone, and they heard only the stillness of the wilderness. They looked and saw their home, standing proudly just as they had left it, smoke rising from the chimneys.

"Please tell me that this time we went home," Matt said hopefully.

"No, we are in Rooksberg. We need to kill another dragon," Eve said, deadpan.

Matt gave an uneasy chuckle.

"She's joking, right?" he asked.

"I've never been prouder of you than I am now," Sarah said, looking at Eve with a smile.

"I've been studying," Eve said seriously.

"Let's get going!" Chris said excitedly, spurring his horse forward.

"Right behind you!" Sarah called, setting off after him.

Matt, who was riding with Sarah, only felt the horse lurch forward.

"Guys, seriously, what's going on?" Matt demanded.

"Dragon slaying, woo!" Cassy giggled.

Echo shrieked indignantly.

"Guys, please," Matt begged, terror in his voice.

"Oh, shut up, you big blind baby; we're home!" Chris called to him.

"Right, of course. I knew that," Matt said with a nervous laugh.

"I wonder if the maids will recognize Mother?" Eve asked.

"Why wouldn't they?" Sarah asked with amusement as they reached the front door.

"You have fewer limbs than when you left," Eve pointed out.

"True, but the rest of me looks the same," Sarah reminded her.

Eve shrugged. Chris tried the door but found it locked. Shrugging, he knocked. They waited several minutes until they heard muffled footsteps from the other side.

"So sorry, but our masters are not home right now. Please come back another time!" one of the maids called.

"It's Chris! Open up!" Chris called.

"Master Shearcliff! Forgive me, it will only be a moment," the maid assured him.

They heard muffled voices speaking hastily behind the door.

"Am I crazy or do I hear Jasheir?" Cassy asked.

"Why would he be here?" Ditrina asked.

"Open the door!" Sarah bellowed.

"Just a moment!" the maid replied hastily.

"Let me!" Eve said excitedly.

She plucked the feather from her hair, and this time it took the form of a massive two-handed sword, blade glittering gold with a grip of ivory. It was longer than she was tall, but with the aid of the banelance's magic, she hefted it with ease.

"Eve, no!" Chris yelled, but it was too late.

"Eve, yes!" Mi cheered.

Eve swung the sword, and the doors blew apart with a blinding flash of light, sending sawdust everywhere. There was a high-pitched scream, and when the dust cleared, they saw a strange sight.

"What the hell is going on?" Sarah demanded, looking into her home with a combination of amusement and disgust, the two emotions wrestling for control of her face.

Flora, or perhaps it was Fiona, stood stunned with a bedsheet wrapped around her, beside an equally shocked Jasheir, wearing only his underwear. They stood looking at each other and Chris's companions mutely, unsure of what to say.

"I have questions," Eve said simply.

"Welcome home," Jasheir said with a sheepish smile.

"Is that who I think it is?" Matt asked.

"Good news, Eve. You're about to have enough skin for your banelance!" Sarah said cheerfully.

"Hurray!" Eve cheered.

"I can explain!" the maid said quickly.

"Good, because I'd love to know why you two are basically naked and standing in the middle of my house," Chris said impatiently.

The maid opened her mouth and closed it several times without saying anything.

"I can't explain," she said meekly.

"Flora, I should go," Jasheir said as he slunk toward the door.

"Not so fast, big guy. Why the hell do I come home to find you banging my maid?" Chris demanded.

"I'm really glad I'm blind right now," Matt said with a shudder. Jasheir shrugged.

"Because you came by in the afternoon," he said as if that cleared everything up.

"I thought I told you not to come dropping by our house!" Sarah yelled.

"Technically, you dropped by on me," Jasheir pointed out.

"You're not helping your case any," Cassy told him.

"Why don't you come in and sit down. I'll catch you up on what I've been up to," Jasheir told them as he beckoned them inside. "Flora dear, please get dressed. I presume your masters have work for you," Jasheir told her.

Flora nodded and left quickly, an impressive feat considering she was dressed only in a bedsheet. Jasheir led them into the waiting room, and they sat on the assorted chairs and sofas.

"So, aside from Flora, what have you been doing?" Matt asked, trying to break the ice.

"Fiona," Jasheir replied.

"Ok, next question!" Matt exclaimed.

"Why are you still here? I thought you were going to look for work after the elves dropped you off here?" Ditrina asked.

"I found work already," Jasheir told them.

"Really? Where?" Cassy asked.

"I'm working in an inn down in the village as a server. It is good work, and whenever the drunks get too rowdy, I can bash their heads together," Jasheir said with a content hiss.

"There's only one inn in town..." Matt said, trailing off.

"Sam, you rat bastard!" Sarah cursed.

"Sam is a good man," Jasheir said firmly. "He is giving me food and a place to sleep in exchange for my service!"

"What about gold?" Cassy asked.

"He said something about paying my debt first. I think it may have something to do with me destroying most of the bar when I first came to the village. The ale in Desgail is much stronger than Gishkar," Jasheir said meekly.

"Well, remind me never to stop by Sam's place ever again," Sarah said with a disappointed sigh.

"So, can you explain how you ended up in our house shagging our maids?" Matt asked.

"Well, one of them stopped by the bar one evening, and I began to flirt with her. Needless to say, I was successful, and she spent the night in the inn with me. The next night she returned, and I once again had the pleasure of her company. On the third night, both of them showed up, and I realized that it had not been one person, but two. To my relief, my charms proved up to the task of wooing both of them, and that night, I had the pleasure of both their companies," Jasheir explained.

"What do mean when you say pleasure of their company? They're boring," Eve told him.

"You're just not being creative enough," Jasheir told her with a sly smile on his snakelike face.

"That's enough of that!" Sarah yelled. "Let's try to save the *one* shred of innocence she has left!"

"I will find this shred, and I will feed it to Echo," Eve grumbled.

"In any event, I will leave you to whatever you are getting up to. I believe there is to be a wedding soon?" Jasheir asked.

"Wait, what wedding?" Sarah asked with confusion.

"That's right! We never told Matt and Sarah!" Cassy exclaimed.

"Cas and I are going to get married," Ditrina told her.

"Congratulations!" Matt exclaimed.

"When did this happen?" Sarah demanded.

"She proposed while we were en route to rescue you," Cassy explained.

"Halfway across Targoth, surrounded by bloodthirsty monsters, half of your family enslaved, and you decide to propose?" Sarah demanded, looking at Ditrina with outrage.

"That is funny, Chris said the same thing!" Ditrina exclaimed.

"I will be going now. You are all insane," Jasheir said as he walked toward the splintered remains of the door.

"Don't come back!" Sarah called after him.

"Be prepared to have to track down your maids then," Jasheir called back over his shoulder as he walked down the path, still wearing only his underwear.

"Asshole," Sarah muttered.

She turned her attention back to Cassy.

"As for you, why didn't you tell me?" Sarah exclaimed with excitement.

"I feel like it's time for a tactical retreat," Matt whispered to Chris.

Chris nodded and began to sneak out of the room, leading Matt by the arm while Sarah was seemingly distracted until her hand reached out and snagged him by the hood of his cloak.

"Sit down. We have planning to do!" Sarah exclaimed.

"Can't their wedding be like ours?" Chris asked hopefully, recalling their impromptu ceremony that required no planning other than finding rings.

"No! Unlike me, I'm sure Cassy wants a proper wedding, right?" Sarah asked, looking at Cassy.

"Well, there are a few people I would like to come," Cassy admitted.

"See? That means there are invitations to send out, dates to plan, and arrangements to be made. We have work to do!" Sarah exclaimed.

"Can't we just relax? We just got home!" Matt begged.

"Shut up, blind boy! Ex-cleric or not, you're still presiding over the ceremony. Start memorizing the lines," Sarah ordered.

Matt groaned and slumped back into a chair. Chris looked around for a way to escape but saw none.

"Good luck," Mi told him.

"Stay strong," Al advised.

"I'm going to die," Chris thought as Sarah launched into a detailed discussion with Cassy and Ditrina about things he couldn't care less about.

One month later, their valley had undergone a transformation. The large, open area by the lake was now covered by chairs and had a small stage installed beside the shore. The maids had been hard at work cleaning the grounds, and Chris and Eve had been grilled time and time again on how to behave. As Sarah put it, *be anything but yourselves for today.* They each agreed that that was rather unfair.

The guests had begun to arrive over the course of the week, and for the first time, Chris was glad that the maids knew the estate as well as they did. They found accommodations for each person as they arrived, sticking people in rooms Chris didn't even know existed.

Not all of the guests they invited were able to make the journey to the valley, however. Cassy and Ditrina received a lovely letter from Baron Francis congratulating them on the occasion as well as apologizing for having to miss the ceremony, along with a sizeable bag of gemstones as a gift. Chris was unsure if Cassy even read the letter, given how entranced by the gift she was. Ditrina invited her father, much to Cassy's displeasure, and he arrived in the village the day before the wedding, along with all of Ditrina's brothers.

"Di, I notice that you never mention your mother. Why is that?" Cassy asked when she saw that she wasn't present at the wedding and remembering how she saw no sign of her in the city.

"My mother has been dead for a hundred and sixty years," Ditrina said sadly.

"Oh, I'm sorry to hear that," Cassy said as her heart jumped into her throat, cursing herself for asking such a question without thinking.

"My father said that she was a lot like me. My own memories of her are a bit hazy. I was barely fifty when she died. She was a Gel, but she refused to follow the rule about staying in the city. She left one day to explore, and she never came back," Ditrina said with a small, sad smile.

"Maybe she's still alive then, exploring somewhere far away," Cassy said hopefully.

"Unlikely. Scouts found her remains in a ruin several months after she left. Given the burns and how much blood they found, it is safe to assume she was eaten by a dragon," Ditrina said bluntly. "She never came home because there was not enough of her to bring home."

"Di, I'm so sorry," Cassy said, taking one of Ditrina's hands.

"Why? You did not kill her," Ditrina said, not understanding Cassy's grief.

Cassy had no reply to that.

"You must be Cassy," an elf said as he walked toward them. "Pleasure to meet you," he said as he shook her clawed hand.

"Who might you be?" Cassy asked, surprised by the kind greeting the elf offered.

"Morilana Figinoma Gel. It is wonderful to see you in the flesh. My sister has told me much about you," he said.

"I am glad that they allowed you out of the city, Moril," Ditrina said as she embraced her brother.

"Well, when my older sister is getting married, exceptions have to be made," Moril chuckled.

"You said you were a Gel?" Cassy asked with surprise.

"That's right. Of my siblings, I'm the only one unlucky enough to be stuffed in the city all day," Moril sighed.

"Won't you be the next king though?" Cassy asked.

"That's right. I'm the crown prince," Moril confirmed.

"Forgive me for asking, but why are you being nice to me? Most of the elves I've met hate me," Cassy told him.

"Well, I won't lie and say that I was thrilled when I learned my older sister was engaged to a naga, but while Ditrina was in the city we talked quite a bit, and she told me all about you. If even half of the things she said were true, then you will hear no complaints from me," Moril told her.

"What type of things did she tell you?" Cassy asked cautiously.

"Only good things, I swear," Moril said with a laugh as he walked away, off to speak to Sam, who had closed his shop for the day to attend.

"Oh, would you look at that. It is Jasheir," Ditrina pointed out, spying the naga near the edge of the crowd.

"Did you invite him?" Cassy asked her.

"No, I figured you did," Ditrina replied.

"Let's hope Sarah doesn't butcher him," Cassy sighed.

"Agreed. Come on, let us go see who else came," Ditrina said cheerfully as she led Cassy among the guests.

Cassy followed eagerly, her eyes scanning the crowd. There was someone she was looking forward to seeing.

"Well, judging by what I hear, the party is going smoothly," Matt told Chris.

"The brides are happy, and Sarah hasn't killed anyone yet. So far, so good," Chris agreed.

"How do you feel that Sarah's wearing a dress to your sister's wedding when she didn't wear one to her own?" Matt chuckled.

"I regret telling you that," Chris sighed.

"Can I go play now?" Eve begged, tired of having to sit with Chris and Matt.

"Not yet, sweetie," Chris told her.

"But the other kids are playing!" Eve protested.

"Other kids?" Chris asked, looking around in confusion.

Sure enough, he saw a pair of young boys racing around the edges of the crowd. Recognition flooded across his face, and he smiled.

"Matt, you'll never guess who made it," Chris laughed.

"Are you talking about our night-loving friend?" Matt asked.

"The same," Chris confirmed.

His eyes scanned the crowd and settled on a woman wearing a large sunhat and long-sleeved dress, standing beside her husband. The man caught sight of Chris and waved, leading his wife and children toward them.

"Rob, Ophelia! I'm so glad you could make it!" Chris called happily.

"Are you kidding? She would have killed me if we had missed this!" Rob laughed.

"I would not have," Ophelia said with a disapproving frown.

"Hello, Mr. Shearcliff," one of the boys said.

The other, who was identical to his brother, save having longer hair, echoed his words.

"Hello, boys. How have you been?" Chris asked kindly.

"Demmi has been teasing me!" the long-haired boy cried.

"Mom, make Jake stop lying!" Demmi protested.

"I'm not lying!" Jake yelled.

"Boys, behave!" Ophelia snapped, and Chris caught a glimpse of her fangs.

"Why is she pale?" Eve asked, and Echo gave a warning hiss.

"Well, who's this cutie?" Ophelia asked, kneeling before Eve.

"I'm not cute! I'm scary!" Eve yelled, and Echo screamed in agreement.

"I'm terrified," Ophelia laughed.

"Eve, Ophelia is a friend of ours. She's a vampire," Chris told her.

"No, she's not. Vampires can't be in the sun," Eve said firmly.

Ophelia laughed.

"We're vampires, too!" the boys yelled, feeling excluded.

"Half vampires, which is why you don't need hats today," Ophelia reminded them, gesturing to the afternoon sun.

"If you're a vampire, show me your fangs," Eve ordered.

"Eve, don't be rude," Chris chastised.

"It's fine," Ophelia said with a laugh.

She smiled a big toothy smile at Eve, giving her a good view of her long canines.

"Echo has big teeth, too," Eve said defiantly, and the tiny dragon opened his fang filled mouth wide, revealing row after row of razor sharp fangs.

"Impressive." Ophelia laughed, ruffling Eve's short hair.

"Can we play now?" the boys begged their mother.

"Fine, be good," Ophelia replied.

"Me too?" Eve asked hopefully.

"Fine, but if I see one drop of blood, then you're in huge trouble," Chris warned her.

"They won't hurt her, I swear!" Ophelia said hastily.

"Believe me, I know. That's not what I'm worried about," Chris assured her as the children streaked off across the field, Echo flying above them.

Their laughter floated thought the valley, mingling with the babble of conversation.

"So, Matt, what happened to your eyes?" Rob asked.

"Long story short, I had the worst vacation ever," Matt summarized.

"I can't imagine what could have happened to you," Ophelia said with concern.

"Ophelia!" Sarah called as she hurried toward her.

"Hello, Sarah!" Ophelia said as she waved back.

Her eyes widened as she realized Sarah was missing a hand.

"What happened to you all?" Ophelia demanded.

"We were captured by slavers," Sarah told her.

"Oh gods, that's horrible!" Ophelia exclaimed.

"It's ok; we burned their city to the ground," Sarah said cheerfully.

"Well, that's one way to get even, I guess," Rob said with a nervous chuckle.

"I hear you and Chris got married. Why didn't you invite us?" Ophelia asked with mock offence.

Sarah laughed.

"It was a really small affair, we really didn't invite anyone actually," Sarah admitted.

"Wish ours had been the same," Rob said with a sad smile.

"In any event, I think it's time for the ceremony. Matt, get up there," Sarah said, gesturing to the stage.

"You know I can't see whatever I'm sure you're pointing at, right?" Matt said irritably.

"Just shut up and follow me," Sarah said as she dragged him away.

Ophelia smiled.

"Congratulations, Chris. It looks like you've done well for yourself," Ophelia told him.

"Thanks, but what about you? Have people been giving you any trouble?" Chris asked.

"No! None at all! Ever since I publicly came out as a vampire, people have been coming from miles around to see me, which is great for business. We've had trouble staying stocked with all the customers we've had," Ophelia laughed.

"I'm glad to hear that. I was worried that you might have started drawing the wrong sort of attention," Chris admitted.

"We've had a few of those to be sure, but the soldiers have dealt with them," Rob told him.

"Soldiers?" Chris asked.

"Yeah, after the feast, Baron Francis decided to leave a small garrison of guards in the village. They've done a great job of keeping the place safe," Rob said.

"If you have a garrison, it must mean that Torville's growing pretty quickly," Chris said with mild surprise.

"More people every day. Lots of nonhumans to be specific," Ophelia said with a smile.

"You can't go saying there are no nonhumans in Torville anymore," Chris said with a chuckle.

"A giant moved in last week. He doesn't talk much, but he seems like a decent fella. The whole town pitched in to help build a house big enough for him," Rob told him.

They heard a scream from the crowd and saw Eve and the twins had cornered one of the maids and were circling her like hungry wolves, while Echo dived for her hair.

"Oh no, I need to stop that. My boys' blood makes them rowdier than most. Getting them to behave is…challenging," Ophelia sighed.

"Oh, believe me, I know. Eve's quite a handful," Chris told her.

"Forgive me for asking, but is she yours? You look a little young to have a child as old as her," Rob remarked.

"Rob!" Ophelia exclaimed with disapproval written across her face.

"It's a fair question!" Rob defended.

"Sarah and I adopted her. Her village was wiped out by a dragon, and she was the only survivor," Chris told them.

"That's horrible!" Ophelia gasped.

"Well, that explains the scars," Rob said.

"What were you going to do with her if you didn't take her in?" Ophelia asked. "Having children isn't a decision you could have made lightly."

"To be honest, we were thinking about asking you to take her in at first," Chris said sheepishly.

Ophelia laughed.

"Well, any time you're in the area, feel free to stop by and Eve can play with the boys. They seem to get along well," Ophelia said, pointing to the children tormenting the maid.

"Likewise. You're always welcome here," Chris told her. "Speaking of that, it must have taken a week for you to get here—at least! Would you like to stay and rest a while before you hit the road?" Chris asked.

"Oh, we couldn't possibly ask that of you!" Ophelia exclaimed.

"We would be grateful," Rob told him, cutting off Ophelia's polite refusals.

They heard Matt clearing his throat from the stage and saw everyone was moving to their seats.

"We should probably get our kids and find a place to sit. I think it's time for the main event," Chris told them.

"Good plan," Rob agreed.

"Eve! Let go of the maid's hair and get over here!" Chris called to his daughter.

"Coming, Father," was her disappointed reply.

Later that evening, long after the ceremony, Cassy sat with her wife, looking out over the lake in the last rays of the setting sun.

"Well, that was enjoyable," Ditrina summarized.

"I'll give Matt credit, he can play the part of a priest well when the need arises," Cassy agreed.

"Many of the guests left already. I expected at least half of them to stay the night," Ditrina remarked.

"Well, considering most of them were elves and can teleport, I don't think they felt the need to impose," Cassy laughed.

"I believe the only people to stay were the Tuxons. You invited them, correct?" Ditrina asked.

"Yeah, they were some of the few I invited," Cassy confirmed.

"Like you said, most of the guests were elves. Who else did you invite?" Ditrina asked.

"Just one other, and he didn't come," Cassy said quietly. "I kept looking for him, but I didn't see him."

"Do you not have many friends?" Ditrina asked.

"Aside from all of you, not really. I count Ophelia and her family as friends, but really, that's it. Before I started traveling with Chris, I was a bandit, after all," Cassy reminded her.

"The man you invited, the one who didn't come, who is he?" Ditrina asked.

Cassy smiled.

"His name is Samuel Cogwell. He's an old drunk who lives in the Shearcliff village."

"Why did you invite him?" Ditrina asked.

"He was the man who raised Chris and took me in. He was something of a father to us, I guess. He wasn't what I'd call a good role model, but he did his best," Cassy said with a sigh. "I haven't seen him in years."

"Perhaps we could pay a visit to your old village?" Ditrina proposed.

"I'm not exactly welcome there. Naga are fairly scary looking, and they drove me out after my scales grew in," Cassy told her.

"Still, if you miss him, you should try to find him. It is something to consider," Ditrina told her.

"I'll talk to Chris about it," Cassy told her. "Let's not worry about that right now, though. For now, let's just enjoy tonight," she said as she rested her head on Ditrina's shoulder.

"I like this idea," Ditrina agreed as she took her hand.

"Come on, this'll be fun!" Eve said as she led the boys away from the house.

"Isn't it getting a little dark?" Demmi asked.

"Yeah, we probably shouldn't be sneaking out like this," Jake agreed.

"Don't you want to have a little fun?" Eve asked. "Or are you scared?"

"Jake might be scared, but I'm not!" Demmi proclaimed.

"I'm way braver than you are!" Jake declared indignantly.

"Good, then come on! Echo smelled something really fun for us to play with," Eve said as she led them along.

"Can't we eat dinner first?" Jake protested, looking nervously around the shadows of the evening.

"What do you mean? You two ate dinner with me earlier," Eve told them.

"Yeah, but Mom never gave us any blood to drink, and we're kinda hungry still. Food only does so much," Demmi told her.

"Follow me, and there'll be more blood than you could ever dream of," Eve said with a gleam in her eyes, her scars hiding half of her face in shadow.

Echo circled them once before landing on her shoulder. He nuzzled her face.

"Good, it's still there. Come on," Eve said, before setting off into the night.

The boys exchanged nervous looks with glowing red eyes but shrugged. Young as they were, they were stronger than the average human and had magic at their disposal. What could the ugly human girl possibly have found that was of any threat to them?

CHAPTER SEVENTEEN

"Master Shearcliff, do you know where Eve is?" one of the maids asked as she walked into the parlor.

Chris, who was currently sitting with the others catching up with Rob and Ophelia, looked up in confusion.

"I put her to bed an hour ago. She should be in her room; look there, Fiona," he told her.

"My name is Flora, and I already checked there. When I went to put her clothes for tomorrow in her room, I saw her bed was empty," Flora told him

"That's not good," Rob chuckled.

"It may interest you to know that your boys were also not in their rooms when I went in earlier," she pointed out.

"Why didn't you tell us?" Ophelia asked angrily.

"I figured being vampires, it was normal for them to be out and about during the night," Flora said nervously.

"No! They should have been asleep by now!" Ophelia exclaimed.

"Do you think they went outside to play?" Cassy asked.

"If it's Eve's idea of a game, then we need to find them as soon as possible," Sarah said quickly.

"What's wrong with Eve's sense of fun?" Rob asked.

"It usually involves violence and is backed by dragon fire," Ditrina pointed out.

"Eve was asking lots of questions about vampires today, I figured it was just because Ophelia piqued her interest," Matt admitted.

"What type of questions?" Chris asked cautiously.

"How they fight, what their abilities are, and so forth. You know, the stuff Eve's into," Matt told him.

"Are my boys in danger?" Ophelia asked nervously.

"Unlikely. Eve seemed to like them, so I doubt she's planning to hurt them. She's probably using them for something," Chris said as he stood up.

"Eve has her banelance. What could she possibly need help with?" Sarah asked.

"Nothing good," Chris said as he ran toward his room to grab his sword.

"Where are we going, Eve?" Demmi asked as they walked.

"Farther up the pass," Eve replied.

"What's up there?" Jake asked.

"Not much, really. There's a house this way where the watcher lives," Eve told them.

"Who's the watcher?" Demmi asked.

"He watches the pass for the King's men. If he sees them, he rides back to the village and warns everyone," Eve explained.

"Why does he warn them?" Demmi asked.

"I dunno. I never really cared to ask," Eve said with a shrug.

"So, are we visiting this watcher man?" Jake asked.

"Nope, he's dead," Eve said cheerfully.

"What? What happened to him?" Demmi asked with shock.

"A monster ate him," Eve said eagerly.

"When?" Jake asked nervously.

"During the wedding. Echo was flying around, and I watched through his eyes. I would have asked to go watch myself, but Aunt Cas and Aunt Di were too cute, and I didn't want to miss the ceremony," Eve sighed.

"What if the monster is still there?" Jake exclaimed.

"Of course, it's still there! What do you think we're on our way to kill?" Eve demanded.

"Why would you want to go anywhere near a man-eating monster?" Jake asked with terror.

"Aren't you two vampires or something? I thought you were cool," Eve said, pouting.

"Hey, we're cool!" Jake yelled.

"Yeah, the coolest!" Demmi agreed.

"I think you're scared. You're so scared that you're gonna let a girl go fight a monster all by herself," Eve said with a sniffle.

"I'm not scared, I'll keep you safe!" Demmi insisted.

"Me too! I'm way tougher than him!" Jake said eagerly. "Let me protect you!"

"Whichever of you brings me the monster's head is the bravest. You two can have the blood and meat and things, but I want its skin and bones," Eve told them.

"Why?" the boys asked.

"Girly things," Eve said with a smile.

"Maybe she's making a mask to hide her scars?" Demmi proposed.

"Why would I want to hide my scars?" Eve demanded.

"Because they're ugly," Jake told her.

"So are your stupid fangs, but I'm not telling you to cover them up!" Eve shouted.

"Our fangs are awesome!" Demmi yelled back.

"Yeah, you're just jealous!" Jake told her.

"Ok, yeah, they're really cool, and I want fangs like that too, ok?" Eve yelled before crossing her arms. "It's not fair," she said with a sniffle.

Jake and Demmi looked at each other nervously. They hadn't meant to make her upset.

"We're sorry," Jake told her.

"Yeah, your scars aren't that ugly," Demmi assured her.

Eve buried her face in her hands and began to sob.

"Don't cry! Please, don't cry! Look, we're going to kill the monster now!" Jake promised her.

"Yeah, just you watch. We'll kill it just for you," Demmi agreed as he and his brother raced down the trail.

Eve continued to sob until she heard their footsteps fade away. When she lifted her head, her eyes were dry, and she wore a sinister half-smile.

"We need to hurry," Chris told them as he raced down the trail.

"I can smell my boys, they went farther down the pass," Ophelia told him as they ran.

"I'll run ahead and see if I can find them," Cassy said as she put her inhuman legs to work, sprinting far faster than humanly possible.

"I'll come, too!" Ophelia said as she kept pace easily with Cassy.

Chris fueled himself with magic and caught up with them.

"That's new," Ophelia said as she looked at Chris's glowing red eyes, eerily similar to her own.

"Rob and Matt stayed back at the house in case they turned back and we missed them, and Sarah and Di went down to the village in case the kids split up, so I'm sure we'll find them, but I still don't understand. What could have possessed them to run off like this?" Cassy asked as they ran.

"Eve likely found something she wants to kill," Chris said with a frown.

"But she has her banelance. Why does she need help?" Cassy asked.

"What's a banelance?" Ophelia asked.

"Whatever she wants it to be," Chris said grimly.

"So, Eve found something so dangerous that she doesn't feel confident that she can kill it with a superweapon and a dragon," Ophelia summed up.

"Pretty much," Chris confirmed.

"Gods help us," Cassy said as they ran.

"There it is," Demmi said, pointing at the house.

The door had been torn off its hinges, and the sound of something large eating could be heard coming from within.

"Eve, are you sure about this?" Jake asked.

"You promised," Eve said with a fake sniffle.

"Ok, ok. What's the plan?" Jake asked.

"Plan?" Eve asked as she walked toward the house, her tearful façade fading away. "Who needs a plan?" she asked as she plucked the feather from her hair.

The twins watched in awe as it morphed into a massive longbow in her hands, with an ivory curve gilded in gold. She pulled back on the string and an arrow of pure light formed in her hands.

"We're not here to plan; we're here to have fun!" she called as she released the arrow.

It streaked away like a bolt of lightning and flew through the open door. There was a flash of light and a deafening boom, and the house was reduced to splinters, revealing a hulking monster standing within.

"Is that a fell boar?" Jake asked with horror.

"Fun time!" Eve shrieked as she charged forward, her banelance now taking the form of a spear.

Echo launched himself into the sky, circling the beast expectantly. The fell boar was a sight to behold. The twins decided that while it shared a name with a boar, the resemblance ended there. First of all, it was far too big, easily the size of a large bear. How it made its way into the house was a mystery to them. It had no fur they could see; rather, it was covered head to toe with thick, knobbly skin, with massive plates of bone protruding from its back and shoulders like a spiked suit of armor. Its shape was more akin to a gorilla than a pig, with massive front arms sporting enormous sickle-shaped claws. Its head was repulsive, encased by an armored plate that would put the strongest shield to shame. Its immense mouth was filled with fangs covered by a thick coat of slobber and blood, with two razor sharp tusks extending from its lower jaw, like daggers. The bone plate on its head covered so much that if the creature had eyes, they were hidden and useless. Rather than rely on its vision, the creature had a disgusting nose like that of a pig, which oozed snot as it snuffled in the air, likely what had given the creature its name.

Despite Eve's assault on the house, the creature seemed oblivious to them and continued to feed on the remains of the watcher. This didn't last long as Eve plunged her spear into the beast's side.

The fell boar squealed and reared back, swiping in the direction of the pain. Eve leapt back out of the way of its slashing claws and prepared to attack again. The boar hunkered down and snuffled the air, turning its head in Eve's direction. It squealed again and charged toward her.

"We need to help her!" Demmi yelled as he sprinted forward, running faster than Eve's eye could track, Jake right behind him.

"So, what can you two do anyway?" Eve asked as she dodged the beasts charge.

"We know a few spells!" Jake called.

"Use them!" Eve commanded.

Jake and Demmi looked at each other before shrugging. They rarely got a chance to use their powers, and this was as good a time as any.

"I know!" Jake yelled as he raced toward the boar. "Distract it!" he yelled.

Eve didn't need an excuse to cause the monster pain, but all the same, she yelled:

"Sure!" before stabbing her spear into the beast's shoulder.

The fell boar screamed and slashed vainly at her, but Jake intercepted it. He reached out and slashed at the boar with his hand in the shape of a claw, and to Eve's shock, he cut a bloody rend in its thick hide. The boar didn't give them the chance to celebrate, rather it slammed Jake into the ground with a massive fist.

"Well, that's unfortunate," Eve said flatly, looking for the smear that she was sure Jake had become.

A bat fluttered up next to her, and suddenly, Jake was by her side.

"I cut it!" he said with excitement.

"Great, what else can you do?" Eve asked, mildly disappointed he hadn't been reduced to paste.

"What do you mean? That's our strongest attack!" Demmi exclaimed proudly.

"You two are boring. Forget I invited you on my adventure," Eve said with disappointment in her eyes.

"What do you want from us? We're only five!" Jake protested.

"So? I'm six," Eve said as she walked purposefully toward the fell boar. "Watch and learn, boys!" she called as she twirled her spear and morphed it back into a bow.

The boar was busy snuffling the ground in confusion where it expected Jake's corpse to be when it felt a burning impact explode against its armored back.

"Here, piggy, piggy, piggy!" Eve called as she fired several more arrows to little effect.

The boar squealed in rage and charged at Eve, kicking up clods of dirt as it raced toward her. Eve calmly stood her ground, and her bow became a massive axe, too large for even her parents to wield. Right when it looked like the boar would barrel her over, Eve swung the axe, delivering a crushing blow to the boar's skull, accompanied by a brilliant flash of light. The boar crumpled to the ground and skidded through the dirt. Eve smiled and turned to the boys.

"And that's how you slay a monster!" Eve said proudly.

"Behind you!" Demmi yelled as he saw the boar rising unsteadily to its feet.

Eve rolled her eyes.

"Relax, I'm sure it's just twitching or something," she said dismissively.

The boar reared up on its hind legs and screamed in rage.

"Or not," Eve said with a sheepish half-smile.

The fell boar stepped forward and reached back to slash Eve with its claws, when suddenly it found one very angry Echo latched to the front of its face, determined to defend his mother. The boar squealed in pain and stumbled back as Echo tore at the sensitive flesh of the boar's nose, spattering the ground in blood. The boar pawed at its face, all thoughts of Eve forgotten, and managed to knock Echo to the ground. With a screech of pain, the dragon was sent crashing to the dirt.

"Echo!" Eve screamed, spinning to face the monster.

Before the fell boar had a chance to recover from his brief victory over the dragon, Eve's fury was upon him. She twirled the axe, and the banelance became a spear once more. Eve cocked back her arm and launched the spear like a golden missile. The twins saw a streak of light, and suddenly everything was very still. The boar still stood upon its hind legs, though the gaping hole through the center of its head rendered it senseless. As if in slow motion, it toppled forward with a crash, bony plates clashing together. Too concerned over Echo, Eve barely notices her victory.

"Echo, Echo! Are you ok?" she begged as she knelt beside her small friend.

She already knew the answer. From the moment Echo felt pain, she had shared it with him. She knew one of his wings was broken.

"Is he ok?" Demmi asked nervously.

"This is your fault!" Eve screamed at him. "If you were a better fighter, then Echo wouldn't have gotten hurt!"

"You made us come! We're not fighters!" Jake yelled back.

"Just leave me alone!" Eve screamed as she held out her hand.

With a flash of gold and ivory, the banelance returned to her grip.

"Eve!" Chris bellowed as he raced toward his daughter at superhuman speeds.

"Father, Father, Echo is hurt!" Eve cried.

"What do you think you're doing?!" Chris demanded, looking at the carnage.

"Please, Father, he's hurt!" Eve sobbed, cradling her injured friend.

Seeing his daughter in tears tempered his anger slightly, and Chris approached the wounded dragon. His eyes glowed red, and with magic, Echo's wing was repaired. Eve gave a sigh of relief and held her friend close, her banelance clattering to the ground.

"What in the gods' names do you think you are doing?" Ophelia yelled as she streaked toward her sons.

"She made us!" Demmi yelled quickly.

"It's not our fault!" Jake agreed.

"When we get back to the house, your father will have words with you," Ophelia said menacingly.

The twins already pale faces lost the last of their color.

"Please, don't tell Dad," they pleaded.

"You think he doesn't already know?" Ophelia demanded as she began hauling them back toward the estate by the ears.

Cassy, who was the last to arrive due to her lack of magic, sprinted into view.

"Oh, thank the gods you found her," Cassy said with relief.

"Why did you run off, Eve?" Chris asked softly.

Eve sniffled, still hugging Echo tightly.

"I wanted to kill a monster, like you and Mother!" Eve exclaimed.

"You shouldn't have run off without telling anyone, and you definitely shouldn't have brought the boys with you. You could have gotten hurt!" Chris scolded.

"I know," Eve said softly.

"How did you convince them to sneak out anyway?" Cassy asked.

"I told them that they could have the creature's blood to drink if they came with me," Eve admitted.

"What did you want with this monster anyway?" Chris asked her, looking at the massive corpse.

"Well, Echo found it, and I thought it would be cool if I made it into armor," Eve told him.

"If you make it into armor now, you'll just grow out of it," Chris told her.

"Then I'll get the supplies and wait until I'm older!" Eve insisted.

Chris sighed.

"Fine. I'll get a cart, and we'll haul it down to the village tomorrow, on one condition," Chris told her.

"Anything!" Eve exclaimed.

"No going out without permission ever again. Do you understand?" Chris told her.

"I promise," Eve said seriously.

"You're too soft on her. She needs to be punished," Al told him.

"Shut up, Al. you were going to kill my wife. You get no say in how I discipline my daughter," Chris thought irritably.

"Harsh," Mi laughed.

Chris ignored him.

"In any event, your mother isn't going to be happy with what you did," Chris told her.

"Oh, I don't know. Eve did kill this giant thing all by herself. I think Sarah might be proud," Cassy told him.

Eve's half-smile widened, and Chris shot Cassy a disapproving look.

"Oh, right! Yeah, she's going to be mad," Cassy corrected hastily.

"You're lucky Echo didn't get killed," Chris told her.

"I know," Eve said softly.

Echo crawled free from her viselike hug and reclaimed his perch on her shoulder. He began rubbing his head against Eve's scars while purring in a strangely catlike manner.

"It seems Echo's forgiven her, though," Cassy remarked.

"He's just happy I'm ok," Eve said as she scratched behind his horns with her clawlike hand.

"So am I. Come on, let's go home," Chris said as he took her hand.

Chris kept his promise and had the fell boar hauled down to the village the next day to be skinned and butchered. Like Cassy originally thought, Sarah was far too impressed to be angry, going so far as to praise Eve's handiwork. The twins were less lucky and found themselves thoroughly scolded by their parents for being so reckless and stupid. Still, Eve made sure that they got what they were promised, and even though they were confined to their rooms for the rest of the visit, they each had as much boar blood as they could drink. As it turns out, fell boar was remarkably tasty, and pork was on the menu for the foreseeable future.

"It's been wonderful here, but it's time for us to head home," Ophelia said one week after Eve's adventure.

They stood in the middle of the valley beside the Tuxons' horses.

"I agree, the shop's been closed too long. We have to get back to business," Rob said as he shook Chris's hand.

"You will always be welcome here," Ditrina said with a smile.

"Likewise. The next time you're in Torville, be sure to swing by. It's always a joy to see you," Ophelia said with a smile.

"What do you say, boys?" Rob asked his sons.

"Thank you for letting us stay here," Demmi told him.

"Sorry we ran off and killed things with Eve," Jake piped in.

"Don't worry, she's always off killing things," Chris said with a smile.

"Lucky!" the boys said, looking at Eve.

Eve smiled a smug half-smile.

"In any event, it's a long ride to Torville. We should be going," Rob said.

"I could take you there," Ditrina told them.

"What do you mean?" Ophelia asked.

"I could teleport you and your horses back home. I have been there before so I can teleport there," Ditrina explained.

"We couldn't possibly ask you to do something like that!" Rob exclaimed.

"It is nothing, really. I do not mind!" Ditrina insisted. "Gather around and hold onto everything you wish to bring," Ditrina instructed.

Rob and Ophelia shrugged and gathered by their horses. Once everything was touching that needed to be teleported, Ditrina vanished along with them.

"She should be back soon; let's wait inside," Chris said as he led the others back into the house. "Wrong way, Matt!" Chris yelled as he saw his friend walking farther away from the building.

"I knew that!" Matt snapped irritably as he spun in place and proceeded to walk in a different, albeit incorrect direction.

"Closer, but still no!" Sarah called.

"Is anyone going to help me, or are you just going to let me fumble about outside all day?" Matt demanded.

Eve stepped away from Sarah and walked quickly to Matt's side, taking his hand.

"Come on, Uncle S, let's get you inside," she said kindly.

"It's sad when Eve has the most compassion out of all of you!" Matt called over his shoulder as Eve led him by the hand.

"I know, I love you," Eve said as she led him toward the lake.

"They grow up so fast," Mi said, and Chris was sure the spirit had a tear in his eye.

"Hey, Chris, I have something I wanna ask you," Cassy told him later that afternoon.

"What is it, sis?" Chris asked.

"I wanna go to Shearcliff," Cassy said bluntly.

"What? Why? They drove you out! Why in the world would you wanna go back there?" Chris asked.

"Mr. Cogwell didn't come to the wedding. I wanna go and make sure my letter reached him. I haven't seen him in two years," Cassy told him.

"The old drunk probably didn't even read it. You know how he is," Chris told her.

"Chris, I'm serious," Cassy told him.

Chris was quiet for a moment.

"You know, I left without even saying goodbye," he said softly.

"He'll forgive you; you were wanted, after all," Cassy reminded him.

"So much has happened since then," Chris said with a laugh. "I got married, you got married; hell, I have a daughter now! What am I supposed to tell him?" Chris asked.

"Tell him what's happened. About our adventures, about Sarah, and about Matt. Invite him to come with us to meet Eve and Ditrina. He took us in and raised us. He's family. Right now, our family should be here," Cassy said, gesturing around her.

Chris thought for a moment.

"You're right; you're absolutely right. When I started adventuring, I wanted to make enough money, so he never had to work another day in his drunken life. It's time to make that happen. Let's bring him home," Chris said with a smile.

"How soon can we leave?" Cassy asked.

"As soon as you like. Ditrina just got back a few hours ago so she can get us to Draclige. That puts us three days away from Shearcliff," Chris told her.

"I don't want them to come to the village," Cassy said firmly.

"Why?" Chris asked with confusion.

"Because I don't need Sarah and Ditrina killing everyone when they start throwing stones at me. Better we get in and out quickly with the old man. No need to attract attention," Cassy told him.

"I see your point. Our wives do lack control when it comes to carnage, don't they?" Chris mused.

"Sometimes it's a plus," Cassy pointed out.

"And sometimes it means they get left behind," Chris laughed. "They can stay at an inn while we head to the village. Hell, maybe they can check on Hal up in the castle and see how he's doing," Chris said.

"When do we leave?" Cassy asked.

"Let's give everyone a day to get ready. After his bath in the lake, I doubt that Matt wants to go anywhere right now," Chris told her.

As it turned out, Matt didn't want to go anywhere at all and volunteered to stay home while they went off on their impromptu expedition. This was overruled by Eve, who insisted that all family members partake in the journey. She was excited for another *vacation* as she kept calling it, anticipating a death toll akin to the last trip. Chris seriously hoped that she would be disappointed.

So, two days later, Ditrina took them to Draclige. They noted the large number of workmen running around and saw that the central castle was still under heavy repair.

"I still can't believe how much damage you caused, Chris," Cassy said as they rode.

"After seeing your wife's little show, are you surprised at anything anymore?" Sarah asked with amusement.

"Ditrina's an accomplished pyromancer; Chris is my idiot brother. Big difference," Cassy pointed out.

"Our leader is a fool at times," Ditrina agreed.

"What did I do to deserve you two?" Chris asked with irritation.

"At least you all can see the castle," Matt said sullenly.

So far, he had spoken very little since leaving the valley. Unable to ride alone without his eyes, he was forced to ride double with Chris.

"Did Father really do that?" Eve asked with excitement from where she sat behind Sarah.

"Yeah, he messed up and blew up the entire castle. Isn't he silly?" Sarah asked her.

Eve giggled.

"There, that inn looks like it'll work," Chris said suddenly, hoping to end all discussion of his past mistakes while in the city.

They dismounted and tethered the horses outside before walking within. Chris spied the innkeeper and walked toward him.

"I need three rooms for a week," he told him.

"All right," the innkeeper said happily, and Chris paid the man.

"A week? How long do you plan to stay here?" Sarah asked with amusement.

Cassy and I leave tomorrow. The rest of you will stay in the city," Chris told her.

"What? Why?!" Sarah demanded.

"Because I don't want you to come," Cassy said firmly.

"Cas, why do you not wish us to come?" Ditrina asked with a hint of alarm.

"Simply put, that town has made it clear that I'm not welcome. It's not going to be a happy reunion for a lot of them, and I just want to find my dad and get out of there," Cassy said.

"Do not worry about that. If they lay a finger on you, I will obliterate them," Ditrina said cheerfully.

Cassy smiled and gave her a kiss on the cheek.

"Which is exactly why you're not coming," she said with a small smile.

Sarah nodded as she saw the logic in Cassy's plan.

"Ditrina aside, why can't I come?" she asked curiously.

"Somebody needs to keep Eve and Ditrina out of trouble," Chris pointed out.

"What about me? Are you forgetting that I'm here too?" Matt asked irritably.

"How much trouble can you get into with no magic and no eyes?" Cassy asked with amusement.

"Like I needed the reminder," Matt muttered.

He turned to walk away and crashed into a table.

"Are you all right, Matthew?" Ditrina asked as she helped him to his feet.

"No, I'm really not," Matt said quietly.

"Do not despair; even though you cannot see, you still have your life. You should take joy in what you have," Ditrina said cheerfully.

"I'm shocked. I was sure you were going to take that literally and start rambling about tables," Matt said with a small chuckle.

"I have been practicing!" Ditrina said happily.

"Well, if that's decided, then tomorrow Cas and I will leave for Shearcliff. Until then, let's enjoy the evening together," Chris said smiling at his family.

"I wanna come with you, Father!" Eve said suddenly.

"Sorry, sweetheart, you're going to have to stay with your mother for a little while. I'll be back soon," Chris assured her.

"But..." Eve began,

"We'll talk about it in the morning, Eve. Let's have a little fun for now," Sarah told her.

"I like fun!" Eve declared, and they saw the bloodlust in her eyes.

"Not that type of fun," Chris said hastily.

"Oh," Eve said sadly.

"Cheer up! We're going to have a great time!" Cassy said as she took a large swig of the ale she held.

"Where did you get that?" Chris asked with astonishment.

It was as if the mug had magically appeared in her scaled hands.

"Not important. Let's have some fun!" Cassy insisted as she signaled for the innkeeper to bring over more drinks.

"I could use a drink," Matt sighed.

"Can I try?" Eve asked with excitement.

Before Chris could say no, Cassy handed her the mug, and Eve took a huge swig. She spat it on the inn's floor, coughing and sputtering.

"That tastes gross!" Eve complained.

"Glad you think so," Cassy said, sending a wink in Chris's direction.

Chris let out a sigh, silently thanking the gods that Eve decided she didn't care for it. She was hard enough to control without the influence of alcohol.

"Come on," Sarah said and led them to a table, helping Matt to find a seat.

The innkeeper set a round of drinks on the table. Cassy drained the one she held and eagerly reached for another.

"Go easy, Cas. We're leaving early tomorrow," Chris reminded her.

The mug that was halfway to her mouth lowered and Cassy's face fell.

"Right, I had almost forgotten," she sighed.

Sarah pulled the mug from Cassy's hands, her own already empty.

"More for me then!" she said and drained the second mug.

"Can Echo try some?" Eve asked, and the tiny dragon's head poked out of her shirt.

"I thought you left him outside!" Chris said with alarm, praying the innkeeper hadn't noticed the little monster.

"He gets lonely!" Eve protested as she tucked him back under her shirt.

"The dragon cannot drink ale," Sarah said firmly.

"Why? Just because I don't like it doesn't mean he won't," Eve argued.

"No," Sarah said, ending the discussion.

"We should have a toast!" Cassy said suddenly.

"To what?" Matt asked skeptically.

"Who cares?" Cassy asked with a shrug.

"What's the point then?" Chris asked.

"It'll be fun," Cassy argued.

"You just want an excuse to drink," Sarah chuckled.

"We should toast to family!" Ditrina said with enthusiasm.

"It's as good as anything to toast to," Chris said with a smile.

"Great!" Cassy said as she snatched another mug of ale

"I want toast, too!" Eve said, looking around for food.

Chris and the others laughed, and together they celebrated the simple things they had and enjoyed each other's company.

The next morning, Eve decided she wasn't content on staying behind as they had discussed.

"I wanna see the village!" Eve yelled for the twentieth time.

"Eve, we're not going to be there long. You need to wait with your mother," Chris said with exasperation.

"No!" Eve yelled. "I need to see where you grew up!" Eve cried.

Chris sighed.

"If you come, you can't kill anyone, no matter what happens," Chris told her, his patience whittled away.

Eve seemed taken back.

"Why would you have to worry about me killing anyone?" Eve asked, giving him an innocent half-smile, ruined by the hungry looking dragon and the gleam in her eyes.

"I'm serious, Eve. Not one person," Chris said sternly.

"I promise, I promise, just please let me come!" Eve begged.

"It'll be ok. She'll be good," Sarah said, ruffling Eve's short hair.

Eve beamed up at her with a large half-smile.

"You're just saying that because you don't have to clean up after her if she gets bored," Chris said with a frown.

"Eve, if you behave, I'll start making the armor for you," Sarah told her.

Eve's eyes became the size of moons.

"You promise?" Eve asked.

"It'll be too big for you, so you'll have to wear it when you're older, but yeah," Sarah said with a sincere smile.

"I won't kill anyone," Eve said solemnly.

"Fine. You can come," Chris said, slightly in shock that he had to have conversations like that with a six-year-old.

"Regarding her armor, I believe I can create an enchantment that will allow it to change size to fit a specific person, so Eve could wear the armor as soon as she likes," Ditrina pointed out. "It is a simple spell. The elves use it with our children all the time, so they do not grow out of their clothes."

"I'm sure Eve will love that!" Cassy exclaimed.

"Because enchanted armor is exactly what she needed," Chris muttered.

"You brought this on yourself when you let her keep the corpse," Al pointed out.

"Shut up," Chris thought irritably.

"Relax; Eve will be cute as a button in armor!" Mi said happily.

"Come on, Chris, lets hit the road," Cassy said as she readied her horse.

Chris sighed and mounted his own horse, pulling Eve up behind him.

"Time to go home," Chris said quietly to himself.

So, their journey began, riding toward the village of Shearcliff. Soon, Chris saw the mountain he had grown up alongside looming on the horizon. As he rode, he smiled to himself, remembering that it was along this very road that he and his sister had been reunited. They made camp in the forest about an hour from Dewbank, the nearest village to Shearcliff.

"Let's try to avoid Dewbank tomorrow. If I remember correctly, they hired you to kill me. Seeing us together might cause problems," Cassy pointed out.

"Why? We could just kill everyone, then we don't have to worry about it," Eve proposed.

"Remember the deal, Eve," Chris warned.

"I promised not to kill anyone in Shearcliff; this is Dewbank," Eve defended.

"No killing at all," Chris told her.

"That's not fair!" Eve exclaimed, and Echo gave an indignant cry.

"I never said it was fair. I said that was the rule," Chris said sternly. Eve pouted.

"Lighten up, Chris," Cassy said from beside the fire, not really paying attention to their conversation.

"Are you implying that I should let her murder an entire village?" Chris asked, raising an eyebrow.

"Well, no," Cassy said with embarrassment, not having put much thought to her words.

"How exactly do I lighten up on this subject?" Chris asked with mild amusement.

"We could kill half the village!" Eve said excitedly.

"No. We're not killing anyone!" Cassy exclaimed.

"I thought you were fun, Aunt Cas," Eve pouted. "You ate people and everything!"

"Fun and murder are not the same things!" Cassy exclaimed. "And I didn't want to eat people!" she added.

Echo let out a very loud and very angry screech.

"Echo say's you're wrong. Murder is great fun, right behind lots of murder, which is the *best* fun," Eve declared.

"We're going to show you other ways to have fun," Chris told her.

"Like what?" Eve asked. "The only other things Echo and I like to do are eat and sleep."

"You like spending time with us, don't you?" Chris asked kindly.

"Well, of course! You're my family!" Eve exclaimed.

Her hand dropped to her dagger sitting in its scaly sheath.

"Family," she repeated softly.

"You can like spending time with other people too. It's ok to have friends," Cassy told her.

"Why do I need friends? My last friends all burned to death, leaving me to rot in my house. Not very reliable friends, if you ask me," Eve pointed out.

"Maybe you could get new friends. There are other kids who live down in the village," Chris told her.

"Then Echo and I can burn *them* to death! That's a great idea!" Eve exclaimed.

"No! No killing! Just spending time with them. Talking, playing games that *don't* involve bloodshed, that sort of thing," Chris told her.

"That sounds boring," Eve said with uncertainty.

"Will you try for us?" Cassy asked. "You'll like it if you give it a chance."

"Are you sure?" Eve asked.

"Positive," Cassy said with a toothy smile.

"Ok. When we go home, I'll try to make a friend. But if they annoy me, I'm feeding them to Echo," Eve declared.

"Or you could try making a new friend," Chris told her.

"Or that," Eve agreed with an indifferent shrug.

She looked at her scarred, clawlike hand.

"What if I scare them?" Eve asked with uncertainty.

"I scared you when we first met," Cassy reminded her.

"I know, but you're not scary now!" Eve insisted.

"Right, so even if they're scared of you at first, they'll learn over time that you're not something to be scared of," Cassy told her.

"But I *am* scary. I like killing people!" Eve exclaimed.

"You're not scary," Chris said softly.

"Echo can sense emotion. Whenever I talk about killing, you both get nervous. If I make you nervous, then I must terrify others," Eve reasoned.

Chris looked at his sister and saw she was just as lost as him for what to say. Eve was not finished, however, and spared them the need to speak.

"That's ok, though. I like being scary; it's fun. Sometimes you and Mother are scary, too. Then we can all have fun being scary together. It's just that sometimes being scary is...inconvenient. Jake and Demmi were scared of me, and they're vampires. I don't think I'll be able to make friends with the other kids very easily," Eve told them.

"You'll just have to try extra hard then," Cassy told her.

"You said that this Shearcliff village drove Aunt Cas out because she was scary, right?" Eve asked.

"Yeah, they did," Cassy told her sadly.

"I'm not going to be driven from our home, am I?" Eve asked cautiously.

"No, you're not going anywhere," Chris assured her.

"Ok, Father. I believe you," Eve said with a content half-smile.

She crawled closer to Chris and rested her head on his lap and was soon fast asleep, holding Echo like a scaly teddy bear.

"Eve confuses me at times," Cassy admitted.

"She just needs the right guidance," Chris said, brushing Eve's hair out of her face.

"And that's you and Sarah?" Cassy asked with amusement.

"Honestly, no, but we're the best she's got," Chris said softly.

Eve smiled in her sleep.

The next morning, they found themselves back in the saddle, cutting through the forest to avoid Dewbank. It took a little longer than if they had gone straight through the town, but most of them wanted to avoid bloodshed, so the detour was worth the time. Several hours of riding later, Al became agitated.

"We'll be able to see it soon!" he said with excitement.

"See what?" Chris thought with irritation.

"Algeminia! My old city!" Al exclaimed.

"It's been a while," Mi agreed.

"We're not stopping by, so you'll have to make do with the view from the saddle," Chris thought.

"Fine, but at least slow down as you ride past it. I want to get a good look," Al told him.

Chris sighed.

"What is it, Father?" Eve asked from behind him.

"Al and Mi are just being irritating," Chris told her.

"Tell Mi hello!" Eve said happily.

"I miss her; she was so much fun," Mi told him.

"Look, Chris, isn't that where you found your sword?" Cassy asked, pointing at the ruins in the distance.

"And the cloak! Why do people always forget about the cloak?" Mi complained.

"Yeah, that's where I found it," Chris confirmed.

"I love this story," Eve said happily.

"What story?" Chris asked.

"Uncle S was telling me a story about how you saved him in the ruins and how you killed a bunch of knights! It's such a good story," Eve told him.

"What else was in this story?" Cassy asked with amusement.

"He told me how they found you, and how you were always annoying, and how Mother almost killed Father, then how Aunt Di saved you all in a mine! It's my new favorite bedtime story," Eve said proudly.

"Has Matt been telling you bedtime stories?" Chris asked.

"Yeah, and my lessons have been going well, too! I can read an entire page now all by myself!" Eve said proudly.

"Better than Chris," Cassy snickered.

"Hey, I can read just as well as you!" Chris defended.

"Who taught you to read, Father?" Eve asked.

"The man we're going to find," Chris told her.

"I can't wait to meet him!" Eve said with excitement.

"Don't get your hopes too high; he's probably drunk," Cassy warned her with a laugh.

"Come on, we're almost at the village. If we hurry, we'll get there around sunset," Chris told them.

Chris's timing was spot on, and as the sun was dipping below the horizon, they entered the forest around Shearcliff. They slowed their pace, and as Chris rode, he was buried under a wave of nostalgia. These were the woods where he and Cassy had grown up, where they had run and hunted together. As the night began in earnest, they reached the village. They tied down their horses out of sight in the woods and began to walk quietly into the town.

"Remember, stay quiet," Chris whispered to Eve.

Eve nodded, and Echo launched himself into the night sky.

"Come on," Cassy said as she led them down the street.

Little had changed since he had gone away, and seeing that everything remained unchanged, drove a tiny dagger into his heart. Eve must have sensed his pain because he found her tiny hand in his as they proceeded down the street. He saw the same houses he knew, the same shops. The Silver Stallion, the inn where he had once worked, still stood on the street corner with a painfully familiar babble coming from within.

"There it is," Cassy said breathlessly as she looked upon the house where they had grown up.

Chris didn't know how to proceed. The lights were dark in the windows, but at this hour Mr. Cogwell would have drunk himself to sleep long ago, so it came as no surprise to them.

"I wanna meet Grandpa," Eve said quietly as she dragged him along.

Her voice roused the siblings from their trance, and together Chris and Cassy approached the house. Chris reached the door. It was unlocked, so he pushed it open slowly.

"Mr. Cogwell?" Chris called cautiously.

"Dad? Dad, I'm home," Cassy said softly as she followed him inside. They heard no reply.

"He's not snoring," Cassy said quietly.

Chris realized she was right. Mr. Cogwell was notorious for his snoring, and they had grown accustomed to the low roar that came with the man's slumber. Tonight, the house was silent.

Chris let go of Eve's hand and raced toward the old man's room, throwing the door open in a rush. It was empty.

"He's not here!" Chris called.

"Check the other rooms!" Cassy said quickly, rushing forward to look inside her old bedroom.

Chris checked his own, and to his despair, they saw no trace of the man. There were no empty bottles, no dishes in the tiny kitchen. The ever-present stink of cheap liquor that accompanied that man was nowhere to be found.

"Someone is coming," Eve said quietly. "Echo can see them."

"Everyone stay quiet," Chris hissed.

A figure appeared in the doorway. His eyes stared at the three of them for a moment before recognition flooded across his face.

"Chris? Cassy?" Mr. Darfew asked with shock.

"Mr. Darfew!" Cassy exclaimed, rushing to the man's side.

"Hello, sir," Chris said meekly, smiling at his old boss.

"What are you doing here? It's been months; nobody knew where you went! And Cassy, I was worried you were never coming back!" Mr. Darfew said as he embraced the two of them.

"Who is he? Is he my Grandpa?" Eve asked cautiously.

"No, this is Mr. Darfew. He's an old friend of ours," Chris explained.

"He helped take care of us when Mr. Cogwell couldn't," Cassy added.

"Oh," Eve said, crestfallen.

She had hoped that they had to silence the intruder or something violent along those lines.

"Sir, where is Mr. Cogwell? We came to find him and take him with us," Chris told him.

The smile fell from Mr. Darfew's face.

"You don't know then? No, you would have had no way of knowing. I'm so sorry," Mr. Darfew told them.

"What are you talking about?" Cassy asked as she took a step back.

As she did, she felt something crumple under her clawed foot. She looked at the ground and saw an envelope addressed to Mr. Cogwell in her own handwriting. The color drained from her face.

"Follow me," Mr. Darfew said as he beckoned them out of the empty house.

Chris and Cassy followed him mutely, Eve trailing behind, not understanding their sudden grief. Mr. Darfew led them a short ways away from the house, into the woods. There, standing in a small moonlit clearing was a small, solitary gravestone.

On it was carved:

Here lies Samuel Cogwell,
Town drunk,
Father of Christian Shearcliff
1452 PC - 1523 PC

They stood in silence and looked at the grave.

"I, uh, wanted to have them put your name on it, too, but the other villagers…well, they wouldn't let me," Mr. Darfew told Cassy quietly.

She said nothing but knelt beside the grave. They heard the sound of a claw being scraped along stone. When she stood, the gravestone read:

Here lies Samuel Cogwell,
~~Town drunk~~, ***Adventurer***
Father of Christian Shearcliff ***and Cassy Shearcliff***
1452 PC - 1523 PC

Cassy said nothing as she returned to stand beside Eve.

"When will I meet Grandpa?" Eve asked, looking between the two of them, not understanding.

"I'm sorry, Eve, you won't," Chris told her quietly.

"Why not?" Eve asked.

"He's dead," Cassy said, more to herself than anyone else.

"Oh," Eve said simply, looking at the grave with renewed interest.

"I'll give you some time alone," Mr. Darfew told them as he waked back into the town.

"I wish I could have seen him one more time," Cassy said quietly.

"I wish I had said goodbye," Chris said.

"It's ok," Eve said suddenly.

Chris and Cassy looked at her. Echo swooped down from the sky and landed on her shoulder.

"He's not your only family," Eve reminded him with a large half-smile on her mangled face.

Chris gave her a sad smile and took her hand. Cassy stepped closer and slipped a clawed hand into Eve's own. They stood for a very long time, saying nothing.

"Come on," Chris said as the sun's glow crept into the sky. "It's time for us to go home."

Together they walked in silence, heading toward the horses.

"Grandpa was an adventurer, right?" Eve asked after a while.

"Yeah, he was," Chris said quietly.

"We need to hurry home then. I wanna be like Grandpa, so I have a lot more adventuring to do," Eve said firmly.

A small smile crept onto Chris's face.

"We all do," he told her.

Printed in the United States
By Bookmasters